What readers are saying ab

"I found it to be both a profound spiritual and faith renewing experience throughout."

"The siege of Hue during the Tet offensive of 1968 and the many hard fought battles around that provincial capital are excellently portrayed. The horrors of the Vietnam war and the scars it left on returning soldiers are well depicted and very accurate. I understand Jack Holden's PTSD better than ever after reading his story. His journey should encourage anyone who has ever suffered from this illness. It is a book I will recommend to my fellow veterans."

"I grew up in a small town just like the one in this book. For many years, it did not have an early warning system in case of bad weather. Living in 'tornado ally,' I witnessed many severe tornadoes like the one in this book. It's depiction here is very realistic, that only a person who had lived through such an experience could have described in such vivid detail."

"It was a page-turning, thoroughly inspirational book throughout. It's the kind of novel that draws you into the lives of its characters and tugs at your heart from almost the beginning, right up to the end. Many complex emotions are masterfully explored: courage and frailty, hope and desperation, love and caring, and what it means to have faith in God. It was a book of epic proportions, beautifully told on an epic canvas."

"Many unforgettable scenes are brilliantly visualized within these pages: Among them, the death of an only child, the destruction of a massive tornado, and the power of war's many atrocities that took place in the Tet offensive of 1968 in Vietnam. But most of all you will remember the scenes of love and faith, how God can work within us to overcome any illness or setback and achieve a positive life."

"A beautiful book, richly detailed throughout, getting me deeply involved from start to finish. Many elements of this novel lingered in my memory long after I had finished it."

... Read the book you are holding in your hands and find out for yourself.

A Return To Meadow Wood

A Novel

By

Sam Rawlins

YorkshirePublishing
www.yorkshirepublishing.com
Write Now.

ISBN: 978-1-942451-42-6
eISBN: 978-1-942451-51-8

Printed in the USA
1st Edition - 2016

Dedication

As this book developed over many years, it was my constant prayer that the Lord would guide me in its writing.

I want to dedicate the end result to His glory and in loving memory to honor a remarkable woman who was my wonderful wife of more than 40 years.

I miss you so much.

Table of Contents

CHAPTER 1
A SOUL'S JOURNEY

The truth of the matter is, I died three days ago. Then I got up from the grave and looked at what my life had been. Something horrible out of my past hung like a shadow over me. It was something I could not run away from nor could I face. Though it tore at me emotionally, I couldn't even remember the details of what happened. Whatever they were, the emotions were deep and troubling. Taking stock of myself, I felt as though part of my soul had died. What brought me to this conviction?

The doctors at the VA hospital explained it to me: In each of us, a trillion or so cells exist that connect to form a recorded memory of one's life. In my brain, though, a certain number of those cells have been corrupted, removing significant memory of specific crucial events. Somewhere within the cerebral cortex, the effects of war had damaged my brain. My memory was fractured. Important pieces were missing.

Facing this grim assessment of psychological paralysis, I found the courage to do something I should've done many years ago. I resolved to complete some unfinished business, a promise to a dying man. He had been my closest friend. The more I thought about my unkept promise, the more it weighted me down. It was a terrible thing I had done, or rather had not done. The idea of doing something about it was gaining momentum within me.

My life had come to a crossroads. I rose out of this grave of depression and rallied. I found a renewed sense of purpose. It was still not too late to do the right thing. The truth of the matter was that I could do something about my life. In the spirit of new found optimism, I got on the phone and made reservations for a journey across the country. I just knew everything I wanted to accomplish on this trip would make me feel better about myself. Taking this step was the beginning of the single most positive thing I had done in a long time.

During the course of this bus trip, I kept hearing an inner voice. My eyes shut, I thought about the words being spoken inside my head: Everything that had gone wrong in my life might be corrected in this single act of atonement. What was my life worth? It would be of any significance only if I could accomplish something positive, really meaningful.

I was a good and decent man but also a broken man. My long, slow descent into this state had taken place over several years. Depression, that I barely noticed at first, was always with me, lurking somewhere in the back of my mind.

Though I had been firm in my plans at first, a lot still bothered me and weighed heavily upon my mind. The longer I pondered the past, the waning strength of my resolve became more apparent to me. I was wavering, struggling within myself. Such was the eroding nature of the conflict building up inside me. Negative poison had been attacking my brain cells for nearly two decades, far too long. Trying to refocus on my journey, I jolted myself, declaring *Enough!*

Getting my attention, the bus seemed to go into another gear. The road was becoming steeper, climbing up Winding Stairs Mountain. Reaching the top, it leveled off before beginning its descent.

Trying to escape my inner thoughts, I looked out the window. Up ahead, the sun was suspended just above the horizon. Below it, the highway cut through a thick forest and over a mountain range beyond. As the bus plunged into it, tall trees rose into the heavens on both sides of the road. Thinning out, they soon gave way to a clearer view of the valley below. It was my first glimpse of the little town that lay shrouded in the evening mist of so many years ago.

Scattered pockets of frame buildings became visible and drew my attention. They appeared to have survived the ravages of many decades. Even in the dim light of dusk, the sparsely populated countryside radiated peacefulness. It was like a small rural community locked in a time capsule out of the past.

The sun passed beyond view as the bus turned down a lonely stretch of country road. Rapidly, the sky was turning a metallic gray, getting darker.

February had only just begun, and its chill surrounded everything. Even with the bus's heat turned on, the cold penetrated deep into my overcoat. Forcing my thoughts inward again, I unwittingly found myself back in those places I had wanted to avoid.

Eating away at me, my self-examination was of such an unrelenting nature it became magnified and made even worse in the strange dark atmosphere surrounding me. I was beginning to have more doubts about everything. My inner strength was slipping away. The bad memories out of my past came rushing back into my mind. These thoughts carried me into a downward spiral. I felt myself unraveling.

On the surface, I thought I appeared quite normal. To the casual onlooker, a quick glance in my direction might not have revealed much beyond the physical. But there was much more to me. I was 39 years old then. Outwardly, I was a man of sharp bone structure. I had been told this accentuated my piercing eyes. I was on the thin side from not eating, tall and dark headed. My hair, though, was not as dark as the thoughts inside me.

I realize now I was a profoundly disturbed person. Memories of unsettling images were going through my mind. These were embedded in both my conscious and subconscious. A nightmare from out of my past had filled my sleep, leaving me with a shaky feeling. I felt the weight of it becoming a heavy pressure upon my chest. The restless ribbon that had been my life was shredding apart. I knew I was not well. Yet, I felt powerless to do anything about it.

A throbbing headache filled my brain. I had gone over and over about my shortcomings, even questioning my worthiness as a man. My feelings of guilt remained with me, constant and unabated. Something grimmer was beginning to take shape within my thoughts. I was becoming suicidal. There could be only one solution. It would be swift and absolute in its finality.

The negative voice had come back. This was what I was most in fear of happening. It spoke to my mind and asked me, *Why don't you end it all?* This was not the voice of my conscience, but I still couldn't get it out of my head. It kept on belittling me, making me feel worthless. A fearful sensation shot through me that I was not alone inside myself. Try as I might, I could never rid myself of this other voice that was haunting me. Rather it was once a month, or once a week, it was always the same voice. Was some sort of demon inside me? I didn't know. All I felt at the time was a struggle going on between two entities inside my brain, one good . . . one evil.

Getting past it would be a challenge. This other presence inside me persisted and continued whispering to my mind. Badgering me, it got to the point where I couldn't think straight anymore.

Needing help, my eyes went seeking it, staring into the dark faces of other passengers sitting near me. The shadows of the night created strange expressions on them. In their own little worlds, they all seemed so unaware and oblivious to others. This seeming indifference was overwhelming, making me even more desperate.

As I sat there in my aloneness, the apprehension was building inside me. I thought no one had the faintest idea who I was, that no one cared. But as I looked around, I realized this was not quite true.

On this particular bus, where a group of passengers were brought together in tight quarters for a prolonged length of time, perhaps the prying eyes of someone might linger on me. Then such a person might see the truth of what lay just beneath the mask I presented to the rest of the world.

Sudden movement in the seat directly across the isle caught my attention in that direction. My gaze settled upon the man's legs extending from the shadows. I was immediately convinced their owner was studying me, even though I could not yet see his face.

Reacting to me, the man leaned forward out of the shadows. He was older, 70 maybe 80, wearing thick glasses. A little smile formed beneath his equally thick mustache. He nodded, then reclined back into the shadows again.

Now I was sure the old man was watching me. What could he be thinking? He hadn't said anything, but his eyes had given me a strong once over. He seemed to be asking, *Who are you? What's your problem?* Of course this was all in my mind. I had looked too closely into the old man's face and came away feeling intimidated.

I was suspicious, rapidly filling up with even more imagined stress. I could feel my anxieties becoming visible. Fine beads of perspiration formed on my forehead and rolled down my face. A clammy coldness spread down my back, bringing on a more severe chill. I could not suppress it. I started shaking and couldn't make it stop. Not realizing what was happening, a full-blown panic attack seized me. The thought of what to do raced through my mind.

Marshalling all my force of will, I tried to calm down. It was useless though. I thought I could ride out the storm raging inside me, but I couldn't stand it any longer.

The voice that was not my own worked its way deeper inside my brain. It gave me orders, telling me what I must do. Its words were more demanding this time, *I thought you'd crack up one day. Well, that day is today. Desperate situations require desperate solutions. Take out that thing you have in your pocket. Use it!* The words were hypnotic, difficult to resist.

I was chilled to the core, shaking more than ever as I listened further. *Go ahead, kill yourself!* Fear told me I must obey.

I found myself zeroing in on something I could not see but knew was there. The desire to end it all had seized me. Knowing that this was a very real possibility, I had brought along something to help me. Working a trembling hand inside my coat pocket, I fumbled for the instrument of hoped for relief. My cold fingers wrapped tightly around a loaded revolver. Pulling it out, my eyes looked straight into the dark barrel. I hesitated. Caught up in a terrible internal struggle, I wondered what to do, *what to do!* I tried to reach out. This moment of quiet desperation blurted out as a barely audible whispered plea, "Someone please! I need help!"

So focused on the gun barrel, I did not notice a hand coming over and down on my shoulder. I jerked around with a surprised expression.

Out of the darkness, a savior of sorts emerged. From the seat across the isle, the old man had come over right next to me. Leaning into my field of vision again, he spoke with quiet authority, "Son, whatever you were thinking about doing—it isn't worth it."

I was rattled. My train of thought was short-circuited. "Who are you?"

"I've been observing you for awhile from my seat. You seemed a little uncomfortable about something."

"I, uh . . ." I was at a loss for words.

"Oh, pardon me, it's just my natural curiosity about people." The old man smiled, extending his hand in an offered handshake. "I'm Doc Peterson, from the little town we're about to come into."

"I'm Jack Holden." I responded without thinking, raising my hand instinctively to receive Doc's handshake, forgetting my fingers were still wrapped around the revolver.

"I'll take that!" In one fast fluid motion he'd swung his arm around behind me, coming up over my shoulder. With lightning speed, surprising for a senior citizen, the old man yanked the weapon from my hand, slipping it into his own coat pocket.

"Hey!" I reacted, caught off guard.

"Now Jack, keep your voice down. You don't want to disturb these other good people on this bus." The old man continued to speak in quiet tones of authority as he made strong eye contact with me.

Obeying, I lowered my voice in submission, and spoke more softly, "Very well . . ." There was something special about this old man that commanded my respect. It was elusive, almost invisible, but it was there in his expression and in the sound of his voice.

As it happened, we were both immediately aware of a sudden jerking sensation as the bus made a turn off the main road. The old man took note, "We're going to be pulling into the bus station soon."

I glanced out the bus windows, but it was too dark to see anything. Turning back to Doc, I asked, "Just what is this place, this spec in the road?"

Doc eyed me closely through his thick glasses. Taking into account my impertinence, he emphasized, "This 'place' is where I get off."

I looked down, caught up in my own dark thoughts as I spoke, "It would've been the last stop on life's highway for me."

Doc studied me silently for a brief moment, then his eyes lit up with an idea, "Son, why don't you get off with me and we'll talk about this some more? I might be able to help. I've been a doctor all my life, and helping people heal is what I do best. You know, Jack, sometimes all the roads of the world can become as one. Perhaps in your case, it's Fate showing you this is the road for you to take today. Consider it."

I looked up and stared back at the old man. There it was again, some-thing in him that suggested wisdom and compassion. Whatever it was, I hung on it and couldn't get it out of my mind.

I thought about the old man's offer for a moment, searching my soul. There was still a lot of turmoil swirling around inside me. Was I going to stop punishing myself for what happened in the past and take advantage of an opportunity here? I wanted to find peace. Could this be the place where I might find it?

As he stood up to get off the bus, Doc looked over at me and spoke as if he could read my thoughts, "Jack, I want to leave you with one last thought. Consider the possibility that meeting in the way we have was no accident. I want you to really think about it. Then you might see the hand of God at work here tonight."

As Doc left, I did really think about it. *Why should I get off here with this old man?* Maybe he could help me. He certainly seemed to have the desire to do so. Yes, an opportunity was presenting itself to me.

I glanced over at the bus door. It was still open. Looking out the window, there was the old man staring back at me from the dimly lit station platform. As if he were a beckoning savior, his motionless image drew me like a magnet.

Sometimes God puts people in our lives for a purpose. Was what hap-pened tonight, divine intervention? There comes at least one time in every-one's life when one must make a profound decision that will affect one's whole life. I had reached just such a moment. My soul's journey had begun.

CHAPTER 2
THE ARRIVAL

S o it was, one evening in the winter of '89 two men sat alone in a quaint little bus station. It was actually early in the year, but winter weather had hung on since the fall of '88. Something else though immediately got my attention, something unusual about this building. It was a throwback to a simpler time, perhaps the 1940s or the early 1950s. Largely dark, the lobby was dimly lit just enough to illuminate two old wooden church benches facing a long counter. Late night had found the place empty. It was just as well, though, because the two men needed to talk to each other freely and uninhibited. I—Jack Holden—was one of those two men.

Getting off the bus, I couldn't fathom what was going to happen next. I was ashamed of myself for what I'd almost done. If ever a person needed help from someone, it was me at that moment in time. Following Doc, I slumped down on one of the benches. Looking over at him, I listened.

It was though my outer self was transparent as the old man's eyes seemed to stare right through me. Peering through the thick lenses of his steel-rimmed glasses, he considered my emotional baggage. His gaze remained on me as he thought out loud, "Do you believe in God?"

"Of course I do."

"Then you know our Creator gave you life. Think about it. God has blessed you with His greatest gift. Wouldn't it be a shame to put an end to what He's granted you?"

"Doc, I'm so ashamed." I went silent again, sitting there in brooding self-reproach, avoiding eye contact with the judgment I saw written across his face. Feeling drained and wrung out, I was barely able to see him through burning, bloodshot eyes.

Doc sensed the suffering that I felt just below the surface. Moving closer, he put a comforting hand on my shoulder.

Appreciating the gesture, I whispered, "I just want one person to understand what's going on inside me."

"Son, I want to do more than understand. I want to help you if you will let me." Doc's deep soothing voice had a calming effect on me.

I looked up at him, thinking this old country doctor was remarkably perceptive about people. I felt drawn to his kindly nature, starting to open up to him as I spoke, "Three days ago I took stock of my life. I had to face the truth. I didn't like what had happened since the war, the Vietnam War that is. My 39th birthday was a week ago. That's when it hit me hard. Over the years, a part of my soul has died. Flashbacks and repeated nightmares have taken their toll. Memories became all consuming, killing off pieces of me a little bit at a time. They've defined my life. I'm a veteran, and this is what war has done to me. Though I survived it physically, I am yet its casualty. Some doctors say I have PTSD. To be less clinical and far more personally precise, I would say I've been living within my own nightmares since the war ended for me."

"What has that been like?"

"They never really go away. Instead they linger in sort of a shadowy background, waiting for an opportunity to come at me again. Did you know I can still hear the mortar shells come down? But that's not the worst. That's when I see the wounded and the dying. I can still smell their burning flesh. That odor stays with you. For as long as I live, I'll never be able to forget it. My mind hasn't been working right for some time, but in a rare lucid moment I decided to do something positive. I thought about changing my surroundings, taking this bus trip. That's when . . ."

Doc could see I was having a tough time. Yet, I wanted to tell someone, and he was listening.

Pausing, my eyes flickered a bit. The lights of a bus pulling out—the one we came in on—penetrated the window and bounced straight into my face. Avoiding the beam of light, I leaned forward, continuing, "While sitting on the bus, a lot of those memories that have been tormenting me came back all at once. Wounds not visible to the human eye were piling up inside me, about ready to hemorrhage. I lost hope. It became too much for me. I was like a pressure cooker about to pop open and explode. Then everything reached desperate proportions, and the lid came off. It seemed the only answer was to use that thing."

I gestured toward the revolver that still rested in Doc's pocket. Even though it wasn't visible, the gun and my actions on the bus were clearly still very much on my mind, and he knew it. "But why Jack, why did you want to take your life now?"

"In my mind, the war never really ended. I found myself questioning why I was still alive while others were still fighting and dying over there. I wanted desperately to go back as a combat medic, saving lives. Because I couldn't, I sunk lower and lower in my own eyes. I found myself unworthy to be alive. Doc, why am I still here?"

"I believe it was meant to be, Jack, that we were to meet the way we did so that I might help you to some other destiny. Surely, there's more than this one way to solve what's troubling you. Won't you entertain that possibility?" The old man's voice was one of reason and hope, "You don't need to rush into death. It'll come along soon enough in its own good time. You have your whole life in front of you. I couldn't permit you to use that revolver and throw it away."

I sat motionless, listening carefully to every word he spoke to me. Feeling a bit more hopeful, I blurted out, "I'll try to do better, Doc. That is, with my life."

"That's the spirit, son. I see it right now. There's a lot of good in you. Just remember, every moment you live counts for something. Make that 'something' *positive*."

"Is it possible for me to change the course of my life?"

"My boy, if one really wants something, there's nothing one cannot overcome."

"Do you really think so?"

"You can overcome anything if you set your mind to it. Call it an old man's instinct, I think you have a lot of potential. You can change your life Jack, but you have to want it. Cleanse your mind of negative thoughts. Pursue the positive. Make peace with your past. When you've done that, you can look to your future and set your sights on what you can accomplish. Every word you say and every deed you do will count for something. Whatever you do, make sure it's a step forward, not backward."

I found myself listening to him. What he said were some of the most compelling words I'd heard in a long time. Reaching out to him, I asked, "Will you help me, Doc?"

"Sometimes each and every one of us needs a helping hand in their lives. Yes son, I'll help you find inner peace."

I saw the compassion in the old man's eyes and was grateful beyond words. A surge of emotion came over me.

Doc's sensitivity was such that he saw the silent cry of thanks in my face. He knew that I needed his support. He whispered quietly, "I'm here for you."

"You're an unusual man, Doc. You're a doctor but yet much more than that."

"I'm a man of many interests that make up the whole of who I am. I like to help others solve their problems, helping them up on a road that leads to fulfillment in their lives. In doing so, it adds a sense of purpose to my own life."

Once again, I saw the good in the old man and had to ask him, "How is it that you know so much about people?"

"After I finished medical school, I soon found the hospital environment was not for me. A doctor there didn't really get to know his patients and adequately understand their individual needs. For me to be a more effective physician, I came to feel I needed to start my practice in a small town. So I came here where I could really get to know my patients. Quickly though, they became my friends and neighbors as well. I've learned all I know about people right here in this little town. As a doctor, I've seen the lives of some of my patients from the cradle to the grave, being the first person they ever saw and the last. Nothing could equal the satisfaction and sadness of some of those moments. My practice has become my life. Over the course of it, I've been exposed to fifty years of human nature, seeing the essence of what makes people tick."

There it was, the summation of a lifetime of knowledge distilled in a few words. I knew then, in Doc I had met someone who would become my friend. For sure, great good would come out of this.

He explained further, "Jack, when all is said and done I can't think of anything more satisfying than helping others, and in a way that brings us back to you and me. Won't you come into town with me?"

I immediately thought only good could come from his invitation. This kindly old country doctor had helped ease the weight of the world I'd been carrying upon my shoulders. The total conviction of his words had won me over and lifted my spirits.

Wanting to thank him, I reached over for his hand and answered him, "Doc, I believe in you and trust you. Sure, I'll go into town with you."

The old man received my hand in a warm handshake, putting the seal on what would become more like a bond of lasting friendship. He looked into my face and saw the exhaustion I knew was there. "My young friend, you look tired. Come, let's go into town. I know a place where you can stay overnight, get some rest, and come around to see me in the morning. Then we will talk again."

"I will, Doc." I was ready to follow him anywhere, even to a place that did not appear on most maps but nevertheless existed.

Silently, we walked toward the door of the darkened bus station. Getting closer to it, the cold night air penetrated the drafty old building. We stopped just inside to fasten our coats.

"By the way," I questioned as I bundled up, "what's the name of this place?"

"This place is my world, it's a little town called Tyler Junction, and it's just down the road a piece."

I went with Doc into his world, filled with unexpected anticipation. Life had been a long winding journey that led me to this place. Now I was beginning a new sort of journey, one that would lead me into uncharted waters to places foreign to me. With a sense of curiosity, I went through the doors of the old bus station eager to explore what lay beyond cloaked in the shadows of the night.

At first, only a few far off scattered lights were visible. As we got closer, I could see Doc's little town up ahead. Through the night mist, it was though I was peering into a snow globe, viewing a mirage of images from an era of innocence and charm long since vanished.

We made our way up a muddy dirt road that led from the old bus station to the main street going into Tyler Junction. This was one of those old cobblestone roads of almost a century ago, illuminated by a few scattered Victorian-style street lamps. Giving off a rich golden glow, they cast isolated pools of light. In this almost surreal atmosphere, falling mist created a shimmering appearance on the street giving it a glossy sheen. In the night's stillness, the world was asleep except for Doc and me.

I was curious, "Where does this street lead to?"

"For you, my young friend, it leads to a new life."

"Really." I wasn't sure of how prophetic those words would be.

"Really son," Doc added reassuringly. "This is Market Street, and there's a nice old hotel a little ways on down."

I could see this was Tyler Junction's one main thoroughfare, with just a handful of buildings lining both sides of the street. It was even more apparent that most of them were built many decades ago.

"Did you ever visit a small town?" Doc continued to make conversation as we walked.

"No, I can't say I ever have."

"Well, my boy, you're going to, at least for the next two or three days. That's when the next bus stops here. The town's a pretty place. A little stream runs through it. It's bordered by rolling hills all around that block us off from the main highway and the outside world. Maybe that's why not much has changed in this town for many years."

"Sounds like the whole town is in sort of a time capsule. It looks like something out of the early 1900s," I observed. "It's strange, but in an odd way it sort of makes my whole bus trip worth it."

"Why were you on that bus trip?"

"Searching for answers, I suppose, to something in my past."

"What sort of answers?" Doc was getting curious.

I didn't mean to be evasive, but I was not prepared to say more about something that was difficult to talk about anyway. "I'd rather not speak of it right now. I'll discuss it with you tomorrow."

"Very well then. We're here anyway." Doc let it go, nodding in the direction of a building just becoming visible up ahead of us. "The Tyler Inn is our only hotel. It's a nice place where you can stay the night, sort out things, and come over to my house in the morning."

We approached the front of a nostalgic looking two-story structure. It was obvious that it had been built when the town had seen far better times.

Doc started up the steps but seeing I was hanging back turned to reassure me, "Don't be afraid, just follow me." Extending his hand toward me, he announced, "We have arrived. Come, let's go in. It'll be okay."

That little bit of extra urging jolted me. It was like a lifeline tossed to me. Listening to him, I was ready to turn things around. From that moment, hope was finding its way back into my life.

Realizing I was at a crossroads in my life, I was beginning to believe Doc's intervention was no accident. Both authority and goodness came together within the figure of this wise old man. I looked up at his outstretched arm beckoning to me.

Fate had taken a hand in what happened. After those dark moments on the bus, maybe I was getting a second chance at life. Something positive was beginning to take hold inside my mind. Any hesitancy I may have had left me. A sense of purpose returned. I had traveled across three states to get to where I was. There was no turning back now. Surrendering to this new destiny, I started up the steps with a good feeling to face the future.

Sometimes though, Fate acts in strange ways. I could not know that the person waiting on the other side of the door would change the rest of my life.

CHAPTER 3
A PLACE OF MEMORIES

Doc Peterson entered the lobby, with me following right behind him. Without looking up, I turned to close the front door behind us. The bell above it made a distinct series of rings.

As I looked up, my eyes took in the surroundings. Again I was struck by the thought that I had gone back in time. The atmosphere was very nostalgic. Pictures reminiscent of a hundred years ago lined the walls, while the furnishings had a definite antique flavor. My gaze traveled up the steps of the staircase immediately in front of me, leading to the second floor. They ascended from the light below into dark shadows above. Over all, the lobby was shrouded largely in darkness, being dimly lit by only a couple small lamps.

The hotel was silent with the single exception being the tick tock of a nearby grandfather clock. Breaking the silence, Doc spoke to me in a very low voice, "I want you to meet the night manager here. She's one of the most truly good people I've ever known. I think you'll like her."

Leading the way, Doc crossed the lobby, passing a high back sofa that faced the front desk. I followed close behind him. A single muted light barely lit the counter up ahead of us.

Advancing toward the front desk, something got my attention off to one side. I zoned in on it. As I got closer, the object came into focus: it was an old cane resting against a chair.

Doc peered over the counter, looking for someone. He speculated in a low voice, "Now I wonder where that Mattie Sullivan is?" Tapping the call bell on the counter, he called out a second time, only louder, "Mattie!"

"I'm right here, Doc." A female voice answered from behind us.

We turned from the counter to face the sofa we had just walked past. It had fallen into the shadows. But now as we focused on it, we could see a reclined figure, more of an imperfect image in the dark, coming to a sitting position.

She explained, "I finished my cleaning and was resting here a bit." Her voice was soft, yet firm and full of character.

"I'd like to get a room for my friend here," Doc said, gesturing over at me. "I'll take care of it."

Coming to her feet, Mattie Sullivan emerged from the shadows into the light. Her face could not be seen clearly because her long flowing hair fell over it. Using her fingers like a comb, she pulled her hair back to reveal a pair of large blue eyes looking straight into my face.

I had been very ill at ease at first, not quite sure what I was walking into. But then I saw her—the woman that would change my life—there was instantaneous strong eye contact as a wealth of unspoken thoughts and curiosity passed between us. It was an extraordinary moment. Even I did not recognize its full importance.

As a spectator, it was plain to Doc we both saw something in each other. He went about introducing us, "Mattie, I want you to meet Jack Holden. We struck up a conversation while riding back from the city together on the bus. He's decided to stay a few days with us here in Tyler Junction."

As Doc spoke, I remained silent, nodding only in acknowledgement. Just staring, I noticed something about her. I wasn't quite sure what it was, but I was going to find out.

Reacting to me, she responded with a nod. Her face came alive with a glowing radiance. Thinking back, it was this response that initially attracted me.

Making her way around the counter with an almost imperceptible limp, Mattie's hand reached for the old cane. Gripping it, and with its additional support, she moved to take a seat in the chair behind the front desk. I sensed at some time in her past she had lived a hard life.

I remained transfixed on her through all of these movements. I was trying not to be so obvious, but I could not help myself. I definitely saw something familiar, but yet new, wrapped in the form of an entirely different person. Was this meeting meant to be? I wondered if this was Fate as well. The more I studied her, the more I thought she might be the one. But I had to be sure first, absolutely sure.

From her seat Mattie's gaze fell upon me. Our eyes made contact again. She gestured to the sign-in ledger, "If you'll sign right here, Mr. Holden . . ." She hesitated, looking over at the room key rack. "I can give you room 206."

As I signed in, Doc leaned across the counter, closer to Mattie. "Thanks for taking care of my friend. You know, you're my special girl, always."

"I'd do anything for you, Doc, anything."

Observing them, I thought she was more than just a casual acquaintance to Doc. Rather, their bond might be through the memories of a lifetime.

Hanging on Mattie's words, Doc looked over in my direction, "And I'll do anything to help you my boy."

I was feeling more at ease with this kindly old man in every passing moment and told him, "There's so much I want to tell you Doc."

"Son, there is so much for me to know. When you're up and about in the morning, come over and see me."

"I will, Doc."

Doc reminded me, "Remember, just go on up Market Street here, past the general store, then take a left onto Olive Road. My place is the second one on the right."

"I understand," I said, confirming I would be there.

Satisfied, Doc reached over and whispered, "Take care of yourself, son."

As we talked, Mattie came around the counter, up alongside me.

Doc fastened his coat, bundling up again. Preparing for the cold outside, he looked up at both of us. "Well, I'll take my leave now. Good night, kids."

Mattie smiled, "Good night, Doc."

As the door closed behind him, the bell above it gave out its familiar ring, and then there was silence.

Transfixed in Doc's direction, Mattie continued, "He's a good old man." Hesitating for a moment, she turned around facing me, continuing her thought, ". . . a good old man who means well, Mr. Holden. He never meets a stranger."

"I understand," I responded, still staring after Doc myself. Then turning to Mattie with my mind on her now, I continued, "It's Jack. Please call me Jack, Ms. Sullivan."

In her own intuitive way, Mattie's probing eyes searched my face. Her voice was warm and unknowingly prophetic as she said, "Jack, I hope you have a rewarding stay during your time here in Tyler Junction."

"Thank you, I hope so too." I meant it in ways she could not even begin to understand.

Glancing over to the staircase that led to the rooms on the second floor, her attention quickly returned to me. Extending a closed hand, clinched fingers unfolded, revealing the room key in her open palm. "It's the second room on the right at the top of the stairs."

Reaching over, in the process of taking the key I gently squeezed her hand. "Thanks Ms. Sullivan, good night."

Crossing the lobby, I was stopped at the base of the staircase by her voice. "Oh Jack . . ."

Looking back around into Mattie's face, I realized her eyes had followed after me. Her gaze was focused on me, more strongly than ever before.

After a lingering moment she broke the silence with a certain personal emphasis, "To you, it's Mattie."

I understood and said softly, "I'll remember." Then I added with a bit more personal emphasis, "Good night again . . . Mattie."

I looked at her one last time for the night and thought she had an interesting face, reflecting something from deep within her heart—something I couldn't put my finger on. For some time, I would carry this memory of her within myself, a certain unexplained quality wrapped in a mystery.

Starting up the stairs, I advanced without hesitation at first. Mattie followed to the base of the stairs. From the lobby below, she stared after me again for a moment, then returned to her work.

Ascending the stairs, I started thinking about what I must do and when to do it. Only I knew the real reason that brought me to Tyler Junction. But for now that must remain a secret. Fate had taken an unexpected hand in the course of events. For this I wasn't prepared. In the meantime, I would watch and wait for the best opportunity to complete my mission.

20

Doc Peterson's encouragement meant well. But he could not fathom the depth of anguish locked inside me. I couldn't seem to forget a past full of upsetting memories. Yet I knew I must come to terms with them. With each succeeding step up the stairs, the thought of that prospect became more and more unsettling to me.

It was an old building full of sounds. The creaking of the wooden stairs, even though muffled under the carpet, was a fresh reminder of something faraway. I could not remember what it was, but the shrill sound put me in the thought of a different place almost immediately. It morphed into the sound of incoming bombs. They exploded in my brain with the impact of a pounding headache. With each step, it grew ever louder in my ears. It made me breathe harder. Gasping, I felt like I was suffocating inside. The sweat trickled down my spine, making me tremble again. I forced myself to suppress it and keep going. At last, I was at the top of the stairs. The tightness within my chest loosened, giving me instant relief. The flashback was gone.

Even so, I barely made it down the darkened hallway on the second floor. Scanning the door numbers for the correct room, I finally saw it, room 206. The large black numbers on the door confirmed it. I inserted the key and unlocked the door. As it opened back slowly, I entered the room cautiously, not wanting to experience any more such episodes.

The room seemed quiet enough. A single small light setting on a dresser had been left on. It was directly across from the bed, facing it. I glanced about the room, realizing that it too, like the rest of the hotel, fell into many atmospheric shadows.

After the room door closed automatically behind me, there was silence for only a brief moment. Winter's wind was gathering strength outside. Whipping the outside walls of the old building, it generated another series of ominous creaking noises. The sound clashed with the complete silence inside the room, magnifying the sense of aloneness I felt within myself.

A pinging sound drew me to the window. Pulling the curtain back, I peaked out and saw the rain had picked up. Turning from the growing storm, I quickly sought the warmth of the interior of the room.

I was alone with myself again and whatever was inside my brain. This could be a dangerous place for me to be. I had read up on it. Within the human mind exists the greatest unknown area of exploration on earth. Man uses less than ten percent of its full potential. What strange and fascinating wonders might be there? Or in my case, would I really want to know?

Speaking of exploration, I felt strangely drawn to the dresser in front of me. Oddly familiar, I gently ran my fingers across it. One of those old large mirrors was anchored to the top. Moving right in front of it, I stared directly into the glass. There was something magical about it. The more I gazed into it, the dimly-lit hotel room reflected in it seemed to disappear. Beyond my own reflection, other images were forming within its dark shadows, becoming figures familiar to me. Springing from the deepest reaches within my mind, they took shape as I remembered them. Each and every moment was taking place as if it was just happening. The mirror had become a window to my past.

I whispered to myself, "It's just like the one Dad used to have in his bedroom." Many years ago, a much younger version of me would often look at the series of framed pictures lined up on my father's dresser. They recalled a passage of time that spanned my family's entire lives. Standing there, I tried to remember some of the memories those pictures represented. My eyes strained, and once more they became real . . .

It was the Vietnam era of the 60s. Twenty years ago, I stood there in a military uniform running my fingers across my father's dresser until they touched an old yellowed picture. Taken many years before during a far simpler time in a much less complicated world, it depicted a lovely young woman. In the course of time she would become my mother. I whispered softly, "She was beautiful."

Then my fingers moved on to the next picture, that of a much older man. This time I picked it up. "I see you've had a new picture taken Dad." I turned to my father, who was sitting on the edge of his bed, "You must've had it made while I was away."

My father confirmed it, "Yes, I had it taken while you were in medical school at Fort Sam."

"It's a good likeness, Dad, but something's missing."

Dad held out his hand and I passed the picture over to him. Briefly, he gazed at the picture of himself in silence. Looking up at me, his eyes filled with tears as he spoke, "You know, Mom would've been in this picture with me if she hadn't . . ." Dad choked up, not able to get the words out, swallowing hard on the emotions that had welled up in his throat.

I sat down on the edge of the bed beside my father, taking the picture from him, finishing the words I knew he was going to say, ". . . if she hadn't had her stroke."

Nodding yes, he agonized, thinking out loud, "It's this war! You know how sensitive and frail she's been in recent years. Your mom loves you so much, son."

Torn up inside, struggling with his thoughts, he stood up and walked over by the dresser. Looking down the row of photographs sitting upon it, his mind reflected upon the succession of images and the lifetime of memories surrounding them.

Remaining on the bed, I saw my father was struggling to say something. I kept silent, preparing to take in his every word.

Rising above a wave of sadness, he managed to continue, "I guess it was after you left for basic training, Mom started watching all the news reports about the war in Vietnam. Every day, she would see those films of the young men wounded and dying. She would cry and grieve over them, saying, 'They could all be Jack.' Then one evening after one of those war reports, I found her on the sofa with a fixed blank stare. She had suffered a massive stroke."

Tears filled my father's eyes. He could not go on. Seeing this, I rushed over from the bed. Coming up behind him, I put a comforting hand on his shoulder. "Oh Dad . . ." I stopped, not being able to get past my own heartbreak.

"Son, you remember don't you? You always did seem to have that special gift. You could look into someone's heart, almost right on into the soul and see the pain that was there. You could talk to someone for awhile, and by the time you were finished, the person felt better, sort of healed. I always marveled at the gift in you."

"I had forgotten, Dad." I lied somewhat. Many friends used to echo my father about what he called my gift with people. But the war had killed it, erasing a lot of those memories. Seeing so much pain and suffering sort of drained it all out of me. What I experienced over there blocked out a lot. But I remembered enough to try to help my father. I told him, "Dad, I wanted to be here for you and Mom. Even though I was half a world away in Vietnam, you and Mom were in my prayers every single day."

"I love you for that, son." He turned around, tightly embracing me. In the shared grief of father and son, the emotional bond strengthened both of us.

My father wiped his eyes, regaining his composure, "When we go visit Mom up at the hospital today, don't tell her I was crying. I've got to be strong for her."

"I won't, Dad. I'll be strong too." I spoke reassuringly and then explained, "You both taught me something very important—the right way to live."

"Your mom would be proud of you. We raised a good son."

"Dad, when the war came, I prayed about what to do. I wanted to do the right thing. I felt a presence around me, greater than us. I believe it was the Spirit of God, guiding me. That's why I joined the Army Medical Corps and became a medical specialist. I wanted to save lives, not take them."

"Son, you did do what was right. War is a terrible thing, always resulting in suffering and in lives being destroyed. But you made it back, healthy and whole. My boy you're home, just as you once were."

For a few seconds, I was somewhere else, staring into a nightmarish darkness. I was still a good person, but the young man my father knew before I left for Vietnam didn't exist anymore. The innocence was gone. What I had seen and experienced in the war had destroyed that part of me forever. Thinking about it, I asked my father, "How long will it go on?"

"As long as we let ourselves engage in more and more wars, we will see our world plunged into turmoil."

"I wonder, when will it all end?"

"When man lets go of hate and anger within himself and instead turns to goodness in his heart to solve his problems. When, instead of resorting to violence, we embrace our fellow man with compassion, understanding, and brotherly love. Then we will find peace."

"Dad, I experienced so much over there. Do you think I'll ever find peace?"

"I see it in your face. The answer is inside you. In the course of time, you will discover a place where you will find inner peace."

"Do you really think so?"

"I know so son. I know so . . ."

I took it all in. Absorbing it, I moved closer to the dresser as he looked on. Running my fingers past the photos of old memories again, I lost myself in the lingering words of what my father had said. Trying to hold onto them, I whispered, ". . . you will discover a place where you will find inner peace."

Something distracted my thinking. The lonesome wail of a train crossing distant tracks at the edge of town persisted, growing louder. The mirror abruptly turned black, and my vision of times past dissolved back into the present. The sound of that far off train continued for a brief moment. Then everything became silent.

Trying to recapture the vision, I heard my father speak again, "Son, you will find inner peace." Nothing but silence followed. I found myself alone back in my hotel room. Closing my eyes, I attempted to focus my mind on traveling back through my past again. I was searching for those memory cells in my subconscious mind that would take me back to the time of lost innocence in my life. Try as I might, I met only with frustration. I couldn't do it, not even in thought. Looking into the mirror, I whispered sadly, "If I could only go home . . . I miss you, Mom and Dad, so very much."

I did not know it then, but what just happened was only the beginning of many strange events that would be part of my future in Tyler Junction. This little town had already become a place full of unexpected surprises for me.

Not wanting to think further about my past, I turned away from the mirror that had become sort of a time travel device for me. I looked around the room trying to find something else to occupy my mind, but it was too late. I was alone with my thoughts again. In the extended quiet, a wave of loneliness rushed over me. I tried hard not to think about those sad times, but their memory hung there in the back of my mind, pulling me down into a place of pain and suffering. Sitting on the edge of the bed, I was depressed even more now. Once more I felt drained, like only a shell of a man.

It was a lonely moment for me. My whole world seemed so empty, gone forever. I had gone looking for a part of my past in the dim light of a mirror and found some fond images of my father. But also, something felt unsettling. Not sure what it was, I tried to put it out of my mind. It was too late though. A door had been opened to the past, and I could not close it. Other ghosts could come through it and engulf me in a nightmare.

I sat there surrounded by ominous shadows of the room. As I was getting in bed, a strange premonition crept over me. I felt like the four walls of the room were closing in. I was in the eye of a storm encircling me with increasing chaos. However, in the eerie silence of the moment I tried to block it out and shut my eyes.

The troubling evening had left me in a restless state. My mind was overloaded with many thoughts. For quite some time, I laid there in the cold darkness surrounding me. Sounds of the stormy evening outside calmed down into absolute quiet. But shortly, the room's silence was broken again. From far away, the cry of another train could be heard. Its whistle became more distinct, transforming into a loud screech.

Much turmoil started churning inside me again. A suffocating feeling returned. The room's chill penetrated the covers. I lay shivering in the bed, fine beads of perspiration forming on my brow. Struggling to awaken myself from an uneasy sleep, my body was trapped in a painful spasm. I felt myself becoming icy and saw my skin color was turning pale in a death-like grip. What was happening to me?

A small red dot penetrated the curtains, searching the room. Beamed from some unseen light source, it came to rest right on my forehead. I tried to shut out what was widening rapidly over my entire face. The intense flash of red penetrated my eyelids causing them to flare open. I looked around, taking in my surroundings. They were surreal, but again never more real, for they were from across time itself.

I found myself dressed for combat. The never ending war I told Doc about had returned to my mind. Huddled in a bunker, it was stifling, unbearably hot. BOOM! A concussion shook the earth, followed by a succession of red and deep orange colors flashing over me. I was caught up in a series of deafening explosions, for this was the country-wide invasion that was the month-long Tet Offensive of 1968. All of South Vietnam was in danger of being overrun in a time when human life was valueless. Shelling had been going on non-stop, day and night, never seeming to end. Because of this, where I was, we were forced into underground bunkers. It had become so intense that many Americans were killed in shelters within our own defensive positions.

I was older than most of the men in the trenches before Hue. Even though I was barely nineteen years old, I was considered the old man of the bunch. Others were only sixteen or seventeen. Not quite old enough to legally be in Vietnam, they were there nonetheless. Being young like that, they were more susceptible to the enemy's mind games. Many were worn down and became demoralized. In that mental frame of mind, quite a few of the younger guys came to see me in the med bunker. Being who I was, I tried to help and support them.

The med bunker became the last stop in this life for so many. It was where I did all my dirty work as a combat medic trying to save lives. It was heavily reinforced, buried deep in the earth, until we hit solid rock. It was built to withstand everything—everything but a direct hit as it turned out. At the time I prayed to God that would never happen.

A loud screeching sound reached into my eardrums. It was the shrill flight of incoming mortar shells getting closer to the med bunker. I was doing my job, giving emergency treatment to the wounded and dying. The number of incoming casualties was unrelenting, rapidly filling up the space around me.

The bombardment was shaking the structure clear down to its foundation. Dirt would break loose from the support timbers within the bunker, dust floating downward upon me, usually when I was trying to save someone's life. Constantly nerve racking, I thought it was only inevitable till the enemy would hit their target.

BLA-A-AM! Another loud crashing sound from behind caused me to jerk around as the door to the bunker opened. Another young soldier rushed in, almost falling on top of me. Just outside, a red flaming explosion flared close behind the young man. Even though he was wearing his helmet and flak jacket when he came in, it wouldn't be enough if we received a direct hit from one of those mortar rounds.

In the flash I recognized him, even though his face and uniform were smeared with the dust of combat. "Johnny! What is it?" My voice was both a question and a startled demand.

Johnny was a friend of mine who had just turned eighteen. I could feel the sense of urgency in him as he spoke, "It's the VC! They're shelling the camp and attacking the perimeter!" Even though he was young, he had become a Vietnam veteran in the year I had known him. While I did my work in here, I trusted my life with him and other young men like him in the trenches out there. During our time together, we had grown close, more than comrades. We had become like brothers.

Experiencing all we had this last year, our faith in each other and in God had grown. I often felt the good Lord was watching over us. I felt it most strongly when I was working on the wounded. Trying desperately to save them, I could feel His Spirit all around, strengthening me so I could save lives.

Everyone was suffering from battle fatigue in varying degrees. The last 72 hours had been full of bombardment, punctuated by intermittent human wave attacks. They had been driven back. But they were regrouping for another go at it, soon.

Johnny looked about frantically, pulling some of the boards away from a peephole. It was big enough for a flash of red from outside to be reflected on his face. He had not been exaggerating. "They're getting closer with their rockets," he whispered, almost fatalistically.

The battle would shortly be upon us. Another explosion followed by the chatter of machine guns and other small arms fire was almost on top of us. It seemed that we'd soon be facing the whole blasted North Vietnamese Army.

Johnny whipped around toward me, his helmet having fallen off after the last explosion. Looking very worried, his face was clearly visible now. Our eyes connected, and I could see the effects of the long battle in his hollowed-out, blood shot eyes. He was right at the edge of shell shock, beginning to break under the strain. Young and vulnerable, Johnny was like so many men of his generation that were lost in that horrible war.

His eyes fixed on me in a searching stare, "Jack, where have you been? They've been calling for a medic out there. Everyone along our trench line is either wounded or dead. The VC are regrouping to overrun us!"

"Listen to me," I interrupted. "A radio man was just in here. He said there's a relief column of Marines on it's way up Highway One right now."

While he listened and digested this information, his vision adjusted to the bunker's dim light. Now he clearly saw the heavily blood-stained operating table behind me. He asked, "What's been going on in here?" Before I could answer, I could see in this young man's expression that he was receiving a sudden dose of reality.

More than ever before, I realized the limitations of one person. The nature of being a medical specialist was when fighting was going on, I worked around the clock.

So I explained, "This is where I do my work. I've been busy, treating the wounded in here for the past 72 hours. One after another, after another . . . covered in blood. Get the picture. They were some of the most horrible wounds I've ever seen, too awful for me to fix, too fragile to be medevaced out. Young guys just like us, except . . ." I stared down at my hands in futility before continuing, "It was almost overwhelming. Shaking in the final throws of life, they all became like brothers to me. It became like a Holy duty to do all that I could to comfort them in the last minutes of their lives. All I had left was morphine syrettes, and I've been using a lot of them."

"What are they? What are they used for?" Johnny was curious.

I explained, "A morphine syrette is a tiny injectable hypodermic needle fitted into a small collapsible tube filled with a single dose of morphine. Enough morphine stops the transmission of pain from the point of origin of the pain to the brain. Enough syrettes can produce a state of euphoria and drowsiness, which can lead to the final drift off into eternal sleep. In the most horribly wounded where there was no hope, I thanked God I had those syrettes. At those times, I felt more like an angel of mercy than a combat medic. When many of them did die in my arms, and these hands could do nothing to save them, I cried and prayed for their souls. There's been so many wounded and dead."

Johnny looked around uneasily and asked, "Where are the dead?"

"See those bags over there." I gestured across the room behind me, without looking around. I couldn't.

In the dim light of the bunker, Johnny focused on the massive stack that covered the entire wall, from floor to ceiling. I could see the horror forming in his eyes as he reacted, "My God . . . Death is all around us."

"Down here it's inescapable. I did all I could do. As each one of them died, the memory of that death was permanently etched into my mind. I suppose I'll have to live with those memories for the rest of my life. But when you're the only medic within miles, you've got a lot more to think about. So many brought in here, their lives just hanging on by a slender thread . . ." I think in that moment I had about reached my own breaking point. I insisted, "I tell you, I did all I could do."

"I'm sure you did Jack."

"It's got so the smell of death is very familiar to me. If you stay in here long Johnny, you'll pick up on it too. It's one of those intimate details that few beyond us medical specialists would know about. Loading so many casualties into those army issue body bags, I've begun to notice a defect."

"What's that?" He asked, but with an expression of dread, almost really not wanting to know.

I was past holding back though, needing to get it off my chest. So I told him, "It was the zipper. No matter how well I zipped those bags closed, body fluids from the remains seemed to always seep out."

Johnny stared more closely. Finally taking it all in, he felt the full weight of the horrific scene. He could barely whisper the words, "Oh my God."

"Yes," I said. "They are in God's hands now."

Looking over at me, Johnny's expression became even more intensified as he asked, "Jack, are you all right?"

"Not really. As they were dying, each one of those men screamed out in pain that they didn't want to die. But the inevitable happened, and they died anyway. Being stuck down here for so long, I can still hear them crying, begging me to save them. There's been no getting away from it for me. All I've seen are the wounds inside those bags, and bodies that won't stop bleeding. I can't take the odor in here much longer."

My attention fixed on Johnny, I could see something grim forming in his expression as he spoke, "It's awful, just thinking about what must've happened to those guys." Then his tone turned much darker, "Jack, are we going to wind up like that? I don't want to die!" Not able to hold it in, he started crying.

I recognized what was happening. Moving closer, I put my hand on his shoulder, trying to snap him out of it, "Johnny, you need to get hold of yourself."

Pulling away, he held out his hand in protest, "No Jack! It came to me a few hours ago. I'm not going to survive this. Please, just listen." Pulling a sealed envelope from inside his flak jacket, he explained, "My folks died when I was little. I don't have anyone left back home, except a baby sister.

We've been separated the past few years. I stole a few minutes and wrote this letter. I want her to know I was thinking of her and I was right with God."

I disagreed, "You are going to survive. When this is all over you can tell her yourself."

"No Jack, I'm going to die today. But you, you're going to make it through all of this and return to the states."

"What makes you so sure?"

"Because God is with you."

"Why do you say that?"

"You don't curse. You're always kind and outgoing to others. When you're alone in the quiet moments, it's been noticed you are always reading your Bible. If there's anyone prepared to meet our Maker, it's you."

"I'm not so sure, Johnny. I don't feel ready to meet God. I'm just like the rest of you guys, just as afraid that I'm going to be killed over here. I don't feel I'm ready—not by a long shot—to meet the Lord. Maybe that's why I read my Bible so much."

"You don't have to worry, Jack. At least that's what the Voice told me."

"What voice Johnny?"

"The Voice of God. You see He told me I'm not going to make it, but you are."

"How did God tell you this?"

"When I was alone last night, in a fox hole out on the perimeter, it was all so quiet. That's when He whispered to my mind. He said, *Get ready, be prepared. Your time is almost here.* As soon as I got back within our trench lines, I wrote this letter to her." Johnny paused for a moment, his eyes closely studying my reaction to what he'd told me. Continuing, he was just as insistent, his mind already firmly set. "You've been my best friend this last year. Won't you do me this favor? Please, take it." He held out the letter toward me.

"Okay Johnny," I said, finally relenting, "I'll deliver it to your sister." I reluctantly reached out to take it, my fingertips almost touching the envelope.

Johnny's face was filled with emotion. Behind him the distant sound of exploding shells slowly became louder, coming closer.

"Thanks, Jack, you're truly my friend. I can never tell you how much this means to me. You know, I ran out of ink before I could write her name and address. It's . . ."

The loud shriek of an incoming mortar shell drowned out everything else. In that same instant the letter passed into my hand.

The door of the bunker burst open in a ferocious explosion. Johnny was consumed in a blinding flash. It enveloped both of us in its burning, radioactive light. A fiery blast followed, ripping the bunker apart. Shredded debris with the force of bullets flew all around us.

Johnny was propelled forward, his lifeless form flung into my arms. Going into a bit of shock myself, I struggled to piece together what just happened: Apparently a mortar shell had come down outside, almost directly behind him. His body had taken the full force of the blast and impact of the shrapnel, protecting me.

Debris had gone flying all around me, but I had escaped with barely a few scratches. It was a miracle. I didn't think about it right then as things were happening far too quickly.

I was far more concerned about Johnny. Examining him, I discovered he was in horrible shape, blood gushing from multiple wounds. They were so massive, he had only seconds left.

There was only one thing I could do. Gently and tenderly, I took him into my arms, cradling his head. I saw he could no longer speak, but his eyes told me he still recognized me. Opening up my heart to him, I whispered, "I love you Johnny . . . my brother."

He responded with fingers of one hand forming into the *I love you* sign that hearing impaired people make.

Comforting him, I whispered, "Go with the Lord. He will heal you now." I held my friend's body tightly in my arms as if it would staunch the flow of blood. My efforts were in vain though. Bleeding out quickly, he stopped breathing, dying in my arms.

Inside I was shaking. Shock waves of the explosion still vibrated through me. I knew I would never be able to erase the images that filled my mind in that moment.

"OH GOD, please no!" I cried out for help. Looking about frantically, there was no one. Nothing could undo the horrible finality in the smoking wreckage of that destroyed bunker. But there was one thing I could do. Making what I considered a sacred promise, I held the envelope tightly and whispered, "I promise you my friend, I'll deliver this letter to your sister. I promise . . ."

Scanning this strange world of dust and rubble, I realized the remains of the bunker were on fire. We had taken a direct hit. The concrete walls were melting away. Even the sandbags were burning and blown open, pouring hot sand across the bunker floor. I knew it was time to go or be burned to death.

Encroaching darkness seemed to be closing in on me. I tried to focus on an object becoming visible in the distance. I could see an older version of myself lying in bed, uniform gone. A chill ran through me as I fell into a seizure, shaking all over.

It felt like my soul was being ripped from my body, pulled out and plunged through time itself. Struggling to wake up, I labored painfully. My eyes flickering open, I bolted up in bed. Waking up like that was very painful. It was like a razorblade was cutting me open from the inside. Finally I had freed myself from this nightmarish sleep.

I was not fully awake though. Getting possession of all my faculties was more of a slow motion process. Blurred vision began to focus. Darkness gave way to a distant light penetrating the window from far off. Even through closed curtains it was too intense, too much light. I was hurting all over. The first few rays of the sun blasted my eyes with throbbing pain, filling my head with a pounding headache.

Blocking the offending light with an outstretched hand, I staggered from the bed over to the window. Deciding to brave it, I peeked out for a brief second. Just rising above the eastern horizon, the sun's early morning glow was painfully unbearable. My hand trembled as I closed the curtain again, restoring the room to a certain amount of darkness.

I was becoming weak. Mustering my remaining strength, I turned and went over to the dresser, clicking on the small light. This made the room just right. But now I encountered something I was not prepared to see. The reflection of myself in the mirror had an even more unsettling effect on me. The whole experience of reliving Vietnam had left me feeling horribly sick. Being devoid of color, with beads of perspiration on my ashen face, only intensified the sick queasy feeling rising inside me.

Somehow I made it back to the side of the bed. I barely sat down when I started shaking again. This time it spread through my entire body. Every muscle seemed to ache. Red eyes full of sadness had all been too apparent even in a quick glimpse in the mirror. As I silently reviewed the events that had brought me to this place of old grief, I whispered, "Oh Johnny . . . Why did you have to die?"

I was in country, in Vietnam, for thirteen months. Many days running 24/7 became endless days, running into endless months. Vietnam was hard duty that broke many a man's spirit, both mentally and physically. Twenty years later in this hotel, I was still trying to get over it.

I realized in a strange way I had once more bridged the unbridgeable distance across time to my wartime past. In a sense, it was more real and vivid than ever before. It seemed the events I had just experienced were not those of twenty years ago but rather of twenty minutes ago. They were more like time travel episodes with everything new and fresh.

The Tyler Inn had become a place of memories, many of which I had not wanted to revisit. Ghosts from out of my past had gotten into my mind again and brought me to the place where I was now. I was ill more than ever, and I knew it. Whatever glue that holds most people together was coming apart at the seams inside me. Feeling like a drowning man, I couldn't go on like this. PTSD had me in a vice-grip that wouldn't let go.

Collecting my thoughts, I decided what to do. If there was one person on earth who could help me, I knew who that would be. A determined thought above all others rose inside me to a verbal whisper, "I must go see Doc Peterson."

CHAPTER 4
JACK'S ILLNESS

G hosts from out of my past visited me last night. Those memories ran through my head as I put on my clothes the next morning.

Leaving this strange hotel, I went down the stairs and out the door. It had provided a window into an earlier time in my life. I thought, *You have born the crosses of your past long enough.* I must get free of it and start a new life. Perhaps it would be here in Tyler Junction. A vision of what I wanted to do was becoming clearer as I whispered, "I can do something positive here."

Fastening my overcoat, I looked around. The morning sky was clear and deep blue. As the cool morning air brushed against my face, I inhaled it into my lungs. There was a fresh, unpolluted smell to it. In the light of a new day, I saw a whole new world unfolding in front of me. The old cobblestone street I'd walked last night now stretched into a world from that same era. Such was the style of the buildings that lined both sides of the street before me. These structures appeared just as new as when they were built, yet rich with nostalgia and memories.

I soaked up this atmosphere as I walked on down Market Street, headed toward Doc's place. The people I passed were simply dressed country folk. It seemed I was truly in the heart of a place hard to find that actually no longer existed. It made me feel good to be here, where all the pollution of the outside world was being cleansed from my system. Over the course of time, I would discover there was no place on earth quite like this town and the valley that surrounded it.

As I got to the corner, the old buildings thinned out. I stood across the street from one last free-standing structure. This was where Market Street stopped, dead-ending into a dirt and gravel country road. Across from the last of the cobblestone street was a long frame building, an old fashioned general store.

Turning slowly around, I saw the store faced a vacant landscape that stretched into the rolling hills and mountains beyond. It reminded me of a simpler time, out of my childhood. This was rural America, a place where I could feel at home.

I stood there relaxing, taking in this scenic view. There was something wonderful about it, growing naturally out of the earth, rising up into the heavens to meet the morning sky. I was at peace but just for a moment. Reaching absentmindedly inside my coat pocket, I felt something oddly familiar that had been with me for a lifetime. Pulling it out, I became more serious when I realized I was holding the old blood stained envelope containing Johnny's letter. Inserting it back into my coat pocket, I whispered to myself, "You're finally home . . ."

Crossing the street toward the general store, I walked past it. Stopping at the corner, I noticed a faded wooden sign marked the end of Market Street. Looking up, I took note of a many decade's old rusted sign that nearly covered the side of the building. The sign advertised nickel-a-bottle pop. I thought it was one more bit of nostalgia to be found here. Not so obvious though, was a much smaller 'HELP WANTED' sign, which I completely missed. It was obscured in a side window, and of no significance to me—at least then.

Crossing the dirt road here, I saw an even more faded Olive Road sign on the other side. Continuing on past the first farm house, I walked along a picket fence bordering the road until reaching a second structure that sat back a little distance on its property. Entering through a gate, I approached this modest frame house with a significantly weathered exterior.

Getting closer, I saw Doc Peterson standing on his front porch. Puttering around a swing, he turned in my direction. As he did so, the morning sun enveloped him in a ray of sunshine. This was a sign to me. Doc was fast becoming a ray of hope that could help change my life.

As I approached, Doc's face took on a welcoming expression. His voice was full of enthusiasm, "Jack Holden!"

Coming up on the porch, I shook hands with him. The old man smiled warmly. "Son, I'm glad you decided to come and see me."

"I'm glad too, Doc. This morning I looked around your little town. It's like nothing I've ever seen. I feel good about being here."

Doc gestured out toward the rolling hills rising up into the snow-capped mountains along the horizon, explaining, "It's quite a sight on a clear morning. Tyler Junction is centered right in the middle of a series of valleys that surround and contain it. We town folks here call it the junction of the three valleys"

"What a stunning view. It's like I'm inside a vision."

"When the ice melts up there in the Ozark Mountains, the water forms into a continuous stream that runs down through the valley east of town. It's quite beautiful to see, especially after winter ends and spring begins to break."

"You make it sound like a place I'd like to become a part of."

"Perhaps son, it could even be a place where you could do some positive thinking."

"Maybe even overcome some things in my past."

"Now you're talking. In time you'll be able to wrap your mind around your problems. What you will experience here is unequaled anywhere else. You just might be starting down the road that will lead you to inner peace."

"I hope so, but, I . . ."

Doc picked up on my hesitancy. He immediately sensed there were things bothering me. In broad daylight he could see me clearly. The physical evidence of a washed out man with a lot of problems stood before him.

I was quit ill. My slender figure revealed that I had not been eating properly in some time. Most all color had left me. My pale complexion was only an outward manifestation of how sick I really was within myself. I tried to hide it. Putting on my best face, I tried to appear cheerful as I spoke, "Well, Doc, here I am just as I promised."

Doc would have none of it though. He saw through my fake smile, coming straight to the point, "What's wrong, son? Tell me about it."

The smile quickly evaporated from my face. "I just had one of my worst nights ever."

"I can see it in your face," he said, his eyes carefully studying me.

I admitted, "I haven't been able to get a good night's sleep for months. I have dreams, actually very bad nightmares. I had one while I slept in the hotel last night. It was a memory that has come back countless times to haunt me over the years. Every time my mind works back around to thoughts of the war I can't handle it. I start suffering stress. It gets to going full throttle, like an engine that does not want to stop no matter how much I apply the breaks. Like a vicious cycle, it keeps coming back. I can't shake it. Doc, I don't know what to do. You're my only hope—my last hope."

I'm sure my face reflected my emotions, as fear and desperation struggled for domination within me. Beyond the spoken word, I felt a silent plea forming in my eyes. I was reaching for a lifeline.

Doc saw this, waved toward the door and said, "Come inside." That cold February morning he not only let me into his home but also into his heart.

Taking my overcoat, Doc hung it on the coat tree just inside the door. I followed him into the living room, where he motioned me to take a seat close to the fireplace. Pulling up another chair, he sat down directly across from me.

Warmth from the crackling fire put me at ease as Doc made the first move, "I can start by explaining your condition scientifically."

"I'm interested, Doc. Go ahead, give me the scientific explanation."

"Very well. Jack, there are several chemicals inside the body that act as neurotransmitters to the brain. Among them, adrenaline and cortisol are the most likely culprits in your case. If the motor inside you gets stuck in high gear, then too many of these chemicals reach areas of the brain that trigger old memories, unwanted thoughts, even dangerous emotions. A sense of no longer being in control of oneself takes over. So now it's going to be up to us to reverse this process within you."

"Sounds like a tall order, Doc."

The old man leaned forward into my space, emphasizing his sincerity, "Jack, I believe with all my heart we can get you back on the road to recovery. With the proper therapy and medications, I believe we can begin to turn your life around."

"I'm ready," I responded, believing in Doc's sincerity and conviction.

"Very well, tell me about your dreams. Begin wherever you feel like starting."

I sat there for a moment, thinking. I knew I would have to talk about my past, including some things that were even hidden from me, buried in my subconscious. Pressing my fingers against my forehead, I attempted to focus, feeling the need to unburden myself. It would be a difficult conversation, but Doc's encouragement swayed me, so I would try. I started talking, edging closer to those forgotten memories I knew must come out.

"It all began for me twenty years ago, less than a month after I'd returned from the war. I started having these nightmares about Vietnam. I thought they would go away in time. Instead they became more frequent and intense. I felt embarrassed and ashamed to talk about it. So I withdrew inside myself, went home and shut out the world. They haven't stopped in the years since then. My life was in a crisis. Eventually I had a breakdown. I saw a succession of doctors. Six months ago, I was admitted to a veteran's hospital. It felt like I was being used as a guinea pig there. I had waited so long to get in, knowing something was wrong with me. Then it seemed like they were ignoring me. They weren't really helping me. I couldn't take it any longer, and tried to kill myself. All they did was put me on some medications and release me. The meds didn't seem to work right. They only helped a little at first and later not at all. After leaving the hospital, I sought escape in taking a trip. I got on the bus where I met you."

Doc could see Vietnam had truly been a horrible place for me and that I had undergone a difficult time since the war. "Let's talk about the VA hospital. What specifically brought on the episode when you tried to take your life? Why did you really want to kill yourself?"

I'm sure I was visibly straining, trying to remember something I would prefer to forget. "It's hard for me to talk about it, but I'll try. My greatest fear had come down to just trying to get through each day. It just got to be more than I could take. It's especially bad when I experience another one of those nightmares or hear that voice again."

"What voice? Tell me more about the voice Jack."

"It's something inside, trying to undermine me. The voice is inside my head, talking to me, trying to make me think it's the voice of my conscience.

But *it's not*. It's an outside presence trying to take control of me. It's tried to make me kill myself on more than one occasion. It takes all my strength and force of will to resist. Even then sometimes I can't. Doc, I'm not insane, but sometimes I don't know what to do."

"Son, I don't think you're insane either. There's one thing though, if it's not the voice of your conscience, whose voice is it?"

"That's one question I wish I had the answer to, but I don't. It sounds familiar. I've heard it before, but when and where I don't know. I *just* don't know."

"What about your tour of duty in Vietnam? Could you have heard it during your time over there?"

"Doc, I have spent years trying to remember all the events of 1968 and exactly what happened over there. It's sort of a mystery. A million things happen in a person's life, and Vietnam was such an intense experience for me. I remember most of what happened during every day I was over there in great detail. Yet, a huge chunk of one particular day is a blank for me. I remember I lost one of my very best friends on that day, but beyond that I remember little. The more I try, the more I have nightmares about those events. It's got to where I don't know what's real and what's not. It's all become a blur of imperfect images. Why is that?"

"Losing a best friend can be heart wrenching, even catastrophic to many of us. Brain science is not an exact science. With each individual it can be a different road map. The human mind is often mysterious. There are no easy answers. But we do know something inside it works as a built in protective mechanism, keeping us from recalling incidents too painful to remember. Memories of them become deeply embedded in the cells of the subconscious."

Doc's explanation notwithstanding, I still asked myself what was locked inside my head. My mind had erected a mental wall, firmly blocking a complete recall of that day in 1968. I honestly did not have any answers. Thinking about it, I accepted his diagnosis, "I guess you're right, Doc. A barrier in my mind keeps me from remembering. If only I could get past it. Actually, it's a strange sort of door, large and adorned with some artifacts out of ancient times. Try as I might, I can't seem to open it."

"If only you could, son. I wish you would try just a little harder. Whatever is causing your memory loss, the answers may be on the other side of that door. It could've been an event so intense that your conscious mind has repressed it. Something seems to have traumatized you during the war in Vietnam. To find out, you must go back in your mind and face that event head on. Then you will learn what happened to scar you so severely."

I sat there, again trying to think back. I ventured deeper into my own subconscious, trying to pry it loose. It was a strenuous exercise. Beads of perspiration were breaking out on my forehead.

I talked to Doc as I mentally regressed myself, "Everything I did as a field medic in Vietnam was to save as many lives as I possibly could. But during the Tet Offensive, and in particular the siege of Hue, we were all wore thin and found our own individual breaking points. Those were the roughest days, with one complicated wound after another brought to the bunker where I was set-up. Too many multiple wound victims brought in at the same time went bleeding to death right in front of me. There was no end to it. Some lived though, especially when I could perform a life saving tracheotomy here and there, or medevac them out. But more often than not, they died. As the body bags were piling up, the heavy humid air inside the med bunker was making it difficult to breathe. It was a most uncomfortable place to be."

I paused as a fog seemed to lift, and a window opened up inside my brain. I was filled with an adrenaline rush as a dark figure came rushing into view right in front of me. "I see something," I announced excitedly. Just as the words escaped my lips, a shaft of exploding light penetrated my mind's eye, surrounding me in its brilliant aura.

My eyes flickered as I tried to look over at Doc. He leaned forward in his chair, questioning, "What is it, son? Describe it."

Through a blur I tried to explain, "There's someone moving in the shadows. I can't see him clearly, but he's coming. He's coming closer. He's got a machete. It's the enemy!"

Panic and fear ran through me in the flash of an instant. I was struggling within myself. Whatever was taking place, it was though it were happening for the first time. "He's right there!" I yelled, pointing at someone not in the room, someone else across time in another place.

41

A strange thing happened to me during that very moment. From my point of view, the reality of Doc's living room was fast receding from me, becoming a small far away dot on a vast battlefield. Events within my mind's eye were becoming my new reality.

It was at first an unfamiliar place I'd been plunged into, far removed from the present. The aura around me turned a pulsating red, and the whole horizon lit up in bright red flashes. I could hear nothing but the high-pitched screeching sounds of descending mortar shells. They became increasingly shrill, tearing into my eardrums as they got closer. Reflecting off everything around me as they detonated, the explosions sent blinding flashes of light through the destroyed bunker.

Still having the presence of mind, I tried to communicate with Doc. I whispered, "It's 1968, I'm nineteen years old and back in Vietnam. I'm in the bunker. I see the body of my best friend lying on the floor. His blood is all over the floor. Perhaps because we were so close, I'm torn emotionally. It is a horrific sight, seeing him suffer so much in his last moments of life. Yet, somehow I know it can't hold a candle to what I will encounter later that day. I stagger out of the bunker's smoking ruins. As its shattered door opens, my eyes fill with images that have haunted me ever since. They are only a blur. A mental wall has closed over whatever I saw, concealing those images from my conscious mind. Trying to block it all out, I shut my eyes."

For a moment there was only darkness, then slowly I opened my eyes again. Refocusing, I followed a comforting hand on my shoulder back up into the face of Doc Peterson. I realized then, this was a man imminently qualified at reaching into the souls of his patients. I was back in Doc's living room. The tension within me seemed to relax a bit.

"You left me for a minute, son."

"Yes, I relived the same nightmare I've been having for years. Beyond the incident described to you, I'm not sure what I saw. It's mostly a complete blank. To this day I only see split-second flashes of what happened beyond the bunker. I wake up and it's gone. I don't know how it ends. Lately, I've gotten afraid if I ever get to the end of the nightmare, I'll die."

"Jack, what do you remember beyond the bunker, that is in the days after the nightmare?"

"I woke up in the hospital a week later. The doctors said I had some sort of breakdown or had suffered shell shock. At least that's what they called it then. All I knew is my best friend died in my arms. Even though he was a good man who passed into the good Lord's hands, I still couldn't handle his loss then, and I can't handle it now. Just the thought of it fills my mind with sadness that won't leave me."

"Jack, your friend is in God's hands now. He's no longer suffering. He's healed."

"I wish I could know that for sure . . ." I paused, trying to suppress the heartbreak.

Doc sensed it and tried to console me. "My boy, the war was such a tragic experience for so many. I'm not surprised that many awful things from it still linger inside your mind."

"Whatever it was, I saw something horrible that day, *really horrible . . .*" Pausing again for a moment, I was shaking inside.

Getting a better understanding of my problem, Doc wondered, "If only we could find some way to jolt those memories loose, some mechanism that would pry them out of your subconscious. In any case, I'm glad you came to the valley so that I might help you overcome them."

"What do you think it is, Doc?"

"It's something that has woven itself into the fabric of your mind and has you in its grip. Finding out what it is can't be any worse than the way you're living now, if you want to call it that. Think about it, the sort of prison you go to in your sleep. It's a torture chamber."

"Putting it that way, I understand what you mean. I'm still more than a little scared of what I might find out."

"It's only natural to be frightened of the unknown. In our heart of hearts I think we all are." He looked at me thoughtfully and added, "You're not alone, Jack. I did some reading last night to see if I could help you."

"What did you find out?"

"Out of more than a million Americans who fought in Vietnam, many thousands came back suffering with some form of the same problems you're dealing with. Quite possibly, more than a quarter million soldiers from the war have PTSD. Think about it."

"To tell you the truth Doc, when I first heard that term—PTSD—I didn't want to admit I had it. Any weakness made me feel ashamed."

"There's nothing to feel shame about. It's one of the unavoidable side effects of a hard, cruel war. The seeds of post traumatic stress disorder have taken root in nearly one in four veterans returning from Vietnam."

"They took root in me. When I came home I was full of guilt and grief for my lost comrades."

"Why guilt, Jack?"

"Because I lived and they did not. I saw so many of my friends wounded and killed. Every medic carries a little guilt around with him for those he couldn't save. I always wanted to do more. All of them together made up a cross section of our country: small town farm boys to big city boys, blacks, whites, Hispanics, whatever. It didn't matter. In the stress of war we became like the old saying, *a band of brothers.* As each one of them died, it tore at me a little, until there was no more to tear out of me. Somehow though, I survived and made it home. But as it turned out, I haven't been so lucky after all. In my sleep, I still hear them cry out. I'll never forget those days in the bunker as a medic for as long as I live. Since my father died, I've had no one I could turn to. No one really understood me."

"You do now."

"Doc, that means so much to me. Thank you, with all my heart."

"Tyler Junction is a place where peace and quiet can be found. I think it's possible you'll find what you're looking for here, the healing your soul needs."

"You really think so?"

"One thing is for certain, I'm going to look after you till you're well. Jack, you might not have chosen me, but I have chosen you. I feel it in my heart. I've spent my life doing what I feel is my calling as a doctor, touching a few lives and leaving them a little better off for knowing me. I believe in your case it's what God wants me to do."

Once more, I was deeply moved by this kindly old man. His words always seemed to come straight from his heart. I told him, "You're a good man, Doc, as good as they come."

"Son, there's so much of a need in this world for good." He leaned forward in his chair, studying me closely again, "That force for good is in you too. I see other things as well, things you might not see in yourself."

"What things?"

"I see the courage that has brought you here, to this town and to me. I see faith too, a faith that even now you're reaching out for. It's a faith that will help you see this thing through and find the answers you seek."

Doc's words were having their way with me. I hung on to them, considering their every possibility, "Courage and faith, those are qualities I would certainly like to have. I hope you're right."

"I know I'm right, Jack. Like I keep saying, there are certain healing qualities that especially exist around Tyler Junction. Only good will come from you being here."

"I really want to believe that." As we talked, I was beginning to feel positive again. What began at the bus station last night was continuing to form into a bond of lasting friendship between us. So it began. Many sessions with Doc led me into the world of psychotherapy which started helping me to let go of my fears and anxieties. This became part of what opened the door to the unique environment of the world around Tyler Junction. Its tranquil healing effect soon took hold within me.

Suddenly though, a winter chill in the air invaded the warmth of this new friendship. Feeling it in his bones, Doc reacted, "I think I'd better add a couple more logs to the fire."

Standing up, both of us walked over to the fireplace. As the flames rose, I warmed my hands, reflecting on things, "You know, what a difference a day makes. Yesterday I thought I was at the end of my life. But now, things are different."

"It's a new beginning for you son. Here in Tyler Junction you will meet people that you'll want to know forever."

I thought about it, gazing into the crackling fire. "Strange, isn't it Doc?"

"What?"

"Even after one loses parents and friends, there's a heartache that stays with you, that never really goes away."

"Nothing strange about it at all, that's if one is a compassionate person and honestly cares for other people. That's why I became a doctor."

"Good old Doc," I remarked, smiling as I returned to glancing around the fireplace.

Looking up, my view took in a beautiful landscape painting elaborately framed and mounted on the wall. Then my eyes traveled along the mantle right above the fireplace, coming to a framed photo sitting at the very end. The picture was familiar. Thinking of someone I might care about, I looked at Doc questioningly. "Is it . . . ?"

"Yes, it's Mattie Sullivan."

I stared at the photograph, studying her image closely. "How is it that you know her?"

"I was Mattie's guardian for several years. When her relatives died, I took Mattie in and raised her just as if she were a child of my own. She's been like a daughter to me."

"She appears to have an inner strength," I said, actually feeling it radiate from her picture. My gaze remained fixed on her face. It was though I could see even more, "She's not let that limp stop her from succeeding and leading a normal life."

"It was a tragic accident up at the state capital several years ago." Doc remembered, a tone of sadness entering his voice. "She was much younger. Crossing a street, she was hit by a car. Specialists at the hospital there said she'd never walk again. But I knew better. Her force of will could not be crushed, either by that car or all the other things that have happened to her."

"Other things?"

"A lot of unthinking people in the world sometimes say things without regard for other people's feelings. When she was finally able to return to school, two such young boys—the Barnett brothers—chided her unmercifully and made fun of her. A lesser person would have given up. Not Mattie. She stood her ground, stayed the course, and finished school. You know, she's more than just a night clerk at the Tyler Inn. She became a school teacher and works over at our school during the day."

"Oh really?" I took note, my eyes finally leaving the picture. Focusing on Doc, I asked, "Where exactly is this school?"

CHAPTER 5
THE SCHOOLHOUSE

As I got closer to the old schoolhouse, I could still hear Doc's voice giving me directions: "Keep on going west, down Olive Road about half a mile till it dead ends in front of the schoolhouse gate. You'll know you're getting close when you come across another picket fence—on this same side of the road—which runs a couple hundred yards right up to the school. It's a small but simple brick building built back in the 20s or 30s when Tyler was in lot better times."

After a short walk, I stood at the gate in front of the school. The building was in plain view about 40 or 50 yards back from Olive Road. Behind the school only a few scattered farm houses were visible, rising out of the rolling hills along the horizon.

I went inside, feeling a lot better about myself, relieved after talking with Doc. At least for the time being I was no longer hurting within myself. However I did not know I was about to feel sympathy for someone else's hurt.

Most of the children were still in their classes since it was only a few minutes after eleven. But in the main hallway one little girl stood all alone. Her body was pale and emaciated. Here was an unfortunate child who was composed of all the elements that make up a terminally ill person. I would later find out her name was Laurie Marsh. Gathering her things from her locker, she seemed to be struggling with something that was too much for this small child to deal with. Her whole body jerking, she sank to her knees crying.

A woman approached from the opposite end of the hall, walking with some difficulty, using a cane. It soon became clear the woman was Mattie

Sullivan. As she got closer, Laurie looked up, tears streaming down her face.

Just then the strong arm of good drew near, filled with kindness and understanding. Leaning her cane against the next locker over, Mattie's whole focus was on the child as she knelt beside her.

Laurie raised her arms in pleading fashion, outstretched toward Mattie. A fragile innocence could be seen in the little girl's face. "Oh Miss Mattie," she agonized.

Their eyes connected. Unspoken feelings of the heart passed between student and teacher.

"Come here," Mattie said as she beckoned to her.

The little girl went over to her. Mattie embraced the child, comforting her. More than just professional kindness came together within her as she ever so gently took the frail little girl into her arms. Equal parts—wisdom and understanding—were perfectly fused together in Mattie, visible in her every word and gesture.

It was something amazing for me to behold. In my eyes, in that instant she became so much more than just a schoolteacher. She became a remarkable human being whom I admired.

The little girl reacted with a sad expression. Her mouth quivered as she spoke, "This is the last time I will ever come to my school."

"Now Laurie, look at me. You have it here," Mattie said reassuringly, pointing inward toward her own heart. "All the good thoughts of your school, the fun that you've had, the love of your friends, all the things you've learned here are golden memories. No one can take them away from you."

A flickering smile tried to form on Laurie's face, reflecting the struggling feelings inside her. "You're more than my teacher, you're my friend. Remember when you took me out into the valley last year? It gave me hope and you were part of that hope. I love you for that, Miss Mattie."

The two embraced again, completely unaware that a little ways farther down the main hallway I was a concealed observer just around the corner. As I watched and listened, I thought Mattie had a beautiful soul. It was a special kind of beauty, mixed with goodness that made her the person she was. As she comforted Laurie, I admired her more than ever.

Witnessing everything, I assumed I was quite alone. That was the case until a hand came from behind, clasping firmly on my shoulder. A male voice followed, but in low quiet tones, "May I be of help to you?"

Startled, I turned sharply, coming face to face with a man in his fifties, wearing thick lensed, horn-rimmed glasses. He was smartly dressed in a dark blue suit, looking like he was in a position of authority.

I responded quietly so I would go unnoticed by Mattie and Laurie. "I'm Jack Holden, new to your town. But I'm a friend of Doc Peterson and Miss Sullivan."

This man who had been eyeing me suspiciously, carefully scrutinizing who I might be, was now more open. Looking at me over the top of his horn-rimmed glasses, he spoke more cordially, "Anyone that's a friend of Miss Mattie and Doc is a friend of mine." Extending his hand toward me, he introduced himself, "I'm George Peabody, the Principal here."

I shook hands with him, adding, "It's good to meet you, Mr. Peabody."

The Principal nodded in Mattie's direction, "Mr. Holden, I see you've been observing Miss Sullivan's handling of the little Marsh girl."

I glanced briefly in Mattie's direction, then back to Mr. Peabody. "Yes I have."

"It's a sad case," he responded.

"Really?" I felt a strange urge to know more about this little girl.

"Yes, it's been a sad time for the Marsh family." Mr. Peabody's voice took on a somber tone as he continued, "What with poor Jerry Marsh just losing his wife two months ago, he's now trying to cope with his daughter Laurie's problems. It's been hard on him the past few years, being out of work too. Lost his job over at the old iron works plant when it folded. Then his burden got worse when he found out."

Mr. Peabody was abruptly silenced by the sound of an approaching figure coming down the hall. Recognizing him, the Principal nodded in his direction while alerting me, "Here he comes now."

Both of us looked up to see a man wearing a very worn cap, getting closer. In his early thirties, he was already a wasted looking, shell of a person.

Jerry Marsh had not noticed us. Not slowing down, his mind was preoccupied with the weight of the world on his shoulders.

"Oh Jerry, Jerry Marsh."

He stopped a couple of steps past us, recognizing the Principal's voice. Turning around, he responded, "Oh, Mr. Peabody."

"How are you doing, Jerry?" He asked, very concerned.

"I'm sorry." Jerry was apologetic, removing his cap.

Getting a good look at him, I could see a face full of overwhelming seriousness. He was very pale, very weak, and far too slender for his frame.

He then confirmed it, his voice sounding tired as he spoke, "I don't eat so well lately . . . I've come to pick up Laurie."

Mr. Peabody gestured past us, "She's just around the corner, down at her locker with Miss Sullivan."

Jerry nodded silently, his eyes full of redness. It was obvious he'd been crying and was just barely holding together. Without another word, he turned and continued on, around the corner and out of sight.

At the same time, Mr. Peabody headed back to his office, leaving me alone with my thoughts. Going through stress myself, I could easily recognize that quality in other men. Seeing the visible lines of anguish burrowed deep in Jerry's face, they betrayed the emotional struggle going on inside him. I could identify with this man, clearly understanding him more than most. Already feeling a premonition, I knew I was going to like this fellow and would one day be his friend.

Returning to the corner, I peered around at Mattie again. She was still helping Laurie get her drawings and school papers together, quite unaware of Jerry Marsh walking up behind them.

"Miss Mattie . . ." Jerry spoke softly, placing one hand against a locker, needing to brace himself in order to stand. He continued, barely loud enough for me to hear him, "I've come for Laurie."

She rose from her knees, standing up in a trembling, weakened state. Observing this, her father opened up to Mattie, "I've watched her body give out, a little bit at a time over the past several months. It's become more than she can take, certainly more than I can. She may just have a little time. I guess I'm kind of selfish, but I want to spend that time with her."

"You're not selfish. You're just a father who loves his child. Mr. Marsh, you and Laurie will be in my prayers always. I mean that with all my heart."

He understood, gazing into her eyes for a long second. "You're truly a good person, Miss Mattie. You have the ability to understand people's feelings, better than most folk. I thank you for that, most humbly."

Laurie looked up, her mouth quivering again, as inner turmoil spread visibly across her face. Reaching out to her, she went into her teacher's arms, crying, "I'll love you forever."

Mattie went to her knees again, getting on eye level with the child. Hugging her tenderly, she gently stroked Laurie's hair, trying to calm her. But nothing could stop the big tears that were rolling down the little girl's sad face.

Mattie reached into her pocket for a tissue, wiping the tears away. Then, holding up an index finger, she signaled her to stop crying. Her penetrating gaze got the child's full attention. "Now Laurie, you've got to be strong. Your father needs your strength now."

Laurie nodded as words escaped her lips ever so softly, "Yes, I understand."

Satisfied, Mattie looked up at Jerry Marsh as she rose to her feet.

In gratitude, he reached over impulsively for Mattie's hand and kissed it gently. He spoke respectively, "I'm deeply beholdin' to you Miss Mattie. We've clung to shreds of hope for so long, believing things would not be so bad. I . . ." Jerry's voice trailed off and faded into silence. The suffering inside him had become too great. He was unable to continue. Putting his arm around Laurie, he turned to leave.

Wanting to say something else to help him, she called out, "Mr. Marsh."

Stopping, he turned back around. "Yes?"

"God be with you. He knows what you're going through and will never forsake you. Please Mr. Marsh, keep the faith."

"Thank you for those words." Hesitating a moment, he added something very profound, "They will help me with the road I must walk upon." A brief smile formed among the sadness etched across his face. With his arm still around Laurie, finding support in each other, they walked through the main foyer and out the school doors—never to return again.

As they walked away, Mattie looked after them with a concerned expression. It was part of what marked her as a deeply caring individual. Following them, she reached the main foyer where a side hall intersects it.

Movement of someone off to one side caught her attention. She glanced around and saw me. Surprised, she was full of questions, "Mr. Holden?—Jack?—What brings you here?"

"I was just visiting with Mr. Peabody."

"Oh, I didn't realize you had business with the Principal of our school."

"I've known George for sometime now." I lied. Avoiding her gaze for a brief moment, I tried to decide how to begin. As our eyes met, I told her the truth, "Actually the nature of my business is with you."

"Really?"

I could see questions forming in her expression so I quickly changed the subject and spoke almost apologetically at first, "I don't mean to intrude. But that man and his little girl, I couldn't help notice how kindly you treated them."

"Jerry Marsh is one of those whose life has been caught up in a very large tragedy still playing out. He was a job foreman over at the old iron works plant till they closed up a few years ago. He'd been barely scraping by with a small farm when his wife died of pneumonia a couple of months ago. Now it's his daughter Laurie . . ."

"Yes," I broke in, "That little girl seemed so frail."

"Yes she is. I've been giving that little girl all the love and support I can, but it's not enough—not near enough." Mattie paused, that concerned expression returning to her face. "It's so sad. Laurie is like a big bright shooting star being snuffed out way too quickly. She was recently released from the hospital over in Raleigh, sent home without much hope. They said there was nothing more they could do for her. Laurie has inoperable terminal cancer and will more than likely not be alive much longer. It's an awful thing to happen to one so young, so gifted. She's an extraordinary child, fully aware of what is happening inside her body. It's as if a power greater than herself is inside her, guiding and helping her at times. If you could only know her, you would understand what I mean when I say she is one of God's children."

"I wish I could know her." My response came from deep inside, surprising even myself. It was something I didn't fully understand then, but I knew I would in the course of time. A glimmer of a thought hit me just then, one that would have far reaching consequences. I would start helping others, freely and unselfishly. In doing so, I would help myself by making my life count, becoming sort of a good deed doer. From that afternoon, I had a new awareness and feeling for people, especially this little girl. There was a great urge within me to do something, to say something. I told Mattie what was on my mind, "I want to help her somehow, some way."

She looked at me questioningly, "Why you, Jack?"

"If you listen to your heart, you have to do what you believe is right. Don't you agree Mattie?"

"I can't recall when I first realized it, but a long time ago I made it my life mission to instill something special into the minds of young children, opening up whole new worlds for them. That's why I became a teacher, so I could be there for those like Laurie with compassion and understanding. I did listen to my heart in doing so. Yes, I agree. But somehow you already knew that, didn't you?"

"Yes, because I see you're a caring person who likes to help people."

"Thank you, Jack. It's nice of you to say that."

"It's true," I insisted. What drew me to Mattie was the fact she opened up her heart and was up front to me with her thoughts about people and things. It was this quality I first admired in her. I felt more like an old friend, rather than a stranger who had just came into her life.

Mattie had taken in my words, silently studying me. Later, she told me of feeling an attraction when we met the previous night. She felt there was something in me reaching out to her that she could not identify nor turn away from. She was curious. Who was this stranger that Doc had brought into her life? Why was he really in Tyler Junction? These were intriguing questions. She told herself she would talk to Doc about me. For the time being she decided to put all these questions aside, explaining herself further, "Jack, I love people. You see, these children here are going to grow into the people who are our best hope for the future."

I saw an opening here and added thoughtfully, "Speaking of the future, would you do me the honor of having dinner with me tonight?"

She looked at me curiously, processing what I'd just asked. "You know, Jack, you're something of a mystery. I'm not sure exactly what it is. It surrounds you and pops up in everything you say. But things get clearer every time we're together."

Moving closer, she looked into my eyes and could almost see the idea seize me as I spoke, "Then let's explore this mystery together. I'd like to hear more of what you have to say tonight."

I do believe it was then, the laws of mutual attraction were never more at work than they were that day. Looking at me, her expression filled with an odd sense of wonder and curiosity together. "Okay," she said, "I'm willing to go down that road to find out more about you." Mattie smiled, but as she took another step toward me she lost her grip on the cane and it slipped from her hand.

CHAPTER 6
THE CAFÉ

M attie's cane laid on the floor as I reached down to pick it up.
"I'll get it." I retrieved the cane, hanging it over the back of a nearby chair.

She was apologetic, "I'm sorry. Even now, after all these years I'm still sort of awkward with it at times."

"There's nothing to be sorry about," I said, reassuring her. "I'm glad you decided to have dinner with me. I'm really a pretty decent guy as guys go."

"I knew that when I first met you," Mattie observed.

I was seated directly across a small table from Mattie. We were at the Tyler Junction Café, overlooking Market Street. The evening sunlight reflected off the cobblestone pavement of the town's main street and shined through the restaurant's windows, bathing its customers in a golden brilliance.

I began to look over the menu while Mattie's eyes looked me over. "Everything on the menu is all homemade, cooked from scratch," she noted, her gaze remaining fixed on me.

I felt relaxed, lost in a place where all time seemed to stop. Walking over here with Mattie, I found myself more keenly aware that the rhythm of this little town was strikingly different from the fast paced rat race of the city. Tyler Junction did not belong in our present world. It was a place ripped out of time from a much simpler way of life.

Soaking up this tranquil setting, I found myself in what would be my most peaceful experience in some time. All my bad memories floated away into the world of the forgotten.

"A penny for your thoughts," said Mattie, noticing my distraction.

"Oh, it's this place. I'm so fascinated by this town," I responded, focusing back on her. "It harks back to another era. Places like this just don't exist anymore."

"I know," she agreed, echoing my own fascination. "Very little has changed in Tyler for several decades. It's a place where cobblestone streets, illuminated by old-fashioned lamps, still survive. This town is like something out of the early 1900s."

"It's as though I've found a lost time capsule."

"If you open it up, you'll find everything inside is alive and still the same within its boundaries. It does put some people off though, those more attuned to the modern world."

"Strangely, it's just what I've been looking for: a small town with old-fashioned values. The modern world's headlong rush into an abyss has gotten to me in recent years. I'm glad I got off that bus with Doc. I'm so glad I'm here with you," I said, feeling quite satisfied.

As we ate dinner, feelings of contentment filled me. It was like a fresh cool breeze had blown in my direction. I soaked up the small town atmosphere, enjoying the sound of a nearby harmonica playing songs flavored with Americana.

Listening to the music, I found myself staring into the face of someone who might be part of a bright new future for me. The evening sunlight had reached our corner table, forming a golden aura around her. It made such a beautiful vision in my eyes. Shutting out the rest of the world, everything around her blurred into the background as I looked at Mattie.

It was a magical, stolen moment in which I wondered many things. There was something about her. Had I quite by accident stumbled upon the person who would mean so much to me? Was this the girl I had been looking for? The gathering power of each succeeding second drew me closer. I was staring and couldn't help it. If this moment could last forever. If only . . . At that point I drew back, realizing Mattie was looking at me. Though other local customers were laughing and talking at tables near us, I was oblivious to these distractions. From the moment I'd heard her name, I could not take my eyes off her. She was my total focus.

"What is it?" She noticed I was staring, quickly adding, "Doc thinks you're interested in me."

"I am."

"Why, Jack?"

"There's something fascinating to me about a young woman who works at a hotel at night, teaches school during the day, taking an interest in little children."

"I sometimes wonder why I do all that I do. I suppose it has something to do with dedication and a promise."

"A promise?"

"A long time ago I believe the Lord inspired me to become a school teacher. I promised Him I would dedicate my whole heart and soul to becoming the best teacher possible. Then in the grand scheme of what has become my life, He made it all come to pass."

"Your plate should be full, but yet you found the time to make a lonely traveler feel not so lonely."

"You don't need to be lonely anymore."

"That's a penalty for living alone as long as I have."

"You don't have to live alone anymore. After all, you've met me."

"Mattie, you make me feel like I never want to leave Tyler Junction."

As our conversation progressed, I had unwittingly re-awakened a forgotten memory inside Mattie. Silent for a moment, she searched my face. Trying to remember something, she was not quite able to put her finger on it. She asked, "Jack, when we first met there was something vaguely familiar about you. Is it possible, have we ever met before?"

"I'm sure I would remember it. No, I think not." In my heart of hearts I thought differently. Leaning forward into her space, I whispered, "Oh, how I wish I had met you."

Now I had her attention. Curious, she asked, "Who are you, Jack Holden?"

"I'm a good man who cares for others—or at least I try to be."

Studying me closely, staring deep into my eyes, she responded very slowly, "I believe you are."

"I guess I'm actually a mixed bag, the best and the worst woven together imperfectly as a flawed individual."

"You're not as flawed as you might think, at least that's my opinion."

"Bless you, Mattie. At least I'm someone who doesn't feel so alone anymore." I spoke truthfully from my heart.

"Why did you come here, to this valley?" She was still pressing me for answers.

I was getting a little uneasy now, picking my words carefully, "I suppose . . . searching for someone, for a place to begin a new life. But really, I'm not quite sure I know myself."

"I do," Mattie said, quickly adding, "Or at least I think I do."

"Then why?" I was fascinated to learn what she thought.

"You're here to do good," she said.

"Okay . . ." Considering the thought for a moment, I liked the idea. "You're correct," I added, "I'm a good deed doer. But I'm curious, what makes you think that?"

"As you said, you're a caring person. I saw it last night. And today, I saw it in your eyes and in your actions." Staring at me, she continued as if she had a vision of things to come, "You're life has a definite purpose. You're here on a mission to help someone."

"Now how do you know all that?" I asked, feeling like she was fast becoming some kind of a psychic.

"I'm not sure how I know it, I just do," she said, trying to explain. "My mind works in unusual ways sometimes. I come to conclusions that contain more truth than anyone realizes at a particular moment. From time to time, I have premonitions that become reality."

Listening to her, I thought she seemed satisfied for the time being. One day though, she would have more searching questions. But thank God today wasn't that day. I was not yet quite prepared for her to delve any deeper into my reasons for being in Tyler Junction.

"What a difference a day makes," I reflected. "Yesterday I didn't know a soul here. If I needed to talk to someone, there was no one."

"During our greatest need it's good for someone to be there." Honestly caring about me I thought, she added, "I'm glad I can be here for you, Jack."

Her words of support made me feel good. I confided in her, "I feel like I'm on some sort of strange journey. Sometimes I think I'm Don Quixote."

"My grandfather often said that too."

"Said what?"

"That in a sense he was Don Quixote."

"I'd like to know more about your grandfather."

"There's so much I could tell you. Let me just say he was a man constantly in search of a vision. But what sort of 'Don Quixote' are you Jack?"

"Instead of chasing after windmills, I think I'm on a quest to find my sanity."

"Sanity can bring you peace of mind and be good for your soul. Perhaps here in the valley, you will find some measure of peace."

"I would like that. I need to uncomplicate my life. Yes, I would like to stay here awhile."

"If you do," Mattie reacted very positively, "I would like very much to help you, Jack. I hope you don't mind me saying this, but when you came in the hotel last night you had the look of a person who had suffered a lifetime of nightmares."

I accepted her remarkable insight, "You don't know how close to the truth you are."

"But it doesn't have to be that way," she pleaded with renewed sincerity.

Leaning forward in my seat, I could see she honestly cared. Lines of heartfelt communication had opened up as we were becoming truly comfortable in each other's company.

The more we talked, the more she seemed to become interested in me. I think she saw something in the mysterious stranger aspect of my character, deciding she would try to help me on my journey. Along the way, I thought she might even find some answers to questions from out of her own past.

Silence fell between us for a moment as we searched each other's faces. Now I looked deeply into her eyes, just as she returned it with the same intensity. A wordless union blessed this beginning to a blossoming relationship.

Slowly, she leaned forward into my space, remarking, "I see something in you, not easily seen."

"What's that?" I asked, feeling like I had fallen under a scrutinizing microscope.

"It's just there's a lot more to you than what's on the surface."

"What do you see, or what do you think you see?"

"I see a much more complex person than what you reveal to the rest of the world. You're sensitive and kind but someone whose been hurt by events in your past."

"Mattie, I'm very fortunate to know you. Please, be my friend," I said, extending my hand across the table.

Accepting my hand, she squeezed it tightly, observing, "This is going to be the start of a very special friendship."

Over dinner, we had both picked up on something. Feelings of affection for each other filled both of us and would remain in both our memories of that moment. Drawn together, we had unknowingly begun to heal the hurt I knew existed in both of us. It was a mutual attraction that neither one of us yet realized the full implications.

"Jack, I hope you will stay for at least awhile here in Tyler Junction."

Throughout dinner, I had listened to Mattie with complete attention, opening up my heart and mind to what she was saying, soaking up her every word like a sponge. Getting to know her had been a good thing, filling the emptiness inside me with her friendship. Just being with her made me feel good about myself.

I knew then, I would stay because something beautiful, indefinable, had happened between us that evening. It was as if some invisible force was making it happen. And of course, it was.

Yet there was one consideration I would have to resolve. So I told her, "If I stay here, I'll need to find a job."

CHAPTER 7
THE HEART OF TYLER JUNCTION

The next morning found me outside the general store. It was at the far north end of town, being the last building before the cobblestones of Market Street dead-ended into a dirt and gravel road.

I was standing in front of a large tin sign anchored across one side of the building. Admiring the old soda pop advertisement in all its glory of rusted decay, my eyes traveled downward, coming to rest on a small window below it. Something sticking up, though partially obscured, got my attention this time. I zeroed in on it to be for sure. It was a small HELP WANTED sign.

Confident in myself, I walked back around in front of the building. Another sign above the door announced in large letters, RUSSELL'S GENERAL STORE. Beneath it, standing on the porch to one side of the front door, was a mustachioed middle-aged man wearing an apron. He called out, "Howdy stranger."

"Hello," I responded, advancing up the porch steps toward him.

The mustachioed man strongly eyeballed me as I approached, a questioning expression forming on his face. "Jack Holden?"

"Yes—Yes I am." I was surprised the man knew my name.

"Kinda thought you were," the man responded. "Miss Sullivan and Doc Peterson called me. I'm Dan Russell."

I nodded, acknowledging the general store owner, "Mr. Russell," thinking to myself, my friends have already put in a good word on my behalf.

Looking past me, out across the vacant land across the street and the horizon beyond, he commented, "We don't get many strangers in the valley anymore. Tyler used to be about 5,000 population in its heyday. But now, we've only got about 500 folks living here, spread out thin, all over the valley."

"You've got 501 now," I corrected, adding, "That's if you'll have me. I need a job."

Opening the store's front door as he spoke, Mr. Russell gestured, "Come on, step inside." As we entered, the door closed behind us, causing the bell above it to ring briefly.

"So you need a job you say."

"I sure do."

"Mattie and Doc say you're a good man."

I thought for a moment, this could be an opportunity, maybe a new start in life. Then I answered with firmness, "I am *a good man.*"

Sizing me up, I think he saw something he liked in me. Then he committed himself, "Come with me then."

I followed him over to the small window where the HELP WANTED sign was. Removing it, he said, "If Mattie and Doc say it, that's good enough for me. Jack, it looks like you're my new clerk."

"Thank you, Mr. Russell," I responded, erupting in a grateful smile.

He held up an index finger, slightly objecting, "Since I feel like we're gonna be friends, just call me Dan."

I could see right up front, Dan was a decent man. I immediately appreciated his kindness to me. "Thanks, Dan, you won't regret it."

"I don't regret anything, so tell me a little bit about yourself."

So I told him about my upbringing, "I was brought up an only child in a decent family, believing in God and country. They instilled their patriotic values in me. When the flag was raised, we stood up, came to attention, placed our hands over our hearts, and swore allegiance to it. No sacrifice was too great. That's why it was easy for me to enlist when the war came."

"Come with me. I want to show you something." Waving toward the rows of merchandise in front of us, he continued, "We'll get to it as I take you around the store."

For the first time, I got a clear view of the interior of this long rectangular-shaped building. Like the café, a nostalgic small town atmosphere was everywhere. As we walked past the long wooden counter, I took it all in.

From the old fashioned pharmacy behind it, to one of those old ornate cash registers sitting on the counter, it was a place out of step with modern times.

Walking down isles of farm supplies, we stopped in front of a large bulletin board. Gesturing to it, he said, "Now here's something I think you can identify with." Tacked on it was one of those old World War I 'Uncle Sam/I WANT YOU' posters and many photos of young servicemen from various wars.

He was right. They got my attention immediately. I was frozen in my tracks, fascinated by what I saw. Scanning the pictures, I became deeply moved.

Dan explained, "These are just the young boys from this valley, those who have fought in our nation's wars from the Spanish American War on up to the present. Every one of these men stood up for what they believed. They gave all they had. Many of them did not return, instead making the supreme sacrifice. They were *all* patriots in my view. You see, this is more than just a bulletin board to me."

I was transfixed in the moment. This was like a shrine, deserving an act of reverence. Moving closer, gently touching some of the photos, I whispered aloud, "It's a wall of honor."

Dan was moved as well, adding, "I'm so very proud of these young men. This is my own way of honoring them, in sort of a memorial." Then almost as an afterthought he asked me, just to make sure, "You say you were in the military?"

"Yes, I served in Vietnam as a medical specialist during the 1960s."

"So you saved lives?"

"Some, those that I could."

Dan echoed what I was remembering, "Those were hard, violent times over there."

"Worse than you could ever imagine." My voice trailed off, lost in so many thoughts running through my mind.

"Jack," Dan called out to regain my attention.

Reacting, I snapped back to the present. "I'm sorry, just thinking about those years is still hard on me."

"Nothing to be sorry about. Actually, I understand more than most," Dan explained. "I know that over 50,000 of America's sons and daughters were lost in Vietnam. But many more came back still suffering from wounds."

"That's right," I told him. "In some—like myself—those wounds are not visible. They are inside, within us in the form of flashbacks and nightmares. In fact, Doc is treating me right now. I uh . . ." I paused, thinking maybe I'd said too much.

"It's alright son," Dan interrupted, seeing I was agonizing about it. "Doc told me. As far as I'm concerned it's just between us. In my book, you're just as much a hero as those on my bulletin board. In fact, I'd like to put your picture up here too, that is since you're livin' here now."

"Dan, you don't want my picture here." I could see he was caught by surprise. I felt unworthy and explained, "The real heroes were the ones who died in Vietnam, like those on your bulletin board, not like me. I got to come back."

"That's right, Jack. But just think about this: you survived so you can be their voice now. They have no one else who can really tell their story. Just think about it, that's all I'm asking."

"I will, Dan." We shook hands, and that's where we left it, at least for then.

I felt like this was something he wanted to do but had decided to wait to discuss it further, at least until he knew me better. "Well, that's okay, for now," he added, knowing he would return to this issue another time. Changing subjects, Dan got back on his tour, "Come on, I want you to see the rest of the store and meet some friends of mine."

Following Dan, I went past a section of tin signs and other memorabilia hanging from the ceiling. Around another isle, we came to a secluded corner midway back in the store. In the heart of the building stood an old fashioned potbellied stove. Nearby was a barrel with a flat game board atop it. Sitting opposite each other, with the barrel positioned between them, two men were playing dominoes.

I immediately thought these were two regulars who hung out at the store. But they were more than just customers.

Looking up as we approached, Dan introduced me, "Fella's, I want you to meet my new clerk, Jack Holden." Gesturing to a bearded man wearing a baseball cap, "This is Zeke Wilcox, former truck driver and citizen in our little town these past seven years."

Zeke looked up, grinning, "Please to meet you, Jack."

I nodded in his direction, "Zeke."

"So you're a newcomer to our valley?" Zeke questioned.

"That's right. I came in on the bus a couple days ago. There's something special about this little town. I want to stay, at least for awhile."

"I know what you mean. Like Dan said, I used to be a truck driver. This was part of my regular run, over the Winding Stairs Mountains, into the valley. One winter the roads froze so bad that I couldn't get my rig back up the mountains. I was stuck here in Tyler, the very last stop on my run."

"What'd you do?" I asked.

"I got another job that winter." He turned in his seat just enough to reveal a badge on his belt. "I'm Deputy Sheriff here now. I fell in love with the town and sold my rig the following spring. I've never looked back. Jack, you can't go wrong here. It's a good place to live."

"And it was this other man here who hired Zeke," added Dan.

My gaze traveled across the barrel to the other man sitting in the corner, whom I now realized had already been keenly eyeing me. He was a man with penetrating eyes, staring at me over a thick mustache.

"This is Dwight Bodeen," Dan continued, "The law here in Tyler Junction."

The Sheriff smiled, a slight twinkle forming around his eyes. "It's good to have you here, son. Doc Peterson called me about you last night, says you're his friend. Any friend of Doc's is a friend of mine."

"Thanks Sheriff," I reacted gratefully.

Moving in his chair, Sheriff Bodeen glanced around for someone not there. Leaning forward in my direction, his expression changed into a steely-eyed stare as he spoke a few words of cautionary warning in a low voice, "He's not here right now, but you will need to watch out for Leroy Barnett. He's been known to become like a force of nature. In the eye of a storm, HE IS the hurricane." Thinking for a moment, the Sheriff put it even more bluntly, "The man is a trouble making bully."

"So you get the picture, Jack," interjected Dan.

"I'm fast getting it."

"His brother Kyle ain't no picnic either," observed Zeke, putting in his two cents worth. "He's just as bad in his own way."

I nodded in full appreciation of the warnings, remembering what Doc had said about the Barnetts mistreating Mattie.

"They're right," agreed Dan, giving his own opinion now, "Leroy is a man who can't control his temper. He is mean as they come, trying to pick a fight every time he comes in here."

"More than that, he's just an evil man," concluded Sheriff Bodeen. "That's why you'll be seeing a lot of Zeke and me playing dominoes, hanging out here. And, if the Barnetts get out of hand, I've got a 'persuader' that will put them back in line fast and just the place for them to go and cool off."

As the Sheriff relaxed back in his chair, his jacket opened up just enough for me to peer down and see what he meant by a 'persuader'—a very large revolver protruding from an otherwise hidden shoulder holster.

Thus, I had been introduced to two men who were the law in the valley. As time passed, I came to realize that Russell's store truly was the heart of Tyler Junction. This was so because, sooner or later, all the folks of the town and surrounding valley came in, visited, made purchases, carried on a little conversation, and left a bit of themselves here. That is, all save one person, and over time I would find out that story later.

The grand tour continuing, we went through a swinging door in the rear of the store. It opened back into a darkened room. Flipping a wall switch, Dan turned on a light in the storeroom.

He explained, "This is where we keep all the surplus merchandise, back stock for the store." Pointing toward the back door of the store, he added, "Now I want to show you what's out back."

"What's out back?" I repeated the phrase as a question.

"I reckon you can stay in the cottage out back."

"What?" I was surprised.

"Didn't you know room and board went along with the job?"

"I didn't realize—"

"Oh yeah," Dan cut in, elaborating further, "I've got a little bungalow out back here. It's sort of like a little efficiency apartment. I used to live there. But since I bought a home, it's just been sittin' back there empty. You might as well make use of it."

"I really appreciate it," I said, being truly thankful. "I knew I was going to have to find something. I couldn't afford staying at the hotel. Dan, I'm grateful. Things just seem to keep looking up for me."

"They're gonna get even better, Jack," Dan added, a little grin forming on his face.

"What do you mean?" My curiosity was building.

"Well uh . . . let's go on out and I'll show you."

Dan unlocked the back door, leading the way. Following him, I wondered what else was out behind the store?

CHAPTER 8
A LITTLE BUNGALOW

Dan Russell and I emerged from the back door of his store. Taking just a few steps, we both came to a dead stop.

Inhaling a foul stench, I'm sure my face took on a repulsed expression as I asked, "What's that odor? Rotten eggs, methane gas, or perhaps something else?"

Dan was disgusted too, explaining, "I know, I know. It's this bad only on days like this, when the wind picks up and carries it over here."

Scanning the horizon, my eyes came to rest on the horrible dark presence of a decaying building, setting far back, barely within view. "What is it?" I asked.

"That's what's left of the old iron works factory. It was abandoned in a state of bankruptcy, putting a lot of good people out of work, nearly killing the town. Even after five years, that building still gives off foul odors, and brings back a lot of bad memories."

I recalled how close I'd come to it. "I went down Olive Road on my way over to the schoolhouse yesterday. I guess I didn't notice it."

"And you wouldn't." Dan explained, "It can't be seen from the main road. It sets back far enough. But you can sure see it from back here—and sometimes smell it." Dan's face reflected he was also getting a deep inhalation of something bad.

Now I wanted to know, "Can anything be done?"

The frustration could be seen on Dan's face. "We've contacted the state health department. They're gonna do something, but I don't know when. I think it's some kind of bio-hazard. Needs to be leveled, it's the only eye sore in the valley. I wouldn't go over there if I were you. It's dangerous. The roof collapsed over parts of the factory a year ago last winter. An ice storm and too much snow caused it to cave in. Since then the stench has grown worse."

Moving on, we ascended steps, actually carved out of the rock, and on up a small incline in back. Reaching the top, I got a clear view of the bungalow for the first time. I'm afraid my expression changed decidedly upon first look, as the structure appeared terribly dilapidated.

Dan read my mind, "I know, it looks a little run down. But that's only on the outside. Someone's worked most of the night and into the morning, fixin' and cleanin' the place up inside. In fact, the cleaning person is in there right now."

Taking my eyes off the bungalow, I turned to Dan, "What? Who?"

"Well . . ." Dan was hesitant, motioning toward the bungalow, "You go on inside, get moved in, and come see me a little later."

"What?" Something about his tone and the way he said it was making me even more curious.

Dan motioned to me again and repeated himself, "Just go on inside and check it out."

I complied this time, heading toward the bungalow's front door. Before going back to the store, Dan focused on me for a moment, as if he was anticipating something.

I reached out, extending my hand toward the doorknob, turning it, pushing the door inward.

From inside, the door continued to open. As it did, a strong shaft of sunlight advanced through the doorway with me. Emerging through this light, I advanced a couple steps into the bungalow. Pausing for a moment, I did not know an answered prayer awaited me.

My vision had to adjust. The first thing I noticed was that everything was cleaned nice and neat.

My eyes traveled the room, settling on a figure stepping from the shadows into the room light. As her hand propped a broom up against a wall, the cleaning lady turned toward me, revealing her face. It was Mattie Sullivan.

As she looked up, I could clearly see every nuance and facial gesture. Seeing me, the features of her face reflected a glowing recognition. I suppose I fancied this, but it did seem her whole expression changed rapidly, becoming full of feeling for me. At least I know I wanted it.

Caught by surprise, I had to ask, "Why are you here?"

She stood still for a moment, focusing on me before answering, "I wanted you to stay. Last night after dinner I prayed to the Lord that you would. This morning I was awakened by a voice speaking to my heart, telling me to come here and do this. Jack, I took it to be the Voice of God."

"Bless you Mattie, you're a wonderful woman."

In the silence that followed, I could see there was something very powerful about her gaze. I knew she could see the hole that was inside me, that I was incomplete, full of loneliness.

We both felt the common bond of unspoken feelings drawing us together. It was though cosmic forces had a hold on both of us. We were on the same wavelength, both wanting to console each other.

Crossing the room, I moved forward till I was standing right in front of her. I studied her face carefully and saw that all her feelings for me were indeed mirrored there. I'm sure she saw the same in my face. Our eyes made a connection, looking deep into each other's souls. I think we both knew this was one of those special moments that just occur a few times in people's lives.

Moving a hand closer, my fingertips ran gently down her facial features. Even though her face was smudged from cleaning this place, I thought she was beautiful. Caring for her more than ever before, I told her, "Last night I thought we were becoming rather good friends—and now I know it for sure."

Mattie's hand moved toward mine, our fingers touching. As our hands intertwined and came together, I drew her closer. We held on to each other, both of us feeling the special connection that had begun last night. It was as if something beyond our understanding was taking an active role in cementing the bond that was beginning to form between us.

Again as our eyes connected, I whispered to her, "Mattie, you're a very special person."

Later, we would find ourselves standing in the opened doorway of the bungalow. Facing each other, we both reached out and exposed our feelings once more.

I wondered out loud, seeking her advice, "What should I be doing with my life?"

"Exactly what you're doing right now, trying to improve it."

"What you've done here today means so much to me." I spoke sincerely, adding with heartfelt feeling, "You've helped me far more than you'll ever know."

Looking up at me, she confessed again, "I had hoped whatever brought you here would make you stay."

"Mattie, you're the reason why I'm staying." I admitted, meaning those words with all my heart.

She was drawn, as if by a magnet, into my arms. Our feelings exposed, we embraced and held on to each other once again.

In our minds, we both made an unspoken commitment to each other. It was more than the expressions on our faces and the look in our eyes. We both could see the truth and sincerity there. It was though our feelings for each other were made sacred in that moment. What lay beyond this spec of time would change both our lives.

I stood there in the doorway, staring after her as she left. I had looked deeply into Mattie's soul and saw what few people may have ever seen. I saw a lot of suffering there. I knew in my heart, I would have the opportunity to help her some day. *I just knew I would.*

My hoped-for life had been like a lost dream, and I pondered if this was part of that dream. But I knew this was real, and my mind rejoiced in that fact. The dream was coming true in Tyler Junction, and Mattie Sullivan had become a huge part of it. I had finally found someone. I felt a measure of peace that had been so unattainable in my life. Seeing a foreshadowing of what could be my future in her face, I became more convinced of that fact in each succeeding moment. A new life had begun for me. I was sure of it. Humbled, I whispered, "Thank you Lord."

At the end of the day, I laid in bed, alone with my thoughts. Tired, I still managed to whisper her name once more, "Mattie . . ." All the threads of my life seemed to be coming together here. In a rare moment I felt free of past memories as my mind drifted into sleep.

I would rest for awhile. But I did not know even then something was there watching me.

CHAPTER 9
FACE OF EVIL

I slept, but as the evening turned into night my mind's eye had taken over. The thoughts inside me were not peaceful. Suddenly, I remembered what the 'something else' was in the repellent odors Dan and I encountered outside near the bungalow. It was the smell of burned flesh, very reminiscent of what I first encountered in Vietnam. A familiar unsettling feeling was coming back again. A shudder traveled down my spine. All of a sudden I was awake. It seemed all too soon. I did not know how long I'd been asleep when my eyes flew open. Something unnatural was happening.

My heart was racing. I was full of anxiety. The overwhelming sense I was not alone seized me all the way down to the pit of my stomach.

Lying on my back, I remained absolutely motionless for a moment. Listening very carefully, I could hear movement nearby. I was not alone. Aware of a presence, I glanced around the room. Light of the full moon shown through a nearby window, enabling me to see something lurking in the shadows.

Staring up into the blackness of the ceiling, it started cracking open. I tried to make sense of what was happening. In the opening, a shapeless mass was forming together and descending down toward me. Fear seized me in its grip to the point I could not move. Something was emerging from the billowing darkness hovering above me. What could it be?

Plunging downward, it landed on top of my body, straddling me. I found myself staring straight up into the crazed face of a machete wielding Viet Cong soldier—or was it? In one of those split second moments that seem to last an eternity, I struggled to understand what I was looking up at. The face was barely skin stretched over bone. Never had I been confronted with a more horrifying vision of the enemy. It was almost other worldly.

Whatever he was, his heavy weight on top of me pressed against my chest and ribcage, making it hard to breathe. I found myself struggling underneath him.

Reacting, getting a free hand I smacked him hard, square in his skeletal bony face. The tremendous force of the blow sent him toppling backward. Hitting the floor, he let out a loud, shrill screech.

Bolting up to a sitting position, my eyes were wide open now. I was perspiring heavily. Looking around, the apparition was gone. Alone now, I was immediately engulfed in absolute quiet.

Swiveling around on the edge of the bed facing the nightstand, I flipped on the lamp. A roller coaster of thoughts rushed through my brain, amplifying my emotions. I was shaking. Nerves frayed, I tried to focus. It was an effort to think clearly.

Sitting there motionless, I stared at the front door caught up in the night breeze, opening and closing on its own. *Was it a hallucination? What was happening to me?* I asked myself repeatedly, grasping at the complexities of what had just happened.

My nightmare world was becoming real. Descending more and more into the grip of my own fears, it felt like my heart was beating out of my chest. An uneasy feeling rose within me. Something terribly sinister was going on inside my head, unleashing this ghost of a Viet Cong warrior. *What else lurked inside my mind?* The answer came quickly, my PTSD was back.

Just the thought of that prospect was profoundly unsettling. It would linger in my mind for the rest of the night.

Quiet desperation lurking inside me formed into a question. Finally, it escaped my lips as more of a plea, "Can I ever have peace?"

The next morning I looked up from this dark pit of despair, full of questions, "Is it possible? Could something out of my war experiences be so powerful that it could get inside my head and work its way so much so into the fabric of my mind?"

As I begged for answers, the blackness around me lightened from the bungalow into the warmth of Doc Peterson's living room. Wrung out, I slumped into a chair, still persisting, "Is it possible, Doc? I must know."

Standing in front of me, he explained, "The human brain can act very strangely at times. Within your inner mind, the rivers of your own subconscious run deep with possibilities. Many things are possible there. Do you understand?"

"I'm not sure, but I'm trying so I can cope with my illness."

"Let me explain it more scientifically. Within your brain are about 100 billion nerve cells called neurons. They affect so much within the realm of the human senses, what you think and feel, all the emotions within you. So you see, if these neurons get damaged—and well they might under the stresses of combat—they could send out incorrect information. What with the multiple traumatic experiences you suffered during the war, these faulty neurotransmitters may have poisoned the rest of your brain with distorted versions of what really happened over there. Consequently, they have taken the form of these frightening nightmares you are experiencing."

"Then some sort of neurological perversion has taken place within my brain. It's trying to destroy me from the inside out. Doc, I don't sleep well anyway. What I saw really frightened me. I can barely describe this thing, but it had a face of evil. The figure from my nightmares that I couldn't quite see clearly before was right above my bed last night. I finally saw what I've been afraid of. It was a ghostly apparition of a Viet Cong soldier. Yet, it seemed so real."

"The destructive effects of PTSD can make many things become all too real to the mind. What you experienced last night is a living monument to the strength of your illness that has interwoven itself into the brain cells of your subconscious. No matter how vivid it seemed to be, this was only a nightmare brought on by the trauma of war. Perhaps though . . ."

"Perhaps what?" I picked up on Doc's hesitation. "I haven't seen the likes of what I saw last night for more than twenty years. But it was real enough to me, closer than we are now, right up in my face." The reality of what I believed I saw I'm sure was clearly reflected in my eyes, even as I asked, "Do you believe in evil spirits?"

"Listen to me very carefully, son. Science tells me what you experienced is only as real as your mind will allow it to be. But on the other hand, as a small town country doctor who believes in God—and that both good and evil exist—I think it could be more. Evil exists in many forms. Coupled with your PTSD, some form of it could have found a way inside you. Perhaps far more than we realize, even far more than our minds can grasp, the forces of good and evil are woven into our brain chemistry, fighting for control."

"Perhaps you're right." I was beginning to accept Doc's line of thinking ever so cautiously. The mere concept raised a chilling feeling within me and more questions. "How do you interpret that billowing mass descending from the ceiling right above me and the VC dropping out of it? Where did that come from?"

"Your inner mind. It was your repressed subconscious memories finally coming to the surface, only distorted. I think the billowing mass represents the smoking battlefield. The VC emerging from it may come from your experiences during the Tet Offensive of 1968. That was an intense campaign, full of up-close fighting with the enemy. It must've been frightening, especially so for a young man just out of high school. Rather real or imagined, what you went through has profoundly shaken you."

"You're right. It was a frightening experience. But understand, I do know what's real and not real. I know I'm sane. It's just that my mind keeps testing the limits of that sanity. What's happening to me Doc? What can I do about this nightmare and the Viet Cong soldier within it?"

"You can destroy it. You can erase it from your memory," Doc responded, having a very definite thought.

"How?"

"You can overcome it through resolve. Since Vietnam, life has been a struggle between reality and what is going on within the emotional upheaval inside your mind. For you, the task will be to go beyond the walled off memory within your brain, break into your subconscious, air out the cobwebs, and reveal its secrets. Then you must confront them."

"Confront them?" I asked, shaken by the very thought of it.

"Yes, it's going to take courage on your part son. One day you're going to have to relive this nightmare one more time, stare this Viet Cong figure in the face, and confront this thing. Find out what it represents. Then—and only then—will you be able to free yourself from this ghost forever and experience a complete healing of your PTSD."

I sat there silent, taking it all in. Threaded into the circuitry of my brain was something insidiously evil. It was a sobering thought. Perhaps one day I could marshal the courage to face this ghost and overcome it.

For the moment though, I was again overwhelmed with thoughts of the war and personal guilt. I could not hold them in. "Doc, what you've got to understand is that for me Vietnam wasn't a traditional war. It was a dirty little twisted affair where anything goes. The most horrific things possible happened there, much of which I can't recall. I do remember so many innocent lives were lost."

"Why is it you remember that?"

"One by one, I still see them dying, right in front of me. I can't forget it. It may have been my fault that some of them died. I often wonder about that."

"Like I've said, you have to face what happened in Vietnam was not your fault, Jack but the fault of the war itself. The guilt you feel is from events that were out of your control."

I considered what Doc was saying, "I just need time to clear my head and think about it. My whole life is changing, becoming a contradiction to my past. I'm no longer a loner. Since coming to Tyler Junction I'm finding myself reconnecting with the human race."

"You know son, I see something very clearly."

"What's that?"

"There are forces for good forming around you here that will help you alter your perspective and reshape your life. I truly believe you can be healed and become a new man."

I wanted that. Memories I could not remember were trapped within me and had become burdens inside my mind. I wanted to unravel those mysteries so I could begin to find some sort of semblance of lasting peace. I found myself asking again, needing Doc's validation, "You really think so? You think I can be healed?"

"I know so. I really believe the fact that you can't remember beyond the bunker is a gift from God, giving your mind a chance to heal in some ways and find a degree of peace."

"Yes," I agreed, "Maybe it is a blessing from God—in some ways."

"Dan Russell called last night and thanked me for sending you his way. You impressed him. Mattie thinks the world of you. And you know I'm pulling for you. We're all for you, supporting you. You've got a support system here, some friends for life, if you want them."

I felt deeply humbled. Expressing my gratitude, I told him, "You're a good friend, better than I deserve."

I could see it made Doc feel good that he was appreciated. Getting cold though, he leaned over to warm himself above the crackling fireplace. This gave me a clear view of Mattie Sullivan's picture on the mantle. Rising from my chair, I was drawn to it again. Coming up beside Doc, I focused on her image.

Noticing it, he observed, "Mattie's a very caring person, and she cares about you."

I added, "I don't believe there's a thing she wouldn't do to help me. And you know something else, Doc?"

"What?"

"I think I'm falling in love with her."

"You are?"

"Yes, I am." I was even more definite, my eyes remaining on the picture, "Her image lingers in my mind constantly."

"I saw that look in your face the other night," Doc pointed out, studying my features more closely now.

"What kind of a look was that?" I responded, feeling his eyes on me.

"A look of someone very lonely, looking for love."

I did feel very lonely, admitting it, "I've been alone for almost twenty years, since my dad's death. That's when the nightmares intensified and I withdrew inside myself. I didn't have anyone. Things have changed though, since coming here. I want to find peace of mind and share what's left of my life with someone else."

"Science is making progress, gaining knowledge of how to heal the brain. But sometimes I think it may take the greatest Healer of them all."

"What do you mean, Doc?"

"From your physical appearance I can visualize sort of a long cerebral atrophy going on inside your head. It makes me think something beyond conventional medicine might help in your situation."

"What could that be?"

"Going to a place where many have found extraordinary faith and inspiration. It's a special place, one that is quiet and tranquil, where you can find yourself and lasting healing . . . and perhaps even God."

"I know it's just a dream for me right now, but do you really think there is such a place in the valley, or for that matter anywhere else where I could find lasting healing?"

Doc placed a comforting hand on my shoulder as he glanced up into the painting above his mantel. "I think I might know just such a place," he said, staring at the scenic flow of nature etched across its canvas.

"It's beautiful," I said, truly feeling it. Being drawn into the painting's vision, it struck a chord deep within me. Reacting to this feeling, I added, "I believe it's calling my name."

"Jack, there is a certain unspoken power in art that can motivate and inspire us. But why do you think my painting is calling your name?"

"It's perfect. Every brush stroke communicates something to me. If only it were real, not just imagination. It's an inspired picture of the dream I hope for in my mind, peace and tranquility, and one thing more, a place where the presence of God resides."

"His presence *does* reside there. In fact, it's near here."

"What do you mean?"

"This painting is the work of a local artist, one Joe Catlin, who lived a little ways outside Tyler Junction, east of town. He gave me this picture, in the last golden days of the 30s, just before I was supposed to go to medical school. Joe loved nature and believed it gave off a certain aura that blessed our lives. He often told me this world belonged to the Creator but was sort of on loan to us while we were here. There were those that scoffed at the way he lived, but it worked for him."

"How so, Doc?"

"Many credited his longevity to his being one with nature most of his adult years. Since he did most of his work there, he made Meadow Wood valley his permanent residence. In constant contact with nature, he came to know the Creator of all things as few ever could. His life transcended to a different level of living as he walked with God daily—or at least so he said. As he described it, living in the presence of the greatest physician of them all had its definite benefits. I believe that relationship blessed him with pro-

79

longed life. From that closeness, he came to understand what he said was the flow of positive energy throughout our bodies. That's what he believed to be one of the keys to a long life. He was 104 years old when he passed away."

Listening to Doc, in one incredible moment came one of those urges that comes to a person once in a lifetime. Hearing about this place that had the potential of enhancing one's life made me want to experience it myself. I blurted out, "Going there just might bless my life too. I wish I could find such a place."

"You can." Turning from his picture, Doc explained, "Joe Catlin painted from life. The scene in this picture actually exists. He took me out there. It's a place of such natural beauty that it knows no equal. It's sort of a lost Eden. Old Joe must've known something. He saw I was struggling with some career choices that could have life changing consequences for me. I soon found it was a place where one could sort out things that were bothering one's self. It changed my life. The Spirit that exists out there got inside me and transformed me. My priorities changed. I decided to return to Tyler Junction and become a country doctor. Some things can't be measured in money, the way they warm our hearts and bless our souls. After making that decision, I never gave it another thought, and I've never been happier. You know, son, it's not how long you live but how well you live the time God grants you."

I had listened carefully to his every word. Perhaps the atmosphere there could help change the emotional compass of my life. I wondered. I hoped. Getting closer, I looked back up at the brilliant sun within the painting. It was almost as if I could absorb its warmth from the picture itself. "Doc, it seems to explode across the canvas, revealing the flowers of the meadow in all their rich colors."

"Joe Catlin was a master artist. He always looked for what was not visible to human eyes, more to the spiritual if you will. He seemed to achieve that feeling in all his paintings. Some have even said that God must have surely guided his hand with each stroke of his brush."

I was thoroughly mesmerized by then, ready to go see the real thing. "Where is this place? How do I get there?"

"It's over east of town. Mattie can help you find it. She used to live over in that part of the valley with her parents, that is before they passed away.

You follow the stream that cuts across the field, away from the main road. Follow it down in the valley where it forks into two other valleys. Some folks around here call it the junction of the three valleys, others call it God's country—but it's a place called Meadow Wood."

CHAPTER 10
LEROY BARNETT

S ince that morning at Doc's, he started me on extremely low doses of Lithium, which greatly helped me. Additionally, we started having at least two evening sessions per week over the next month. They provided food for thought and helped alleviate much of the turmoil inside me. I felt myself settling down. His efforts, together with Mattie's support, helped to calm and strengthen me. With these two stabilizing influences anchoring me, I felt like I was turning a corner. I experienced no further anxiety attacks or flashback nightmares.

Genuinely improving in the weeks that followed, I opened up my mind and heart to Tyler Junction. I was changing. Being around Dan Russell, Sheriff Bodeen, and Zeke, I was no longer the introverted person who first came here. I was evolving into a more outgoing human being. Without consciously realizing it at first, I was becoming deeply committed to helping others, becoming that good deed doer I had talked about.

Time passed peacefully at Russell's store, and my job there made it an excellent place to get to know these simple people of the heartland. Interacting with them, I met so many that were good. This was a time of peace and contentment for me.

I was growing in understanding of my inner emotions and how best to keep them under control. Try as I might, though, I would soon learn that in certain intense situations such control would not be possible.

One eventful day arrived when the world's ugliness in the form of a monster came walking through the door. It would be a day that would test me for sure.

That particular morning found me behind the counter looking out the front window. I got caught up in a shaft of morning sunlight, daydreaming about that part of nature called Meadow Wood. I'd been thinking about it increasingly so since Doc had told me about the painting. The old man's words made a special connection with me as part of the hoped-for healing that filled my mind. Lost in thought of this prospect, a loud jarring slam at the front door soon brought me out of my hypnotic-like trance.

I looked up to see an enormous baboon of a man with a large mustache. Grinning wickedly, he stood just inside the door. This was a stocky man with a weather-beaten, hard face that reflected he had lived an even harder life. With the exception of myself, everyone in the store knew Leroy Barnett and feared he was up to no good.

Leroy was so big that he almost blocked from view his puny looking companion following right behind him. Trying to peek around, this smaller full-bearded man was grinning widely, displaying an ugly set of teeth. He was Leroy's ferret-faced brother, Kyle.

The two potential troublemakers ambled over to the counter in a confrontational manner. They stared at me with hard expressions through bloodshot eyes. It was obvious to me that these two men were drunk or well on their way there.

"I'm Leroy Barnett, and this . . ." Pausing, the alcohol induced fog was getting to him. Resuming very slowly, he completed his sentence, "is my brother Kyle."

Kyle flashed his ugly snarling grin again, "Howdy!"

As soon as they opened their mouths, I took a step backward. Their breath was rank, with a hot foul odor.

Before I could speak, Leroy leaned over the counter into my space. Pointing with a half empty jug of corn whiskey, he flashed an arrogant expression and roared in a raspy voice, "You're new!"

Leroy and Kyle didn't move, hunched over the counter. Both men had the appearance of having been wallowing around in the dirt before entering the store. Hovering there, they were there long enough for me to get a deep inhalation of their foul smell, resulting from a twenty-four hour binge. The combination of booze and chewing tobacco made their hot breath light years far worse than any snorer's breath ever imagined. Add to that, they carried with them the scent of old stale whiskey, which had dried on their clothes. It permeated the air all around them with unsuspecting rancid smells.

Even so, I decided to brave it anyway and leaned forward, trying to be friendly and head off trouble. "Hello fellas," I said, extending my hand toward Leroy, "I'm Jack Holden."

Refusing my hand, Leroy's expression formed into a tough snarl, as he responded hatefully, "No thank you! I don't shake hands with strangers." Just under the surface his mercurial temper was almost visible.

I quickly became aware this was an unstable man. Though I tried not to let on, my instincts told me this was someone I would have to keep an eye on. The man's attitude was already befitting the troublemaker the sheriff spoke of.

Sensing something too, Dan Russell spoke up from the far end of the counter, "I want no trouble, Leroy!" Russell poked the air with the tall broom he'd been using to sweep the floor.

"No trouble, Russell." Leroy replied coldly, then repeated himself in a deeper, more intimidating voice, "NO TROUBLE."

The two brothers turned from me, moving on down to the end of the counter, closing in on Dan Russell.

Getting right up in Dan's face, Leroy whispered contemptuously in a low voice barely containing its volcanic rumblings, "I see you're startin' to use STRANGERS round here. Us out of work town folk ain't good enough for you to hire!"

Right across from them, Sheriff Bodeen had been sitting in a shadowy corner of the store, listening intently. He spoke up, "Leroy! I believe Dan said NO TROUBLE."

"Sheriff?!" Surprised and startled, Leroy jerked around in the sheriff's direction, "Didn't see you sittin' over there."

"I'm sure you didn't."

"Well uh, what you doin' round the store this early in the mornin'?"

"Oh, just enjoyin' a game of dominoes with my deputy here." Sheriff Bodeen glanced across the barrel to a pair of boot clad feet protruding from the dark corner.

Zeke Wilcox leaned out of the shadows from the opposite side of the barrel, grinning, "Howdy Leroy."

Glancing over at him, Leroy's face transformed from a frown into a rare grin. "Zeke, you no good, dead beat truck driver! How you doin'?"

Zeke's face mirrored a look of strained thought, "Ohhh, I'm just restin' a bit, enjoyin' some peace and quiet."

Sheriff Bodeen drilled Leroy with a silent stare, adding, "I wouldn't take kindly to someone messin' up my game. You understand my meaning Leroy?"

Leroy shook his head, protesting, "You got me wrong Sheriff. I'm just wantin' to be peaceable."

The sheriff was not to be fooled, and still looked at him suspiciously.

Turning to his brother, Leroy motioned to him with the jug he was carrying, "Come on Kyle."

The two brothers, without another word, turned and walked back up along the counter. Near the front of the store, they sat down at a little table just inside the door.

Seated along the opposite wall from me, Leroy slammed the jug down on the table between him and Kyle. The noise got my attention. Our eyes locked. We stared at each other for a long moment. I think we both felt an instant dislike for each other.

My attention drawn to the sight of these two brothers, I immediately felt something sinister and evil was going on in the mind of Leroy Barnett. Instinctively, I knew here was a dark force that would have to be reckoned with.

Turning to his brother, Leroy observed in a low voice, "There's too much law in here today."

His ferret eyes darting about, Kyle looked around and agreed, "That's a fact."

Leroy thought some more, and the first sensible words he'd said that day came out of his mouth, "Maybe Sheriff's got a point. We ought to just kick back for awhile."

It wasn't long, though, before something else caught Leroy's eye and demanded his immediate attention. He found himself looking at every troublemaker's friend, the half-empty one-gallon jug of corn whiskey. "Hey Kyle, pass that bottle of rot-gut over here."

Kyle gently pushed the jug across the table till it was almost under Leroy's nose. Hovering above it, he popped the cork letting the genie—or a monster in my point of view—out of the bottle. Taking a big swig, Leroy reacted to its kick, "Wow! That's original old-fashion bust-head for sure!"

Leroy and Kyle continued their drunken descent, passing the jug between themselves. After downing a couple slugs, Kyle extracted a huge plug of Red Devil chewing tobacco from his jacket pocket. Leroy went to work wrapping his lips around the jug's opening, gulping the clear liquid down his throat. He reacted as though it burned like fire. With each swallow it seemed to fan the flames of anger within him, adding to his undoing.

Leroy in his own crude way had promised he would mind his manners. That may have been his plan for a passing moment, but this day's fate would dictate unhappily otherwise. Sometimes certain people bring back bitter memories through no fault of themselves. That's exactly what was about to happen.

The bell jingled above the store's front door. As it opened, Leroy looked up and the wicked grin on his face turned immediately into a scowl. His inner demons had just been awakened.

As the door closed behind him, a worn down looking man entered the store. He was slumped over with the appearance that the weight of the world was on him. He removed the old faded cap he'd been wearing, revealing the drained face of Jerry Marsh. Looking up, he approached the counter.

Catching my eye, it was immediately clear to me that in the past few weeks this man had quite visibly aged. A grave expression filled Jerry's face, upon which worry lines were deeply etched. He was rundown even more, his clothes becoming large upon his frame. He'd lost a lot of weight from the heartbreak that weighted him down. Nervous, he fiddled with his cap before speaking, "Can you handle medicine refills?"

"Yes sir, I was a medical specialist during the Vietnam War."

"You're new here?"

Sweeping the floor nearby, Dan Russell had been listening. "He's new, Jerry, but well qualified."

Getting his attention, Jerry glanced over at Dan.

He offered more information about me, "Jack, here is a fully accredited, licensed pharmacist and my new clerk."

Hearing this, Jerry turned back around in my direction again.

Pointing to the empty medicine bottle held tightly in his hand, I asked him, "Do you want to renew your prescription?"

"Yes, I do." Jerry was more definite as he passed the small bottle across the counter, "It's for my little girl, Laurie."

Taking it, my pharmaceutical knowledge came into play. I looked at the prescription on file that Doc Peterson had written for her. Beyond what I knew, it confirmed what I suspected about her. The little bottle had contained morphine tablets used in relieving the intense pain related to cancer. Doc had increased the dosage. He knew then Laurie's condition was worsening. Totally focused on this, I turned to retrieve the medicine bottle from the shelves behind me.

As I did so, Jerry leaned forward, resting his weight on the counter, his eyes following me. A lingering question was still on his mind, "You're new here, yet you look familiar. Have we ever met before?"

"Well, sort of," I answered, stopping and looking around at Jerry. "I was visiting with Mr. Peabody over at the school the day you came to pick up your daughter."

Jerry recalled, "Oh yes, I remember now." He paused, sadness becoming even more visible across his face. "I'm sorry, it wasn't a happy day."

"Nothing to be sorry about, Mr. Marsh. You're just being a good father, and you've got your hands full doing that."

Jerry nodded, acknowledging me. A look mixed with both compassion and understanding passed between us.

After a moment, I turned my attention back to the little medicine bottle. "I'd better finish this," I said, returning to the business of filling Laurie's prescription.

Jerry's eyes were on me, but it seemed his mind was elsewhere. Perhaps lost in thoughts concerning his daughter, he was not aware of the evil behind him. He had not noticed the Barnett brothers seated against the wall when he entered the store.

Leroy leaned forward in his chair, his eyes emitting a seething stare through Jerry Marsh. Focused on him, he muttered something to himself. His face grew harder, filling with anger that would not go away. Remaining silent, he was obviously boiling inside. Finally, he could stand it no longer.

It was too late. He had resisted the feelings rising within him all he could. Never mind the sheriff or his promises to him. The thought of what might happen next was of no consequence to him. Leroy was on the move and up to no good. Bent on doing something cruel, he nudged his brother, signaling Kyle to follow him. Rising from their chairs, the two brothers sauntered over to the counter right behind Jerry.

"Marsh!" yelled Leroy, his face flushed with anger.

Jerry spun around, quite startled. Stiffening, he backed up against the counter. "Barnett." He could barely speak above a whisper. Instant intimidation seized him.

"You've got your nerve comin' in here!" Leroy raved on, glaring at him.

"I . . ." Jerry went silent for a moment, seemingly trying to overcome the fear I saw registering on his face. Making an effort to explain, he continued, "I'm here because I had to get some medicine for my little girl. She's been very ill."

"I ain't forgettin' what you done to me!" His hatred quite visible, Leroy would have none of Jerry's reasons for being at the store. Getting right in his face, Leroy's voice filled with belittling contempt, "You know what's wrong with you, little man? You're the coward who put a lot of folks out of work in this valley!"

Jerry backed up a step or two along the counter as he advanced on him.

Sensing trouble, Dan Russell interrupted, tapping Leroy's back with the wooden end of his broom. "Leroy, that's enough!"

"Stay out of this, Russell!" Leroy flared at him sharply, then tried to justify his anger, "There ain't a man alive gonna stop me! This jerk fired me from my job over at the iron works!"

"That was five years ago!" Jerry responded defiantly.

"It seems like it was yesterday, Marsh!" The wicked grin returned to Leroy's face. "But then, you got canned when the iron works folded."

Even worn down, Jerry could stand no more of this. His courage returned. "Listen Barnett! You got what you deserved. You were a troublemaker!"

"Wha-a-at!" Barnett's hand started to form into a fist. It looked to me like he was getting ready to beat Jerry to a bloody pulp.

"Alright, that's enough of this!" I spoke in an authoritative manner, determined this was not going to happen. I got his attention. It surprised even me, but I meant every word. After all, what's right is right.

It worked, breaking the tension momentarily. Everyone turned toward me, including Jerry, who focused on what I was about to tell him.

"Mr. Marsh, it's ready for Laurie." At that very moment, I placed the bottle of medicine on the counter between us.

Jerry looked down at the pills, remembering his reason for being there. "Yes, for my little girl."

All of a sudden, we were completely ignoring Leroy. He glared at both of us, wondering out loud, "What is this?"

"That'll be nine dollars, Mr. Marsh," I said, paying no attention to Leroy.

Jerry felt into his pocket, pulling out a very worn ten-dollar bill. Laying the money on the counter, that weight-of-the-world look returned to his face. "It's my last ten dollars, all the money I've got left in the world."

Before I could pick the ten up, Leroy's hand darted between us, snatching it up. The wheels of evil rolling around in his head were visible in his expression. Flashing that disgusting grin of his, he waved the bill in front of us. Leaning forward over the counter, he yelled at me, "He ain't gonna spend this money in here!"

In that brief instant I got an up close glimpse of the consuming rage filling him completely. While keeping an intense eye on me, Leroy gestured over at Jerry. Acknowledging his presence with an almost seething disgust, he yelled, "No sir! He ain't gettin' those pills!"

I could see Jerry was barely hanging together. Falling into desperation's grip, he begged, "Please, Barnett! My little girl's bad sick." Glancing over at the bottle on the counter, "She needs that medicine! She's in a lot of pain!"

Unmoved, the brute stood there threateningly. More menacing than ever before, Barnett looked at him contemptuously, snickering silently. Cold and unbending, he thought only of himself as he responded, "The pain! What about all the hurt I felt after you fired me?!"

Lowering his head, I sensed Jerry felt beaten by this bully. As he did so though, his eyes came to rest on the bottle. Scared as much as he was, he still extended his shaky hand hesitantly in that direction.

I believed here was a good man with a gentle soul. Listening to his trembling voice pleading with this brute with no compassion had become too much for me. It was a sin the way Leroy was treating him, beating down on an already broken man. It would be a worse sin not to do anything about it. I thought of Jerry as a kindred spirit who had suffered too much, and I could no longer be silent about all of this. I had to do the right thing, or I couldn't live with myself. The voice of my conscious told me, *In the name of good, say something.*

Leaning across to Jerry, I gestured to the prescription bottle, urging him, "Mr. Marsh, just go ahead and take it!" Turning toward Barnett, I added with firmness, "You stay out of this."

His hatred growing for me, Leroy's burning glare was now trained totally in my direction, "He'll not take it! Not now! Not ever!"

In that same instant, Barnett grabbed up the little prescription bottle, viciously smashing it upon the counter. Shattering, the precious tablets rolled every which way.

Jerry was crushed, tears forming in his eyes. He was shaken to the core, full of inner turmoil. Desperate, he thought nothing was too much for him to do for Laurie. He would sacrifice everything for his little girl.

Seeing this, I admired those qualities and wanted to help him. It was time to stand up and be counted. Thinking about it, I hated bullying. I'd seen so many people in the war that had needed my help and circumstances prevented me from doing so. It did not make me feel good about myself. But this time I could make a difference and help give this little girl some relief from the suffering she was going through. I knew what to do. This determination to do something must've shown in my eyes.

Leroy saw it and warned me, "Stay out of this Holden! My quarrel is not with you."

I ignored him, becoming increasingly convinced *this was* my business. This little girl absolutely needed the morphine pills, and I had the power to do something about it. I knew how to instantly diffuse this situation. Reaching around, I pulled the master bottle from the pharmacy shelf behind me. Placing it on the counter in front of Jerry, I spoke with firmness, "Here, take this."

Jerry was surprised at this unexpected action. He looked at the bottle thrusted in front of him and then up into what he perceived as the face of a friend. He whispered, "Thank you, Jack."

Leroy protested bitterly, "You can't do that!" Red faced, hate had taken possession of his soul, and vengeance was all he could think of.

Across the counter, I saw it coming and was now very aware of this possibility. Leaning in closer to Jerry, I urged him, "Mr. Marsh, take it and just leave."

Jerry knew he must act quickly and take advantage of this opportunity. His hand closing tightly around the medicine bottle, he snatched it up. Turning rapidly, he dashed out the door. As it slammed shut, the bell above it rang loudly for a moment, then there was silence.

CHAPTER 11
THE FIGHT

B arnett just stood there, staring at the door for a long moment. Was he going to chase after Jerry Marsh or not? He took a step or two in that direction toward the door, then stopped.

Glancing around, he found himself facing me. I stood directly across the counter from him. Our eyes locked on each other, and neither of us would let go. Leroy shot a glance toward the door, then quickly returned to me. I was rapidly becoming the new focus of his hate.

Leroy's voice though, was still full of ridicule for Jerry, "See how he ran outa here with them pills. Marsh ain't nothin' but a yella coward! Well I for one ain't gonna let him . . ."

"LEROY!" I shouted in a loud voice, interrupting him. Instantly, I got his attention.

"Wha-What?" Leroy stammered, quite caught by surprise.

"I'd let it go if I were you."

"Holden, are you threatening me?"

"Let's just say this, if you make a move for that door, I'll be stopping you."

With eyes enlarged and nostrils flaring, he shouted, "You can't stop me!"

I reacted, trying to get through to him, "Do you know how he feels, Leroy? Have you walked a mile in his shoes? Do you have any idea what he's going through? Come on, answer me!" I snapped my fingers at him, feeling my own temper race past a point I could control.

"No, and I don't care!" Barnett stood there fuming as he responded. Fine beads of sweat formed on his brow, dripping down his unshaven face.

His eyes became white-hot daggers, huge containers full of hate. It was the look of a savage beast directed at his new target, me.

I was not afraid, standing my ground. Sometimes you have to have the courage of your convictions. I knew I had done the right thing. Originally, I had intended to avoid a fight, but violence is the only thing certain men understand. There was no avoiding the unavoidable. I could still do something else positive in this situation and be a real force for good. A day of reckoning was here. It was time to settle accounts with Leroy.

"Holden, you're gonna pay a terrible price for doin' that."

"What do you mean, Leroy?"

"You let that jerk get outa here with what he wanted! You're gonna answer to me."

"No, *you're* incorrect. It seems to me you should be the one held accountable for the way you treated that poor man."

"You don't know what I'm capable of. I could split you open."

"Leroy, in life there's a constant struggle always going on inside our souls between good and evil. Have you ever read the Bible?"

"That's none of your business! Anyway, what's that got to do with it?"

"Somewhere in the Good Book it talks about evil doers, saying, *You reap what you sew* and *the wages of sin is death.*"

"I don't know what you're talkin' about."

"You should, and you will. I made a vow to myself when I decided to stay here in Tyler Junction that I'd try to do what's right in all things. That's what I aim to do right now."

"You're a fool, Holden!"

"I may seem like a fool to you, but you're the one who acted like a fool today." Something had just snapped inside me. Instead of being merely a spectator of the events unfolding in front of me, I now became an active participant in them. Having the strength to do something, I knew I would.

Barnett tried to justify himself, "Listen to me, Holden. Don't you understand? Marsh got me fired from my job!"

"I don't think so, Barnett."

"Say what?"

"Are you sure you didn't get your own self fired?"

"How so?"

"You're so full of hate for everyone. You did it to yourself."

"Just what do you mean?"

"Deep down, I bet you even hate yourself." I explained, talking as I walked along the counter, making my way around to the customer's side. "It's wrong for a big bully like you to pick on a decent person like Jerry Marsh. You ought to be ashamed of yourself. Hate can eat you up like a cancer and destroy you. It takes a lot stored up inside to make one do what you've done. How did you let so much evil take you over? Somewhere along the way you've went down the wrong road in your life. You know Leroy, it's not too late for you to change."

"Who are you to tell me this?"

"Someone who's seen too much evil in this old world and doesn't want to see anymore of it."

"I don't know what you're talkin' about!"

"Then you're going to have to learn a lesson. You need to learn right from wrong. You don't come in here and just take over, picking on our customers. The way you treated Jerry was wrong."

"You and who else's army are gonna teach me anything!" Barnett yelled, mocking me. Seething with rage, the quaking volcano within him appeared about to explode into physical violence. The time for words had ended.

Dan Russell sensed it, clutching his broom tightly. Feeling something bad was imminent, he stepped backward enough to get clear of what was about to happen.

Over in the darkened corner, Sheriff Bodeen leaned forward in his chair, recognizing trouble.

Zeke Wilcox moved around in his seat too, trying to see what was going to happen.

As if by some invisible force, Kyle Barnett's ugly grin wiped from his face, to be replaced by a deadly serious scowl. Moving near his brother, he leaned over, snickering and whispering something to him.

I was in front of the counter now, stopping about seven or eight feet in front of them.

The Barnett brothers stood close together, staring through me. Leroy's contemptuous grin spread over his face again as he revealed, "I get a dollar for you, Holden."

"What?"

"My brother just said he'll give me a dollar if I knock you out."

I glanced over at Kyle, who responded with a big grin, revealing his ugly yellow teeth. Then my attention immediately returned to Leroy, who looked like he was beginning to make his move. I warned him, "Your kind of behavior will no longer be tolerated here. It stops today. Do you understand?"

Leroy sized me up, "You're not half the man it would take to stop me."

I stood firm and persisted, "It was a rotten thing you did, taking that poor man's money. Now, you're going to give it back."

"NEVER!" Leroy yelled defiantly.

"Yes you will, because it's the right thing to do."

"Teach me, Holden! Make me give it back!" The reddening flush deepened in Barnett's face as he yelled. His hands tightened into fists at the same time.

Advancing closer, eyes glaring, he swung with a wide sweeping punch, connecting only with the air.

Lowering his massive head like an enraged bull, Leroy prepared to charge again. In a swift move, he lunged forward, crashing into me. His huge hammer-like fists flying, one scraped past my chin, taking some skin as it plowed across me.

Stinging pain spread up one side of my face like an expanding friction burn. Moving rapidly though, I avoided most of the damage behind Leroy's other lunging blows. Now I was all the more determined not to allow this hulking brute to catch me off guard again.

Kyle Barnett was screaming, "Smack him Leroy! Take his head off!"

The lunge forward though, had caused Leroy to go somewhat off balance. Turning around quickly, I took advantage of this, driving hard and fast into his side with both my fists.

Leroy was turning to meet me, but not fast enough. From my crouched position I shot straight up and connected with his jaw. Making hard contact, Barnett went backward from the impact. His mouth flying open, a red spray spewed forth into the air. Slamming back into the counter, his knees buckled under him, sinking to the floor with a busted lip.

I watched the giant bully closely, hovering above him. Keeping my fists raised defensively, I sensed other danger.

Kyle Barnett had been circling behind me to attack. I spun around just in time as Kyle moved in threatening, swinging viciously at me. Exchanging blows, the punches were heard in a series of bone crunching sounds. I swung a right, plowing up the skin across Kyle's face, then a left directly under his chin. His head jerked backward from the impact as he was sent sprawling on the floor.

Pulling himself together, though, Kyle came up on one elbow. His cold and calculating expression revealed his plans for me. Reaching inside his jacket with his free hand, he pulled out a switchblade knife.

Just as the knife sprung open in Kyle's hand, something long and dark came near his face. Almost immediately, he found himself staring into the business end of a shotgun. Hearing the triggers being cocked back, startled him enough to swallow his mouthful of chewing tobacco. Eyes widening, his point of view traveled up the barrels to see that it was Deputy Sheriff Zeke Wilcox taking dead aim.

"Not today Kyle, give it up." Zeke ordered as his trigger finger tightened.

Kyle's murderous expression instantly disappeared, fully appreciating the 'persuader' stuck in his face. He knew Zeke meant business. Obeying immediately, the knife dropped from his hand in submission.

Meanwhile, Leroy came to his feet. Advancing down the counter, he attacked me. Lashing out, his powerful left swing just narrowly missed clipping my jaw.

"Kill him!" Kyle screamed.

Perhaps because of the whiskey, Leroy didn't act or react fast enough. I maneuvered in close enough to hit hard with a right and then a left to Leroy's mid-section, doubling him over.

Then I came down with my right again, connecting in a sledge hammer blow to Leroy's face, splitting his nose open. He crumpled to the floor in a loud CA-THUD!

"It ain't fair!" Kyle screamed from his subdued position.

"Shut up, ferret face!" Deputy Wilcox commanded.

As he struggled to his knees, Leroy seethed with rage. Blood was streaking down from his split nose and busted lip. He was battered and bruised all over from the pummeling I had given him. Yet, he came back asking for more.

Summoning up his remaining fighting strength, Leroy rose to his feet, exploding in still another ferocious attack. Like a charging bull, he advanced the rest of the way down the counter swinging wildly at me.

I wheeled about, avoiding the intended blows. Getting in close again, I delivered a driving punch that connected with Leroy's jaw in a loud pop, sending him spinning around and downward.

Collapsing, Leroy smashed against the barrel in the corner, atop which the dominos went flying. Though his face was red and swollen, he remained defiant, yelling, "I'll kill you yet, Holden!" Struggling to sit up, he couldn't move fast enough, just looking up in time to see my fist shooting down into his face. Leroy was knocked senseless. Down for the count, at last he lay still.

Standing over him, I reached into his shirt pocket. Retrieving a waded up ten-dollar bill, I remarked, "I believe this belongs to Mr. Jerry Marsh." Taking the money, I stepped aside, backing up against the opposite wall.

The fight was over, but my muscles still ached, tightened with tension and throbbing pain. Holding up my clenched fist, I looked at my lacerated and bruised knuckles. Extending my fingers out, my whole hand trembled. A lot of adrenaline, transformed into anger, had flowed through me.

Presence of mind had helped me regain control, but I had seen something within myself I didn't like. I looked over at Barnett and thought, under different circumstances, I could've been this angry and bitter man. In a sense I had become like him, unleashing the violent beast within myself. Shaken by this thought, it rolled over in my mind and lingered with me.

Leroy's blurred vision refocusing, his eyes met square on with a large revolver and its owner, Sheriff Bodeen. Relishing the moment somewhat, the Sheriff proclaimed, "Oh, how the mighty have fallen!"

Leroy tried to sit up, a little bit of meanness still left in him.

"That's enough, Leroy!" Sheriff Bodeen declared with authority, the familiar twinkle around his eyes changing into a steely-eyed stare. "Now you've done it! Disturbing the peace, engaging in public drunk, and . . ." Glancing down at his bloodstained dominos lying in disarray on the floor, then back up to Leroy, he became even more enflamed, "Add destruction of private property!" Turning to his deputy, "Zeke, cart these two idiots over to the jail. Maybe some time in the cooler will bring 'em to their senses."

"It'll be my pleasure," Zeke said, responding with a good deal of relish in his voice too. Poking them with the business end of his shotgun, he coaxed the Barnett brothers out of the store.

Sheriff Bodeen was following right behind them when he spotted me standing off to one side, just staring at all the mess. He put a firm hand on my shoulder, "Listen, young fella."

I looked up at him, "What, Sheriff?"

"I would've interrupted sooner, but you were doing too good a job teaching them a lesson that was way overdue."

I nodded, and without uttering a word walked out of the store. I told myself it was to get some fresh air, but it was really to escape the thought of what I had done.

The front door opened back and I emerged, brooding silently. I stood on the front porch of Russell's store looking down at my bruised and bloodied knuckles. My hands were still shaking. The struggle within me about my own anger raced through my mind as I looked up and stared out across the horizon.

Though I still firmly believed Leroy deserved a sound thrashing for his evil ways, it bothered me greatly that I had exploded in such a violent way. The fight had left me questioning myself. Did I do the right thing? I wondered if I should pray about it. I struggled for answers when my thoughts were interrupted.

A hand came up from behind, patting me on the back. I glanced around to see Dan Russell had followed me outside. He nodded toward my hands, "I see you got a few nicks yourself in that fight."

I turned around facing him, protesting, "No, it's nothing."

Dan searched my face, seeing something was troubling me. "What's the matter, Jack?"

"It's just me."

Dan persisted, "Come on, what's wrong?"

I tried to put it into words, "It bothered me to do what I did. In Vietnam I saw so much violence, and later on as well. I've seen too much of what hate can do to people, how it can destroy them. I didn't want to experience it anymore. But I just couldn't stand by and let Barnett run over that poor guy. I just couldn't." I looked down, avoiding Russell's gaze. I was brooding again, but this time out loud, "Well Dan, I've made a mess of things. I guess I'm fired."

"No way!" Dan shook his head to the contrary. "Leroy Barnett got what he deserved. A person that mean was going to eventually meet up with the hand of justice. It had to happen. Someone man enough was going to have to stand up against him sooner or later. I believe, whether you know it or not, you were God's instrument in what had to be done. In the end, that's what really matters."

I glanced back at the store, protesting, "But Dan, what about the store?"

"Sometimes the value of a sacrifice is outweighed by what is accomplished. Even if we have a little mess inside, that can be cleaned up. The Barnett brothers were taught a lesson today that will stay with them a long time. It was worth it."

"I certainly hope so," I agreed, adding with sincerity, "I can promise you, I'll pay for all the damages out of my wages."

Dan reacted, explaining what he thought of me, "You're a man of honor, Jack, trying to do the right thing. You know, there are so many things to learn in life. Sometimes it takes a man near forty years to grow up. That's when you really start learning, putting together the pieces of the puzzle that make up your life. I believe that's what you're doing."

"I'm certainly trying to do the right thing," I said, glancing down at my hand still clinching the wadded up ten-dollar bill.

Dan noticed it too, "I see you got Marsh's money."

I held up the old wadded bill, offering it back to Dan. "I want to do something for Jerry Marsh. He strikes me as one who needs help."

"It's gonna be on the house too," Dan said, refusing the bill. Thinking about it, he went on, "No customer of mine should ever have to go through such humiliation as Jerry did today. Things have been hard enough for him lately. I know he's been going without, sometimes not even having a crust of bread for dinner. No sir, I won't keep this ten dollars. It wouldn't be right. Jack, I want you to take that money out to the Marsh place and give it back to him."

CHAPTER 12
PROMISES

Later that very afternoon, a small wooden farmhouse became clearly visible in the distance. As I got closer, I could hear Dan Russell's directions: "It's out from town, north of the Tyler Junction School, over the ridge from it, sitting alone on the edge of the horizon, sort of lonesome."

The landscape flattened, revealing a weather-beaten, worn down house up ahead. It was easy for me to see that last year had been a drought-filled, diseased-ridden time for Jerry Marsh. The land itself revealed it. It was so barren, broken with crevasse lines leading out from the house in all directions. It was though the land was sick too, echoing the illness and heartbreak from within the old house.

Far from being repelled by it, I went on ahead, being drawn toward the people who lived there. I didn't know how, but I wanted to help them and in a strange way to help myself.

Inside that house—as Jerry would later tell me—little Laurie was sitting at a small round table in a modest kitchen of old-fashioned simplicity. He was nearby, keeping a watchful eye on her, having given her a morphine pill when he first got home. Even though it helped her, a side effect was morphine usually made her tired and sleepy. Yet this night was different. Fully awake, it was though she was expecting something, or someone.

Finishing a glass of water, she handed Jerry the empty glass. It shook in her trembling hands. Avoiding his gaze, she knew he was observing her. Feeling his concern, she explained, "Daddy, I'm weak, but this medicine does help take some of the pain away."

Jerry went to his knees beside her chair, comforting his little girl, "I know sweetheart." Gently and tenderly, he brushed a strand of hair back from her thin face.

Reacting to his touch, Laurie's large expressive eyes revealed her love for him.

The love he felt for her in his heart reached into the words he spoke, "You will always be Daddy's princess."

"I will always want to be," she said, having an equal amount of devotion to him.

As their feelings connected, Laurie extended a hand toward him. Drawing her up into his arms, she responded to her father's deep love. Reaching up, she encircled his neck, hugging him. It was though her love flowed into him, strengthening both of them.

Taking his hand, Laurie's fingers traveled down, running along the life-line etched across his palm. Then she touched him on the chest right above his heart. Looking up into his eyes, she said, "Daddy, I love your heart with all mine."

"I love you with all mine, Princess."

"Promise me something, Daddy."

"Anything sweetheart."

"That after I'm gone you'll take care of your granddaughter Peggy."

"My granddaughter?"

A smile flickered across her face as she explained, "You know Daddy— my dolly!"

Reaching over to the chair next to her getting something, Laurie turned back around holding a raggedy doll with a big sewn on smile. "Remember, Mama made this smile with her sewing needle." Centering the doll in her lap, she somehow seemed to take on its same expression.

To Jerry, it was though the shadow of his late wife had reached from beyond the grave to give their daughter a moment of happiness. Tears formed in his eyes as he struggled to speak the unthinkable, "What will happen if you . . . if I lose you sweetheart?"

"All my love for you Daddy will always be right here." She touched his forehead, adding, "I will always be in your mind."

In silence they just looked at each other, both their hearts bonding with the deep love they would feel forever. The spell of this moment was suddenly broken by a knocking sound. Together, they looked around in the direction of the front door.

Outside, I had come up what seemed like an endless dirt road that led me right to their front porch. I knocked on the door two more raps. As I think back on it, standing there on the porch of the humble little Marsh farmhouse, I could not even imagine I was about to meet someone who would have such a staggering wealth of answers to all my questions. Meanwhile though, I waited outside as the knob turned and the door opened back.

As he came outside, Jerry's face lit up with both recognition and surprise. "Holden? Jack Holden, isn't it?"

"Yes, I've come to see you about something."

"Thanks for what you did today. Jack, I'm grateful, most grateful. But what brings you way out here?"

"Mr. Marsh, I'm here to give you this." Reaching into my pocket, I pulled out the ten-dollar bill.

"But it's yours, for my little girl's medicine," he protested.

"It wasn't right for you to have gone through what you did today. Dan Russell said this time it's on the house. Mr. Marsh, I'm here as a friend wanting to do the right thing. So please, take this money back." I held out the ten dollars toward him.

Reluctant, but moved by the gesture, Jerry took the money back. As he did so, he reflected, "I don't have many friends, none that would come way out here to give me anything."

"You do now."

"Thank you, Jack."

"It's my pleasure, Mr. Marsh."

"Why don't you call me Jerry? I appreciate your kindness more than you'll ever know. I'm right beholdin' to you."

"Jerry, I'll treasure your friendship always." It occurred to me that since my arrival in the valley, I had gone from no friends to several in a matter of weeks. Once more I extended my hand in what would be a lasting friendship. Brushing my battered knuckles in the handshake, I pulled my hand back, wincing in pain.

Noticing it, Jerry saw the clearly visible scrapes on my knuckles. "What happened? Is that what you received on my account?"

"I think Leroy got the worst of it. He won't be bothering you anymore. I saw to that. He's a guest, right now as we speak, in Sheriff Bodeen's jail. Sometimes there's more strength in right than in wrong."

At that point, a little girl's head popped around the door into view. Laurie Marsh had been listening. "Daddy, why don't you invite the nice man inside?"

"I'm sorry." Motioning toward the door, Jerry was apologetic, "Forgive me, we don't get many visitors out here. Won't you please step inside?"

"Yes—Yes I will," I responded positively, really wanting to get to know these two. I stepped forward, following them through the door.

Inside, Laurie led me into the kitchen and pointed to a small table and three chairs placed around it. "Please, come and sit down beside me, Mr. Holden."

I obliged, sitting down at the table. Laurie took the seat next to me, while Jerry sat across the table viewing both of us.

With obvious love and pride, he introduced his little girl, "Jack, this is my daughter, Laurie."

Even the full brunt of her illness could not diminish this fascinating glimpse of innocence in its purest form.

I was unusually drawn to her right from the first, perhaps from having prior knowledge of her condition. Sitting next to her, though, I felt the connection more strongly than ever before. I did not fully understand why this was, but I was determined to find out. My voice softened as I spoke to her, "Pleased to meet you, Miss Laurie."

My first close up impression of her was of a young person obviously at death's door. I saw immediately she was courageous in spite of her illness. Her strength was inspiring. It made me ashamed of my own weaknesses. Looking into her face, I saw a radiant smile that was a reflection of the inner beauty of her soul.

Returning my gaze, Laurie recognized something in me. Her large eyes were hypnotic, drawing me in. It was though her thoughts and mine bonded together. Leaning forward in her chair, she asked me, "You were very good to my daddy today, but why did you help him?"

"Because your daddy is a good man and what was being done to him was a bad thing."

"I had a dream last night that a good man, a stranger to our town, would help my daddy and be his friend forever. You're that man, Jack."

"I hope I am. I would like to be."

Her eyes traveled down to my hand, "May I see your hand?"

"Of course sweetheart," I said, holding my hand out in front of her.

With her fingertips, Laurie gently touched the gashes on my knuckles, still red and enflamed from the fight. Concentrating even more, she shut her eyes in sort of a mental mind meld with me, jerking as though she could feel my pain. As she wrapped her tiny fingers around the palm of my hand, I realized in that single instant I had never felt the power of a more focused mind on this earth. The tentacles of a powerful vacuum reached from her hand on through my body, up into my brain, stripping away its memories and absorbing them back into her own brain. Digesting them, she knew everything I knew about myself, and more. Taking a deep breath as her eyes opened, she looked up at me knowing my most personal thoughts, "There is turmoil within you. I sense it. I know you're troubled about the anger that was in you when you fought the man today. But I want you to know something."

"What Laurie?"

"The voice of God told me in my dream that He would use you as His instrument to punish the bad man."

For the second time today someone had told me I had been God's instrument against Leroy Barnett. I wanted to believe her, but something in me protested, "I was just visiting Doc Peterson, and while I was here I decided to take the job over at Russell's store. I don't even know for sure if I'm going to stay in the valley."

"Jack, you're going to be living in the valley for a very long time and in the process change a lot of people's lives. You are a champion of righteousness and defender of the good. There is more at work in your life than you ever realized. The Lord was with you when you got on that bus. He wanted you to come here."

"You really think so?"

"I know so. Something has been troubling you for almost twenty years. That's part of the reason why you came here. But what you didn't know was the shadow of God has been following you all these years, just waiting for you to call on Him. You did answer His calling by coming here, without even realizing it. Think about it. Search your heart and soul and you will find this to be true."

Looking into her face, I was beginning to realize what Mattie had said was true: this little girl was one of those very special people who truly walk with God. Searching for answers, I offered up a confession of an innermost secret, "Sometimes in the quiet moments I hear a voice speaking to my mind. I wasn't sure what it was. At first I thought it was my imagination. I didn't fully understand. I'm not sure I do even now."

"Elements of the spiritual are around us all the time, whispering meaningful words to our minds. It's up to you Jack, if you are willing to believe and accept them. Sometimes you will hear words of wisdom beyond measure."

"I want to believe. Laurie, can you tell me more?"

"There are many voices—both good and evil—that try to alter our destinies. The voice that told you to get on the bus to come here was the Voice of God. He brought you to this valley for His purposes. More than you know and can imagine, your destiny is here. Within everything you've ever done, all things have been connected for a reason. Call it Fate, Destiny, God, or whatever you like, He has been involved in your every decision. He is with you now. This is why you're here to see me."

I could see in Laurie's eyes that she understood me completely. It was though she had peered into my soul and knew everything about me, past, present, and future. Her words were not only spiritual but had their roots in deeply sacred, God-given origins. I felt exposed. In reaching out to her, I was sure she already knew things beyond the words I was about to speak, "Please, help me."

"Yes, Jack, I do feel the true desperation inside you. Your cry for help has been heard. I want you to understand something."

"What is it?"

"A lot of people put up barriers in their lives so they can't do certain things, that it's just not possible. But if they would really look inside themselves, they might find the special something that motivates them to become greater than they actually are. As for me, I found the Holy Spirit of God. I embraced and believed what it taught me, that some part of God is within all of us. He has made me who I am. It is through that ability I know many things that can help you, if you listen."

"I'm listening. What do you know?"

"I see it clearly now, you were wounded when you were a soldier."

"No, I wasn't."

"Jack, I see it—not a physical wound in the body—but a mental wound in your head." Pausing, she touched my forehead as if to confirm something. Sure of herself, she told me, "Yes, it's still there. Unless you let God in to heal it, you will continue to suffer."

"But how do I do that—let God in?"

"You have to believe in Him. You have to open up your heart, mind, and soul—and pray."

"But how will I know if what troubles me is gone?"

"Trust me you will know. When the power of God's Holy Spirit is inside you, you will know."

I knew every world she had told me was true. Now I had to know one thing more. "Laurie, you have a gift straight from God. How did it happen? How did He give you such knowledge?"

Her large eyes took on a beautiful look as the evening sun reached through the window and bathed her with its warmth. They were aglow with a beautiful internal vision. As she spoke, a strange mixture of innocence and wisdom came out in her words, "I'm just a little girl, but I'll try to explain as best I can. In time, you will come to understand it better yourself. God is like a farmer who goes about planting seeds everywhere. Except His farm is the whole universe, and in the field—instead of soil—is every one of His creatures, us included. God's seeds are special. They all have a divine spark. That is to say, we all have a spec of Him in us. We are all His children. It has been so since the beginning of time."

Fascinated, I told her, "I have never quite heard it explained that way."

She continued, telling me more about herself, "Some time ago, God planted one of those seeds within me. It was a kernel of wisdom. Taking root and growing, it expanded the knowledge and understanding I have within my brain. Like a veil being lifted, I see things now in the crystal clear light our Lord provides."

"It's something most people don't have," I pointed out.

"Jack, you need to know that once inside a person His seeds bear fruit, blossom and grow. The fruit is from the tree of knowledge and understanding. You will become more aware because it's growing inside you right now."

She had spoken with wisdom far beyond her years. I believed in my heart what she said was true and wondered out loud, "How will it change me? What do you see in store for me?"

"I only see what God permits me to see. You've been trying to put your life back together here in the valley, haven't you?"

"Yes, with all my heart."

"You have a real hunger for something you don't have. What you don't know is that God is right here by your side, taking every step with you. Something wonderful is going to happen to you."

"What is it?"

Laurie looked like she was staring into a vision as she told me, "He is getting ready to touch you. He is going to heal your broken spirit and make you whole again. His strength will become your strength. It will transform you into a different person, a better person. Your whole life is about to change in every possible way."

I listened to her spellbound. Her words were deeply affecting me. She knew things greater than the combined wisdom of all of the doctors who had ever examined me.

At the same time I was taking all this in, my heart went out to this little girl who was ravaged by disease, wasting away right before my eyes. A rush of good feelings came over me. The words just came out, "Laurie Marsh, I love you."

"I love you too, Jack Holden," she responded without hesitation. Then she said something she seemed to have knowledge of, and clearly understood, "I think you're already getting closer to the Lord."

"What makes you say that?"

"To know love, is to know a part of Him. You see, God *is* love." The more she spoke, the more her words were full of wisdom.

I looked across the table at Jerry Marsh, who had been listening to the whole conversation. "What do you think, Jack?"

"It's remarkable what she knows."

"I guess you see how my little girl affects people in strange ways. Those who have talked to her say it's as if she can see into your soul and know everything that's there."

I knew then she had the gift my father had often spoken about to me. But in her it was far more complex and highly developed than anything in me—at least at that point in time.

It occurred to me there was a similarity between Laurie and her father. There was the same caring attitude and gentile kindness in both of them. Jerry was truly a good man. I already admired him. Knowing for sure now, I was going to value him as a friend. Turning my attention back to her, I observed, "Sweetheart, your daddy is a good man who loves and cares for his little girl and wants her well."

She hung her head, not wanting to make eye contact as she spoke, "But I have so little time. My mommy, who is in Heaven, misses me."

I glanced over at Jerry, catching his reaction.

The strain was clearly visible in his face. Her words had hurt him too much. His voice was full of depression, "It's not been a happy time lately around the Marsh home. I lost my wife, Lana, not two months ago. Doc said it was complications from pneumonia."

I asked her, "How do you know your mommy wants you to go with her?"

"She came to me while I was sleeping last night and told me so. She talks to me all the time now. I hear Mommy's voice in my head—and someone else."

Hearing this, Jerry looked up at his daughter, "Who else, Princess?"

"Daddy don't you be worried or frightened when I tell you this. I've heard the voice of God in more than just my dream last night. He talks to me quite often now."

Gently running my fingers through her hair, I moved the matted, sweaty strands away from her forehead. She looked at me, sensing a burning question. I asked her, "How do you know it's His voice?"

"Because I see Him. He emerges from a brilliant light right above my bed and watches over me every night. I was afraid at first, but He told me not to be afraid, that He will come soon and take me to be with my mommy."

"Take you where?"

"You see, Jack, He told me about Heaven. It's in another dimension, beyond death. It's a spiritual place."

"A spiritual place?"

"Yes, Jack, it's His Kingdom."

Jerry sat there in silence, sinking further into sadness. I glanced over at him and recognized the signs of acute depression I knew all too well. Seeing this, I got up and went around the table behind him, putting a comforting hand on his shoulder.

Jerry spoke to me in a low voice, his attention still on his little girl, "With each passing day, she becomes wiser, beyond her years. I don't understand it all, but it seems like it's God's gift to her." Looking up at me, he tried to manage a faint smile, but the truth was forming on his heartbroken face. The fact that he felt so powerless to help Laurie was only compounded by the increasing desperation filling him. I sensed he was crumbling on the inside.

"Jack." Getting my attention, leaning back in his chair, he whispered, "As in the words of David in the 23rd psalm, *my cup runneth over*, I feel like they apply to me. Do you understand what I mean?"

"Yes, I do, more than you'll ever know," I whispered.

Both of us studied each other's faces in that strange moment of truth. We realized we were kindred spirits. We had both been through a great deal of suffering in our lives. Later on, this connection would be the basis for a real and lasting friendship. He even said, "Thanks, Jack, for being my friend."

I nodded silently, patting him on the shoulder before turning to head for the door. As I left the room, Laurie came up alongside me, placing her hand in mine, and said, "Let me walk you to the door."

Stopping just inside, Laurie stepped in front of me before I could open the front door. Looking up at me, she whispered, "I must talk to you."

I moved closer, getting down on my knees beside her, "What is it, sweetheart?"

Full of innocence and truth in her face, she told me, "I used to be afraid of death, until I remembered what Jesus said, *I am with you always, even unto the end of the world.* So you see, I'm not going to die. I'm going to live forever in Heaven."

"Bless your heart." My own heartstrings tugged at me as I added, "I so wish you could be healed."

"He has already healed me in more ways than you can possibly know. He has lifted me out of the sadness I felt when I had to leave school. He has given me the strength to live each minute of every additional day I live. Without Him I could not exist. I'm at peace."

I truly felt for her, "May you have peace for all eternity, forever and ever."

"Right now my purpose for existing is to help you, Jack. It is for you I pray, that on your journey through life you too will also find peace within yourself."

"It means so much—more than words can say—you thinking of me." I was deeply moved. "I hope I do find the peace you speak of. Laurie, I'm still trying to find myself. There's a lot from out of my past haunting me."

"Jack, there's a lot of people out there searching for meaning, trying to find themselves. If you commit yourself to Him, He will help you find your own identity, one that is uniquely all your own."

"I wish it were that simple."

"It is, if you let it be. It's very important, there's more." She saw that she got my attention more than ever, and continued, "I know two secrets about you, one that you hide in your heart, and one that even you do not know."

"You do?"

"I know why you're here."

"I'm here to help you, Laurie, however I can."

"I don't mean me. I'm speaking of someone else. The one you came to the valley to help really does need your help. You're the only one on earth who can help this person stop grieving."

I pulled back in amazement, quite surprised. She really did know. Fumbling for words, I managed a half-hearted response. "I don't know what to say."

"You don't need to be afraid to talk about it. Your secret is safe with me. Just remember, search your heart and do what's right. When you two talk, you both will gain from it and find support in each other."

Just when I thought she couldn't surprise me further, she did.

"Let me ask you, do you believe in angels Jack?"

"I guess so."

"Did you know you have a guardian angel?"

"What?"

"Well, sort of a guardian angel."

This caught me even more off guard, demanding an answer, "What do you mean, *sort of a guardian angel?*"

"It's someone who was not born an angel, but was appointed by the Lord as a spirit guide to watch over you and come to your aid if need be."

"Who is this spirit guide?"

"It's someone who knows your heart. He is near you, wanting to protect and help you."

"Why?" Will I need help?"

"All I know is that he is one among a sacred list of angels who really want to help you. In a time of great danger, this angel will reveal himself to you and come to your aid. The Creator of all things has ordained angels for such purposes since the beginning of time."

"You seem to know so much about me."

"The Lord revealed it to me when I touched your hand."

"I wish I could know more."

"As time passes you will, but there's one thing you must do first."

"What's that?"

"You must get to that place within yourself where your own soul exists. There you can become more in tune with the infinite. When you do this, you will be able to reach a clearer understanding of your self. There is a force within you, inside all of us. If you tap into it, you will be strengthened. There are so many extraordinary gifts within this force that will help you on your life's journey. Listen to its voice which embodies the good within you."

"Tell me again, what is this force?"

"It is that part of the Holy Spirit of God that exists within all of us."

I was troubled and tried to explain, "I feel so unworthy. I only wish I could talk to Him."

Laurie closed her eyes, touching my forehead again with her tiny fingertips. I could see her lips moving and that she was praying. Barely above a whisper, her voice was so low I could not make out a single word.

I could feel her mind's eye probing me. It was like nothing I had ever experienced. I asked her, "Can anyone really look inside someone?"

"Don't you know?" Laurie asked, her eyes still closed.

"Know what?"

"The eye of the Lord has already searched you. He knows your heart. The potential is within you to accomplish many things. He knows you're a good person. Let Him into your life. Become one with the infinite, and God will be your Savior, just as He is mine." Opening those large eyes, she backed up a step or two, looking me over. A satisfied expression crossed her face. "Now you can talk to Him, and He will listen to your mind. Then, if you try really hard, you will hear His words as thoughts inside your brain. He will be there whenever you need Him."

"What do you think He wants me to do?"

"You have a destiny to fulfill. I think He wants you to help others, and they in turn will help others. It will keep on spreading around the world, until the day comes when His Spirit will exist in the hearts of all mankind."

Looking deeply into her eyes as she spoke, I could see a glow that seemed to capture the brilliance of Heaven. A golden light emanated from them, making connection with the recognition in my own eyes. Reaching into me, its warmth permeated throughout my own psyche. Removing the cobwebs that symbolized my own weaknesses, a new central core of strength began crystallizing within me. I was caught up in her vision and held out my hand, beckoning to her, "I want to be part of that world."

Laurie went into my arms, her small fragile body hugging me in a tender embrace that was heartfelt to both of us. As for myself, I felt some of her energy go into me along with some of her wisdom. It was an extraordinary gift flowing straight from God.

"I see it in your face, Jack. There's a lot of love and compassion inside you."

"Laurie, I recognize this force in you now. It's very powerful around you, encircling you in its aura."

"It's what keeps me alive. More than ever, I feel it every moment of every day. It's in you too now, and will eventually heal you completely. Sometimes, more often than we know, a greater power than our own helps us along in our lives. In time you will be able to help others as I have helped you. Think about it."

"I will, but I'll do more than think about it." I knew I would. Just for a flash of an instant then, I knew my entire life was about to change.

"You're such a good person, Jack. My daddy is a kind father, and full of the same goodness that is in you. Please help him after I'm gone. He will worry about me. Help him to understand that I'll be in a place where there is no pain or sorrow."

"I'll help him. With all my heart, I promise I will."

"Please tell him my soul is going home to the Lord."

"I would be most proud to tell him that." As I said this, I looked directly into her eyes and saw that inner light again. I knew for sure then there was a Heavenly Light inside her, helping her.

Leaning closer to me, she whispered several other things that would be bound by my sacred promise: words of healing that I would later relate to Jerry in what would turn out to be one of the most emotionally moving moments of both our lives.

Getting down on my knees, I gently hugged her again. Feeling another wonderful surge of energy from her, I remarked, "You're an extraordinary little girl."

"I'm no more extraordinary than God allows me to be."

"You're truly a good person, Laurie Marsh."

"And so are you, Jack Holden. It's been a privilege to meet you. I wish I could live and get to know you better. I wish there was more time."

"Laurie, you can talk to me anytime you like."

"Good," she said, sounding satisfied. "Some night after I'm gone, you will hear my voice in your ear. So don't be afraid."

"The privilege to hear your voice will be all mine."

"It makes me feel really good to have met the man who will be my daddy's best friend."

Rising to my feet, I opened the door. Glancing back at her one last time, I promised, "I will treasure his friendship and your friendship all the rest of my life." Feeling the sacredness of the moment, I added, "I mean it with all my heart."

Laurie responded in her soft gentle voice, "Jack, I will remember you when I am with God in Heaven."

She smiled at me, and I felt her love from that smile. At the same time, I smiled back at her, and the circle of love between us became complete for all time.

It was only after I left, in quiet moments of reflection, I thought about this image, realizing I had talked to an angel. Seeing this vision of her, the feelings I walked away with that evening would remain in my mind and heart forever.

CHAPTER 13
AT SUNDOWN

D own the road a piece, I stopped for a moment. Looking back, I could still see the Marsh house. Golden crested clouds stretched across the horizon behind it, like a giant halo over the little girl. Even the heavens were blessing her.

I couldn't stop thinking about Laurie. Her voice lingered in my head, *Open your mind, and you will receive knowledge of things as you need to know them.* I felt so humbled to have met her. She had helped open my eyes to a greater understanding of life itself.

Starting to realize it, I was beginning a journey of self-discovery in the day's last light. Something was transforming, changing within me. I could feel all the pain and anguish leaving me. Something wonderful was happening. I was entering a phase that would take me beyond the boundaries of what I had thought was even possible. But now things were different. I felt as if a strong guiding hand was leading me into a spiritual realm. Already forming around me, I could feel the warmth of its aura.

My first few weeks in the valley had gone from a pit of desperation to a place where hope and faith had started flowing through me. I had found something here, people whom I cared about and a whole way of life that was meaningful to me. The thought of it gave me comfort and filled my heart with a good feeling.

On my journey back from the Marsh place, my preoccupation with Laurie caused me to whisper aloud, "Poor little girl." Scanning the heavens above, I offered up a prayer for the Marshes, "Lord, bless Laurie and her father, and be with them." It was my first real prayer in some time. God had re-entered my life, and I found myself embracing Him. Unknowingly, I had begun the healing process within my own soul.

Getting to the end of the old dirt road, I looked up to see an open field stretch out before me. In the distance beyond it, I could see a rising plateau, upon which stood Russell's store and the little bungalow. Standing there for a moment, I listened to the gentle wind blowing across the landscape. Absorbed in its peacefulness, I found myself listening to the voice of my inner self. Things were crystallizing in my mind. I realized I was at a crossroads in my life. I could feel my morale lifted. A surge of resiliency shot through me, filling me with an abundance of new energy to face the future with.

In the clearing now, I could see the path back to the place I now called my home. At the same time, I began to visualize a new path for me to take, one that would lead to my own salvation.

Crossing the field, I inhaled the fresh evening air, savoring it as it flowed into my lungs. I felt a sense of being liberated. The shackles inside me that had chained my mind and soul to the past were beginning to fall away. I was not going to let PTSD hold me back. Much food for thought filled me.

I had gone out there to meet Laurie and learn a little about her. Instead, I had learned a good deal more about myself. Talking to her, a door cracked open in my mind, letting in enough light to illuminate a new future for me. The little girl's words were inspiring and profound. Seeds of hope had been planted inside me and were growing there now. She had been right. I was beginning to believe there was a reason for everything, especially in meeting her. I whispered aloud, surrendering to her visions and accepting her predictions, "Laurie, you're right. My destiny is here. I belong in this town and in this valley."

When she touched me, her positive energy had flowed into me, setting off far reaching consequences. Most scientists agree that we only use a small portion of our brains. But there are exceptions, and I was beginning to think I might be in the process of becoming one of them. I could already feel dormant cells within my brain awakening to a new understanding of nature. I would soon learn incredible things about God's creation as long as I focused my mind on them.

In a spiritual sense, my whole being was going through a miraculous transformation. Many things I thought were inconceivable would soon become possible. Change was taking place throughout my body and soul.

I was more aware than ever of God's involvement in all things, making a commitment to Him. With a new sense of purpose, I vowed to be a better human being. Setting goals for myself, I decided to do positive things as I went about the business of making this new life a reality. Each day I would do something positive that would bring me another step closer to Him. I walked back to town with renewed determination and dedication to this proposition.

The evening light had faded into a red brilliance streaking across the entire western sky. It hung there in a reddish glow behind me as I returned from the Marsh place.

Coming to the ridge behind Russell's store, I looked up to see someone. In this warm, radiant light I was able to distinguish a figure standing there on the ridge in front of my little bungalow. Getting closer, I could make out the silhouette of a beautiful woman. She stood there, bathed in the setting sun, her hair blowing in the gentle evening breeze.

Advancing up the ridge, I picked up the pace, moving more swiftly. As the woman turned in my direction, she held onto a cane for support. It was Mattie! She had been in my thoughts all day. Now, she was reality again. Up ahead, her lovely face was aglow in the remaining light. An uncontrollable urge seizing me, my fast pace accelerated even more as I ran up the steps leading to the bungalow. Reaching the top, I stopped a few paces in front of her. Both of our senses heightened, we stood there looking at each other, frozen in silence.

Her name formed on my lips in a brief whisper, "Mattie . . ."

"Jack." She whispered back, looking prettier to me than ever before. She was like a flower opening up into full blossom. Her feelings revealed themselves in her voice, "I missed you so very much today."

"I've felt the same way," I responded, feeling the same longing for her.

"I'm here," she explained, "Because Dan called and told me what happened at the store today."

"I was just trying to do the right thing."

"Jack, I'm so proud of you."

We approached each other, silhouetted and bathed in the still visible red light. Taking her hand into mine, I kissed it.

"Hold me," she said, looking into my eyes.

I think the desire was overwhelming in both of us, drawing both of us forward into each other's arms. Clinging together, we embraced. I could see genuine affection reflected in her face as we both turned to look out across the valley. Just in time, we saw the sun's ragged flames deepen into a dark orange as they melted below the horizon at sundown.

"What is it they say about a red sunset?" I asked.

"They say it means warmer weather is coming."

Relieved at her answer, I speculated, "Hopefully that could mean winter is coming to a close and springtime is almost upon us."

"I hope so. The valley is so beautiful in springtime, and there's a lot around here I'd like to show you Jack."

As we viewed the sunset, I had my arm around her, holding her close. I felt a wonderful sense of belonging to this place and the people in it. Longing to share my thoughts and feelings of the day, I wanted to confide in her.

As our eyes met, she must've been psychic, asking me, "How is Laurie Marsh?"

"I went out there to help her, but a strange thing happened."

"What was that?"

"She helped me. I wanted to give her another shoulder to lean upon. Instead, it turned out she prayed for me. It did something for me that I can't even begin to put into words. But one thing I do know."

"What is that?"

"What she said and did somehow stopped some of the hurt that was inside me."

Mattie looked at me knowingly. "Now do you understand what I meant when I told you Laurie is truly one of God's children?"

"Yes, but it's more than that, though. I went out there to meet a little girl. Instead I met an angel. I saw it clearly and felt it all around her."

"What exactly did you see and feel?"

"A more than human power radiating from her. It seemed to form a protective aura around her. I can still sense it, part of a vision I can't get out of my head. She stands in God's shadow and draws her strength from

Him. Her spirit is undefeated in spite of all her suffering. Even though she's wasting away physically, she remains mentally strong. But still, it makes me wonder how long can her frail body hold together? I just wonder." Trailing off for a moment, I'm sure she saw I was visibly troubled.

"What are you thinking?"

As we reconnected, I revealed my thoughts, "I was this close to her, as close as I am to you, and I looked into her eyes. I saw in them how desperately ill she really is. She doesn't have much time left. I was wondering what the future holds for her. What will happen the day after tomorrow?"

"Sometimes it's best not to know our future. The Lord will reveal it to us in His own good time."

"Mattie, I've seen so many sad things in my life. Sometimes I wonder what is keeping me going. Though for at least right now I know: part of it is you."

Drawing closer, she gently ran her fingertips down the roughed up side of my face, touching the gashes there and on my chin. Carefully studying me, she rendered her verdict, "You've been through a lot today."

"I did what I had to do."

She looked at me admiringly, "It took a lot to stand up to the Barnett brothers. I wasn't sure if there was such a man left in the valley who had the courage to face them."

"If I hadn't stepped in and stopped Leroy, I couldn't live with myself."

"Dan said you referred to Jerry Marsh as a fine decent man, but that's how I'd describe you."

"I'm just trying to do the right thing. Maybe that's why I'm in Tyler Junction."

As Mattie searched my face, I felt like she saw something more than skin deep. Gently touching my gashed chin again, it was though she was trying to reach deeper into my soul, whispering, "If these fingers could only heal. I would have them take away all your pain and heal up all those scars lingering from your past."

As a calming feeling came over me—one that seemed to take away some of my pain—I knew in that very same moment the healing touch of Mattie Sullivan was truly miraculous in its own way. I took her hand into mine, kissing it tenderly again. Knowing in my heart that something meaningful was connecting us, I whispered my feelings to her, "Just to know that you are here is more than a comfort to me."

I drew Mattie closer, feeling a cool breeze suddenly pass over us. She moved even more so into my arms, clinging to me.

Lost in the moment, we didn't hear the distant sound of thunder or see the storm clouds moving across the western sky toward us. Clearer and more distinct, a much louder rumble followed, getting our attention this time. We saw a faint flash of lightning off to the northwest. A sharp crackle of thunder followed. It was startling and at the same time darkly ominous. We were both brought back into a reality neither one of us wanted to face.

CHAPTER 14
BELONGING TO GOD

S even days later, a sadness would come into the valley.
I was trying to remain focused and keep control of our vehicle. It was a torturous road, full of unseen chuckholes. Being way out in the country where it was not lit up at all made it even more difficult. The winds of a powerful storm were bringing turmoil all around us that particular night. Our vehicle almost careened off the road at every turn. The driving conditions were highly dangerous. But travel we must, proceeding with all haste.

Many emotions tugged at my heartstrings like a tidal wave as I drove, but I was reassured because Mattie was beside me. I knew her strength would be needed, yet there was silence between us. We both knew we were fast coming to Jerry Marsh's place and the sadness that would be awaiting us there.

A short while before, I had received an urgent phone call at Russell's store from Doc Peterson to meet him at the Marsh Place as soon as possible. Borrowing Dan Russell's truck, I picked up Mattie and drove off into the storm. Driving through poor visibility brought on by sheets of rain, it would be a rough ride.

At last though, I came to a smooth patch in the road as I entered through an open gate onto the Marsh property. Pulling up in front alongside Doc's old truck, I could barely see beyond my headlights. The house was dark except for an occasional lightning flash reflected off the front porch.

Other than the sound of heavy rain pounding against the windshield, Mattie and I sat there in a moment of eerie silence. We were both brooding. Just then, the illumination from a jagged lightning flash managed to reach inside the cab and envelop us. It was as if nature's wrath was somehow echoing the pain inside the house.

I had known about it before we got there. This would be the last day of Laurie's life. Leaning closer to Mattie, I spoke above the sound of the storm, "Doc said Laurie was nearing the end when he called me over at Russell's store." She reacted, and I saw the same hurt in her eyes that I was feeling in my heart.

Just then a severe wind surge came up. A swirl of wind and rain together slammed into the truck. Rocking it about like a toy, all the commotion rattled its frame, making a loud noise.

Almost in response, a light came on just inside the front of the house. The door opened, and a figure emerged onto the porch. Dressed in a raincoat, he pulled his wide brimmed hat down before heading out towards the truck.

Straining to see, I cracked the driver's window. Another lightning flash made visible a familiar thick mustache under the hat. I alerted Mattie, "Here comes Doc."

Coming up by the driver's door, Doc leaned in close. "Thank God you've come!" He glanced back at the Marsh Place, then toward us again. His face was grim. "Why does it always rain when someone dies? Mattie, maybe you can talk to him. Jerry wanted to kill himself after she passed away." Deeply saddened, he went silent for a brief moment. Finding his voice again, it was filled with concern, "I'm really going to need the two of you in there tonight."

A few moments later—clad in our raincoats—the three of us emerged through persistent sheets of pelting rain. Reaching the front porch, which was covered by an overhanging roof, we went up the steps. Out of the downpour, Doc leaned over to me, "You can help me with Laurie." He had not noticed the front door was still ajar.

Jerry Marsh was standing there in its shadows, just inside, listening. As soon as I caught sight of the redness around his eyes I knew what had happened and what was going to happen. Men are often broken by sadness and loss. This was the night Jerry would be brought to that breaking point.

He staggered out onto the porch, only caught by its railing. Grabbing it for support, he shook all over, contorted in his own grief. Just hanging together by a slender thread, Jerry was about to snap. As I turned around, we came face to face with each other. He stopped right in front of me.

I saw a face full of anguish and streaming tears staring back at me. It was so overpowering. I looked down and away, feeling like I had invaded the most personal moment of this poor man's sorrow.

Jerry Marsh was completely shattered, out of his mind with grief. He had kept everything bottled up for so long. But now all his hurt was visible and laid bare before us. Taking a step forward, he braced one hand on the railing while raising the other in the form of a clenched fist. His whole body trembled as he exploded. Screaming at us through tear stained eyes, he yelled, "No! You're not taking my little girl! I won't let you! I'LL DIE FIRST!"

"Now Jerry, you know that's wrong," Doc broke in, trying to reason with him. "You'll never forgive yourself, son."

Jerry went silent, overcome by everything. A floodtide of emotions spilled out. Through trembling lips, he still managed to whisper, "There's nothing left for me."

I could see his heartbreak. Laurie's death had pushed him over the edge. I knew something had to be done. Looking over at the one person who might be able to calm him, an unspoken communication passed between us.

Mattie knew what she had to do. Her caring way of helping others who were in need took over. With the aid of her cane, she moved closer to Jerry. Coming up alongside him, she placed a comforting hand on his shoulder and whispered, "Now Mr. Marsh, your little girl wouldn't want to hear you say that. You know I'm right. Please. Let's go back inside."

Knowing the goodness within Mattie, a calmer expression came over Jerry. He nodded silently, relenting to her request. She followed him, stepping inside. Out of the rain, she wiped the water and wet hair away from her face.

Right behind them, Doc entered and took his hat off. His face seemed to reveal a certain measure of relief.

As Jerry staggered past me, I saw something in his body language, through every movement of his entire frame. Laurie's passing had torn his heart open. His cup was running over with more sorrow than he could endure.

Following behind all of them, I stood in the doorway for a moment. Behind me the rain was still coming down heavily. Other than the rumble of thunder in the distance, there was silence. But inside my head a rush of feelings for Jerry filled my thoughts, *Dear God, please be with this poor man. Please, be with him.*

"Jack?" Doc called after me, seeing my distraction.

"Oh, sorry Doc." Snapping back to the matters at hand, I closed the door and followed Doc into the kitchen. It was very dim and shadowy except for one small faint light.

Jerry stood there, shaking all over. Staggering, his legs buckled under him. He collapsed into a chair at the kitchen table. His eyes glistened as the heartbreak within him found release in the tears that spilled down his face. Holding nothing back now, he wept hard. I could see it clearly now, more than ever. Jerry was completely broken, as much as a man could be broken.

Seeking to comfort him, Mattie sat down beside him. It was her compassion, faith, and inner strength that saved him from complete collapse. She felt his pain as much as another person could. Putting her arm around Jerry, she supported him both physically and emotionally.

Trying to focus on her was very hard. Pulling a wadded handkerchief from his pocket, Jerry suppressed his grief as best he could. He tried to explain, "Don't you see, she's all I've got in the world." His eyes then went across the table to Doc and me, "In the name of God, please don't take her." Tears streamed down his face again as he buried his head in his handkerchief.

Wiping his eyes, he avoided her as he continued to talk to Mattie, "I've lost my little girl. I would've killed myself awhile ago if Doc hadn't stopped me. After my wife died, she was all I had left in the world. My Laurie was all I had to live for. You know that Miss Mattie. So don't you see? I can't let her go without me. She'd be alone. If I could sleep, I'd pray to God that I not wake up."

"Jerry, listen to me," she said, getting him to look at her as she reasoned with him. "Please don't talk that way. It's not right to take one's life. Laurie wouldn't have wanted you to be talking that way. And she's not alone. Her soul is with her mother now. Your wife, your Lana, wouldn't have wanted you talking that way either." Glancing across the table at us, she continued,

"Doc and Jack are your friends. They loved Laurie too. Please, won't you let them help?"

Jerry had listened to her, sobbing. He sat there for a moment trying to accept it. Turning to Doc and me, his lips moved as he tried to speak, but the words wouldn't come. The torment within him was too much. Nodding silently, he gave his consent to let us help.

Doc knew what he had to do, "Jack and I, we'll go check on Laurie."

"I'll stay in here with Jerry," Mattie responded. Seeing he was visibly shaking again, she reached over with a firm hand to help calm him.

Grateful for her support, he settled down a bit. Trying to put into words what he was feeling, Jerry opened up, "Miss Matttie, in the past year I've gone crazy with grief. Its penetrated so deep, it cuts me like a knife. My heart is broken. What do I do? How do I go on?"

"Jerry, I know *why* you go on."

"Why, Miss Mattie?"

"Because Laurie would want you to."

"I'm so glad you're here," Jerry responded, touched deeply. "My Laurie loved you. She was all I had. Now I have nothing."

"You're wrong. She projected a light that's still here with you." Mattie leaned forward, touching his chest. "It's right here, in your heart."

"I hope so."

"Your wife and child are still with you. By the grace of the good Lord their spirits will be with you for the rest of your life. I'm not just saying this, I know. Coming here tonight I felt God put that thought in my mind."

"Why would He do this for me?"

"Because Jerry, you're a good person. He has a plan for your life. The good in you is going to help a lot of other people, some that you don't even know yet."

"Oh Miss Mattie, now you're sounding like Laurie." Jerry glanced down, trying to decide what he should do. Looking over at Mattie, he saw the kindness and understanding that was in her face. Knowing now what he needed to do, he asked, "Would you pray with me?"

"Yes I will because He is with you always, even unto the end of the world." They both bowed their heads. She prayed, with and for him, "Lord, please be with Jerry here and show him the purpose You have for him."

God's own words spoken through Mattie, comforted him and eased the pain within his soul.

In another part of the house, Doc and I stood in front of a closed door. Pushing it open, we entered a dark room where all life had been snuffed out. I took the left, and Doc the right, as we moved up along each side of Laurie's bed. For a moment we just stood there in silence, hovering above her lifeless form.

As I looked down at Laurie, I could see the inner light that had once shined from her was now gone. The dark circles that had started forming around her eyes during her illness had now expanded, becoming even darker, closing them forever. Yet, it was strange. I could still feel her spirit reaching out to me. I could hear her little voice whisper to my mind, *Jack, I'm okay now.* After that, I knew some part of her had triumphed over death. This belief would grow stronger within me in the days and weeks to come, eventually comforting me. But right then, I felt the same intense grief that everyone else was feeling that night. I had come to love this little girl in the brief time I knew her. She had reached into my heart and touched me in a way no one ever would.

"It wasn't the cancer that took her," Doc remarked. "It was the effects of a high fever this afternoon. It was all too much for her little body. Her already weak heart just gave out."

Placing my hand on her chest, I whispered, "Bless you Princess, you're at peace now, and for all time."

Doc continued his narrative, telling me more of Laurie's final moments, "You know, I delivered this child into the world. Because of that I always felt a special connection to her. She was a brave little girl, full of courage and comfort for her father, and for me. Near the end, I wanted to give her something for the pain. Bless her heart, she said, 'That's okay, Doc. I can't feel the pain anymore.' Jack, I can't get that moment out of my mind. It lingers with me."

Emotions overwhelming him, the old man leaned down very close to the child. In words that were only meant for her, he whispered, "It's okay, Laurie. You don't have to suffer anymore."

As Doc snapped back from his own grief, I saw the sadness in his face. Feeling his pain as well, I said, "I'm sure you did all you could have done for her, all that was humanly possible."

"I tried to the fullest extent of my knowledge and with all the help of modern science. But sometimes, that's not good enough. Now she belongs to God. But you know something, I think she always did."

As the wind and rain outside raged on, we both gazed for a final time at the frail child, whose soul had already begun the journey down the stream that flows into the river of eternal life.

CHAPTER 15
ON CEMETERY RIDGE

Two days later a rainbow stretched across the valley, as it often does after a long rain. It was as if the glory of Heaven was present during this morning of sadness.

A gentle stream flows around the eastern edge of town. It runs along the horizon until it reaches Cemetery Ridge. A group of those who knew Laurie had already journeyed past swirls of morning mist drifting through the valley to gather there, around her newly dug grave.

Other children from Laurie's class, along with their parents, were still making their way up the ridge. Many were simply dressed farmers. All were sincere, God fearing people. The population of Tyler Junction was in large part descended from the pioneer stock that settled this part of Middle America. Bequeathed by their ancestors, a patriotic, religious fervor still ran in the veins of those here today.

I could especially see this legacy alive in Mattie and Doc. It was a good thing, making me feel proud to be here with them on this morning honoring Laurie.

The word about her passing had spread, and the gathering of a few people grew into a crowd. Tears were in the eyes of one person after another. I could see the sadness in all of their faces. It quickly became apparent to me that the whole town had loved Laurie.

All were quiet and respectful, knowing Jerry Marsh had suffered a season of loss. The people of the valley had come out to pay their respects and support him. In doing so, everyone touched each other's lives.

The funeral service began with the mourners joining together and singing, "We will gather at the river, the river that flows by the throne of God." The song echoed down the ridge into the town below, tugging at the hearts of all who heard it.

Meanwhile, with Bible in hand, Doc Peterson moved to the foot of the grave. Nearby, on one side of the grave, was Jerry Marsh, flanked by Mattie Sullivan and myself. A little behind us stood Sheriff Bodeen and Deputy Wilcox. On the other side of the grave stood Dan Russell and Mr. Peabody, the Principal of Tyler Junction School.

As quiet fell over the crowd, Doc opened the service, "After a long illness, one who was a friend to most of us—little Laurie Marsh—lost her final struggle. We are all heartbroken at her passing."

I think everyone present felt those same thoughts in their own hearts. I know mine was breaking. I thought, *God bless you Laurie, you've touched the hearts of everyone here.*

Doc adjusted his glasses, reading aloud, "Suffer the little children not, and forbid them not to come unto me, for of such is the Kingdom of God." Closing the Bible, he continued, "Laurie Marsh was a very spiritual child. She was raised in poverty and didn't have much in this life. But before God she will be rich beyond measure. Now she has inherited the Lord's promise, and this day is in His kingdom."

Doc had Jerry's attention as he talked about Laurie. But also, something unspoken and powerful passed between them. Jerry was holding it together, but only by his fingernails. I picked up on the strain that seemed to be just below the surface. It was all he could do to keep from crying out loud, barely able to suppress the grief that tore at him.

Mattie stood close to him, providing moral support. But sadness was in her eyes too, as she wept with him in his grief.

Doc held up the Bible he'd been reading from and announced, "This was Laurie's Bible. As I was looking through it I found a note, on the inside front page. It was written by Laurie to her father, and to all of us. It's dated two days ago, her last day of life on this earth. It reads: 'Daddy, I love you with all my heart. Even though I'll be gone when you read this, I want you to know I'm leaving these words to be with you always. I've also been thinking of Miss Mattie, Doc Peterson, and my new friend Jack Holden. By your goodness and unselfish actions, you've proven to truly be my friends. I love you all so very much."

Doc removed his glasses, wiping his eyes. Laurie's words had moved him, as well as everyone else there. Regaining his composure, he scanned the crowd, "There's more about everyone here. You will all have a chance to read it later." Passing the Bible back to Jerry, Doc turned to Mr. Peabody.

The principal of Laurie's school came around to the front of the grave. Taking Doc's place, he glanced at everyone over the top of his horn-rimmed glasses, reflecting on her, "Laurie Marsh lived all her life here in Tyler Junction. Though small in size, her capacity for love was bigger than this whole valley. She made a lot of friends here and had found her way into the hearts of all of us. The life of this one little girl touched our lives and left us the better for it."

As they looked on, the faces of the other kids, her classmates and friends, all visibly mirrored the emotion of their inner most feelings. Pausing, looking over this crowd, Mr. Peabody saw a touch of sorrow in everyone. Reacting to it, he said "We will miss her. We all loved her."

Glancing over at Mattie and Jerry, his eyes kept returning to them as he recalled, "As did Miss Sullivan here, I got to see and know Laurie on a daily basis. Almost every week she'd somehow find a blossoming flower and bring it to my office. It got to where I looked forward to seeing those flowers appear on my desk. She said they represented the beauty and good that was inside all of us. Jerry, I speak for all of us over at the schoolhouse. We will very much miss the beauty and good that was inside your little girl."

With those words the services concluded. Everyone was moved with emotions, now more than ever.

As we all began to sing, "We will gather at the River" again, something unsettling caught the eye of Sheriff Bodeen. He later told me he saw a familiar figure, standing apart from the rest of the crowd a little ways down the ridge. Troubled, I could see a concerned expression cross the Sheriff's face. Quietly, he stepped aside, working his way toward that person.

Leroy Barnett was the lone figure, standing off to one side. Strangely quiet for him, he was so focused on the funeral that he didn't notice the sheriff approaching.

Coming up alongside him, not wanting to disturb the proceedings, Sheriff Bodeen whispered in a quiet voice, "Barnett."

Pulled out of his concentration, Leroy looked over in the direction of the voice. His expression showed more than a little surprise to see the sheriff standing next to him. His face didn't reflect his usual evil grin or trouble-making attitude. Seeming at a loss for words, he barely started, "Sheriff, I uh . . ."

Sheriff Bodeen cut him off immediately, "Before you say one more word to me, I want you to know that nothing is gonna interfere with this funeral and Jerry Marsh's grief."

"I'm not goin' to interfere, Sheriff," Leroy said, lowering his head. Seemingly ashamed, he was not making eye contact. Shaken by the course of events, his whole manner revealed the beginnings of some inward soul searching. His words came out barely above a whisper, "Have you ever noticed that really evil people are those ate up by hatred? I've had time to think about it and it's true. The hate grew in me because Jerry fired me over at the iron works plant. God may punish me, I know. But I'm gonna try to change myself."

"Well, you're certainly not yourself today," Sheriff Bodeen responded, obviously surprised.

"Hopefully Sheriff, you'll never see that man again."

"Just keep remembering this is Laurie Marsh's funeral."

"I've tried not to think about her. It hurts me every time I do. But you see, I must. That little girl didn't deserve my hate. I didn't know how bad off she really was." Finally looking back up into the Sheriff's gaze, he couldn't let go of the thought and repeated himself, "I just didn't know."

Sheriff Bodeen studied Leroy for a moment, seeing the shame and guilt in his face. Satisfied there was not going to be a problem, he turned and left.

A few moments later, Sheriff Bodeen rejoined Dan and me, walking up behind us. Glancing back at him, we also caught a glimpse of Leroy, farther on down the ridge.

"What did he want?" I asked.

"Don't worry, Jack. Barnett's not gonna be causing any trouble today. It seems he may even be developing a conscience."

Our attention returned to the funeral as Jerry moved to the foot of Laurie's grave. Silently, the town folk filed past the gravesite as they departed Cemetery Ridge.

When it came Mattie's turn, she stopped in front of Jerry, gently resting her hand on his shoulder, consoling him.

He responded in an emotion-filled voice, "Miss Mattie, you're truly a good person. God bless you for all you've done for my family."

Doc filed past, stopping as Jerry's eyes met his. He voiced his support, "Son, I'm here for you whenever you need me."

"Thank you Doc for everything but especially for being here with me today." Jerry could not hide his inner pain. It could clearly be seen in his face, never leaving him.

Doc saw it, becoming even more concerned than he already was.

Nearby, Mattie leaned over close to me, "I've got to go back to school now. Doc's going to give me a ride. I have one more class." She halted for a moment as several of Laurie's classmates passed across her field of vision. Observing their sad faces, she whispered, "I'll have some counseling to do this afternoon. They've lost a friend here." Her original thought came back as she looked over at me again, "Will I see you later?"

"I'm going to stay up here and visit with Jerry after everyone's left. Maybe I can help him in some way."

"Maybe you can." Mattie's eyes searched my face for a moment. Seeing something she liked, she told me, "He's indeed fortunate to have a friend like you. We all are."

"I'm just doing the right thing. It's what I should do. After that, I'm just going to stay here and think about some things till you get back."

She confirmed, "Then I'll meet you here."

I nodded, agreeing with her. Then as our eyes froze on each other, a split-second unspoken communication of affection passed between us.

In the next few moments the last of the mourners—Mr. Peabody, Dan Russell, Sheriff Bodeen, and Zeke Wilcox—filed past the grave, paid their respects, and departed.

Jerry barely acknowledged them, his head lowered, lost in his thoughts. Words of sympathy were inadequate against the magnitude of grief that lingered on within him.

The funeral was over, and there was silence on Cemetery Ridge. Two men stood there alone—Jerry and me.

Just looking at him, I could tell Jerry wished he could be anywhere else but there. "My baby," he whispered. Looking down at the burial plot, he looked as if he was sick and empty inside. Standing motionless at the foot of the grave, he stared at the wooden marker. Even though just a few feet separated him from Laurie's body beneath the ground, the very thought of the far greater divide of Heaven and Earth was almost unbearable, or so he would later tell me.

Letting him have some private space, I went elsewhere in the small cemetery. Viewing tombstones and markers of the young and old alike, they reflected more than a hundred years of history here. Walking among the gravesites, I covered the entire cemetery in less than half an hour. As I did so, I had to think about what to say to Jerry. A prayer flowed through my mind, *Please God, guide me. I want to help Jerry, somehow to give him strength. I promised Laurie I would. Please God, help me with the words.*

As I got closer—even though we were the only two people in the cemetery—I did not feel we were alone. I very definitely felt the presence of another. Though I could not see her, the spiritual essence of Laurie was there with us. I had felt her presence throughout her own funeral. Now, I could hear her voice inside my head saying, *Okay Jack, it's time to talk to my daddy.*

Jerry was still at Laurie's grave when I got back. Quite alone and completely silent, he was still brooding. I wondered what thoughts had been going through his mind. Lost in his own world of sadness, his expression spoke volumes. Looking up, our eyes met. I could see the intense grief in his expression. As tears streamed down his face, he said, "I just can't let her go, not yet at least."

Here was my opportunity to help him, to keep a promise that had become sacred to me. I offered a friendly ear, "They say I'm a good listener."

His words were full of quivering emotion, but he made an effort to ask me anyway, "Jack, do you know what I was thinking?"

"What Jerry?"

"I was wondering, what happened to Laurie's soul after she died?"

"She went to be with our Lord in Heaven."

"But our children are supposed to outlive us, not the other way around. Why, Jack?" He tried to hold it together, but just couldn't. His eyes filling with more tears, he asked, "Why do you think God took my baby?"

"God didn't really take Laurie. The way I see it, He healed her."

"What do you mean?"

"He ended her suffering, and delivered her into the loving arms of your wife, your Lana."

"I want to believe you, Jack. I want that with my whole heart and soul."

"She told me if you concentrate hard enough, you will be able to hear her speak to your mind."

He searched my face wanting me to reassure him, "Is that really possible?"

"By His grace, God will allow it. Then you will be able to hear Laurie as clear as if she were standing right her in front of you."

Struggling with his emotions, trying to accept what I had told him, he glanced upward into the heavens and whispered, "Thank you Lord."

"You know, Jerry, in this world of so much that is ordinary, she was an extraordinary human being."

Remaining there, we cried and prayed together, becoming like brothers. In doing so, a bond was forged that would become even stronger over the course of time.

Gaining strength, Jerry was finally able to speak more about the heartbreak he felt, "It hurts so much, Jack. First my wife Lana and now Laurie . . . I'll be honest, I don't know if I can deal with it. They were my whole life, and now they are laid out in front of me." Raising a trembling hand, he pointed to his wife's tombstone just two months old and then over to a fresh grave next to it, that of their only child. "Now at least like you say, they are together."

"There's something else your Laurie told me and wanted you to know."

"What Jack?"

"A very special part of her will always be with you. If you look up in the heavens at night, you'll see her star shining brighter than any of the others, watching over you."

He had listened in silent appreciation. "Bless you my friend."

"Jerry, she wouldn't want you to grieve like this. She told me so."

"What else did she tell you?"

"She said, 'Be Daddy's friend, he's so alone. I don't want him to be sad.' Your little girl loved you right up to her last breath of life here on this earth. But she loves you even more now. She will be with you always, alive in your mind and heart."

"I want to believe it."

"Believe it. Love is sometimes so powerful that it can transcend life and death. If you just close your eyes, focus on her, in the quiet moments you will hear her voice speaking to your mind. She will always be there for you."

"Every single day of her life, I told Laurie that I loved her. If I could only have just one more moment with her, I would tell her that again."

"You can, but you have to have faith. You have to believe. She's listening right now, in Heaven."

"Jack, that's what Laurie used to say to me, *Daddy you have to have faith.*" Jerry's voice faltered again.

"With faith all things are possible. She wanted you to believe and rise above all human doubt. She wanted you to look at these events as if they were pages from a book. Turn from these sad pages, and you will see the remaining white pages representing the rest of your life. In them you will find life with hope in your heart and peace of mind."

"Jack, Laurie told me, that after she was gone you might talk to me about living and dying. You know how I feel, don't you? With everything closing in on you. . . Didn't you want to kill yourself one time?"

I was caught by surprise. "How did you know that?"

"She told me."

"I didn't tell her that."

"You didn't have to. She felt it when she held your hand. Didn't you feel something also?"

"Yes, I did. I wasn't sure what it was, but I thought she was inside my mind."

"She was. Some people thought my little girl was sort of a psychic toward the end. Actually, I prefer to think of it as something very special, bestowed upon her by the Lord. By touching people she knew all their thoughts. She had the ability to look inside you and see not only your future but everything from your past as well."

I thought about it again. Was such a thing possible? My mind was telling me it must be true. Now more than ever, I accepted it, "Your little girl knew things that no one else could. She truly had an extraordinary gift."

"It was more than that, Jack. What she had was given to her by the good Lord for His purposes. I realize now that she was more of a spirit in human form, sort of a gift to all of us from God."

I understood more than ever what Laurie had said about helping her father. "Jerry, there's one other message she wanted me to give you. She said, 'It takes far more courage to live than to die. Tell my Daddy he has to live.' If you could have only seen her face when she said it."

"She said that?"

"Yes, my friend. You may not know it right now, but you have a lot more to contribute in this old world than you realize, helping a lot of people you don't even know yet. You will be loved and adored by many."

Jerry listened very carefully. Thinking about it, he added, "It's odd."

"What's that?" I questioned.

"Your choice of words are strangely familiar. You sound so very much like her. I think a part of my little girl will always be with you too. I see it in your face and hear it in your voice. I'm deeply beholdin' to you."

In the rush of feelings that followed, I leaned over and hugged him tightly. I felt something unusual. It was as if someone else's hands were working through me, using my body. Laurie's spirit had become one with me, reaching out, touching her father. Jerry felt it too. He said, "When you touched me, it felt like Laurie's familiar touch, reaching from beyond the grave to give her daddy one last hug."

"See Jerry, all things spiritual are true. You just have to have faith and believe."

"I believe now." Then putting all his feelings for her in a single thought, Jerry turned and looked down at her grave, whispering, "I love you sweet-heart, forever and always."

As Jerry stood there, I could see in his face that although he had been strengthened by this experience, he was still struggling with heartbreak. I leaned over and put my hand on his shoulder, supporting him. It was then we both became more aware of a God who cares for all mankind, part of His creation. Jerry and I both felt the healing warmth of the Holy Spirit around us, comforting the intense grief we both felt.

Later, as we were walking out of the cemetery together, I reassured him, "If you ever need me, I'll be there for you."

Jerry stopped for a moment. Turning to me, he revealed something else that had just come to him, "One more thing: You, Doc, and Miss Mattie have all been good Samaritans to me. That's something I'm going to always remember. I want you to know the same is true for me, if you ever need someone, I'll find a way to be there."

Staying at the top, I looked on in silence as Jerry walked slowly down Cemetery Ridge. As he did so, I saw that he was bathed in the morning's sunlight. Its warmth felt good. I know it was comforting and helped lessen the sadness that was still inside him. His healing had begun, for this was God's light. One other thing taught me from this day forward. He is truly the greatest comforter of them all.

I was alone now as a morning breeze brushed past me. Turning around, I walked back into the cemetery. Looking down at Laurie's grave, I thought about her touching me and what it meant. I knew now that the special something she gave me was much more than a gift. My mind, though, was only beginning to comprehend the full extent of it.

Just then, another bright shaft of morning sunlight broke through a passing cloud and bathed the cross marking Laurie's grave. More than ever, I realized how much her passing had affected me, just as I knew how much her life had inspired me. These feelings led me to one other thought, which formed in my mind. I whispered it aloud, "God must've wanted another angel in Heaven."

CHAPTER 16
THINGS REMEMBERED

In another part of the valley, events continued to unfold that same morning. Later, Jerry revealed to me what happened when he got back to his farm.

He stood there on the porch for a moment, feeling a sense of great dread suddenly come over him. The very thought of going inside alone was not something he wanted to do. But he knew he had to do it. Summoning up the courage, he stepped forward.

The door to the farmhouse opened slowly. As it swung inward, bright morning light filled the doorway. Emerging through this light, Jerry entered a house that was no longer a home. Closing the door, he had almost expected to hear his daughter's little voice. She gave the place so much warmth and life. Now though, this pathetic little house was just an empty shell to him. He had lost his wife and now his only child. The last remaining spark that gave this place life was gone. He started aching all over, weighted down with sorrow.

Jerry had felt a little better before entering the house. My words had lifted his spirits a bit. But now he was back in the very heart of where tragedy had torn his life apart. A loving family had lived here. Now they were gone forever.

This rush of things remembered hammered him repeatedly and pulled him back into a depression that hadn't completely let go of him. He looked around in the cold silence that abounded here. There were layers of it as well as a certain unnatural stillness that lurked within these walls. It seemed to close in all around him. Like a thief in the night, death had entered this little house and stolen the joy of life out of it. There were too many ghosts here. A season of sadness had turned his home into a house of lost dreams.

At first he truly did not know what to do. He had nothing left except memories. In this frame of thought, Jerry's mind reached back, recollecting a particular conversation between him and his little girl. This silent review sparked a ray of hope. Clinging to it, he wandered through the house searching.

He was a man with a purpose now, looking for something. But with so many things coming at him at once, he could not remember what it looked like or where it was. His eyes traveled around the living room. He pondered as a succession of images past played in his mind. Then it crystallized into a mental picture. "Where is it?" he whispered allowed, as he continued through his small house.

Stopping in front of Laurie's room, which had been closed since her death, he hesitated and took a deep breath. Reaching out, he opened the door, and this barrier to happier times opened. Standing in the doorway, the thought seized him that there was some part of her soul, not wanting to let go, still living and existing in this room.

Jerry entered, glancing about as something in the room beckoned to him. Advancing slowly along the wall, he approached several of Laurie's toys gathered together. His fingertips moved slowly across her rocking horse and Jack-in-the-box.

Then he suddenly froze, his eyes settling on something in the corner of the room. He had found what he'd been looking for. Sitting there on a box, Laurie's big raggedy doll with the sewn on smile was staring straight at him. Moving closer, directly in front of it, he went down on his knees and gently touched the doll's face.

As Jerry picked up the doll, tears started to form in his eyes. All the memories concerning it came rushing back to him, especially what Laurie had said about it and what he had promised her. He whispered softly, "I'll take care of your dolly, sweetheart." Just holding it gave him comfort.

But the overwhelming sense of loss was still with him. Caught in the grip of sadness, he cried aloud. Feeling her invisible little hands tug at his heart, his view traveled down and took in the doll's face. It stared up at him with an expression that was a reflection of his own little girl's wide-eyed innocence. It was though some part of her spirit was reaching out to him through the doll. Feeling this, he whispered a prayer, "Oh God, please take care of my baby."

In the silence that followed, Jerry felt a gentle rush of wind through a nearby cracked window. It blew a paper off the dresser from behind the doll. Gliding across the floor, the folded sheet came to a rest right in front of him. He reached down, his fingers slowly touching the piece of paper. Wondering what this was, he picked it up. Unfolding it, he saw something far more profound and meaningful than most people would ever realize.

The simple crayon drawing was a picture of Laurie's doll holding a card with a few brief words printed in large letters. The card said, DADDY, I LOVE YOU ALWAYS. Just five little words printed in her own hand, they spoke volumes of the feelings she had for her father.

She had loved her father her whole life, but forces greater than the two of them were about to make their relationship reach beyond the boundaries of life itself. As he looked at the picture, another whoosh of wind carried a familiar little voice into his ears. He thought he could hear her words so clearly now, speaking to his mind, *I told you Daddy, I would find a way to reach you.*

It was just as I had said, if he tried hard enough he would be able to hear Laurie again. Such was the power of God letting it happen. His little girl's soul was truly close to the Lord. Jerry felt uplifted, for now he knew for sure that a part of her was still with him. Grateful to God, he whispered, "Thank you Lord."

While still on his knees, he heard the sound of a truck pulling up in front of his house. Almost immediately, there was a series of sharp knocks at his front door.

Rising to his feet, he wiped the tears from his face with his hand as he went to the door. Opening it, Jerry found himself looking straight into the face of Doc Peterson staring back at him. It was impossible to hide his heartbreak. Inside the doorway, the kindly old physician became immediately concerned.

Doc's worried expression did not waver, remaining as a steady gaze upon him. Seeing Jerry's sad countenance so deeply etched across his face, his observation was immediate, "You've been crying again."

"Yes, I was. Doc, I tried to be strong today, but I can't hold it in any longer."

"I know son, that's why I'm here now. I felt like God wanted me to come and see you."

"Bless you, Doc. You've always been here for me and my family. But now my family is gone. I lost Lana and now Laurie. As long as she was alive there was hope. She was the shining light of my life. It's more than a man can take."

Doc could see the strain was still unrelenting within Jerry. The day's heartbreak had taken its toll. The emotional wall inside him had cracked open, and all his inner turmoil was quite visible again. He sought to comfort him, "I loved Laurie like she was a child of my own."

"I know you did. She loved you too. She would've appreciated you being there for her today."

"Son, I was also there for you today. I was praying for you, as were a lot of other people at the funeral. We were all there to help you make it through this thing."

"Doc, I'm grateful—most grateful—to you and everybody else."

"Do you remember what you said to me when your dad let me take you over to Meadow Wood, when you were twelve years old?"

Jerry remembered it like it was yesterday. "Yes, I recall it Doc. You pointed out all the beautiful flowers coming into bloom, and I said something about life renewing itself."

"You knew that, even then when you were young. I know this is hard to take, but death is part of living. It's part of God's master plan for us, the human race, and all nature."

"It's still so hard for me to understand."

"With Laurie gone, I think the Lord has a different journey planned for you during the rest of your life on earth."

"What could that be?"

"Only He knows for sure. But you're a decent man, and I think your journey could only be for the good of mankind."

Jerry listened, thinking I had said something similar to him after the funeral. He thought there must be some truth in what we were saying. It helped him to hear Doc's opinions and he would think on it. But for right now, there was something more immediate on his mind. He wanted to show Doc his recent discovery. "I found something I need to talk to you about."

He followed Jerry into his kitchen, sitting down opposite him. Doc's attention was immediately drawn to the raggedy doll still in his hand.

Jerry set the doll on the kitchen table, making it the subject of his conversation, "Laurie came back from the dead and kept a promise to me."

"How so?" Doc asked, quite surprised and more than a little curious.

"She told me if there was a way, she'd find it and contact me from the other side."

"Son, how could she keep such a promise?"

"I was looking for this doll earlier. It was one of Laurie's favorites. Near it, I just found this." He extracted a folded paper from his pocket, carefully opening it, laying the drawing on the table in front of Doc. "After I saw this I heard Laurie's voice in my head, comforting me."

He examined it closely, commenting, "God works in mysterious ways sometimes, and this is one of those times." His eyes rose from the drawing meeting Jerry's, "Son, I believe your little girl wanted to see you heal and this proves it. I'm truly amazed, but then again knowing Laurie, I'm not surprised. With this drawing, she has reached across death itself to you."

"I thought so too when I found it. Coming home and seeing all her things still lying about, it just got the best of me. But this time it was in a good way. When I'm here alone, I find her love surrounding me, and like you said, helping to heal me. Her aura still exists within the walls of this house. I realize it now."

Glancing around the kitchen, Doc could see Laurie's drawings taped up everywhere. He agreed, "Just sitting here I can feel her spirit still in this house. With that kind of help, I think in time you're going to be okay."

"It may not be today, tomorrow, or even next week, but I will get to feeling better. I know that now because it's like you said, my Laurie's spirit is with me."

"It's more than a doctor or any other mortal man can do for you." Realizing something very important, Doc picked up Laurie's crayon drawing. Feeling the love radiating from it, he added, "You've just tapped into a hidden reservoir of strength, a gift from your little angel."

Jerry felt comforted. Everything Doc, Mattie, and I had said helped him make it through the roughest day of his life. Most of all though, it was his little girl that lifted his spirits. It was true, her light had gone out to the rest of the world. But in his heart and mind, just as I had told him, he could still see and hear her just as clearly. Her image had burned itself so deeply into his soul for all time. In the months and years to come, in some of the most crucial times of his life, this would be true. In a very real sense, she would never leave him for the rest of his life on this earth. Because of her, because of his friends, he started remembering good things and letting go of the sadness that had been pulling him down.

Later he walked Doc out onto his front porch and waved at the old country physician as he left. At last Jerry was settling down. A measure of peace and tranquility had begun to fill him. The Lord in His infinite wisdom and mercy was at work, healing him. Over time, he would become a stronger, better person than he'd ever been. Standing there, he looked upward at the bluest sky he'd ever seen in the heavens and projected this thought, whispering it aloud, "Thank you, Princess, for being my little girl."

CHAPTER 17
A PIECE OF HEAVEN

An aura of sunlight still illuminated and surrounded the home-made cross anchored in the ground with this inscription:

LAURIE MARSH: MY LITTLE SWEETHEART

Two cemetery workers had come to clean up around Laurie's grave. The turning of the earth by their shovels, packing the ground solid around the grave, carried with it a finality even I couldn't face. Turning away, one profound thought ran through my head, *From dust thou art, to dust thou shalt return.* Nothing of our bodies is ever permanent on this earth. But words of wisdom, such as those that Laurie had spoken, will last forever. What she had said to her father and me would stay with us all the rest of the days of our lives.

Finishing their work, the grave workers left the cemetery. Alone again, I had time for more reflection. My steady focus on Laurie's grave had not dimmed as I whispered, "I only knew you briefly, but you touched my heart. You made a difference in every life you ever came in contact with and made their lives more meaningful in the process." In the past few weeks, I had gone from desperation to the place where I was now, full of hope and encouragement in my life. In no small way, Laurie had been a force in this change. This brought me back to thinking about her, "You suffered so much in your short life. I suppose there is a reason for everything that happens. But only God knows for what purpose."

Contemplating it, I looked up and walked across the ridge to a vantage point where I could stare past the little town below, on out across the entire valley. My eyes traveled upward and searched the sky as I continued in sort of a communion with God, "Since meeting Laurie, I've felt closer to you Lord. I want to go to a place where there is peace and no sadness, a place where You are."

"Do you want to go where God is?" Interrupting, a familiar voice came out of nowhere.

Startled, I looked around for the source of this voice. Coming up from behind, I saw Mattie. She smiled at me as she approached. A breeze caught her hair, blowing it back, revealing a face glowing with warmth and hope. "I told you I'd be back."

My spirits were instantly raised. "I'm glad you're here."

She pursued her original question, "So would you like to go to such a place, where few human eyes have ever seen? What do you say?"

"You don't have to ask twice. The answer is yes, of course . . . That is, if it's a place where I could find a faith like Laurie possessed."

"Yes Jack, you just might find such a path to faith there. It's called the pathway of God, and it can be found over where the junction of the three valleys comes together."

I responded enthusiastically as my curiosity peaked, "How do I find this place?"

Mattie pointed down the ridge, "You follow the stream that runs just below us here, through the open meadow into the forest beyond. It will take you to a truly magical place."

"Sounds wonderful, that is so long as I'm with you. When do we go?"

"I'll take you this weekend."

"How about meeting me just inside Russell's store?"

"No . . . I-I can't." Mattie seemed strangely reluctant for a brief moment, then quickly offered an alternative meeting place, "I've got a better idea, I'll meet you at the front door of your bungalow, bright and early, at the crack of dawn."

"Okay, but what's the name of this place?" I inquired.

"It's a place called Meadow Wood. It's a piece of Heaven on earth."

I recognized the name from the painting in Doc's living room and was immediately intrigued by the very thought of going there. Yet, right at that moment my thoughts were also drawn to someone else. Thinking of her, I glanced back in the direction of Laurie's grave. "May God have mercy on her little soul. I hope she has found her Meadow Wood."

Much later that same evening, thoughts of Laurie were still with me. I was at Doc's place, just inside his front door.

Doc still had her on his mind too, telling me what he thought, "I believe that she is in Heaven now. But I found out something when I went over to see Jerry after the funeral."

"What was that, Doc?"

"So much of Laurie remains on this earth. Her spirit is still very much in that house, helping to heal him."

Her shadow still weighed heavily on Doc and me as we stood in his little hallway. Glancing up at the antiquated phone mounted on the wall, Doc recalled, "I answered this old phone here in the hallway the other night. It was Jerry begging me to come over and see Laurie. So I went to check on her the day before she passed away. Jack, I brought that little girl into this world and loved her as much as if she were a child of my own. This case, more than most, makes me glad I'm a small town doctor. It's helped me not to be cold and impersonal like some big city physicians. I just can't help it. I have genuine feelings and love for people. But maybe I'm a relic of the past, out of step with modern medicine."

I interrupted, "You must not talk that way. You're the physician best suited for this town, like no other doctor could be. You were put here for a reason and a purpose. I think just by being here you're fulfilling your destiny."

"I only wish I could have done more for her."

"You did all you could, Doc. No human being on earth could've done more. Besides, she was already in the Lord's good hands."

"Yes son, you're certainly right about that. When I got there, I looked down at Laurie and could see how bad she was. She had become so emaciated that with every breath she took her chest would rise and fall in such a way as to reveal skin barely stretched over her rib cage. She was struggling to survive, but the light was going out of her. I just didn't want to admit it to myself. But you know, even then when her struggle was about over with, she thought of others. I think I will remember that evening for the rest of my life. I still remember it very clearly." Doc closed his eyes, visualizing it again.

Laurie had asked if I would put her to bed. I obliged and followed as she went to her bedroom. After examining her, I looked in my medical bag hoping I might find some miracle in there for her.

"Doc," she said, "there's nothing in there for me. The Lord's already told me what's gonna happen."

"Child, isn't there anything I can do?"

"Just one thing."

"What?"

"Pray with me."

"I feel honored you would ask me."

"Doc, God is here right now, with us. You see, He comes and listens to me every time I pray, and then He talks to me. He loves you for what you are trying to do to help me—and I love you too."

"Oh my child, I love you right back."

She smiled, her big beautiful eyes becoming even bigger. "He wants you to know everything will be okay because I won't be here after tomorrow. I'll be going home with Him."

I looked at her and thought I saw a more than human presence reflected in her eyes. It felt like we were connecting on more than one level. I will take the feelings of that moment with me till the day I die.

She saw the concern in my expression and said, "Don't worry, Doc, I don't. Long ago, I exchanged my fears for faith. He has taken away my weakness and given me His strength. Now, I'm going to get down on my knees and pray." As she did, she reached over and clicked off the light on her nightstand, putting the room into darkness except for the moonlight that shown through the window. But it was enough for me to clearly see her pleading eyes as she knelt beside her bed and asked again, "Doc please, will you say my prayer with me?"

I reassured her, "Of course I will Princess."

Clasping her hands and bowing her head, she told me, "I've said this prayer on my knees every night since I was three years old." I closed my eyes, praying along with her as she prayed aloud, "Now I lay me down to sleep. If I should die before I wake, I pray thee Lord my soul to take. God bless Daddy, Mommy, and all my friends. Please Lord, be with all of them, even after I'm gone. Amen . . ."

Doc opened his eyes from praying, but back in the hallway of his own home again. Looking up at me, he continued, "I looked around her room and saw nothing. But something *was* there. I saw it reflected in her face. I can hardly explain it, but I could feel a presence. There was this invisible energy in the room with us, projecting a warmth and reassurance. It was all around her. Jack, I believe this was the Spirit of God."

Going on into the living room, Doc and I sat down in front of the fireplace, facing each other.

"You know, son, there are those in the medical profession that will tell you her visions were just hallucinations brought on by the morphine pills. They're wrong. Some things have to be accepted on faith. She said she saw and talked to God, and I for one believe it. Laurie was one of the most truly good people I have ever known." Doc's eyes were blurring up, but he got hold of himself and continued, "I'm going to miss her so much. Even the thought of her makes me wish she were here right now."

Seeing it was my turn to help Doc, I spoke up with a few words to comfort him, "Sometimes no matter how much we want a thing, it's just not possible. Somehow, I know in my heart the Lord had greater plans for her that are beyond our understanding. Laurie knew how you felt and loved you for it. Those feelings are what you have here right now, to comfort you for all time."

"Thank you, son."

Doc and I bonded more closely than ever before in that moment. In our shared grief we helped heal the sadness that was in both of us.

I think Doc sensed the growing faith in me and asked, "Have you thought about praying for help with your own problems?"

"Quite recently in fact, since that night we talked at the bus station. That's when I started thinking about God in my own life again. Then after Laurie talked to me, I began believing in God more than ever before. There has to be a Greater Power than all of us, who created this world, and the entire universe. But yes, Doc, I do need to pray more."

"Sometimes prayer can do the soul a lot of good. It took me many years to really learn that, but over time it changed my whole life for the better."

I listened and knew in my heart Doc was right. In fact, I was already sure the day would come when prayer could help set me free from my past. Today though was not that day because my thoughts were suddenly pulled elsewhere. Abruptly, there was a change in my face. A response to something in the room had gotten my attention.

Doc saw it too, and was not quite sure what had mesmerized me. "What is it, son?"

I did not hear him, sitting there in trance-like silence. Everything was blocked out except the painting above the mantle. It had caught my eye again, beckoning to me. I stared at the picture, focusing in on that part of the frame where it was entitled, 'In the Mouth of Meadow Wood Valley.' My concentration was rewarded, revealing so much more detail from the canvas this time. It was almost alive, fully dimensional, coming out from the painting, as if it were in 3-D. I spoke out loud, but really whispering to myself, "It becomes so real, drawing me into its world."

"Jack?" Doc called out to me again, seeing that I was lost in my thoughts. "You're not going into one of those dark places, are you?"

Breaking the trance, I heard him this time. Turning back to Doc, I protested, "No, I'm going to a place that will take me into the light."

"What?" Doc didn't quite understand me.

"I was just staring at Joe Catlin's painting."

This got him to wondering about what significance it had for me, "Tell me again. What does my painting mean to you?"

"I'm not sure, but I believe the Lord is speaking to my heart and soul through your painting. The whole concept that the splendor of this place is a reflection of God's glory intrigues me. If it be so, I want to experience it."

"Son, if there is any place on earth where you might find what you're looking for, it's Meadow Wood. If you seek a spiritual experience, you will find it there. In doing so, you just might hear the still, small voice of God in your mind and heart."

"That would be a wondrous thing, to discover His healing in such a place. But Doc, I think I may already be hearing His voice."

"You have? I see it more clearly tonight. Something about you is changing."

"A month ago I wouldn't have believed things could've turned around so much for me. My whole life is being redefined for the better. You're right, I do feel myself changing. I've been feeling this overwhelming resolve building inside me, to go out and find the destiny that Laurie talked to me about. It's as if there's a voice in my head urging me on to do the things I'm doing now."

"A voice?"

"Laurie told me I would hear it. She told me it would be the Voice of God."

Doc marveled, "You seem very convinced of this."

"More than that, I know where He lives."

"You do?"

"Yes, in fact I was just thinking about what I'm going to do next."

"What are you going to do?" Doc inquired.

Looking back up into the bright sun within the painting, my mind was caught up in its blazing vision again. I nodded toward it. More resolute than ever before, I explained, "I'm going to this place, where you said His presence could be found. I'm going to Meadow Wood Saturday morning with Mattie."

CHAPTER 18
INTO THE VALLEY

The bright sun of the painting became real in all its early morning brilliance. Positioned in a clear blue eastern sky, it cast its illumination upon two figures as they approached from a distance. I was the man carrying a picnic basket, while the woman who walked with a cane was Mattie.

We were just two moving specs across a wide stretch of earth. It was an epic canvas with golden shafts of sunlight illuminating the road ahead that would lead us into the valley beyond.

Almost immediately, other elements were coming into play. An early morning mixture of mist and fog hugged the ground around us as it drifted across the winding road. Emerging through this haze, we drew closer to our intended destination. True to what I had told Doc, this was the beginning of our Saturday morning trip.

Mattie and I had been making our way down an imperfect country road when we came to a stop. We had come to at a point where the road turned more into an old trail that ran across the rolling fields.

"I'm glad Dan let you off for the weekend," Mattie said, obviously satisfied.

"He felt like with all that's happened lately, I deserved the time off. I told Doc too, and he was glad you were taking me."

"I'm glad you came. I've wanted to show you the junction of the three valleys almost since the beginning of our friendship. If God still lives in any one place on earth, it's in a magical place nearby. It's called Meadow Wood. His Spirit flows through everything that lives and breathes there."

"Why do you suppose that is?"

"Only He knows, but I like to think after Adam and Eve left Eden, God somehow took that place—or at least the essence of it—and put it right here in our little valley. You see, Jack, this is the secret of Meadow Wood."

"Have many people come here?" I asked, now very curious.

"Not many," she explained, "Because everyone that's ever been here has kept it a secret. Early explorers like Daniel Boone came through here but never revealed its exact location. In the early 1900s Teddy Roosevelt came here but swore everyone in his party to secrecy about its existence. It was so special to him that he resisted all attempts to make it a national park. He thought if civilization came here, it would bring pollution that would eventually destroy Meadow Wood. So those of us that come here have sort of become protectors of it."

"Have you ever showed this place to anyone else?"

"Yes, I brought Laurie here two years ago. That was before she got sick. Jerry and his wife were going through hard times then. We could all see it was weighing heavily upon her. He asked me if I could help, so I offered to bring Laurie out here on a weekend outing. Jack, she was never quite the same after she'd been to Meadow Wood."

I was curious, "How did it change her?"

"She was always a spiritual child, but after coming here it could truly be said she walked with God. All her senses were heightened. She became the little girl you met."

"So she felt God's presence in this valley?"

"At least that's what she thought. You'll know for sure though once you've experienced it yourself."

Feeling total conviction emanating from her, I expressed my equally sincere commitment, "I'm here with you, and that's what counts. I wouldn't want it any other way."

Mattie understood, reacting with a smile. Pointing our way across the field, I followed. The land rolled gently upward to a slight ridge. Stopping for a moment, our view took in a shimmering stream cutting across the land. Scattered patches of Blue Bonnets were in bloom, running wild in blue and purpled splendor, glistening in the sunlight. Seeing this, she agreed, "You're right. One shouldn't come here alone."

As we stood there looking at each other, key elements of nature came into focus. A breeze passed over us with the first scent of spring. The melody of the birds, the rustle of the trees, the trickle of the stream, and all the other sounds around us blended together to provide a perfect setting, instantly calming and peaceful. Both of us were caught up in its atmosphere as we took it all in.

In my search for inner peace, instinct told me I was getting closer to my goal. I marveled, "Before I came to Tyler Junction, I could no longer hear the birds singing, but now they're like voices out of Heaven."

Being immersed almost totally in the moment made my spirits want to soar. I had such a good feeling inside myself. All the old war trauma had faded from my conscious memories. This was truly among the happiest times of my life. Something magical of the earth and sky had fused together in perfect harmony that day.

Mattie steadied her free hand in mine while using her cane with the other hand. Together, we started out across the field. The old trail was more a worn path of many years' use. The stream flowed nearby and swirled among the green of the field, meandering on throughout the valley beyond.

I took it all in but did not stop as we kept moving forward. Our goal was just up ahead. It was somewhat a steep climb up the ridge that would over-look the valley, but we did not let this deter us. We were both too energized, getting closer to a place that would hold many questions as well as answers for both of us.

Arriving at the top of the ridge, we reached a knoll of shade trees and came to a stop. Our vantage point gave us a stunning, panoramic view of the junction of the three valleys. Scanning over it, I began to understand how God was everywhere at once. Yet at the same time in my observa-tion, His Spirit was with a single blade of grass, helping it to bask in the energy of the Sun's rays. The same attention was extended to every living thing throughout the valley. Confronted with this thought, I was filled with admiration for the Creator. Surely this must indeed be so throughout the Universe. His Presence is truly infinite, beyond the realm of human under-standing. I was silent for a long moment while my senses attempted to pro-cess the succession of images before me.

"Jack, can you feel it?" Mattie asked as she looked over at me.

"I feel something," I responded, feeling a gentle wind passing by. Inhaling it's coolness and freshness, I felt it go deep into my lungs.

Mattie explained, "The soul of this land is alive. It swirls around us in the breeze."

I realized it immediately. Existence here was nature in its purest form. "All the elements here—the tress, the rolling land, and the sky behind it— are so clean and pure. It all seems to be just a step away from their Creator."

"Yes Jack, His essence is here in Meadow Wood, sustaining it as long as this earth exists."

Gazing over the lilies of the field that flowed through the valley below, I knew in that one brief glimpse I'd never encountered nature quite like this before. Vast patches of multi-colored flowers meandered endlessly. The incredible richness of these colors was a thousand times more intense than anything I'd ever seen. In every direction within my field of vision, it was so incredible I could not absorb it all. I was never more keenly aware of the intelligence beyond human comprehension behind all of this. It was indeed truly a magical place.

Imagining it or not, clear and unmistakable, inside my head I could hear Laurie's voice, *Before this day is over with you're going to resolve to become one of the protectors of this most sacred place—Meadow Wood Valley.*

I stood there transfixed in the moment, moved both by what I saw and what I heard. Speechless, I could only utter one word, "Look." With a slight hand gesture, I waved across our view of what lay beyond.

"Yes, Jack, look around you."

"It's so beautiful. Such colors, I have never seen the like anywhere."

"This is what I'd hoped you would see. They are the colors of the Lord. You know, very few people from the outside world have ever seen this place or even know of its existence."

"It's truly wonderful," I responded.

"It's more than that," she added, and went further, "The Presence that created the world can be felt in every living thing here."

"Yes, I feel it too," I said, agreeing with her more than ever.

A golden sparkle seemed to be reflected off of everything. It was the beginning of a new season. From the ridge, I focused on the valley below. Flowers were exploding into full blossom. Bathed in the warm glow of sunlight, its energy penetrated and strengthened every fiber of their petals. From them to the unfolding limbs of distant trees, every single piece of nature was interconnected, pulsating with life.

In time, I came to believe this cosmic energy that blessed everything was an extension of the Creator. This was all happening according to His good grace. His love was reaching out to preserve nature, holding the entire universe together.

In a very real sense the atmosphere that was unique to this place had already surrounded me. Here in this valley, the whole world was finally coming clearly into focus for me. What I saw made me think if we as human beings would only open up to absorb God's light and allow it to penetrate our bodies, then our souls would be energized and revitalized too. A conscious decision entered my resolve again: to give up what I had been to become a better me. Feeling different inside, I already knew I was being reborn into a better life that day.

For a moment, I thought about how all of this happened to me. I had been caught up in a spiritual experience that started with meeting Laurie Marsh and now was taking me another step on my journey. In my heart, I knew what the implications were. I was making a deep connection with the Creator of all living things.

"What is it, Jack?" Mattie could tell I was not just taking in the scenic view but that something more was going on inside me.

A new sense of understanding crept into my voice as I told her what I was thinking, "This place has helped clear something up for me. I see now that I'm on much more than a Saturday morning outing. I feel like I'm on a spiritual quest as well."

"There's so much here that I want to show you, Jack. Every time I come here, I feel like I become one with God." Mattie took my hand and looked up into my eyes, whispering, "I told you this is a place to share with someone."

Feeling an inner peace like I had never known, I was undergoing a special kind of healing. Even more, I could feel her love for me. Not knowing it then, it would prove to be the catalyst that would heal the unhealable within me. I was finding peace through love, and was beginning to believe it could be the greatest force for good in my life. I looked at Mattie, seeing her radiant smile form again and knew this to be true.

The feelings she had for me filled her face. As she gazed into my eyes, we shared another rush of unspoken communication between ourselves.

With each succeeding minute, this journey to Meadow Wood was taking on more meaning. Mattie went into my arms and drew close to me. We were both caught up in this most wonderful of moments, full of genuine feelings.

As we stood there, the sun bathed us in all its morning glory. Stretching down from it, the shimmer of its heat floated across the entire length of the valley floor, blessing it with much needed morning warmth. Admiring this, I gestured out across the valley and told her, "I've been searching for something like this all my life."

Mattie, still close in my arms, whispered, "Isn't it astonishing—astonishingly beautiful?"

"Yes," I said, meaning more than the word implied. As I gazed back over into her face, I thought she was beautiful. My focus totally on her now, I added, "It's something I want forever."

"What's that, Jack?"

"Happiness, in a place I thought could never exist."

It had been a quiet, personal moment for us alone. Reinforcing that, the morning mist was beginning to clear away, revealing for sure we were the only two people in the valley at that particular time of day.

I could clearly see past the valley floor now. Beyond it, on the other side, a vast wide range of tall trees bordered Meadow Wood, extending in an infinite line all along the horizon. Thick and impenetrable, this forest formed into a solid wall, protecting and cloaking the entire valley from the prying view of the outside world.

My enthusiasm pushing me forward, I turned to Mattie, urging her, "Come, let's cross over the valley and rest under the trees on the other side, beside the still waters of the stream." Holding up the picnic basket I'd been carrying, I added, "Let's have our picnic over there."

She looked at me questioningly, "Didn't someone famous say something like that?"

"Yes, sort of. It was Stonewall Jackson during the Civil War. I've always admired him for being a God fearing man during time of war. He never let go of his faith. That means a lot to me now, especially here where I'm beginning to find my faith again."

"I'm so proud of you for that, Jack."

"Come on, let's go over there," I said, getting eager to cross the valley floor.

As I held out my free hand toward her, Mattie stood there motionless, momentarily reluctant. Avoiding eye contact, she seemed lost in thought ever so briefly. There was a flicker of sadness as she stared across to the other side, whispering, "There's something I want to show you over there anyway." Looking back up at me, her radiant smile quickly returned as she agreed, "Yes, let's go." Stirring into movement, we made our way down the ridge, walking together into the valley.

I felt exhilarated, sensing it would be a place of enchantment. But I had no idea as to what extent it would be a place of miracles as well. In a way that almost defies human explanation, the Presence existing there beckoned me forward.

Advancing across the open meadow, I walked across the valley floor for the first time. Remembering what Mattie had said, I did feel like I was on the pathway of God, walking in the footsteps of the Creator. I thought this was the way it must've appeared when He brought this world into existence. I was in the heart of Meadow Wood, seeing a place largely untouched by human hands.

I got my first up-close look at the sea of life living there. As roses and other intensely colored flowers opened up, a breeze carrying their many fragrances passed over me. At the same time, I could hear the tranquil sound of birds singing again, this time in the distant woods beyond. Getting closer to the tree line, I could make out the branches of huge trees older than man, rising up to meet the rays of morning light. I knew in my heart this was the finger of God touching all nature and leaving His autograph upon it.

Walking through this sea of budding flowers, it occurred to me that I had found myself in a living, breathing extension of Joe Catlin's painting. It was a unique moment in which I saw the reality of what had been the painter's artistic vision. The two images morphed together inside my mind, burned into my memory for all time.

Reaching the edge of the meadow's far side, we picked a spot on the crest of a plateau that overlooked the valley below. In a strange way, taking in this view helped to relieve one of my biggest problems, the emptiness inside me. Setting the picnic basket down, Mattie began to spread a blanket out on the ground. At peace with myself, here I was about to bond with her in ways I could only imagine at that point.

As I looked on, a brilliant light caught my attention. Hitting me in the face, I turned around and sought its source. Following the shaft of light back up through the limbs of a towering oak, and beyond that to its point of origin 93 million miles away—the Sun itself. From that infinite distance its rays touched the surface of Meadow Wood. Reaching down, they became the essence of God's own healing warmth penetrating me. This was truly a miraculous instance in which I felt like I was in a place that was the center of the Universe.

I had reconnected with nature in the purest form of all its beauty and splendor. A conscious awareness of the divinity of this place filled me. But something even more life-changing was happening. I was making connection with the spiritual entity that inhabited this valley. It was a moment of Divine recognition in which I knew its name. It was the Holy Spirit of God.

From the little things she had said, Mattie was already well aware of its presence in Meadow Wood. I would come to recognize it more and more that she had Divine insight herself. It was just the beginning for me, though. My connection with all things spiritual would open new doors of enlightenment all day long.

Just then Mattie broke the spiritual hold and called me, "Hey Jack, come over here."

Mattie and I sat beneath a cool shade cast by the great trees that climbed into the sky near us. With the picnic basket in front of her, she retrieved some sandwiches and passed one to me. We would share lunch and later bare our souls to each other.

After lunch, I lay there on the blanket resting a bit. As a cool breeze passed over me, I was filled with a state of calm I had not felt since before Vietnam. It was more like a merging of nature and man. I was at peace with the earth beneath me and the sky above me. Body and soul, my whole being seemed to drift away. Shutting my eyes, I dreamed of a better future. Somewhere deep within myself, I realized God would illuminate my every step throughout the rest of my life. An invisible spiritual force that could only be felt was entering me again, merging with me, becoming part of my soul. In every way humanly possible, I truly felt one with God. It was a moment of perfect peace.

But the moment passed all too quickly. Something broke in to take possession of my senses. Darkness cast it's shadow over me. In a jarring flash, the war was upon me again in a series of unsettling images. In what followed, I felt the presence of something I'd like to forget. Something unseen that was the epitome of evil was fast approaching and upon me once more. I could not escape. Springing from my subconscious, the embodiment of painful memories too long denied crept down my spine. Startled, I bolted up to a sitting position, bathed in beads of cold sweat. Trembling severely, I must've been visibly shaken.

"What's wrong, Jack?" A startled Mattie was down on her knees beside me at once.

"I'm not quite sure." Breathing hard, I felt like I was out of breath. I tried to explain, "At first I saw this shaft of golden sunlight, descending down through the branches, almost touching me. But then in a flash, I was back in Vietnam. Explosions were all around me. I was running to escape them. Then I saw all those people who did not survive the war, among them the faces of my friends who never came back. I wanted to help them, but it was too late. Looking around, I saw something evil lurking in the shadows. It was their killer, a Viet Cong executioner." I wanted to speak further, but I couldn't, quite overcome by a combination of sadness, sorrow, and fear. These emotions that were all bottled up inside me fused together in a knot of tension.

Mattie seemed to understand what I was going through. She held out her hands, reaching toward me. Overcome by my emotions, I went into her outstretched arms. Surrounded by her strength and compassion, this PTSD episode made of events from long ago drained out of me. A moment of silence passed, then she asked, "Do you feel it?"

I was calming down, far from the sights and sounds of war. I was feeling something else too. I wondered aloud, "What is it?"

Mattie pulled back just enough so she could look at my face. Her eyes searched me. Then she knew what it was and told me, "It's the peace of God."

"Yes, I agree," I said, fully aware of what she meant now.

Later, while Mattie folded the blanket and repacked the picnic basket, I walked out to the edge of the clearing. The inner calm I had felt earlier was still coursing through me. Thinking about what she'd said, I scanned the valley. As she had told me, this place was truly a piece of Heaven on earth. Somehow I knew it even then. I would come to know it intimately in the fullness of time.

Standing there, inhaling the coolness of Meadow Wood's air into my lungs, I was now convinced God had wanted me to come here. As my eyes took in the valley once again, I started seeing more clearly how His Spirit was so interwoven with the intelligence of nature here. So much beauty and splendor was all here under the Creator's watchful eye. In ways I can only speculate, I believe it's His home on earth.

Thinking about these things, I was becoming very aware my thought processes were sharpening and expanding. Encompassing far more details than I had ever been able to, my perception of all nature was changing rapidly. It was then I knew I was receiving the beginnings of a gift. In time, the reach of my senses into the hearts and minds of others would be just as what Laurie had done to me.

Mattie had come alongside me, taking in the same wide panoramic view. From the tiniest flower to the tallest oak, I could feel the Lord's presence here. Together, we experienced God's love for this 'Lost Eden.' at the same time.

Slipping her hand into mine, she got my attention, "I had hoped the valley would help you."

"It has . . . But you knew that for sure all along, didn't you?"

"Yes, Jack," she conceded, "I did know it was a place that changed people's lives. But I've been thinking about something else concerning you for sometime now. It took me awhile to figure out what you meant over dinner that night, but I think you may have found it."

"What exactly was that?"

"What you said about being like Don Quixote, about being on this journey, searching for a better life. I believe you've found it right here in Meadow Wood. Don't you still feel it, the aura that is here?"

"Yes I do. I've been feeling it since the moment we set foot in the valley."

"Every time you come here you'll feel the Presence of God, like no place on earth."

Accepting those words in my heart, I squeezed her hand affectionately, adding, "You know, I want to complete Don Quixote's journey—here with you today."

The moment I said that I felt the invisible presence of something sent from God. I thought surely there must be guardian angels at work here, protecting this patch of earth called Meadow Wood. Gazing upward into the heavens, I saw something soaring high over the valley. Large and brilliantly white, it circled us. I whispered aloud in recognition, "An Eagle. See how it turns its entire head to keep us in sharp focus."

Bearing down on us, the eagle descended lower, until its eyes frozen into an intense stare became plainly visible. As it got closer, I felt it wasn't an eagle, but rather something else altogether. As the great white bird grew still nearer, something very strange happened. It seemed to be studying us closely, in a manner most uncharacteristic of eagles. Then, in the flash of an instant, it broke contact and soared upward again, back up into the heavens beyond our view.

I looked over at Mattie and she added, "An eagle's vision is truly miraculous. They can see up to eight times better than us humans."

"I think it's more than that in this case," I insisted. "Perhaps for only a few seconds, mind you, it seemed like there was more than just an eagle's intelligence behind those eyes staring at us like it knew us."

"You picked this up in only a few seconds?"

"Yes, I saw it very clearly. I have a keen eye for quick observation."

"Then I have the same gift because I saw something in that bird that told me it was more than just an eagle." It was though she'd read my mind, explaining as only she could, "It could have been some sort of heavenly creature on a mission. It could have been a guardian angel watching over the whole valley."

"You really think so?"

"I do. Angels don't have an exact physical form. Their essence is spiritual in nature. As such, they can take many forms in the human world. They are all around watching over us."

I wanted to believe her, "I wish I could have such an angel to help with some of the things that have been bothering me."

165

"I wouldn't be surprised if there wasn't such an angel watching over you right now."

"You're not the first to tell me that. A week before Laurie passed away, she told me I had a guardian angel watching over me."

"Then it must be true. I told you how close she was to God."

"I wish I knew for sure."

"Perhaps you will, one day. Jack, I think we all have guardian angels. We just don't know it."

Thinking about it, I believe we both felt comforted by the peace and protection we had found here. At the same time, the eagle that we believed was a guardian angel continued to circle above, watching over us and every living thing throughout the entire valley.

Looking out across the scenic view that spread across the horizon in front of us, I whispered, "I don't think there's hardly a place like it on this entire earth."

"As I said before, except for a few from Tyler Junction, and even fewer outsiders, it's our secret from the entire world—or at least I like to think that."

"You know, Doc told me Meadow Wood was special, but I already knew that from his picture."

"What picture?" Mattie questioned.

"That painting he has hanging above his living room mantle. It really spoke to me when I first saw it. I thought it was such a vision of peace and beauty that I had to see the valley for myself."

"Sounds like his painting made quite an impression on you."

"It did, but Mattie you must've seen it too?"

"Oh, I'm quite well aware of it."

"Doc says it was painted by this artist who lived here back in the 1930s, a fellow by the name of Joe Catlin. It reminded me of something out of my childhood, in a happier, more innocent time that no longer exists. It's hard to explain, but for me Catlin's painting captured nature's beauty in a way that few artists have ever been able to put on canvas. I can tell he was more than a gifted artist. He must've been a very special person. I wish I could have known the man."

"Jack, in a way you do."

I looked at Mattie questioningly, "How so?"

166

Her face was sparkling. There was a strange twinkle forming around her eyes. Then she told me, "Joe Catlin was my grandfather."

"Your grandfather?" I was caught by surprise. "I didn't know."

"Yes, Catlin was my mother's maiden name," Mattie explained. "Doc was his best friend. They often spent time together here in the valley. Doc's told me he sees a lot of my grandfather in me, that I have his insight and love of nature. So you see, in a sense you do know him."

Looking at her more closely for a moment, I saw it too. "Now that you mention it, I see those qualities in you."

"My grandfather's gift to me—his insight into others—tells me a lot about you too, Jack."

"It does?"

"Especially now, here in the valley, when I look at you I see the same expression of wonder I saw as a child in my grandfather's face. It's fascinating. In many ways you may be kindred spirits with him. Just as his life was fulfilled here, so I believe you will fulfill your life here too."

What I'd seen that morning had already convinced me. "Mattie, I believe you with all my heart. Inside, I feel like I'm already changing for the better. I know it. I just know it."

She seemed to light up at my acknowledgement, adding, "I believe everything and everybody on earth is here for a reason. You're here in Tyler Junction for a specific purpose." She was more correct than she could've possibly realized.

I knew this but at least for now still tried to explain myself a little differently, "You've said something like that before, and I've been thinking about it ever since. You could be right. Since I came here, I've felt like I'm on a mission to be a force for good."

"You are such a force already." She searched my face again, "I see kindness and compassion, as well as strength and courage in you. If you continue using those qualities in what you're doing, the good you do now will become as seeds that blossom into the flowers of tomorrow."

"I hope what you say will come true. When I came here, I only wanted to escape from the world, to find a place where there was no pain or sorrow. In the past month, I've found a new life in Tyler Junction."

I smiled at Mattie. The feelings I felt for her I'm sure were visible across my face.

She looked at me with the same caring emotions, as though she was looking into my soul. Gesturing toward the winding path through the maze of trees that had shaded our picnic, she reminded me, "The special place I wanted to show you is just a short distance through these woods."

"Lead the way, my lady." A sense of discovery had filled me throughout the day. I was aware of it again as we journeyed up the old trail. Glancing over at Mattie, I felt the calm reassurance of her hand in mine. This feeling stayed with me every step of the way.

The trail disintegrated into an imperfect and winding path that was grown over. Surroundings changed, and the woods became more dense and dark.

I glanced about and something caught my eye. "Just one minute," I said, stopping to pick up a partially hidden object, barely visible amongst the tall overgrowth. Retrieving it, I turned back toward Mattie, revealing a blossoming flower. Gently placing it in her free hand, I whispered, "For you, this is a reflection of how I feel about our relationship, that it's blossoming into something special."

"Oh, Jack," she whispered back, her face positively absorbing the glow of the beautiful flower.

I couldn't help staring for a moment, and told her, "I was just thinking how wonderful the world is with you in it."

Her eyes made contact with mine as she responded, "The world is wonderful so long as I can carry the memory of today in my mind."

Just then, a loud rumbling sound jerked our attention to the heavens above. Ominous storm clouds were moving in from the west, spreading quickly across the sky. Looking back in the direction we had come from, the once golden valley was no longer visible through the trees, deepening into dark shadows cast from above.

I reacted, "Bad storm's coming up fast, out of nowhere."

Mattie pulled on my hand, getting my attention, "I know a place of shelter nearby. You'll have to follow me."

Hearing crackling thunder in the distance, both of us looked skyward at the same time. A bright flash of lightning went streaking across, high in the heavens. Knowing speed was of the essence, we left the trail immediately, cutting through the woods. Winds were rapidly picking up, blowing tree limbs and tall grass all around and past us.

"Are you sure about this?" I questioned, as the winds blasted ever harder against us.

She reassured me, raising her voice to be heard, "It's not far, I know exactly where it's at!"

We pressed forward, squinting our eyes from the dust kicked up. Scrambling through heavily wooded terrain, we plunged deeper into the dense forest until it suddenly opened up . . .

Pushing ahead, Mattie saw what she'd been looking for and got excited, "There it is!"

I strained to see and could barely make out a dark black mass jutting out of the ground, maybe thirty yards ahead of us.

We both rushed forward, eager to reach the shelter. But we did not know that abiding there were some ghosts out of both our pasts.

CHAPTER 19
A SECRET PLACE

We made our way from the woods into a small clearing in front of an almost hidden, dark rotting structure—a secret place harboring an abundance of its own secrets. Without knowing it at the time, we had reached our trip's final destination.

Caught up in nature's destructive clutches, it was an old shack in the advanced stages of decay. Abandoned for many years, it still stood defiantly against the elements. Choking vines and wild roots had encircled it, straining to pull it down.

Making our way through the tall weeds, lightning was reflected off of them. Removing blowing limbs and twisting vines from our path, we were caught in a downpour. Fighting our way to the front porch, we were protected by its overhang, partially sheltering us from the pelting rain.

A quick glance and I became quite frustrated, "Its been boarded up for years!"

Mattie agreed, but in a strange way, "Only ghosts live here now."

I wondered, *How did she know that?* But I didn't have time to think about it further. It was more important to get inside as soon as possible. I examined the front of the place, getting a closer look. Confirming my earlier assessment, I found all the windows had indeed been thoroughly boarded up. The front door had also been nailed shut. In frustration, I protested loud enough to be heard above the storm, "No one was meant to get in this place easily!"

Stepping backward, I took in a full view of this darkly shrouded structure once more. Little did I know that there was a full measure of mystery and wonder awaiting us within its walls.

Looking around, I spotted a solid strong limb that had been snapped off by the force of the storm. It was sharp at one end. Reaching for it, my hand closed tightly around the big stick. "This might prove to be useful!" I announced, holding it up in front of Mattie, feeling more optimistic about our chances of getting inside.

Jabbing furiously with the pointed end, I wedged nature's version of a crowbar between the boards across the nailed up door. Pressing down and pulling back, I repeated the process several times, prying boards away. Feeling the door giving way as well, it quite literally moaned as it loosened. Putting all my strength into it, the door uttered a loud snapping pop. Creaking on its rusted hinges, it began to open.

From inside, the old weather-beaten door opened inwardly, revealing two drenched people, Mattie and me. Entering the shack, we arrived there at a point in time that only Fate could have ordained. What was found there would have far greater significance than either of us was prepared for or expected.

We strained to see in a place that had known only darkness for many years. The only illumination within was from the storm clouded sky piercing through the doorway. Beyond the boundaries of that natural light, things faded into blackness. As we walked inside, the floorboards creaked as well, making strange haunting sounds. What we could see of the interior had an almost ghostly appearance, full of long forgotten memories.

Just inside, Mattie and I turned toward each other, out of breath, in silence. We looked at each other, soaked to the bone. Seeking an emotional release, we found it, breaking out in a sort of laughter. Out of the storm now, the tension was finally gone. She smiled at me and spoke with a sigh of relief in her voice, "Safe at last."

Our laughter quickly became silence again, and things became more serious. The whistling wind working its way through the boards of the old shack got our attention. I took her hand, and the mood dramatically changed. Shivering from the continued cold penetrating through our rain soaked clothes, drove us into the warmth of each other's arms. Moving even closer together, we peered deep into each other's eyes for an instant. But almost immediately the storm announced its presence again. A loud crackle of thunder startled both of us as a massive lightning strike ripped across the skyline just beyond the door.

Jerking backward, I felt my foot brushing up against something. Looking, I saw the picnic basket I'd sat down on the floor. "I managed to keep it covered," I said.

Another object behind me caught Mattie's eye. "Look!" Excited at her discovery, she noticed, "There's a lamp over there." An old kerosene lamp sitting on the floor was leaned up against the wall, barely visible in the dim light. She picked it up and examined it more closely.

"Maybe we can get it working again," I said.

Several hours later, light had virtually left the sky, and it was almost nightfall. The lamp was now cleaned free of the dust and dirt that caked it, and working. Sitting on a crude dining table, it helped to light up the room.

Nearby, Mattie was wearing an apron and sweeping the floor with a broom she had found. As she did so, her eyes traveled across the room and fell upon me. She stopped, her eyes not moving from me. The expression on her face revealed she was struggling with something on her mind.

For an instant, I felt like I was invading the private space of her thoughts, so I turned my attention to the window near me. Since walking into this old place, I'd been aware of a strange odor. It smelled like old paint and plaster somewhere within the walls. In an effort to let in some fresh air, I pulled the last board away and pushed the window up, about halfway open.

As I peeked out the window, there was a flash of distant lightning. After a delayed clap of thunder, the rain still persisted but far more gentle in its falling sound. I stood absolutely still for a moment, listening. It was almost as if I could hear a voice in the rain speaking to my heart. I thought about it, remembering what Laurie Marsh had said about a voice whispering thoughts to me. There had been signs of this all day, leading me to a deeply profound conclusion. Not knowing how I knew it, I just did: that a Higher Power was about to change my life.

It was fast becoming clear how much was on my chest. I knew I would have to speak of something soon, but knowing this did not make it any easier.

Turning toward Mattie, I told her another conclusion I had been coming to, "It's so bad out, I guess we'll have to stay the night here."

She didn't mind. "That's alright, really. I've cleared a space over here and made a pallet with the blankets from the picnic basket, and there's enough food left for a small dinner."

Mattie gestured down to the pallet on the floor. She had placed it against the back wall of the room opposite the front door. It was bathed in unusual patterns of warm light and dark shadows created by the lamp.

I glanced about the room, seeing that the interior of the shack was in an equal state of decay. Peeling wallpaper revealing bare walls prevailed throughout the rotting structure. But this process of decay had revealed something even more important, thought provoking . . .

"If only these walls could talk, this old place could probably tell a lot of stories." I paused. Looking over at Mattie, I sensed something was troubling her, "You never said. How did you know about it being here?"

Slowly she revealed the ache in her heart, "This is the special place I wanted to show you. Jack, I came from very humble beginnings." As old memories came to the surface, a sad look filled her face, but she continued, "These walls could tell plenty. I unfortunately know all their stories. I used to live here. This was my home, that is until my folks died several years ago."

"Your home?" I responded questioningly, wanting to know more about this woman who now so obviously needed my compassion and under-standing. As I waited for Mattie's answer, something behind her got my attention. My eyes were drawn along the wall to something that looked familiar. Sticking out from behind some peeled back wallpaper was the corner of a crude rough sketch. Reaching over, I pulled more of the cracking wallpaper away, revealing more of the sketch on the wall itself. I knew what it was immediately. My hunch was confirmed when I saw the faded writing below the sketch. It said: 'IN MEADOW WOOD VALLEY as drawn by Joe Catlin.'

"This place originally belonged to my grandfather." She explained, "He built it with his own hands. It was from here he journeyed around Meadow Wood Valley to do his paintings back in the 1920s and 30s. That's when he did most of them, though he painted right up to the end of his life. He even died here in this old house. There was so much love here. Even though I was very little at the time, I still remember him clearly, the good times we shared, and how much he loved me." She glanced around the room once more and then back to me, revealing something, "I feel his presence, even now. A part of him still lives within these walls. This is a house with a soul."

I understood her more than she knew. "So this place has a lot of memories for you?"

"Memories that I would not have wanted to return to without you, Jack. I'm so very glad you're here with me."

I looked at her with a great deal of compassion, whispering her name, "Mattie."

Silent for a long moment, she just looked at me before responding with a single word, barely spoken, "Yes."

"I will always be here for you." I said it, meaning every word with all my heart. Taking a few steps toward her, I paused beside the crude dining table, meeting her half way.

Mattie must've felt something also. Crossing the room, she stopped right in front of me, looking up into my face.

Standing there in silence together, we looked into each other's eyes. Up close, I think we both saw the shared truth of our mutual feelings. Surrounded by the warm light projected from the lamp on the table, it only seemed to reveal more clearly the sadness and other heartfelt emotions that were inside both of us.

Her face was full of vulnerability. Deep hurt from long ago was only beginning to reveal itself.

I saw all of this clearly in her haunting expression. Totally focused on her, this image intensified inside my mind.

Reaching out to me, she explained, "I've felt so alone for so long."

Feeling for her, I took her hand into mine. Reassuring her, I spoke softly, "You'll never be alone again. I'll never let go. After all, I stick like glue."

CHAPTER 20
VISIONS OF LONG AGO

L ater that night, my eyes opened, glancing around. Leaned back against the wall behind us, Mattie and I were sitting on the pallet where we had dozed off against each other. She had fallen asleep, her head on my shoulder, her hand closed around mine. The growing closeness between us was never more apparent to me than right then.

While she still slept, I had awakened, thinking about our day together and what was said between us. I was tired, but my mind wouldn't shut off. My thoughts drifted back to an earlier time that no longer existed, of coming home after the war.

Abruptly though, I was interrupted from the quiet of my thoughts. Outside, the storm had picked up again and was shaking the old shack. Mattie slept through it all, totally unaware as a howling wind grew louder, rattling the front door directly across from us. Beyond it, I knew things were different in this valley, more so than anyplace on earth. I sensed something was about to happen, something beyond human understanding.

My full attention was drawn to the source of this noise, staring at the door. I felt the glowing lamp becoming like hot coals burning in my eyeballs. The wind's force even caused the table it was sitting on to shake. The lamp's flickering light mingled together with the reflection of lightning streaking across the sky, casting strange and surreal images that moved around the room.

Just as quickly, the wind diminished into silence, only to be replaced by something even more strange. Whispering sounds carried along in its force, penetrated the rotting walls of the old shack. They were very faint at first, but steadily increased in their volume. Getting closer, they were coming from the darkness just beyond the front door.

Becoming clearer now, they were echoing voices from some other-worldly place, working their way to me. Forming into a powerful life force, they reached inside me. Once there, they found the keys to unlocking the subconscious memories of my brain.

The soft voice of a little girl was inside my head. It was Laurie: *Open up your heart Jack. Let me talk to your mind and you will learn much from many voices this night. Listen . . .*

I rubbed my eyes for a moment, not sure if what I heard was real or imaginary. Trying to clear my mind of the cobwebs, I listened again. This time I heard a trio of voices. First, it was Mattie whispering, "It's like coming home again, returning to Meadow Wood." Then Doc spoke to me, "It's a place where you can sort things out and find peace within yourself." Finally my father imparted a pearl of wisdom, "Home is where the heart finds peace, son, a place where rainbows end, and all of life's turmoil becomes a distant memory."

In the silence that followed, I asked myself, why have these voices out of my life come to visit me this night? Could it be because of this strange old shack? Mattie had said this was a house with a soul. Was it even possible? Some psychiatrists might call it a form of schizophrenia, or could it be something even more profound? Was it possible these voices were sent by the Lord, reaching inside my mind with advice and words of wisdom to help me?

While contemplating all of this, an amazing sight unfolded right before my eyes. The door opened back directly toward me, revealing a glowing arc of light advancing from the darkness outside. Working its way through the doorway and into the shack, the pulsating energy form hovered right above me. Feeling myself being pulled by an all-powerful magnetic force, I was rapidly drawn forward into it. Trying to shut this vision out, I closed my eyes. My mind, though, could not keep it out. As they whizzed past me, the succession of flashing colors were so brilliant and intense they penetrated right into my brain. I had the sensation of being hurled through sort of a black hole at the speed of light. Just as quickly, the colors and arc of light were gone, but so was I . . .

Opening my eyes again, the shack had vanished, and in its place darkness surrounded me. It was like dusk, very dimly lit. I took a few shaky steps. I was in some other place beyond the world of the flesh but not quite the world of Heaven. A powerful invisible magnet grabbed me, pulling me toward a distant figure. Instantly, I was standing in front of an old man sitting at a table with his head lowered.

Appearing familiar, the old man looked up, and the darkness surrounding him transformed into a warm early morning light. It was my father. I now was in my old military uniform staring down at him, sitting there in front of me.

The ability to transcend time that I first experienced in the hotel room had returned. Intensified by the flow of energy from Laurie's touch and further enhanced by the powerful aura that existed in this valley, I was back in my past again.

"Son, you're finally home." My father's voice was full of emotion. The expression on his face said it all, revealing his broken heart. He had quite visibly aged. His hair was now all white. The spark and inner fire had totally left his eyes. He appeared drained of energy, seated at our kitchen table of so many years ago. Barely hanging on, in the twilight of his life, I could see that the war had taken its toll on the home front as well.

Coming around beside my father, I got closer. Obviously glad to see him, I announced, "Dad I'm home from Vietnam, for good." Wanting very much to do it, I leaned downward, warmly hugging him.

His watery eyes were full of both sadness and joy as he spoke, "Maybe I don't say it often enough, but I'm so very proud of you. I love you, son." Weighted down by his own grief, he lowered his head again. Staring at a small-framed picture, he cradled it ever so lovingly in his hands, gently touching the image of the person in it.

Feeling my father's silent heartbreak, I whispered, "I'll always be here for you, Dad."

"Thank you, son."

Getting a clear view, I recognized the photograph. "I see you've got a picture of Mom."

Looking up, he handed the picture to me. Taking it, I carefully held the photograph under a nearby lamp light to study it more closely. It was taken in the winter of her life when she was so sick. But even in the worst days of her illness, she still had the familiar expression of the mother I always loved. There, etched across her face was the warmth and affection that she had always comforted me with as far back as I could remember.

I had always loved my mother. Like little Laurie, she was always a truly good person. Her loss had left a huge hole in my heart. Someone special to me was lost forever. As my eyes lovingly absorbed her image, I whispered the feelings that would stay with me for the rest of my life, "You're gone now, but your memory will live on in my heart. I miss you so very much."

I put the picture back on the kitchen table in front of my father. He stared at it, his voice still fresh with hurt, "It was while you were away at war that Mom had her stroke. At least though, you made it back home before she passed away." There was silence for a moment. Then he looked up at me, continuing, "She wanted you to know how much she loved you, and something else. There was one other thing she wanted me to tell you." He had a strained expression, struggling with his memory, "It was really important too."

"What was it, Dad?"

Getting past the turmoil inside himself, it finally came to him, "I remember now. It was what she said the Lord told her in a dream. She wanted you to know that there is a beginning and an ending to everything except in certain matters of life and death. Life doesn't end with death, but goes on beyond it, in the memories within our minds. She also said for you to just think of her, and her spirit would be with you."

I pulled another chair over and sat down beside my father. Our eyes shared the same grief. The sadness that had filled our souls boiled over. Leaning closer, I wrapped my arms around him. We warmly hugged each other as both of us cried aloud.

More than any other time, I realized words were sometimes inadequate, but I said them anyway, "Oh Dad, being home with you means everything to me."

He looked at me through tear stained eyes, caring for me as well, wanting me to know something else, "I feel the same way, son. It's so good to have you home. You know, the subject of home brings to mind something I want you to always remember."

"What is it?"

"That no matter where you go, home is where your heart is. It's a place where you keep all the memories of your life. As you live it, your life will become an accumulation of seasons, each succeeding one bringing its own happiness and heartbreak. This is what life is made of. Accepting both the good as well as the bad is one of the hardest things a human being has to do in life. But I'm learning—just as she told me—to keep the memories of your Mom's life in my heart where I'll treasure them forever. Remember this, son. It might help you some day."

"I will. I promise." I reassured him, truly feeling like I'd picked up another one of his pearls of wisdom.

Drawn back to Mom's picture, my father spoke directly to her image, "My sweetheart, it wasn't so long ago. We were young then and had our whole lives ahead of us. We thought we had forever, but our bodies finally got old and gave out. I wish we could go back and start over, and I could somehow eliminate all your heartbreak."

"Dad, I wish there was something I could do to help you," I said, knowing my own pain must be more visible, becoming aware of a blurring sensation in my eyes. Strong feelings were already tearing at my heartstrings

"You've done more than you know by just being here for me. Bless you son. You always seem to try to do the right thing."

"I hadn't really thought about it that way. I just want to live my life doing unselfish things, giving of myself."

"Son, what you're doing is all part of growing into the man you will become." He paused for a moment, seeing something far off, yet to happen in my life. Something prophetic came to him in those few seconds of silence that would profoundly affect me, "You know," he said, "Maybe you might be able to help someone else some day, and be a good deed doer."

"I promise you, if I ever have the opportunity to set things right for someone and give them peace, I'll do it."

"And you will do more than that." My father's eyes took on a strained look, just like little Laurie's expression so many years later. It was as if he was staring into a vision as he spoke, "I see it very clearly. You will meet a young woman who harbors a terrible heartbreak deep within herself that only you can heal. Don't let this opportunity slip away from you. It will be the right thing for you to do. God will bless you for all the good you will do. He has a plan for you and a purpose for your life."

The power of his words from long ago filled my mind anew, genuinely moving me. His wisdom was once more sealed in my memory. As this bonding between us took place, powerful forces were closing in again. The warm light of that morning so long ago faded into the stark reality of the present stormy evening.

I felt myself yanked back by the same powerful magnetic force that had sent me into the past. Pulled back through the blackness, I heard a rumble of thunder surrounding me. A powerful invisible force propelled my body through the front door of the shack, slamming it shut behind me, making a loud noise.

Laid out on the floor, I bolted back up to a sitting position. I could see that continued pounding of stormy winds had loosened the door from its frame. Opening and closing repeatedly, it creaked continuously on its rusted hinges making a horrible noise. Rising to my feet, I crossed the floor and stared out into the storm, seeing nothing but darkness. As quietly as possible, I wedged the door closed so it would stop banging.

I was back in the present, in the old shack again, returned from my journey to a time and place of long ago. Just how much of this was a dream or a vision, I could not say. But no matter, it was something wonderful, almost spiritual in nature. Some long forgotten advice having great relevance had reawakened in my memory. I took heart that in some way, from across the chasm of life and death, I had made contact with my father one more time.

It still felt like an odd moment though. Something was not quite right. Carefully, so I didn't wake Mattie or creak too many of the old floorboards, I turned around slowly and walked softly back into the room. It was then, I saw myself lying on the pallet with Mattie. So if there was my flesh, what was I? A spirit perhaps? Feeling weak, I fell forward, collapsing into myself, rejoining my own body.

CHAPTER 21
SECRETS REVEALED

I felt my whole body shake as I opened my eyes, quite unsettled. The sudden movement awakened Mattie. Concerned, she touched my shoulder. "Jack, wake up."

"I'm not asleep." I looked over at her, admiringly. She was such a warm and caring person. I couldn't help thinking, if only there was something I could do to lift her spirits. Of course, tucked away in my heart of hearts, I really did know what that one thing was. Acting upon it, I said, "We have to talk."

Sensing it was important, not able to put her finger on it, she asked, "Is there something wrong?"

"No." Hesitating, I looked away for an instant. But then again, I knew I must talk about it. Being full of new pain and old memories made fresh, I started over, "Yes, there is something wrong. I just talked to my father, at least I think I did. I guess I had a dream, perhaps some sort of a flashback, or a time travel episode—if that's even possible. It's happened before, where I've talked to my father. Each time it has become more real."

"What happened this time?"

I was taken back to 1968 when I first came back from Vietnam. I got home just before my mother died. My father took it hard. After that—little by little—he went into an irreversible decline. He died less than a year later."

Mattie understood the heartbreak of losing someone. "Oh Jack."

Feeling her compassion for me, I looked back up at her and continued, "This experience stirred up a lot of old memories, things I had forgotten. There was a lot of pain and sadness all around me in those days. Mattie, when am I going to accept my Mom and Dad are gone forever, that they're never coming back? Do you know what I mean?"

"Yes, but in a sense they're not gone. The best of who they were will always be in your memories. I know the good that is in you." She paused, thinking about my words as they also awakened old memories within her. She genuinely understood my feelings, "You're a loving son who misses his loved ones. I know I certainly miss mine. It still hurts, even now."

"I keep asking myself, though, was this a dream or did it really happen? I suppose I'll never really know for sure, but the whole thing didn't seem like a dream. My father seemed so real, just as if he were standing in front of me right now."

"Perhaps he seemed real because your mind made him as real as you remember him. Then again, there are so many strange things that we don't know about the afterlife. Perhaps he wanted to talk to you again, and God let him."

I took Mattie's hand and agreed, "I want to believe it happened. I miss him so much. Since Doc and I have been talking about my dreams and flashbacks, I've been doing a lot of reading. The ancient Egyptians believed we have an astral body which could take you to the other side and another world of existence beyond death."

"Who can say, but maybe God let it happen and made it all possible."

"I think you're right, Mattie. Rather real or a dream, perhaps in some way God did allow this in order to help me. After all, my father offered me some important advice. Dad told me I could start over and be a good deed doer. That is the person I'm becoming right now."

A smile formed on her face. "So becoming a good deed doer was your father's idea?"

I conceded, "Yes, but there's something else I see very clearly now."

"What's that?"

"After coming to Tyler Junction and to Meadow Wood with you, especially after this vision tonight, I think a Higher Power has been trying to tell me something for some time."

"I know this much," she said, explaining, "I feel like God brought you to this valley because of the positive way you affect people's lives. Some people go through life spreading good will and making it a better world for everybody else. You're one of those people."

"Bless you for that, but there's more. It's from my past, something we have to talk about. It's gonna be hard. When I came here I decided to start over and change my life."

My words had hit a nerve with her. She looked at me, revealing her feelings, "I started over too. It can be a positive thing, to start a new life. But I want to know about you. Tell me more about Jack Holden, about his life before he came into the valley and who he once was." She leaned over and in her reassuring manner took my hand into hers. "I want to know the whole truth about you. I do care. Tell me what weighs so heavily upon your mind and heart."

Again feeling her compassion, I knew we would talk for a long time that night. "I suppose because of what happened in Vietnam and in the years afterward, I came to feel emotionally paralyzed. After my father died, I had no one to turn to. I became very withdrawn, resigned to being alone for the rest of my life."

"But you're not alone anymore," she protested, "I'm here." I'm sure she could feel the gaping hole of loneliness in me. Taking my hand that she'd been holding, she kissed it with genuine feeling that came straight from her heart.

I tried to explain, "Mattie, it's because you're here that I'm here."

She managed a flickering smile, not yet comprehending the full meaning of what I was saying. From the beginning, she had been so wonderful to me, giving me her support. Her strength had become my strength. Now things were coming full circle and my strength would become her strength this night.

I continued on, avoiding her gaze at this point, peering into my past that had begun to unfold in my mind's eye, "I've thought about my situation often. In the quiet of the night, I realized I had nothing. My nightmares about the war got progressively worse. I was running from myself. But there was no escape from what was inside my mind. Finally, everything sort of fell apart all at once, and I had a complete breakdown a year ago. I was committed to a veteran's hospital . . ." My words trailed off into silence. For the moment I felt weak and ashamed. It was just too much to think about.

"What did the doctors say was wrong?" Mattie was persistent.

I continued, explaining, "They said it was PTSD, which is Post Traumatic Stress Disorder. That's where you see or experience something so horrible that you can't come to grips with it. You have flashbacks and nightmares of those events triggered at the most unexpected times. They tried to help, putting me on medication. I recovered some. After that, they released me. That was two months ago. It was then I started making plans for a bus trip."

"Why did you come to Tyler Junction?"

"Originally, I got on that bus because I had lots of regret about something. I was going to set things right and seek some sort of forgiveness for what I had not done. But the trip sort of changed into finding out what was wrong with me, to find myself and my destiny."

"Some sort of forgiveness? I don't understand."

I was looking at her now. From the way she stared at me, I could tell she was still trying to make sense of what I said. Having her full attention, her eyes remained locked on me as I continued, "While on the bus, my nightmares came back and overwhelmed me. I felt alone and forgotten, like no one cared. It changed everything. I couldn't cope with it anymore. I decided I was going to take my . . ."

She had put a finger to my lips, continuing for me, "And Doc stopped you. I know, he told me everything. But you see, Jack, you were not alone. The Lord knew you were there. He cared. That's why Doc was there. We may not realize it, but more often than not, in the grand scheme of our lives, sooner or later, God's hand is there."

"I believe you, more than ever now. Since coming to Tyler Junction, I've begun to feel the Lord's presence around me. I'm glad Doc told you. I was reaching out, and he helped save my life. Then I met you. Instead of death as an answer, I've found and received much more than I bargained for—a new life."

Her reaction was plainly visible as she spoke, "When I first met you, I saw a good man who had been hurt. You were reaching out, and I wanted to reach right back and help you."

"I have many regrets in my life, but knowing you is not one of them."

"Jack, nothing could change my opinion of you."

"And what is your opinion?"

"That you are a kind and gentle person, whom I cherish."

What she said touched my heart. "Before I found the peace I've come to know here in Tyler Junction, the world had become an unsettling place full of angry people. Then I met you." Leaning closer, I whispered, "You've brought meaning back into my life."

She unfolded my hand, looking at my palm. As she traced my lifeline with her fingertips, something unspoken came over her. The warm look on her face suddenly disappeared, replaced by a sad expression. Withdrawing her hand, she seemed preoccupied with something forgotten out of her past.

I watched her as she got up from the pallet. Without a word, she walked over to the open window near the front door. Even in silence she could not hide her pain from me. It was deep within her, but I knew it was there and was sensitive to it. I wondered aloud, "What's wrong?"

Mattie did not respond to me, so obviously caught up in memories of her deepest grief. She looked out the window, but her thoughts were about events far beyond the darkness of the storm.

Getting to my feet, I stood there beside the pallet, thinking. Sometimes the worthiness of one's whole life can be summed up in a single act of kindness. I knew if there was one thing within my power to do, I would help take away her hurt.

I could see that just below the surface a wound from her past was still there, unhealed and too long uncomforted. In her silence, the pain was more intense than ever before.

Seeing this clearly now, I knew there were things I could say to get it all out on the table. I knew I must. Staring across the room at her, I tried once more, "Mattie, what's wrong?"

Turning around this time, her eyes traveled about the room absorbing memories of many years ago. They were still very much alive in her mind. It was like an old wound had been reopened. Looking about for someone who was not there—who could never be there again—her search came to rest on me.

In the collective silence of those few moments, her expression seemed to say she wanted to open up her heart to me. She was ready to talk. Hurt she had kept bottled up for so many years revealed itself in her cracking voice, "You know this is the first time I ever really studied your hand. It reminded me of my brother's hand. I said earlier I had started over. That was after I left here to go live with Doc in Tyler Junction."

Mattie took a few steps back into the room, stopping beside the old dining table. A glimmer of a smile formed among the sadness that was spread across her face. She ran her hand over the nicked and heavily worn surface, recalling past memories that had taken place here. She spoke of those times in an almost nostalgic tone, "It was all so long ago."

"I know what you mean."

"That's right. You said you've re-visited your own past and your father."

"More than just him. My first night here at the hotel I also relived some of my war time experiences. It's never easy. There's so much sadness in some of those old memories."

"It's easier with you being here." She spoke, reflecting the reassurance she felt from my presence as she continued, "This is the first time in years that I've actually come back to the old place. So coming here today has been sort of a return to Meadow Wood for me. It's good to be back where my brother and I spent our childhood."

I thought this was the perfect opportunity to talk to Mattie about this subject. Moving closer to the table, right in front of her, I wanted to make sure, "You said you have a brother?"

"Yes, I had a brother. I miss him greatly. For a long time after he died, my grief was all consuming. Because he wasn't here to enjoy life, why should I have that right? It was a rough time until Doc took me in and raised me. He helped me to see things in a different light. If I became a teacher—helping others—I might be doing something positive, something my brother would've wanted me to do. Just thinking about it now is almost too much. I have endured so much pain and sadness over the years. I guess I'm sort of a survivor. I've always pulled myself together and just kept going."

"Inside, you must be one tough customer, Mattie," I observed.

An aura of grief hung over her as she spoke, "Jack, I want to tell you why I never come over to Russell's store to visit you. Up near the front of the store is a certain bulletin board across from the counter."

"I've seen it. It's a wall of honor."

"Bless you for referring to it that way. Then you know it's covered with photos of American service men just from this valley. Among them is a photo of my brother. Every time I see that picture it breaks my heart."

"I know. I saw his picture there."

"How'd you know which one was my brother?"

"I'll tell you, but you must look at me."

She complied, and our eyes locked on each other. I was silent, my entire attention focusing on her. What happened next pulled me in completely. It was like the gates of Mattie's brain opened up, revealing a world of past memories existing there. My spirit became one with hers, seeing whatever her mind's eye saw. As she thought of a time in her past many years ago, I could visualize every detail inside my head.

A powerful force pulled me back to that time in the valley, several years before I was ever here. I was actually inside this vision with her now, becoming a spectator. We were in a place that was neither dream nor sleep but as real as could possibly be from millisecond to millisecond. It was a moment that truly reached into the innermost recesses of her subconscious memory, made possible by the Lord through the energy I had received from Laurie's touch. It had awakened and empowered a gift that had laid dormant within me for many years. Now tonight, this time traveling, mind melding gift had returned.

Probing her mind, I could see her inside Russell's store. She was getting closer, coming down the aisle, stopping in front of the bulletin board with all the pictures of young soldiers who were never coming back. Reaching up, she slowly extended her hand, softly touching the surface of a particular photo. Tears spilled over her eyelids and down her face as she whispered, "Brother, I'm here. I still love you. I haven't forgotten, and I'll never forget you. I pray that God will be with your spirit and comfort your soul."

At that very moment, in this small corner of Mattie Sullivan's universe, the Lord had mercy upon her and answered her prayer. The anguish and pain she was suffering went away and in its place the peace of God poured into her soul.

As I looked on, this vision made visible the greatest heartbreak inside Mattie's soul. I shared her sorrow and prayed for her. If there was ever any doubt, it was clear to me now that I was there to help heal this wound inside her and be the good deed doer my father had told me to be. This was my mission and reason for coming to the valley.

Sensing a presence near her, Mattie turned from the bulletin board and was startled to see a stranger staring at her—a stranger that would become Jack Holden in her future. But of course, in her past she did not know me. She rubbed her eyes, and the background of Russell's store behind me melted into the background of the old shack as she was drawn back to the present.

Mattie's startled face relaxed as she came out of her vision. Knowing I had seen what she'd seen, she looked at me a bit frightened. But suppressing the fear rising within herself, she spoke of it and questioned me, "You were inside my brain with me and saw what my mind's eye saw. I felt your presence. You were there watching me, inside Russell's store. That was several years ago, but you were just as you are today, unchanged. How did you do that? How is it possible?"

I tried to explain, "I'm not quite sure I know or even want to know. It's nothing less than a miracle. Ever since I touched Laurie Marsh and got a little bit of her spirit inside me, I've been having these time travel-like visions, even more so since I've been here with you today, here in Meadow Wood Valley. I experience a heightened sense of knowing things about those I've come in contact with. It's as though some of her God-given psychic powers have passed on to me. I've been able to see things, reliving events—both past and present—in people's lives."

"Jack, it's a remarkable gift to be able to tap into something deep within someone's soul. Surely it must be God given."

"I wonder though, why me?"

"He knows your heart, Jack, and knows you would only do good with such a gift."

"For me, there's something very profound about going on an inner journey into someone else's past. I remain in awe when it happens."

"Jack, something else frightened me when it happened." The fear was quite visible in her face. I could sense it too, an unsettling feeling still bothering her.

Seeing this in her expression, I tried to help relieve her of any apprehensions she might have, if I only could. "Don't be frightened. It's like you said, you thought God brought me to this valley. I believe that now. But also, please believe, I'm here to help you because I love you."

In her mind's eye, she had not only relived an incident out of her past but had finally connected all the dots and solved the mystery regarding me, or so she thought. "I've always known, since the night you walked into the hotel, there was something special about you, linking you to me. I just wasn't sure what it was till now. When I saw you in my vision, this really happened several years ago in Russell's store. Now I know, you were the mystery man I saw that day. You vanished right after I rubbed my eyes."

"So much of it I don't understand." Thinking about it, I offered my thoughts, "Being there with you then, and here with you now is stranger than Fate. It all has to be ordained by a Higher Power for some purpose."

"There is still more," she said, breaking in. "Something else was lingering from that memory, haunting me all these years. There's one more thing I haven't told you about my vision." The unsettled feeling was rising back up within her again.

"What's that?" I asked, feeling it too.

"Yours wasn't the only apparition that appeared to me that day. There was another . . ."

I pressed for an answer, wanting to help her, "Mattie, who was the other figure?"

Overcoming her hesitation, she told me, "Standing a little behind you was my brother. I felt like his spirit was trying to reach out and make contact with me. I was young, and it frightened me. I've never set foot in Russell's store again. Doc has picked up my groceries for me from that day forward. Oh God, what do you suppose it means?"

"I'm not sure." All kinds of thoughts raced through my head, as I pondered the meaning of what she had told me. Was it her brother's ghost? There had to be an answer. "Let's try to work through this together," I suggested, wanting to help her. But in my heart of hearts I truly felt any answer concerning her brother would somehow be tied to me.

"Why do you think the spirit of my brother was standing beside you, watching me that day?" she asked again, not able to forget the images she saw years ago. "Jack, please help me."

"Come sit by me, and I'll tell you what I think and what I know." I reached over for two old rickety chairs pushed up against the wall and pulled them along side the dining table. Sitting down facing each other, the chairs creaked, as did the floor beneath them. It spread throughout the shack, as if the old place itself was letting out an odd sounding sigh of relief, letting go of the tension built up from the force of the storm. But there were other forces here. I glanced around, feeling the presence of old Joe Catlin himself, along with little Laurie, and even my own father. Perhaps this shack was alive after all, with some part of their souls witnessing this conversation.

I wanted to tell Mattie everything, not only to free her from the past but to also free myself. Something the Lord spoke to my mind made me realize what I had to do, *As you come to know the truth, the truth will set you free.*

I moved my chair closer, directly in front of her. I took her hand, beginning to reveal what I had held in for so long. I couldn't help it, my voice was punctuated with emotion. I spoke sincerely, reaching deep into our shared heartfelt memories, "There's something I want to tell you so that we can get the past behind us. Let's start with when you and your brother last lived here."

She recalled, "It was early 1967, and both our folks had died. I was eight, and my brother was eighteen. There was no work for him in Tyler Junction. He went to the city—over to Raleigh—to find work. Doc Peterson came by, saying he owed my grandfather many favors. One of them he explained would be not to allow Joe Catlin's little granddaughter to live way out here in the valley by herself. Doc took me in, and the place here was boarded up."

"What did your brother do?"

She sank back in the chair, reliving the saddest days of her life. Wiping tears from her eyes, she told me, "My brother joined the army and was later killed in Vietnam. I didn't know it for a long time. His records were lost somehow. Such things happened in those days."

I was trying to be sure of the date, "That must've been in 1968 when he was in Vietnam?"

"Why yes, you're correct." She was puzzled, but too many sad memories were flooding through her mind. "I was a little girl then, just nine years old when I lost my brother. He was the only blood kin I had left alive in the whole world. A huge hole was torn in my heart the day I got official confirmation he was killed in Vietnam. It still remains as a lingering sadness that never quite goes away. There's not a day goes by that a little part of me doesn't hurt because he's not here. I've never truly felt complete closure. If you could only understand."

"Bless your heart, I do understand." I said, truly knowing how she felt.

Her face revealed the heartbreak she had been holding onto for so long. "I loved my brother, but I'll never see him or speak to him again."

Feeling my own anguish in her grief, I wanted to help her more than I wanted to do anything in my entire life. I knew it was time to speak of the unspoken things I'd been keeping from her. "There's something I haven't told you, something I can no longer keep from you. This is not easy, but it concerns someone we both loved. I feel that a promise made is like something sacred before God. A long time ago I made such a promise."

"I don't understand. Jack, what are trying to say?"

"That night in the café you asked me who I really was. I didn't know how to tell you. Even then, I had started caring for you and your feelings. I wondered over dinner that first time, if you were the girl I was looking for. I had to be sure. Then Doc unknowingly confirmed it, later in our conversations about you. But by then I cared too much. Reopening old wounds was not what I wanted to do. I didn't want to hurt you. That's why I hesitated about giving you something I have in my possession."

"What could you possibly have that would hurt me?" she asked, having listened to my every word, taking it all in.

"I knew your brother. We met the first day we both arrived in Vietnam. After I returned from the war, I tried to find you for years to give you something." With that said, I reached down, retrieving a faded blank envelope from my pocket. Even in the dim light she could see it was bloodstained. Extending it, I handed the envelope to her.

Taking it, she looked at me questioningly, "What is this Jack?"

"Mattie, you were wrong. Johnny will speak to you one more time. I promised him I would find you and deliver this letter, his last words to you."

As she carefully examined the envelope, a powerful sense of closure finally came over me. Down deep in my soul, I felt good about myself being able to do something for the woman who had come to mean so much to me.

Watching her as she noticed the envelope was cut open at the end, I commented, "I opened it to see if I could find an address from the letter itself, but it only mentioned this state. That was all I knew because Johnny never mentioned anything about Tyler Junction or this valley."

"And he wouldn't. Grandfather had sworn us to secrecy about the valley or any information that would lead others here. But Jack, I'm so glad you found me."

Mattie's attention returned to the blank envelope, then gently pulling the faded letter from it. Slowly and lovingly, she unfolded the pages to read them. As her eyes traveled over the words, a heartfelt expression spread over her face. "It's his handwriting, I recognize it."

Appreciating her reaction, I watched her silently for a moment. Then I mentioned, "It was only two months ago that I finally located your where-abouts after all these years."

Mattie looked up from the letter, commenting, "I *was* hard to find. When Johnny's records were lost, he was buried in the military cemetery at the state capital. It was months later before they located me and I found out. By then I was nearly ten years old. Walking from the cemetery, I was crying so badly that I didn't see what was coming. I stepped in front of a car, and it ran over my leg. Doc never forgave himself for not being right at my side. Bless his heart, he's been sort of overprotective ever since. Doctoring me back to health, he's been so very good to me. That all happened a long time ago, but it seems like yesterday."

"He's been a good old soul to me too. Doc didn't know it, but when I got on that bus I was already coming to Tyler Junction for a purpose—to find you."

"And you did." She went silent for a bit, frozen in her thoughts. Slowly, she returned to the letter. Getting to the end of it, she looked up at me with a question I knew was coming, "He wrote he was giving this letter to his very best friend. Jack, was that you?"

In that quiet moment, I recalled my own memories of Johnny Sullivan. "Mattie, what do you know about your brother's death?"

"They only told me he was killed in action in Vietnam."

I nodded toward the letter, "It was just over twenty years ago, during the Tet Offensive of 1968, at the siege of Hue Citadel. When the Viet Cong had overrun our position, Johnny brought this letter to me. He wanted you to know he was thinking of you and loved you so very much, even on the last day of his life."

"Oh, Jack ..." Her mouth quivered, just thinking of Johnny was becoming emotionally overwhelming to her. Even so, she looked over at me, wanting me to continue, "Please go on."

"I must tell you, the reason for my PTSD was that I saw many things so horrible I couldn't live with them. Among those things, I saw a friend killed." I paused, choking with emotion, my own heart full of pain. "Johnny was that person, my very best friend. We slept in the same tent together and talked about our hopes and dreams, about all we wanted to do when we got home. Though he never told me your name or where you lived, he talked a lot about you. During our year together in Vietnam, we had become like brothers. More than that actually, he *was* my brother. He died in my arms, Mattie. He loved you so much, and I loved him too. I'm honored to be able to give this letter to you."

"I'm the one who's honored to be able to receive this from you." Tears were filling her eyes. She had listened to me, totally absorbed in my story, thinking about what it meant to her. I had reached right into the core of her soul and touched her. Shaking with emotion, her feelings became words, "I'm glad he was with you when he died."

"By the grace of God, He let me survive Vietnam so that one day I might find my way to you. Finding you was the beginning of a new day for me."

"Why do you say that, Jack?"

"Because at the same time I was trying to put my own life back together, God was leading me to you. I'm convinced of that now."

Supporting each other, lifting each other up made me feel stronger. It was the beginning of re-defining what the rest of my life could be.

We looked at each other in silence as increasing intensity filled both of us. Just as hurt had brought us together, what we were sharing would keep us together. I took Mattie's trembling hand, closing my own around it. She moved into my arms. Tied together in an emotional bond, we comforted each other's grief, slowly letting go of mutual unhappiness that had haunted both of us these past 20 years.

In this mingling of both joy and sorrow, we clung to each other and our feelings found release. Sadness held in too long was finally released as we cried together. An old wound had been reopened for both of us, and it had been healed by the support we gave each other. The compassion we shared was turning into something else. Special feelings were born out of a moment of truth where we both had laid bare our souls. We never lost those feelings all the rest of our lives.

I looked into her eyes, tenderly wiping the tears from her face with my fingertips. I saw the truth there. It was then I knew. What I felt for her came through in words straight from my heart, "It's a miracle that we have been brought together. I love you more than words can say."

She looked up at me revealing her own feelings, "It's a miracle where my brother could come back and speak to me again. You're part of that miracle. It is the tie that binds us and connects our lives. You've been my anchor here tonight. I cherish you for that—I love you."

Mattie silently raised my hand to her lips and gently kissed it. Then lowering it, she stared into my face, her eyes full of love.

Our whole focus was the love we both felt in one of the most powerful moments of our lives. We wrapped our arms around each other again and kissed affectionately. It was a moment that felt so right to both of us. As we embraced, I could see something in her face that I felt inside myself. All the sorrow and pain of the night drained out of us, leaving only the good feelings we had shared. The hand of God was at work in both of us, calming the turmoil inside us, healing us in ways only the Lord can. We stood there for a long time, just holding on to each other. The world around us seemed to blur away until the beginnings of daylight penetrated the front window of the shack, bathing both of us in its healing rays.

Though we were in a humble little shack, I felt like we were in a place more sacred than a church. Such was the feeling I had, that God had brought us here and bestowed his blessings upon us. His divine will had been done.

Morning had broken through the trees, and I felt like my life had just been introduced into a season of light. An inner cleansing had taken place within me—God's cleansing. Everything around me had just been illuminated with a morning sparkle that resonated throughout the peace and beauty of Meadow Wood Valley. God had just let me have a glimpse of what

Heaven would be like. Taking it all in, I looked over at Mattie and said, "I guess it's time for us to get on with the rest of our lives."

It'll be different, though," she added, knowing something. "We have each other now."

We left the old shack that morning and never came back to it. The decaying structure collapsed during the coming summer, caving in on its own rotting timbers. But Mattie and I took some new memories and renewed some fond remembrances we would both carry within ourselves always.

When we got to the edge of the clearing, I glanced around at the shack one last time. I marveled that after the night's storm, the rays of a morning rainbow had cut across the sky and descended to the ground just beyond it. This was truly a place where the rainbow ends. It had been a place of dreams, where our spiritual ancestors resided, I thought. We had both discovered something about the ghosts out of our pasts and were better for it. Just as I walked away with a little bit of my father's spirit, Mattie retained some of Johnny's spirit within her.

It had been a good thing to see my father once more and find this strange place where all points of my past might lead to a better future. I whispered, "Goodbye, Dad." With that, I turned back to the old path and with Mattie began our journey back through the woods. As we did so, the trees and dense overgrowth shut the old shack off from view forever.

CHAPTER 22
MATTIE'S CLASSROOM

The light of a new day reached through the classroom windows, and its warmth fell upon the face of Mattie Sullivan, the person I cared most about in the entire world. She was seated behind her desk, contemplating. She would tell me later about these events in the classroom, what happened before I came to her later that day.

It was early yet, and she was alone. In such an atmosphere, something important was becoming quite clear in her mind. Her life was changing, and in some ways it would be forever. She already knew this for sure, gut instinct told her so.

As for now, though, she had just finished setting up 'show and tell' day. The display consisted of three paintings supported on easels to one side of her desk. She had arranged them so they would be facing the class but still angled toward her as well.

Coming around in front of her desk, uncovering it, Mattie stood motionless in front of the center canvas. Entitled, *Self-portrait with a child*, her eyes traveled over every feature of the old man within the painting. In turn, he seemed to be staring back at her. Even more so, in a moment that goes beyond the normal senses, he seemed to be listening. Speaking to him as if he were right there in the flesh, she said, "Thank you for everything, guiding that small child's first steps into a world you showed her was full of so much wonder. Now that child is the woman standing before you, passing that wisdom on to new young children. I miss you Grandpa."

"I didn't know paintings were alive," said a familiar voice coming from behind her. Startled, she turned around, realizing she was not alone.

It was Principal Peabody, who continued, "At least I didn't think so until your grandfather showed me paintings could come alive. He was a remarkable man."

"So you knew my grandfather?"

"Right after I came here in 1960, Doc took me out to the valley to meet him. He'd just turned a hundred years old, but even then he was alert and full of advice for a naive young schoolteacher. He helped set me on the path to a lifetime career in education. I only wish there had been more time to know him better."

"I know exactly what you mean," she said sadly. "I was born in late 1960 and was not quite four years old when he passed away in 1964. But there were things he told me and good times we shared that have never left me and probably never will. Even at such a young age, he had an inspiring effect on me."

"Mattie, that's it exactly. I hope his paintings here will have an inspiring effect on the children today."

"I'll pass on my grandfather's own words to them, introducing them to the world of Joe Catlin and his art. I know the children will find it fascinating. As you say, I hope they'll be inspired."

Reassured, the Principal nodded silently, and with a knowing look forming on his face, explained, "I suspicion it will happen because, like your grandfather, you're a very inspiring person. I've seen that quality in you more than once. He would be very proud of you. If only he could see you now."

Glancing over at his self-portrait, she reflected, "You know, somehow I think he still can."

"I would like to pursue why you think that, but . . ." Remembering something, he looked down at his watch, realizing other duties were calling. "I must be off." He headed for the door, leaving her alone with thoughts of twenty-five years ago.

Something lingered in Mattie's mind from her conversation with Mr. Peabody. She concentrated on the center painting again, absorbing all the depth and detail of her grandfather's self-portrait. The intangible elusiveness of his spirit was captured in his own image, just a breath away from springing to life.

Without directly mentioning it, she had felt his presence throughout the night with me in her old home in the valley. He had loved Johnny too. Her brother was fourteen years old at the time and was with her at their grandfather's bedside when he passed away. Now the old man's restless spirit was at peace because his grandson's last letter was finally home, to be treasured by his *little princess.* She smiled as this thought ran through her mind, remembering that was what he used to call her then.

I later learned Joe Catlin had an opinion of me. As Mattie looked more deeply into the mesmerizing eyes of his self-portrait, she could not only feel his spirit right there in the room with her but could also hear her grandfather's words whispering to her mind, *Little Princess, it did my heart good to see you come back to the old place, to return to Meadow Wood. The valley misses you. That Jack Holden is a fine young man. He's a decent fella. Be good to him. He loves you so.*

Stepping backward for a moment, she took in the whole painting, especially the other figure in this picture. It was her, playing on the floor while Joe Catlin was sitting nearby in his old recliner, observing her every movement. Concentrating, all the distracting elements of the classroom disappeared. Her view tightened on the scene, to include only what was within the dimensions of the painting itself. There she was, almost four, staring up at her 104-year-old grandfather. The picture had captured the very moment when their eyes met. It was a world long gone and far removed from the present.

Mattie felt this world of the past sucking her into it. In this quiet reflective moment, the hypnotic effect of the painting was more than powerful. It pulled her back to that very day, to the surroundings it so vividly portrayed, coming alive for her once more.

Even though he was in the last days of his life, her grandfather's advanced age had not slowed him down. Right up to the last, his eyes were sharp and undimmed, giving him the clarity of vision to put the final touches on his last painting, this self-portrait. Her grandfather's snow-white hair glistened as his whole face was bathed in a shaft of sunlight. Turning within this Heaven sent illumination, Mattie saw him and he saw her.

She had been sitting motionless, on the floor nearby. His painting was like magic to her. She sat there awestruck. Maybe because it was one of their last conversations, she remembered every word clearly.

"What do you think, Princess?" he asked, wanting Mattie's opinion, making her feel important. Including her in his creative process was part of a much larger closeness that bonded them together till the end of his life, and now beyond.

"Grandfather, the more I look at one of your paintings, the more it seems so real. I feel like I can almost become part of it."

"Well this time you have," he said, pointing to her image in the picture playing with her Jack-in-the-box on the floor.

"But that's the way I feel about all your paintings. I can look at one of your pictures of Meadow Wood, and it's almost like I can hear a voice on the wind, blowing among the trees, calling my name, leaving me with a good feeling inside myself."

"Child, that's the magic of the valley. When that feeling surges through me, I know I'm finished with a painting. I've worked on this picture for three years now, days and weeks at a time, trying to capture something special, that is until a little voice whispered to me, *This is right.* I knew then, it was done. Now it belongs to the ages, and the enjoyment of viewers that I will never live to know."

"Grandfather, I want you to be here always."

"Oh, I wish I could, but my days are numbered. I've been feeling for some time now that the good Lord is going to be calling me home."

"But how will I know what to do without you here to tell me? Please don't leave me."

"Princess, I will never leave you. My words of advice will always be with you in your mind. Concentrate and think about it real hard, and you will hear your old granddad talking to you. Or if you need help, just look at this painting." Pointing to his own image in the rocking chair, he told her, "I'll be right here."

"I'll never forget. I only wish other people could know what you know, and see all the things that you have put in your paintings of the valley."

"It takes a very special gift."

"What kind of a gift, Grandfather?"

"When I came here, I felt like Don Quixote, a man in search of a vision. I was searching for something too. What I found was food for thought, the bread of wisdom and life. I found I could go to that inner place within myself and find peace. It was like life renewing itself. After each experience, I felt fresh and healed all over, ready to create something inspired by the beauty here. I would spend months soaking up the atmosphere of the valley for my paintings. Then images started forming before my eyes, which I captured, putting them on canvas. I'm convinced these images were given to me as a gift straight from God."

Mattie marveled and told him, "There are so many beautiful things in your paintings. I have to stare at them a long time to take in all the details."

"Actually Princess, it's all the little intangible things existing around us that illuminate our lives. If everyone in this fast-paced world would just slow down and see a thing for what it is, appreciate its beauty, and absorb the inner peace it gives us, then their lives would be better for it."

"I'm trying, but I'm not sure I understand all of what you're saying, Grandfather."

"Don't worry child, in time you will."

Closing her eyes, Mattie thought about what he'd said. Images around her grandfather faded, but the memories of a lifetime away remained clear in her brain.

Becoming frozen in time, the little girl from the painting morphed back into the Mattie Sullivan I knew. As she opened her eyes, she found herself back in her classroom. In the present, she retained something special from the past. Returned from her dream of long ago, the thought lingered within her as she whispered, "I understand now."

A few minutes later, seated behind her desk, she focused on the little faces entering the room. The school children that made up her class were taking their seats. As her class was about to begin, thanks to a few words of wisdom from her grandfather, Mattie was far better prepared for the day than anyone would ever know.

"Class, as I told you, today would be 'show and tell' day. For this purpose I have brought along these three paintings for our discussion. Can anyone tell me who the old gentleman in the center picture is?"

A young boy in overhauls stood beside his desk, and spoke up, "Miss Mattie, isn't he your grandfather, Joe Catlin the famous artist?"

"Why yes, Bobby, you're correct."

The young boy stared at the self-portrait for a long moment. Looking back up in all his wide-eyed innocence, he asked, "What was he really like?"

"He was warm and loving, like what you'd expect a grandfather to be. I remember clearly: he used to chase me around the old recliner in this picture, and play 'hide-and-go-seek.' That was twenty-five years ago, but in my mind it could have been yesterday."

Bobby was becoming even more curious, "Can you tell us more about him?"

"My grandfather was sixty years old when he first stumbled upon the valley. That was in 1920, and he'd already lived a full life, or so he thought. He was not prepared, though, for what he would find there. Revitalizing him totally and completely, it proved to be a life changing, life enhancing experience. Over the next forty-four years, he completed nearly forty paintings and hundreds of sketches, capturing what he saw, embracing the valley that embraced him. Art was an act of self-discovery for him. His Meadow Wood paintings are rich with many different textures and colors that he discovered with each canvas. Living there made his palette of colors almost infinite. Because life was an adventure that never ceased to be a miracle for him, his mind remained alert and active till the last, when he passed away in 1964."

By now Bobby's interest had widened to include the two nature paintings that flanked the self-portrait. He marveled, "His paintings of the valley are so beautiful. He must've loved it here."

"Meadow Wood was an artist's heaven for him. I remember him telling me the valley was God's country. He believed the Spirit of the Lord was working through his fingers, helping him to create the pictures you see here today."

Stopping for a moment, Mattie looked over the top of her desk at the roomful of young students sitting at their little desks. All of the children were completely silent. Their eyes fixed on her, they were all caught up in her words and the story they told.

"Miss Mattie, your grandfather's paintings are really moving," Bobby said, visibly awestruck. "They inspire me. I want to grow up and be an artist just like him."

"Just remember, Bobby, painting is an inspired craft, not a job. It's something that becomes a way of life, as it did for my grandfather. If you want to become such an artist, do as he once told me: 'Open up your mind and let the creative powers of God flow through you, guiding your brush.' A really good painting like you see here is one that reaches within us, into places almost spiritual, inspiring us. If you're not careful, that's a feeling that will come over you from just being here in Tyler Junction. You know class, I'm really glad to be living right here, in the heart of America where it so reveals itself to be God's country."

A young girl, who bore a strong physical resemblance to some very disagreeable people who lived in the valley, raised her hand.

Mattie acknowledged the child, nodding in her direction, "Yes, Nellie Barnett."

She stood up beside her desk, revealing somewhat grimmer thoughts, "It may be America's heartland here, but Miss Sullivan these are hard times. Since the iron works closed down, both my brothers lost their jobs. Work's been scarce around Tyler Junction. A lot of people have been forced to leave the valley for jobs over in the city, over in Raleigh."

Mattie knew she was a bright young student, smarter than her much older brothers. Seeking a more optimistic tone, she agreed with Nellie somewhat, "You're correct in what you say, but there's something else you should think about."

"What's that Miss Sullivan?"

She gestured out the classroom windows, "It's farm country all around us, here in the valley. The land is still good. There is hope for the future. After all, one day that future will be in the hands of all you young children. You are its hope."

Nellie's strained thought was mirrored in her face before she blurted out, "I don't want to be a farmer! I want to do something else."

"You don't have to be a farmer, Nellie. Don't let me or anyone else tell you what to do with your life. If you want something bad enough, study hard and gain the necessary knowledge to become whatever you want to be. You will improve yourself and change your own life for the better."

Again, the young people in the classroom were listening to Mattie's every word, knowing she was giving them good advice. Glancing around, she realized it as she continued, "Children, the valley is such a beautiful place. Aren't you happy here?"

Another little girl, Jenny Harris, spoke up, "Since my folks lost their home in last year's storm, it's been bad for them. But our neighbor, Mr. Jerry Marsh, has really been friends with my dad."

"What are you trying to say, Jenny?"

"I guess, that people really do need people, and if we all help each other, it will make the valley a happier place to live in.

Nellie broke in, getting curious, "Miss Sullivan, how about you? Are you happy—really happy—here in the valley?"

Her mind silently reviewed a lifetime of memories in a few brief moments. Among a succession of thoughts, she remembered the loss of her brother and all the heartbreak that followed. Mattie had lived through a season of sadness, becoming handicapped in its wake. Now she was entering a season of joy. A miracle was taking place in her life. Something good had happened to her, and she candidly shared it with her students, "For a long time I was very sad. I thought I had lost my chance at personal happiness. My whole world was teaching you children here. But recently someone very special has come into my life."

Nellie persisted, "Is this someone a good person?"

"He's a very good person and makes me very happy."

The little girl saw a special glow radiate from Mattie's face. In her own youthful naïve innocence she asked, "Can I meet this nice man?"

She smiled, as this brought out a good feeling in her heart, "Why yes, Nellie, I hope you will meet him very soon."

"Miss Mattie, I want to be just like you."

"How so Nellie?"

"I want to be a school teacher when I grow up."

"When I was your age, I was very poor. I wanted to accomplish certain things bad enough to do something about it. I decided to study hard and change my life, becoming a schoolteacher so I could help others. I care about all you young people and your future."

"I love you for that," Nellie responded with obvious admiration. "You're my hero."

A glimpse of her cane caught Mattie's attention. It brought an important thought to mind that she wanted to convey to the children, "I want all of you to know something. You might not understand this right now, but in the fullness of time you will. The world is full of excuses. At one time or another, in all your lives, you will have your own individual crosses to bare. You can make a crutch out of them and become defeated in life." Reaching over for her cane, she picked it up. Holding it in front of her steady gaze, she continued, "Or, you can remain positive, overcome obstacles, and put away the crutch that has handicapped your life." In the spirit of that thought she leaned the cane back up against her desk.

Becoming lost in the moment, she told me later she thought of me and the growing emotional bond between us. Gaining strength from that, she experienced a glimmer of a new life opening up. Feeling stronger, both mentally and physically, she stood up without her cane and walked around her desk.

Pausing in front of the class, she looked up at her students. They had been following her every step of the way, making eye contact with their determined teacher. She could see awe and admiration in their faces.

Revealing her deepest feelings, she advised them, "All of us have been scared by life's bruises, but that's no reason why we can't recover and enjoy a new and better life. If you're ever so lucky that a good samaritan—a good deed doer—comes along to help you, don't ever turn him away. Children, don't let go of your dreams. Cherish and live them."

As the children digested her words, the silence was broken by the schoolhouse bell indicating lunch recess. She looked out the classroom windows, noticing a band of bleak clouds beginning to form in the distant western sky. Turning to her students, Mattie reacted, "Children, it's time for lunch break. Let's go eat and hit the playground for awhile, before the weather gets too bad."

As she turned to leave, Mattie was distracted by her cane once again. Thinking about it, the morning had been good to her. She felt both the wisdom of her grandfather and the strength of our relationship welling up inside her.

All the kids shot out of the room except one, who kept a watchful eye on her teacher. "Miss Sullivan," Nellie spoke up, getting her attention. "May I walk with you?"

"Why yes, child," Mattie agreed, already very sure in her mind of what she was going to do.

Nellie came up beside her. They had just taken a few steps when the young girl noticed that something had been left behind, "Miss Sullivan, your cane?"

Glancing back at it, she said, "No child, I think I'll try walking without it."

Together they walked out of the classroom, leaving the cane Mattie would never use again.

CHAPTER 23
RUSSELL'S STORE

Less than thirty minutes later, distinctly darker storm clouds were moving along the horizon. I saw them from a window inside Russell's store. But they were just a fleeting impression to me then. My mind was more consumed with thoughts of Mattie Sullivan. There was so much that I adored about her. For me, time had seemed to come to a stand still in Tyler Junction. Since going to Meadow Wood, one day had passed slowly and pleasantly into another as Mattie and I grew closer together.

During this passage of time, new memories filled my mind. I felt a positive attitude giving me strength. It truly seemed that all the warmth and love I'd experienced in the valley had healed me. The past had slipped back into my subconscious and become only a distant memory. I believed I had finally found a measure of the happiness that had always been just beyond my grasp. But fate was going to deem otherwise. For even then, outside forces which man has no control over were closing in on me.

I was thinking of Mattie at that very moment when I heard the bell clang above the store's front door. It would be the start from which I would measure this day as the longest day of my life. I looked around to see Jerry Marsh standing just inside the store. "Hello Jerry," I said, turning and really noticing the western sky. It was then I nodded toward the window, "It looks like a bad storm rolling in."

"Yeah," Jerry agreed. "When I looked out this morning I noticed something was becoming unstable in the atmosphere. I boarded things up before I came over here."

Dan Russell had been busy with broom in hand behind Jerry, listening. Deciding to see for himself, he went over to the west window, directly across the counter from Jerry and me. It was not even midday, and the clear sky of morning was already being replaced by a growing unnatural darkness. Ominous storm clouds were rolling into the valley. There was the distant rumble of thunder, signaling something more severe to come. It was a massive front that stretched clear across the horizon.

Having seen it before, Dan was the first to recognize what was coming. Quickly becoming more concerned, he remarked, "Jack, it's just like what happened to you and Mattie over in Meadow Wood. This time of year, storms have been known to hit the valley all of a sudden like, with disastrous results. After all, this is tornado alley."

I noticed a strange expression was forming on Dan's face. Full of anxiety, it was a look I had seen on the faces of other men a long time ago. Then I realized what it was. I would remember later this was the first time I ever really saw fear in him.

"That's part of why I'm here now," Jerry added, picking up on Dan's comments about the weather. "Last year about this time we had a bad storm that flattened two of my neighbors' homes. You remember, Dan, don't you?"

"Yeah, I remember. It was the Farley place and the Harris place," Dan said, remembering what he didn't want to remember, "It was awful." He went silent, having a flashback of his own, seeing a terrible vision in his mind's eye.

Jerry continued for him, "It blew their windows out, injuring those poor folks. They were cut up pretty bad and almost had their entire farms destroyed."

Dan's face mirrored the pain and sadness he had felt during those events of a year ago. "Right after it happened," Jerry explained, "I went over to see if I could help. Mr. Harris lost an arm. And his little girl . . . she *was* pretty. Now she's got an awful scar that runs from her face clear down her neck. They never knew what hit them."

"Wasn't there some kind of warning?" I wondered out loud, asking, "What about tornado sirens or some kind of early warning system?"

"We have no sirens, nothing," Dan answered in a somewhat grim tone. "After Tyler Junction lost the iron works plant, we've just been hanging on by our fingernails. The town council says we're flat broke."

"If I was mayor, I'd find a way to do something," I responded, quite incensed.

"Then maybe you ought to run for mayor, Jack."

"Maybe I will, Dan, someday."

Not responding, Dan grew silent, looking back over at the window. "Excuse me, I think I'll keep an eye on those storm clouds." He walked back across to the west window, totally absorbed by what was going on outside.

Jerry turned his attention back to me again, "Can I have a private word with you?"

"Sure," I said, gesturing we step down to the end of the counter, beyond earshot of everyone else.

Before he ever spoke, I immediately noticed a glimmer of strength in his expression and in the way he carried himself now. The heavy burden of grief was beginning to lift and a glimpse of hope was becoming embedded in his face.

Speaking in a low voice, he explained, "With the weather getting bad I didn't want to be out there alone, especially now with Laurie gone." Pausing, his eyes reflecting the emotions in his heart as he continued, "I thought about what you said to me that day in the cemetery. It was the darkest day of my life, and what you said about her spirit still near me has been a real comfort."

I reassured him again, "I'm glad, because whenever you think of her, Laurie's spirit is going to be with you—always."

"After I got home, later that night, I found this note stuck between the pages of her Bible." Jerry extracted a small sheet of paper from his coat pocket. Unfolding the note, he read it to me, "It says, 'Daddy, I was reading my Bible and I believe that neither death, nor all the powers that be, will ever separate us or our love.'—signed Laurie."

"Jerry, the more I think about it, the more I feel good that I could help you with Barnett. I just wish there was something else I could've done for Laurie and you."

"But you did, and you have. I feel something of her spirit around us every time we talk. That's the other part of why I'm here. Early this morning while I was still in bed, a strange feeling came over me. I felt like I was not alone. It was Laurie. She spoke to my mind again."

This got my full attention. "What did she say to you?"

"In her own voice, she spoke just as clear as if she were sitting in front of us right now. She said, *Daddy, don't stay home alone today. Go to Mr. Russell's store.*"

"Is that all?" I asked, having the feeling in my heart there was more.

"No . . . There was something else, but I'm not sure I should mention it."

Seeing the reluctance, even worry in Jerry's face, I persisted, "It's alright. Tell me anyway."

"She said, *Jack's gonna need your help today. Warn him about something he must do. You can help save his life.*"

An unsettled feeling rushed through me, rising from the pit of my stomach. I looked at Jerry silently, sensing something ominous was about to happen. So I asked, "Warn me about what?"

"Sometime today you must go over to the school and check on Miss Mattie. If you don't . . ." He halted, looking very reluctant to tell me more.

"If I don't, what's going to happen?" I insisted on knowing the rest.

"She won't survive." Jerry told me with a great deal of dread in his voice. He was relieved that he had told me, yet there was still fear in his face. He was holding back.

I could feel it. He was holding something back. I asked, "There's more?"

"Yes, you must be very careful Jack because your own life will be in danger too."

"Thanks for warning me. You're a good friend, Jerry."

Trying to reassure me, he insisted, "No matter what happens, I'm going to be here for you."

"Look!" Across from us, Dan's raised voice blurted out. Startled by something he saw out the window, he turned to Jerry and me. The approaching danger was mirrored in his face and voice, "There are funnels in those clouds. I'm sure of it!"

We all heard the sudden rise in the sound of the wind outside. In a flash, our attention was immediately drawn toward the store's front door as it rattled violently and flew open.

A howling wind blasted into the store as a lone figure concealed by a wide-brimmed down-turned hat emerged through the opening. Pushing the door closed against the resistance of surging wind blowing against him, the figure turned around. In the process, the brim of his hat had blown up just enough to reveal it was Leroy Barnett.

Approaching Dan, Barnett was full of a sense of urgency, "Russell, you'd better get this place boarded up quick! Bad storm's a comin'!"

Leroy glanced around the store just as Jerry Marsh turned in his direction. Their eyes met. Taking off his hat, Leroy brushed his hair back. Walking toward Jerry, he stopped right in front of him.

I had slid along the counter behind them. My hand tightened around an out of sight baseball bat just in case of trouble. But that would not be necessary as I quickly saw Leroy's whole confrontational attitude had disappeared. For me, this was the first visible sign of a dramatic change in his personality.

Leroy leaned forward, getting on eye level with Jerry Marsh. Looking at Barnett, one could plainly see he was worn down, exhausted from soul searching. "There's been a lot on my mind lately. I've been needin' to talk with you. Jerry, you've got every reason not to listen, but would you hear me out?"

Jerry looked at him closely, seeing the anguish and remorse in his face. This was a distinctively different tone in the usually much angrier Barnett, he thought. He decided to listen to him and finally agreed, "Very well, I'll hear you out."

Leroy had faced the monster within himself and came up with some answers. He spoke in such a low voice, that he could barely be heard above the rising intensity of the storm. "I'm not well educated, but I've been doin' a lot of thinkin' about my life and what I've become. I was so full of vain pride when you fired me. Anger raged inside of me. I couldn't cope with it. Building hate upon hate, I couldn't think about anything but you. I just wanted to hurt you and hurt you bad. If hate transforms us into something evil, perhaps good can transform us as well. After your little girl died, I was ashamed of myself. I cried at Laurie's funeral." His voice cracking, he lowered his head, looking off, not wanting Jerry to see the tears already forming in his eyes.

213

Recognizing this, Jerry said, "That's okay, Leroy. You're a bigger man than you think you are when you show you've got a heart."

He shook his head, "It's not okay. It was then I realized I had said and done horrible things. Nobody was to blame for me gettin' fired but myself. I was a troublemaker. You did what you had to do. I caused you more pain than anyone should have to endure. This may not make any sense to you, but I ain't been sleepin' right. I keep wakin' up in the middle of the night seein' those eyes of your little girl starin' at me. It was as if she were tryin' to tell me something."

"What do you suppose that was?" Jerry asked.

"She pointed to something on a table. I recognized that it was my folks' Bible." It seemed that something had clicked inside Leroy. It was as if this vision of Laurie had given him some insight into himself. Taking another step in becoming a different person, he revealed how much this affected him, "Since then, I've been reading that Bible and learning the difference between good and evil, praying for help." He looked back up, finding Jerry's eyes. His voice pleaded into them, "As God is my witness, I'm truly sorry for all the things I've ever said and done to you. I know it's more than I have any right to expect, but if you can find it in your heart, I'm asking you to forgive me."

Feeling his sincerity, Jerry studied him for a long moment. He told me later he thought he heard Laurie's voice speaking to his mind, *Daddy, do the right thing for me—give peace and love a chance.* He knew then what to say and do, "Leroy, the Good Book teaches us to forgive and forget. I cannot do less."

Barnett stretched out his arm toward him and opened his hand saying, "Be my friend and I'll spend the rest of my life setting things right with you for what I've done wrong."

Jerry could see that Leroy had opened up his heart and spoken with genuine feeling. With that in mind, he held out his own much smaller hand and saw it swallowed up by a gigantic grip. It would be the beginning of a lasting friendship.

In the same instant, these two hands came together, there was a sudden loud boom in the distance. Everyone in the store jerked. The lights flickered and went out immediately.

I reacted, coming up with a big flashlight from below the counter, "Lightning must've hit a transformer."

From the west window, Dan observed, "The storm's snapped the power lines from the electric pole outside." As he looked around at me, I could see that expression of fear in his face again.

"Dan, what's wrong?"

Instantly, before he could answer me, we all felt the source of that fear. The whole building shook violently, right down to its foundation. Something unknown was directly overhead, exerting a powerful force, surrounding and squeezing the store till it was about to explode. In a terrific downburst, wind whipped all around the structure, pounding it relentlessly. Without warning, a window at the front of the store shattered, making a loud noise. All heads jerked around in that direction as another blast of wind penetrated the building through this new opening. In an ironic way, this helped by relieving the pressure that was destroying it.

Being nearest to what used to be a window, I stared out the gaping hole. The force of blowing rain drove through this new opening almost horizontally, forcing my eyes to squint. Not sure, I strained to make out something. Whatever it was had disappeared into a clouded sky.

Coming up right behind me, Dan was returning from the back room carrying another flashlight and a handful of boards. He had seen something too. He reacted, "Oh no! Lord please help us."

I turned toward him, asking, "Did you see what it was?"

"Yes I did! It looked like a twister!" Dan was visibly shaken, as the nightmare from a year ago had returned. He recalled, rendering his verdict as an unofficial weather forecaster, "Those clouds are so massive they could be packed with one gigantic super-cell—multiple tornadoes—just like what we had last year."

"Oh Lord!" Leroy reacted, with fear beginning to take him over.

Dan continued, scaring the be jeepers out of him, "Here we are in late April, and for the last 39 years—since 1950—it has been one of the worst months for tornadoes in our state's history."

"Oh please, don't tell me anymore," responded a definitely spooked Leroy.

I think we were all a bit frightened. For in that moment, through the newly enlarged window opening, we saw a sky growing ever thicker with the rapidly moving cloud formations Dan had talked about. They were forming into a huge black mass along the horizon.

Leroy came alongside me, pointing through the opening. "It's forming over the ridge there, to the northwest, near the school!" He looked around sharply, his eyes meeting mine. Both worry and a sense of urgency were in his voice, "My baby sister is in class there too! I've got to go to her!"

Dan grabbed my shoulder, getting my attention. "Go with him. They may be needing help over at the school." Turning to Jerry, he handed him a hammer. "Help me with these boards!"

Jerry glanced over toward me, remembering what Laurie's spirit had whispered to his mind.

As our eyes met, I knew what he was thinking. Grabbing up my raincoat, I came around the counter right behind him. "Jerry, I'll be alright. I'll take care of myself."

Jerry nodded he understood and added, "I'm going to help Dan with this, but then I'll be over to the school as soon as I can. I won't let you down, I promise."

Then we both turned, and as a group, the four of us headed for the door. Leroy in front, turned the doorknob. As he did so, some invisible force outside grabbed it right out of his powerful grip. A terrific gust of wind flung it open, almost tearing the door from its hinges. Pushing on through the doorway, we ventured into the unknown that awaited us.

CHAPTER 24
THE STORM

The storm's fury had broken loose outside just as Leroy Barnett predicted. Having led the way, he looked back around as the rest of us emerged through the doorway onto the front porch of Russell's store.

Jerry joined Dan to one side of the door as they struggled amidst the blowing wind, boarding up one of the store windows. He pounded with the hammer furiously while it was all Dan could do to hold onto the boards.

Coming from behind, I was hit by a sheet of rain slamming up against me. I quickly fastened my raincoat. Barely able to keep my eyes open, I tried to see. The view in the direction of the school was totally obscured. No longer focused on myself, growing anxiety churned up inside me as I thought of Mattie being there. Since connecting with her in Meadow Wood, she was everything to me. Without her, there would be nothing left for me. Call me psychic or whatever, I just knew she was in danger and that I had to get to her.

Just then, a loud crash vibrated the front porch and got my immediate attention. The noise came from just west of the building where Dan usually parked his truck. We all jerked around in that direction, to see that his truck had been flipped completely over by the force of the winds.

"Oh no!" Dan reacted upon seeing it tossed about like it had been a toy. Turning to Leroy and me, he was apologetic along with a dire prediction, "Sorry men, I guess you'll have to go it on foot, if you can even make it at all."

"Russell, I have to get to my sister!" Barnett yelled, then turning to me, "Come on, Holden, if you're coming."

"I'm coming," I said, following Leroy down the steps, plunging into the heart of the storm. Raw winds whipped across us, becoming like a gigantic hand pushing us backward. Determined, we pressed forward through it. Headed for Olive Road, the sky above opened up with a new sheet of pelting rain of such force that it impacted us like a thousand needle pricks at once. Every step was achieved through total focus. Iron will formed within my mind, willing me forward.

A half mile farther on, we reached the old picket fence line leading up to the school. In the time it took us to make it to this point, we had become completely drenched. New layers of dust joined the rain, blowing straight at us with equal tremendous strength. Smacked in the face, it was both unrelenting and unforgiving, stinging as it hit us. We were being pelted so hard it became hard to think. A persistent force that was now an obsession kept us going though, and we pushed through this wall of nature's resistance. Straining to see, the school finally became barely visible, little more than an outline in the distance beyond the fence.

We were making our way much more slowly now, advancing cautiously by using the fence posts as a guide. Every step forward was becoming dangerous. Broken branches and other debris blew past us in a fury. We found ourselves struggling to just stay on our feet. Somehow, I like to think it was the good Lord's help that kept us moving closer toward the wooden gate leading to the school.

In my own mind, if I had to make the ultimate sacrifice I was okay with it. I thought, there is no greater love than to lay down one's life for the person you love.

The fence posts ahead of us were beginning to strain and bend. The same powerful invisible force that so easily yanked the door to Russell's store right out of Leroy's grip was removing them! Sucked upward from right out of the ground, they went flying through the air.

Not giving an inch, though, we kept going until we reached the gate. It was stubborn at first. The gate was wedged shut by the power of the storm. We strained to open it. We pushed the gate inward. The weakened railing adjoining it started breaking apart. Boards flew in every direction as the rest of the fence gave way and collapsed.

Still leaning into it, pushing with all his strength, Leroy lost his footing. Falling forward, he hit the ground hard, twisting his leg badly. He lay there in a heap, the wind knocked out of him.

Hovering above him, I reached downward to help. Leroy grabbed my hand and made an effort to stand. Putting pressure on his injured leg, Leroy's face contorted. The pain was intense. Sinking to the ground again, I could see he was hurting bad. Resigned to the fact he was not going to make it, he declared, "Holden, it's no use, I've torn something in my leg. You go on without me."

I would have none of it. Equally determined not to leave him, I shook my head no and was insistent, "Barnett, you're coming with me! I'm not leaving you out here!"

Looking up at me, he could see I meant business. Extending his hand toward me, I think he got a new appreciation for my determination.

Leaning over, I grabbed his arm up. Using all my strength I yanked the hulking Leroy to his feet again. With his arm over my shoulder, we hobbled toward the school building together.

Reaching it, Leroy leaned up against one of the two front doors while I yanked on the other one with both hands. It wouldn't budge. I banged on the door, but still no response.

Leroy just looked on, silently studying me. Feeling his stare, I turned toward him expressing my frustrations, "It's not opening. I don't think they can hear us."

Leroy had something else on his mind as he spoke, "I can't always put my feelings into words, but I've got something to say to you Holden when all this is over with . . ." He paused, gathering strength while some of his old redneck fighting spirit seemed to be returning. Then he let me know clearly how he felt, "If we have to, let's break this door down!"

We both began to yell and bang with renewed energy. Stubbornly defiant in the pelting rain, Barnett got red faced as he screamed, "Hey! You've got people out here! Open up now!"

The commotion got someone's attention. For almost immediately, the huge door was pushed open in our direction. The suddenness was surprising. I quickly moved backwards, stumbling to avoid getting hit by it.

There stood Mr. Peabody in the entrance, trying to see over his horn-rimmed glasses. Wide-eyed, he was full of a sense of urgency. At the same time, a sigh of relief came over him. "Oh thank God, someone has come. But quick! Get inside!"

After we staggered inside, Mr. Peabody pulled on the door handle. Using both hands, his grip showed surprising strength. Fighting against the elements outside, he somehow managed to close it once again.

Turning back around from the door, he faced us. We must have been quite a desperate looking sight to him. Both of us were wind blown and wild-eyed, completely drenched with raindrops streaming down our faces.

Immediately, I noticed the lights were incredibly still on. I questioned it in disbelief. "You still have electric?"

He explained, "We have our own light source from the big generator out back, but I don't know for how long."

"Mr. Peabody!" Interrupting, Leroy's already booming voice became even louder, just to be heard above the increasing roar of the storm.

As their eyes met, the Principal found himself looking directly into Barnett's wild stare, still mirroring the pain from his fall. Not knowing about this, he was immediately intimidated. Not sure of what to expect, only one word escaped his lips, "What?"

Glancing about for someone not there, Leroy asked him, "Have you seen my little sister, Nellie Barnett?"

"No, she was in Miss Sullivan's class out back on the playground during morning break when the storm hit!"

We all had to talk in raised voices especially now, to be heard above a new sound—a sharp clattering on the roof. As it passed over the school, I thought I knew what it was, "Hail?"

The Principal confirmed it, "Yes, it's been pounding the school off and on since the storm began. We're trying to get the children to the basement to protect them from flying glass!"

Looking around, I saw that chaos was everywhere. Children and teachers were running past us through the halls. Fear at best and panic at worst was mirrored in their faces. "Where's Mattie?" I asked, echoing Leroy's sense of urgency.

Mr. Peabody was hesitant, not responding immediately. A lot was coming at him at once. Looking past Leroy and myself, his attention was drawn to a line of bruised children covered with dust, coming down the hall toward us. Quickly, he crossed the hall to them. "Children, please hurry on down to the basement." He gestured to the staircase at the end of the hall leading downstairs. As they filed past he urged them on, calmly but swiftly, "Faster. Please children. Faster!"

Eyeing each child strongly, I could see his worst fear building up in him. Glancing back at us as we followed right behind, he looked increasingly concerned. "I can't account for all the children. There may be others still outside!"

I snapped back, "Are you saying Miss Sullivan is still out there?!"

Not answering me at first but hearing the growing desperation in my voice, Mr. Peabody came to a sudden stop. Looking square into my face, he told me what his worst fear was, "She went back out there to find the missing children. She's unaccounted for at this time."

The full impact of what he said hit me hard. It spread visibly over my face as I realized that the person I held most dear might be caught out in this storm's fury.

Leroy, who had been looking on, saw something beyond us that caused a full magnitude of horrifying dread to rise in him also. "Oh no!" he blurted out.

Mr. Peabody and I jerked around and saw what he had seen.

A separate group of kids were approaching us, coming at a fast clip from the direction of the back door. Many were battered and bruised. All had fear and shock imbedded in their expressions.

The impact of this sight was reflected in Mr. Peabody's face. His lips formed words into what was little above a whisper, "Oh my God." Recognizing one young boy from Mattie's class, he stopped him. "Bobby, have you seen Miss Sullivan?"

The young boy who had been asking art questions in Mattie's classroom earlier looked up at the Principal. His overhauls were bloodstained and torn. He now had a bruised forehead and a bleeding laceration along his cheek. He was in tears, crying through his words, "She's still outside! She got us to the back door and then went back looking for Nellie!"

I turned immediately, rapidly heading for the back door. A massive surge of adrenaline filled me as I rushed down the hall. Leroy followed, hobbling right behind me. We were determined men on a mission to save those who were dear to us.

Turning into a short hallway, we saw the back door ahead. As we approached it, the door rattled frantically. Someone was trying to get in from the outside.

We tried to see out through the windowpane in the upper part of the door. But it was caked with blowing dust, obscuring our view.

I tried to get the door open, but I wasn't strong enough by myself. Again, it took the strength of both of us pulling together against the sucking winds to open the door.

The door finally gave way and flew open. A lone young girl was crumpled in the doorway. She looked up, quite terrified, revealing a bleeding cut above her right eye.

As we reached for her, a blast of howling wind and blowing dust surged past, surrounding us. Crouching low, we pulled the little girl inside. I shielded her with my body as the glass in the door shattered. Debris went everywhere, blowing wild.

Rising up, Leroy threw his weight against what was left of the door, closing it again. As he was doing this, I removed my raincoat, which was now covered in slivers of fine glass, tossing it aside.

The little girl looked on and realized what I had done to protect her. Responding with a beautiful smile, she said, "Thank you, Mister." But as she turned full face to me, an older, much more horrible scar was revealed. There on the left side of her face, it ran from her cheekbone clear down her neck.

I remembered hearing of this girl in conversation with Dan Russell. I tried to reassure her, "Don't be afraid, we'll take care of you."

"I'm frightened. You see, I've been through a storm just like this before."

Sliding back down to the floor next to us, Leroy also recognized her now. "It's the Harris girl! Her folks' place was destroyed last year by a twister."

Shaking, she looked up at Barnett. "Please help, Mr. Leroy! Miss Mattie's still out there, at the far end of the playground looking for your sister. I don't think she can make it back without help! I'm very worried, because . . ."

"What is it child?" I asked, sensing something else horribly wrong.

"She doesn't have her cane! She left it in our classroom. She was trying to walk without it!" Tears streamed down the little girl's face as fear and concern filled her voice, "Please help, please."

Focusing on the little girl's pleading face, I knew right then what I must do. Anxiety exploded inside me as I thought about Mattie struggling against the powerful winds outside. Rising to my feet, I strained to see through the opening that used to be a window in the door. I yelled at the top of my lungs, "Mattie! MATTIE!" I knew she was out there somewhere, holding on to something, trying to make it back. I knew with all my heart it was not too late to save her. No power on earth was going to stop me. With determination filling me, I looked down at Barnett and said, "I'm going after her!"

Leroy rose to his feet, protesting, "Not without me, you don't! My sister is out there too!"

We stared at each other intensely. This moment of potential conflict was quickly broken though, as Leroy felt a strange tugging at his pant leg. Looking down, he saw a pair of child's hands reaching up toward him, pleading.

The frightened Harris girl begged, with tears in her eyes, "Please Mr. Leroy! Don't leave me here alone! The storm's gonna tear the school apart!"

"I . . ." He hesitated, not prepared for this. Not knowing what to say, he looked over at me.

"Barnett, listen to me. She's somebody's little sister too. You can save her."

He glanced down at the girl, then back to me. I had gotten his attention. Leroy knew he had to get her to the basement, and finally relented, "I'll do it, Holden."

I turned to the door, knowing I must hurry. The storm had been rolling in on the town in a series of waves, and the increasing darkness in the sky told me the worst was yet to come. Yanking with all my might, the door flew open with another rush of wind. Looking back, I made a promise, "I'll find your sister and bring her back to you."

Our eyes made contact in such a way that Leroy knew these were more than just words coming from me. The sincerity in my tone also made it sound more like a sacred promise. With the unspoken pledge understood, I silently turned and plunged through the doorway.

As the wind raged, Barnett stared after me trying to keep me in view. He did so until I became a spec in the blowing dust that was rapidly blotting out the sky. All kinds of second thoughts and conflicting emotions ran through his mind as he stood there in silence. Finding his voice he shouted after me, not sure then why he let me go it alone, "Holden! HOLDEN!"

He had waited too long. By then I couldn't hear him, and had disappeared from his view, swallowed up into the storm.

CHAPTER 25
A TWISTER

I could barely be seen, emerging through a sea of blowing dust. I literally hugged the earth as I crawled forward. The school behind me, up on the high ground, was obliterated from view except for the most imperfect outline.

The land here slanted downward till it reached the playground and leveled off at the far end in back. I remembered that the Harris girl said she had seen Mattie there. It was a long treacherous crawl, past the clanging flagpole beginning to bend in the wind, continuing on down into the debris-strewn playground itself. Gagging on the thick blowing dust that got in my mouth, it was all I could do to keep moving.

My commitment to rescuing Mattie consumed me. Even if I had to forfeit my own life, I would do so. Again, I assured myself it would be an acceptable price to pay to save the life of the woman I loved. But just as this self-sacrificing resolution was becoming set within me, a Greater Power was intervening, reaching into my mind. All of the storm's deafening roar could not drown out the Voice inside, whispering to me, *Jack, do not fear. Have courage, for I am with you.* I knew this Voice was straight from Heaven, speaking to my soul. It sounded familiar yet definitely not of this earth. It gave me confidence and willed me forward. With renewed resolve and determination, I had found an elusive force not present in all men. Some might call it courage. It was much more than that to me. Pressing forward, it was though a more than human strength was flowing through me, empowering my every move, guiding me toward my goal.

It was still by no means easy. The forces of twister weather continued to fight against me every inch of the way. No matter how level I was with the ground, debris was blowing all around me. It was worth it though because every inch forward brought me that much closer to the life most precious to me on this earth.

Cautiously raising my head, I tried to spot Mattie. The wind blasted my face in retaliation. I tried to yell above its roaring sound, "Mattie! MATTIE!" At first there was no response. I listened some more. Precious seconds passed, then . . .

"Jack, we're over here!"

It was Mattie's voice! She was not far from my present position, I thought. But in the wall of dust moving across my field of vision she might as well be an eternity away. All the pebbles of gritty sand from the playground were being churned up in the swirling winds, flinging into my face with the force of tiny stinging pellets.

"Over here Jack!" Mattie's voice called out again.

"Please help us!" Young Nellie Barnett followed with her own plea.

I thought I knew which way to go now. "Hang on! I'm coming!" I started crawling in the direction of their voices.

Indeed, less than twenty yards away, little Nellie hugged close to her teacher. She was crying, tears streaming down her face.

Mattie was flat on her stomach, barely clinging to a large-shafted limb that somehow still remained rooted in the ground. Fully outstretched across the ground, she had one hand grabbing onto the limb as best she could, while her other arm was wrapped tightly around the young girl's waist. Together, they were both hanging on for dear life by the slenderest of threads.

Mattie's face, caked with granules of dust amidst beads of sweat, reflected the strain that was running down the muscle of her arm. Sheer will power had helped her hold on, but the inevitable was about to happen. The cramping fingers of her hand were about to lose their grip on the limb. Just as the unseen forces of nature pried them loose, I had gotten close enough to encircle her wrist with my own strong grip. It was an extraordinary moment for me when faith and strength of purpose became one, enabling me to come to the rescue. Hugging the ground from the opposite direction, I had saved her with my arm stretched almost out of its socket. Adrenalin fused with energy ran through my arm in a super human effort that was more like a miracle. But then the forces of nature became even more furious. Our clothes rippled all over as the howling wind attempted to pick us up and blow us away.

Straining to hold on to her, my fingers wrapped even more tightly around her wrist. I yelled, "We have to find shelter! Come on!"

Nodding in agreement, Mattie was ready. Staying close to me, she moved as I moved.

We struggled to rise to our feet. With her hand in mine and her other arm wrapped around little Nellie's waist, we moved fast. Making a run for it, we dashed across a playground that now looked more like a battlefield. Plunging forward through it, uprooted bushes and broken branches blew all around us, airborne in the powerful winds.

The storm was becoming much worse, hitting the playground with increasing fury that knew no limit. The wind continued to howl even louder. Reaching a high-pitched level of screaming intensity, it must have almost been a hundred miles per hour. Its sheer power slammed into the building with exploding force, rattling the schoolhouse windows. A shower of shattered glass from the windows sprayed across the playground. Splintered boards and jagged pieces of metal went flying everywhere.

Running past a huge old oak tree, the three of us slid into a ditch that ran just below it. Slivers of glass chased after us, propelled through the air with the cutting force of razor blades. Most of the deadly projectiles passed overhead. But some impacted Mattie and me, producing slash marks across our arms.

Crouching low in the ditch, I managed to look up and see that even the giant tree—surely more than a hundred years old—was bending to the pressure of the storm's intensity.

I yelled, "We've got to find a safer place!" As I attempted to look around, flying dust particles pelted me again. There was no way to avoid them this time. The tiny granules found their way into my eyes, temporarily blinding me.

Mattie and little Nellie managed to look up, though, and saw something that filled their eyes with horror. The old oak was bending even further, much more ominously toward us. Groaning and creaking down to its base, the great tree itself screamed out in pain.

What I could not temporarily see, I could hear. A horrible wrenching sound like none I'd ever heard, even in my most horrifying Vietnam moments, was coming from this source just a short distance away. The invisible fingers of the tornadic winds had the tree firmly in their clutches. It was being yanked from the ground. Roots that had burrowed into the dirt over long decades, anchoring the old oak deep in the earth, were being ripped and torn apart. The groaning sound grew louder with each passing second. It was nature's own cry of agony in the wake of the storm's destructive force.

I forced myself to see through burning eyes, full of pain. Though my vision was blurred, I managed to see the tree finally uprooted. It was lifted into the air, where for a few terrifying seconds it was suspended right above us.

"Look out!" I screamed. My only thought was to protect Mattie and Nellie. Putting my arm around them, pulling their heads down, I shielded them with my own body.

The huge tree slammed back down to earth, crashing into the ground right along the edge of the ditch that we were in. It exploded into splintering pieces of wood and broken limbs, flying in every direction all around us. As we lay flat in the ditch, countless projectiles with the force of bullets, from small specs to large sections, passed directly above us.

After a few moments, we cautiously raised our heads just enough to see over the edge of the ditch and view the fallen tree. It had finally settled but kicked up a lot of dust all around its resting place.

Not even a spec of blue sky could be seen at all now. The storm clouds that had filled the entire western horizon began to separate and a huge mass of destruction emerged from them. Ominous swirls of the growing funnel transformed from a light color to dark gray, then almost black. Moving along the skyline, it was coming closer to the ground, approaching in our direction.

"This is no good!" I reacted, truly alarmed.

Mattie was caught up in this frightening moment, realizing all too well what it was, "It's a twister! Oh Lord, please help us," she prayed. Rising to her feet, she looked around frantically. Searching, her eyes fell on something familiar, reflecting sort of an immediate recognition. Her prayer had been answered. Getting my attention, she pointed excitedly at what could be our salvation.

CHAPTER 26
THE ROOT CELLAR

"Jack, look over there, it's the old root cellar!" Mattie yelled. Even with the blinding dust she knew its general location.

I knew we wouldn't stand a chance if we couldn't get to something underground. Never was there a safer place to be than the school's root cellar, actually more of a storm shelter. I looked at Mattie, encouraging her, "Let's go for it!"

We stood up cautiously again, making our way in the general direction of the root cellar, staying inside this man made trench line. It was actually an old drainage ditch that ran for about thirty yards just below the playground. Advancing its entire length, we had to dodge and duck from all manner of flying objects passing overhead. Slivers of glass, wood splinters, and jagged pieces of metal had all become deadly projectiles due to the lethal force of the storm.

As we reached the end of the ditch, poor visibility made it almost impossible to see much beyond it. Mattie just stopped, motionless for a few seconds, hearing something. Grabbing my shoulder, she blurted out, "Listen!"

Hearing a loud noise that seemed to repeat itself every few seconds, we looked around trying to find its source. Powerful winds had unfastened the cellar's trap door, opening and slamming it shut again and again. All the banging helped us to zone in on it. Recognition registered in Mattie's face as she pointed, "There it is!"

The storm had temporarily subsided, just enough so we could see a little beyond us. The unlocked door to the root cellar was visible now. We realized at a glance that it was still 15 to 20 yards beyond us. We would have to cross open ground to get there. There was no other choice.

The sound of the wind was returning and coming toward us. That said everything. I immediately realized how precarious our situation really was. We had to do something. "Our time is running out. Now is better than later," I said. Looking over at Mattie and Nellie, they both nodded, silently agreeing.

I took Mattie's hand tightly. She, in turn, grabbed Nellie with her free hand. I reassured them, "We're going to make it, together." Hand-in-hand, the three of us crawled up and out of the ditch.

We scrambled to our feet and pushed forward. It was now or never. Determined, we ran across the open space toward the cellar's entrance.

Seeming to chase right after us, there was no let up to the rapidly increasing volume of the screaming wind. It meant the twister was getting closer.

Reaching the root cellar with no time to waste, I leaned forward, yanking the door open. In that same split second, a flying piece of jagged wood shot past right above, just missing me. But Mattie, standing right behind me, was not so lucky.

K'THUD!

I heard an impacting, crunch sound, followed by Nellie screaming, "Mattie!"

Spinning around, I saw her slumped to the ground. I reacted, "Oh God!" My voice was almost lost in the wind's ferocity.

Going down on my knees to check on her, I became sick with worry in a split second. Such was the intensity of my feelings for Mattie. She struggled, trying to rise up to a sitting position, but could only do so with my help. The board's wallop had knocked her off her feet. Nellie was trying to help too, despite the fact that she was shaking with fear.

It was only a terrifying instant of time, but it seemed to last an eternity. In it I realized that the three of us had been hanging together by the most tenuous, slender thread. Its strength had been Mattie. With her down, the thread had snapped.

If it hadn't been for an adrenaline rush and the urging of a Higher Power, we would have all been blown away into oblivion. She later told me a Voice inside her mind whispered to her, *Mattie, you must stand up.* There was tremendous power in the Voice, and it made her focus. She looked around at me, revealing a bleeding gash and a bruise above one eye. Regaining her senses, she saw the worried look in my face. Her inner strength returning, she spoke in a strong voice that in turn had a calming affect on Nellie and me, "I'll be alright."

Taking her hand, I helped Mattie to her feet. Putting weight on it, she felt a strange, but good feeling in her bad leg. It gave out a loud pop that extended into her hip joint, and could even be heard above the storm.

"What was that?!" I asked, sort of half screaming it.

"*That* was my leg—but it's okay."

I was reassured. Then the three of us moved with all haste. As we made our way into to the cellar opening, the winds caused our clothes to ripple all over and our hair to blow about in wild confusion. Nellie descended the wooden steps first into the blackness below. Reaching the bottom, she turned to help steady Mattie as she entered the cellar. I lowered her down the steps as gently as I could.

Catching the door again, I turned in the entrance to pull it down. Looking around, I could clearly see the massive dark clouds formed abnormally low all across the horizon. Riveted there for just seconds, I caught a glimpse of the swirling mass within them coming closer, bearing down upon us. It was a rotating funnel, twisting violently as it rapidly descended and connected with the ground. The wind currents around it were kicking a multitude of objects into the air. The twister chewed them up, spitting them out into shreds. Rapidly moving in our direction, we were directly in the path of oncoming destruction. I was sure of it. Nothing on earth was going to keep it from smashing into the school. I whispered, "God have mercy on the children there."

Inside the cellar, I pulled the door downward till it completely closed. Sliding two large bolts across, I firmly locked it. Shutting out the approaching monster somewhat diminished the sounds of it for awhile. A few shafts of dim light still managed to break through some of the large slits between the boards of the old door. This gave me enough light to finish my descent down the steps. Reaching the bottom, I backed up against the cellar wall, sinking to the floor exhausted. Glancing around, I could see it was a dark shadowy place—seemingly cavernous—but in actuality quite small. Seated next to Mattie and little Nellie, the three of us huddled close together.

Sensing impending doom, Mattie asked me, "How bad?"

"It's a twister headed this way. It's on the ground. I fear nothing above us will fair well."

"Oh Jack." uttered a shaking Mattie. Her eyes dared about nervously. She was quickly looking for something familiar. Reaching over, she pulled back a lantern that was sitting nearby on the floor. Holding it up, she explained to me, "It's the old lantern I left down here during our last twister storm, a year or so ago."

"Let's see if it still works," I said, examining it. Reaching in my pocket, I pulled out some matches. Striking one, I leaned over, lighting the lantern.

"Good! It does work." Nellie reacted with a sigh of relief, glad she was no longer in the dark. Even though still frightened, she managed a trembling smile.

Mattie placed the lantern on the floor between us. As it lit up the rest of the root cellar, it gave us a sense of security all too briefly.

I moved even closer, examining Mattie's face. It had been a very serious blow. Raising my hand slowly, my fingers reached toward her injured forehead, not quite touching it. She smiled, some of her old energy coming back. Deeply relieved, I whispered, "Thank God you're all right." I couldn't hold it back. The emotion in my voice revealed how much I deeply cared for her. As I glanced down at her bad leg, the concern I felt translated into a question which formed on my lips, "Why did you do it—go outside without your cane?"

"In class this morning I felt the nerves and ligaments in my leg mending, getting stronger. I can't really explain it. I feel like something is inside me working a miracle. Jack, it seems like my whole body is being healed in every possible way."

I took her hand affectionately into mine, knowing the feelings I felt for her had become rooted deep into my soul.

As our eyes met, the look of love filled her face. Quietly, she leaned over placing her head on my chest as I gently put my arm around her. Comforting each other, we braced ourselves for the inevitable.

In that same instant I felt the intense stare of little Nellie focusing on me. "I'm scared too," she announced in an obvious panic-filled voice.

"That's why Leroy sent me here, so you wouldn't be frightened."

"You know my brother?"

"Yes—quite well."

We were interrupted by whatever was approaching outside. From a quiet somewhat muffled noise, the sound was changing dramatically. Escalating from a distant hum, it was fast becoming a freight train-like noise. Growing increasingly louder, it was speeding straight toward us. As I looked at Mattie, the recognition of what it was formed instantly across her face.

The earth shook in turmoil, quaking all around and beneath us. At the same time, the lantern trembled and moved about on the floor. All of this movement announced the twister's grip on the root cellar, trying to rip it from its very foundations.

BLAM! BLAM!

Our attention immediately went upward to the cellar door and the source of the noise above us. It rattled and shook furiously. BLAM! BLAM! BLAM! Again, we heard a rapid succession of blows, an invisible fist pounding away outside. The full force of the storm was directly on top of us.

I acknowledged it, "The twister's at our door."

Little Nellie's growing fear filled her face. She could no longer stand it. Rushing into Mattie's arms, she looked up at her. Words came trembling from her mouth, "I'm really scared now!"

"We all are honey," Mattie responded, wrapping her protective arms around the child.

Next to them, I found myself staring upward again. Drawn to the cellar door, it seemed to consume my total focus. Just outside, the wind reached its most elevated intensity, screaming in all the high pitched loudness of a thousand screams.

Sitting there helpless, at the very height of the twister's impact had brought on a double whammie of my PTSD. I had by no means been completely cured, and it was telling me so in no uncertain terms.

An uncomfortable feeling was rapidly creeping over me. Summoning up all my strength to save Mattie, I had lulled myself into a false sense of security that somehow I could be invulnerable to the ravages of this storm.

I was not. It had found a way to cause me havoc. Reaching inside my mind, the constant and unceasing sound cut my nerves with the sharpness of a razor blade. Daggers of intense pain shot through my head. My forehead broke out in fine beads of sweat. I was beginning to feel sick inside, quickly becoming soaked with perspiration. My heart beat so loud I could hear it clearly inside my ears. Looking down at my hands, they began to tremble uncontrollably. In just seconds, I felt the tremors spreading throughout my body, seizing me in their grip.

Full of quiet desperation, my mind tried to exert discipline in a futile attempt to keep a lid on the volcano inside myself. But it was too late. Complete helplessness took me over. I did not know what was happening to me, let alone control it. My whole body was in expanding inner turmoil. Jerking uncontrollably, I felt a powerful vice-gripping force reach into the pit of my stomach, pulling my very soul from my body.

As my subconscious mind sought escape, it collapsed in on itself to an even more horrible place, turning to its own past memories. Something I would never be able to forget came rushing into my mind. All of my nightmares exploded within me at once. Like a thief, they stole all my attention from conscious thoughts. My immediate surroundings rapidly became obscured within a hazy blur. The tentacles of my PTSD had me firmly in their grip. I felt like I was being pulled down into a black hole, sinking into its bottomless pit of swirling blackness.

Mattie had looked over and could see that I was hurting. Realizing immediately something was horribly wrong, she reacted, full of worry in her voice, trying to reach me, "Jack! Jack!"

I could feel my hand grow weak and fall out of hers. Trying to focus, my eyes became locked on her. It was though I had become paralyzed, not able to move a muscle of my face, my eyes set in a blank stare.

Even though I could no longer see Mattie, I could still hear her screams calling after me. They seemed so far off, across a gulf of space and time. Her cries grew fainter, going completely silent. It was no use. I quit struggling and surrendered myself to the forces trying to take me.

Continuing to fall into the abyss, a swirling vortex surrounded me, sucking me deep into it. The flashes of light and darkness were moving around me incredibly fast now, perhaps even faster than the speed of light.

Had I begun a journey into the place where all my memories were kept? Had I had found an inner pathway into the subconscious of my own brain? My questions went unanswered because at this point blackness completely enveloped me. I was fast losing consciousness. Then I knew nothing . . .

CHAPTER 27
FACING DEATH—
THE TET OFFENSIVE

Even though my faculties were returning, all strength had left me. Feeling dizzy and queasy inside, I had been sucked into a place where almost total darkness surrounded me. I had felt myself going far beyond my present circumstances into points unknown. So began my journey from deep within my inner self to places not meant for mortal man. At the time, though, my mind did not fully comprehend what was happening.

I knew this was not a dream, and as greater awareness came back, I was suddenly jolted. BLAM! BLAM! I could hear the sounds of screaming mortar shells. They seemed to be coming from a distance but were getting closer.

The swirling abyss surrounding me disappeared completely. I was once again standing on solid ground. But confusion swirled inside my head: Where was I? Everything was all fuzzy. It was hard for me to think. In a few moments I would have my answer.

Bright flashes of light flared in front of me as a series of explosions went off across my entire field of vision along the distant horizon. They were blinding in their intensity, yet I never turned away for a moment. The flickering light lit up my surroundings, making things more visible. My vision came back into focus as I glanced around. Almost immediately, I knew where I was. Of all the memories that had come flooding back recently, this was the one I didn't want. I was in the bunker again, reliving my very worst days in Vietnam. A growing whisper within me turned into a loud defiance, "This is not real. THIS IS NOT REALITY!"

How did this happen? Waves of hypertension brought on by the circumstances of the moment had piled in on the delicate balance of my mind, thrusting me back into its dark corner where my Vietnam nightmare lurked, just waiting to envelope me. I was helpless, being swallowed up by this mental quicksand.

Glancing about, my eyes fell upon a broken mirror. The flashing light lit up the image. I saw the younger Jack Holden in Vietnam era combat uniform. I knew for sure then I was reliving my past again. Yet I decided to do something different this time. I willed myself to suspend all logic and accept it as real so that I might find out what I had not been able to remember. This helped. Now, I was experiencing some things for the first time. Both past and present were coming together, merging in a strange remarkable way.

Before leaving the bunker, I looked down at the floor and whispered, "This is not goodbye, Johnny. With all my heart, I pledge to you I'll take care of Mattie. I will love and cherish her always, just as I know your spirit will be with both of us always."

Turning, I grabbed up my medical kit, full of morphine syrettes and pressure bandages. Strapping it to my waist, I pushed debris out of the way, making a clear path to the bunker entrance. Moving forward, I shoved against the remains of the jammed door until it flew open. Spilling out into the trench outside, I was determined to face whatever was out there. What lay immediately before me was a honeycomb of trench lines south of Hue. The old imperial capital of Vietnam had been swallowed up into the war.

I carefully peered above the remains of our fortifications, scanning the horizon. Memories were coming back to me. This time, the size of my vision was enormous, all encompassing. In the distance, a vast column had formed into a mass exodus. An endless stream of humanity fled the great city which was but a small spec on the horizon behind them. Hanging overhead were flames licking the heavens. Choking everyone were the airborne ashes of these refugees once proud homes.

Coughing myself, I realized I needed to move from this area of scorched earth and exploding debris. I looked around and saw soldiers coming up from the opposite direction. Even from a distance they looked like a relief column of Americans.

A split-second decision came over me. I had to reach them! Scrambling out of my present position, I clawed my way up and out of the flaming ruins of the med bunker, back on solid ground. Dodging smoking rubble, I dashed across a pock-marked battlefield. Tracer bullets whizzed through the air all around me at the same time. As I ran, for a fleeting instant I doubted the sanity of my decision, but the die was already cast. I kept running and zig-zagging though. Explosions ripping up the ground, mortar fragments tore through the air chasing after me. Not stopping, I ran for my life, toward the imagined safety of what would prove to be elements of the 1st battalion, 5th Marines approaching from the south up Highway One. By the grace of God, I remained just ahead of the VC attempts to kill me.

This was the Tet Offensive of 1968, in which the enemy had invaded the south in full force. Some of the most intense fighting of the war took place here. Whole divisions of North Vietnamese Army regulars and Viet Cong guerrilla fighters had hammered the entire country in a massive onslaught. Even though they were paying a heavy price with each human wave attack, they seemed to regenerate almost immediately. Overrunning American positions, they laid siege to the city, destroying great buildings that had stood for a thousand years, engaging in a reign of terror.

When I got close to Highway One, my eyes were met with a gigantic mass of human suffering. I was immediately confronted with what 30 days of occupation had wrought. From the youngest infant to the oldest adult, shock and pain filled the faces of everyone, making the city of Hue the most tragic place to be on the face of the earth that particular day.

As one refugee after another passed me, I stared deep into the agonized faces of those who had nothing left but what they could carry on their backs. These were the faces of the hopeless that now were truly without hope. It was the grimmest scene of humanity I had ever encountered in my entire life. Overwhelming heartbreak came over me in a tidal wave of sadness. Seeing people broken to the core moved me to tears. Filling my eyes, they spilled down my face.

Unexpectedly, I felt a consoling hand on my shoulder. I turned, following it up into the face of a young Marine lance-corporeal. "It's pretty sad, isn't it?" He remarked, gesturing to the civilians passing us.

"Yes, it's not right. The anguish and the suffering . . . it's just too much. I have to do something about it."

"You can go with us."

"Where are you going?"

"Into the city. Our orders are to engage the enemy."

Silent for a moment, I stared into his face, studying him as well as some of the other Marines passing nearby. Firmly set in their expressions was determination and courage. I could see they possessed the total commitment to see this thing through. This was good because everyone would be putting their lives on the line.

As we stood there, the Marine noticed the medical bag strapped around my waist. "Doc, we could sure use a medic. We lost our corpsman in a fire fight earlier today. Will you come with us?"

I responded without hesitation, "Then I'm your man."

So it was an Army medic joined up with a Marine unit in its journey northward into Hue on the afternoon of February 23rd, 1968. Equipped with only my medical kit and a .45 caliber sidearm, I crossed a mental river of no return that day. Initial foreboding seized me for a moment. I knew we were going into the mouth of certain death. Many would be wounded or killed. Nevertheless, I remained firm in my resolve to be involved with those who were going to make a difference.

I didn't know it then, but I was about to become part of something much bigger than myself, deeply profound. Something weird was happening inside me. A knot was forming in my stomach as we approached a bend in the road up ahead. Some sort of recognition of events passed—yet to repeat themselves—was forming in my mind. I was beginning to remember more. I could already visualize the stretch of road that was beyond my view. Sure of it now, I had been here before. What my mind had shut off for so many years was becoming part of my memories again. The fog was lifting in my brain, and everything beyond it was becoming real—all too real.

Shortly I would be reminded again that I was in one of the most horrible places on earth. The odor of decay up ahead was almost unbearably strong, and all too familiar to me. Perhaps it was from being in the bunker for so long with so many body bags. I knew what that smell was. Only now it was multiplied a hundred times over.

Still on the outskirts of the city, we all picked up on the odor. Even though there was no breeze blowing in our direction, we were all inhaling a foul stench. It was the worst odor I had ever come upon in my entire life. It was the smell of decaying human flesh. It sickened me, just as it had for days in the bunker. It was also my first inclination there had been a blood-bath somewhere nearby. In my heart and in my soul, I knew something monstrously evil had happened up ahead.

We hadn't gone much farther when we came upon several huge burial pits alongside the road. The Viet Cong must have been in a hurry for they were all still uncovered. They were mass graves, full of hundreds of inno-cent civilians: men, women, and children.

I stopped and forced myself to look. I never wanted to forget this, not for all time. Even though Highway One was little more than a dirt road at this point, I wanted to remember where I was. I looked down in one such pit and could still see the shocked expressions on the faces of small children, lives snuffed out all too soon in a single instant. "Oh God, oh God." I whispered it several times, not able to let go of what I had seen.

It was grim and awful, seeing so many souls butchered by machetes, their bodies hacked open, exposing their internal organs. All males—men, children, babies—without exception, had their genitals removed, and were bleeding out. Disgusting and stomach churning, I saw several battle-hard-ened Marines lose it right there.

The Marine lance-corporal standing next to me remarked, "It takes a special kind of monster to do this."

"Yes," I agreed. "We have to stop this slaughter. Lives of the innocent have little value in the eyes of the VC. What was their crime?"

The Marine looked at me thoughtfully and answered, "They were friendly to us. It was a matter of guilt by association."

I brooded, continuing to linger on the subject, "We have to put an end to atrocities like this."

"We will," the Marine added with definite resolve in his voice. Patting me on the shoulder, he silently motioned me forward.

Now more than ever, I had a purpose. I wanted to find those responsible for this atrocity and hold them accountable. Yet, it was more than just helping those poor people, now beyond help. Something else was drawing me forward, something I could not put my finger on.

I glanced upward, trying to avoid dwelling on this horrible site any longer. But even then I couldn't get away from the war. I could see the flashing trails of a series of rockets overhead. Tearing across the sky, they delivered their payloads of rocket-propelled grenades to their intended enemy targets up ahead.

The North Vietnamese regulars had been shooting plenty of rockets at us as well. As they got closer to us, we could hear their shrill sounds too. As they struck a little too close at times the ground shook, sending shockwaves all around us. If I hadn't known better, I would've sworn we were having an earthquake.

As we reached the southern outskirts of the great city, I wondered why it was getting dark so early. It wasn't. Flames were shooting out of buildings everywhere. Thick black smoke from the fire rose into the heavens, replacing the blue sky above us. A thousand years of history in this old imperial capital was systematically being reduced to charred rubble, then pulverized, rapidly reducing it to ashes.

I tried to justify what was happening in my own mind. Considering the atrocities they had committed in the last 28 days, it was necessary to rain fire on Hue to eradicate this enemy from the face of the earth.

It all reminded me of something out of World War Two, when we fire-bombed the Nazi's at Dresden. I thought I'd just entered Hell itself. In a sense, I really had.

It truly seemed like Armageddon, not only to the eyes but to the ears as well. The shelling had increased to the point of a perfect storm of mortar shells and rockets falling from the skies. All around me now, I could hear more of the screeching missiles as their deafening sounds reached ear-splitting proportions.

Even under the heavy bombardment, we continued to advance into Hue. The unit I was with soon got caught up in a massive sweep across the city to regain all Viet Cong held positions. Buildings left standing had been completely gutted. Passing them, the sound of crackling flames could be heard nearby. We were more careful now, moving slowly down smoke filled streets strewn with debris.

Remnants of the enemy forces were not giving up easy. But the will of our forces was just as stubborn. We shot at anything that moved in front of us, pushing the enemy back.

Going after them, we finally reached the Perfume River, which bisects the city. Because the bridge across it still stood, it became a prime target for the enemy's biggest rockets and mortar rounds. Crossing it, until you got off the bridge and found safety on the other side, would become like running a gauntlet of death. Behind Marine tanks, we made our way very cautiously across the bridge.

From my position, crouched low behind one of our tanks, I was able to get a quick glance down the river. I could see the bodies of a lot of dead G.I.'s floating there in the water. In nearly thirty days of continuous fighting during the Tet offensive, many American boys had sacrificed their lives. Now, in the fullness of time since then, I ask myself what was it all for? Was it worth it? What did we get for our sacrifice?

The loud explosion of an enemy rocket hitting a bit too close for comfort brought me back to my current predicament. Fortunately though, they never found their mark with a direct hit. But it was still just enough to scare us. When the enemy hit too close, it would send vibrating concussions into a ripple effect the entire length of the bridge.

It was a miracle we made it to the other side of the Perfume River. But by the grace of God, we did. From that point on, I truly believed the good Lord was with us, watching over and protecting us from certain death.

Regrouping, the Marines I was with got behind three tanks and continued to work our way northward. From then on, every inch of ground gained was a struggle. We almost had to have eyes in back of our heads.

As we made it into the old part of the city, fighting became increasingly intense. This is where we found ourselves fighting not only the Viet Cong guerillas but professional troops from North Vietnam in brand new uniforms.

We were almost immediately set upon, and our progress was halted. From the rooftops of two-story buildings, the enemy was throwing Chinese stick grenades down at us. As they exploded, shrapnel was flying everywhere. Sniper elements from three North Vietnamese regiments were firing at us too. The Marines I was with sought whatever protective cover possible. From behind bullet-riddled, disintegrating walls we returned fire.

The fighting became so bad, most of us thought death would soon be upon us. Enemy bullets whizzed past my head like the sounds of powerful insects. At times they missed me by a fraction of an inch. Thank God for my flak jacket. It saved my life many times that day. In the space of just a couple hours I was once more thanking the good Lord for watching over me.

Even though we had stumbled into a hornet's nest of enemy resistance, we fought our way out of it. After several well-placed mortar strikes of our own, the enemy was finally silenced. After the smoke cleared, I noticed we had also paid a price. There were several Marines sprawled out, dead on the ground in front of us. They had made the ultimate sacrifice so that we might move forward again.

Ahead of us, the old part of the city was beginning to look like a ghost town. No one was on the streets to oppose us. When some shadowy figure did dart out, we shot first and asked questions later.

I think it was then, as we progressed deeper into old Hue, I could feel we were actually breaking the resistance of the enemy. Their will to fight was slipping away. Slowly but surely, we were prying open their grip on Hue.

As the smoke cleared, our journey's destination was revealed. We had found one through street that led straight to the Citadel. Somewhat in ruins from 28 days of shelling, it was still standing. Our reconnaissance had said the stronghold of the Viet Cong had been here. Confirming it, a well-worn, shredded yellow-starred flag of their National Liberation Front could be seen still flying atop the main gate of the ancient fortress.

Seeing it from a distance, we began to close in on it. All of a sudden, though, I went charging ahead. I don't know why I did it, perhaps it was the adrenaline of the moment. But something took possession of all my senses, drawing me toward it. Moving ahead quickly, I got separated from the Marines I had been with. Reaching what was left of the Citadel, I found myself quite alone with no backup support. Immediately, fateful premonition filled me. Somehow I already knew the essence of evil lurked within it.

I looked up the stone walls, and at almost twenty feet high, they were not climbable under the present circumstances. The only other way in was through the massive iron double doors directly in front of me. Racing up crumbling steps to reach them, I pressed forward. Standing before them at last, I could see these were the doors out of my dreams, adorned with oriental dragons!

I knew I had come to the end of my search. All I still couldn't remember about Vietnam was beyond this point. The elusive answers that could unlock the mysteries within my memories would only become known if I went through these doors. They not only barred my way, they protected my subconscious from things that had become too painful. Somewhere deep inside myself I was terrified of whatever might be on the other side of these doors. They were large and loomed high above me, but I had no choice. I must go through them if I were ever going to have complete peace in my life. Keeping this thought in mind helped to diminish my fear of the unknown.

I had to reach whatever was on the other side of this barrier. Pounding on the doors, I yelled, "Open up! OPEN UP!" I continued pounding on them until my hands were bruised and bleeding.

Struggling with my emotions, I thought no matter what was there, the strength and wisdom I had gained had made me strong enough to face it. Then I would know the whole truth. I listened, and the voice in my head told me, *the truth will set you free.* It was a powerful thought and it empowered me. Getting a grip on myself, I became firm in my resolve. My course was set. I had to finish this nightmare. Without that, I would never be free of my past.

Grasping the dragon-shaped, oriental handles with both hands, I leaned into the huge doors and pushed with all my might. It wasn't easy. They resisted, but a sustained effort made them give a little. Making a horrible noise, they stubbornly fought against me. Creaking and groaning as they gave way, they started opening back.

Entering, I stopped just inside. Looking up, I could see the guard towers along the poc-marked, outer wall had been abandoned. The enemy had been forced out in previous days fighting. I was truly alone now. The thick walls cut off all sounds of the war going on outside. It was just me and the unknown. Something bothered me immediately, that is the not knowing what might be lurking within these darkened walls. Because of the swirling nature of this month-long invasion, some Viet Cong guerillas had re-entered this place through secret underground tunnels. With this thought in mind, I had to be fully alert with each step I took.

Moving forward, just a few steps through the entranceway, I was already picking up something very potent. An odor of decay rose from this place that was immediately repulsive. It was the smell of death. Filling the air, the odor of the bunker and the mass graves I had encountered earlier had returned.

A surge of apprehension went shooting through me. I wrestled with an overriding thought that seized me again: I knew my destiny was here. Whatever I had dreaded so much was within these walls. I had been drawn in here as part of this mop-up operation to clean out any remaining VC. It was time for me to do what my whole heart and soul told me to do. I had to complete my mission.

So I pressed on, working my way deeper into the fortress, I entered into a whole other world inside the citadel. I came upon the throne room of the Vietnamese war lords who ruled here hundreds of years before. I later learned they ironically called this place the Palace of Perfect Peace. The room was large, cloaked in the darkness of night. It was like the inner sanctum within my mind, protecting its secrets to the very last. The time had come, though, for those secrets to be revealed.

I looked around, making my way through the rubble of this ancient meeting place. Advancing slowly, I found myself in what had been a large circular gathering area. Bordered by what remained of once ornate columns, it was the great pavilion of the old imperial palace.

Flickering lights from an unknown source invaded from the space above me. Looking up, I saw that like the city itself, the interior of this building reflected the bombardment. Disintegrating under the pounding, most of the ornate tile roof had been blown off revealing a perfect view of the heavens. They were lit up by multiple trails of several rockets and mortar shells racing across the night sky. The illumination also revealed something that nothing on earth could have prepared for me to see.

I took another step and just froze, stopping in my tracks again. Standing there motionless, my eyes traveled over the great chamber, taking it all in. No imagined reality could have been more vivid. Graphic images burned themselves into my senses for years to come. I saw bodies severed and ripped apart in the most horrific ways, tangled together and contorted in the most abnormal fashion. Looking closely, I could see their fixed expressions revealed the painful way they died. It was more than I could stand, being far worse than what I'd seen in the burial pits on my way into Hue, if that can be imagined. A transition ran through my mind, ranging from outright denial into emotions that sent shock waves through me that would remain for many years to come. My eyes had just bore witness to more death than I'd ever seen in my entire life.

Stretched out in unnatural positions, the victims lay the entire length and breadth of the pavilion. The floor of the citadel had become a graveyard of the most graphic sort. This was no longer a temple, it was a slaughterhouse!

"Oh no," I cried. "Take it away, Lord!" But there was no way I could escape it. This time it would not go away nor would I ever forget. It would stay there, lurking in the back of my mind for the past twenty years, until now.

The exploding shells in the sky gave off just enough light for me to be able to clearly see countless human shapes, young captured GI's and innocent Vietnamese civilians. There they were: men, women, and children, even babies, strewn about on the floor. They were so many.

Killing was an awful thing and a sin. I kept hearing, *Thou shalt not kill* from the word of God. Seeing these victims, never had killing revealed itself to me to be more cruel and inhumane. Without exception, I found each victim in pools of their own life's blood. So much in fact, it ran like water across the entire floor. Truly, this had to be the work of evil in the sight of the Lord.

Moving forward, I had to be careful where I stepped. As I did, my eyes adjusted to the darkness, and I saw clearly what my mind had withheld from me for so long. They all looked like they had been slashed with something sharp, their lives taken without mercy. A mass execution had taken place here. It was the most horrible scene of genocide I had ever seen or would ever see.

Such was the mind sync and style of the enemy to do this thing, time and again throughout the Vietnam conflict. War is a cruel uncompromising thing where evil often corrupts and wins out over the hearts of men.

Seeing the slaughter, I absorbed all of the vacant stares and pallid faces glaring up at me. Expressions of the last moments of life for these unfortunate souls became an indelible memory buried within my mind. Death had become part of my life in Vietnam, but this was never more true than on this night.

The overwhelming grief I felt for all of the fallen here was swift and immediate. They would leave fathers and mothers childless, wives would become widows, and their children would become orphans. Grief unimaginable would grow out of this place. Hurt and anguish filled me. A sick feeling moved from the pit of my stomach to the knot forming in my throat. I couldn't hold it back and cried out, "God have mercy on their souls."

Suddenly, in the moment of unnatural silence that followed, I sensed I was not alone. I felt an ominous presence in the chamber. I didn't know from where, but I knew I was being observed, perhaps even being stalked.

My eyes were still absorbing the carnage on the floor when a shadow crossed in front of me. The sudden movement caused my whole body to jerk tight with tension. My heart was almost beating out of my chest. Searching the shadows, I saw nothing. But I still believed I was being watched. Then from across the room, something sprang up and moved among the shadows. Something life threatening was in this place. Just from the thought of it I recoiled, quite startled.

I could not clearly see who or what it was. It spoke to me in chilling tones, "I've been waiting for you . . . for a long time now." The voice was grim but yet familiar in a strange way.

From deep in the shadows of the great room, a pair of cold eyes followed me menacingly. Seething with hate, they were flaming red. In predator-like fashion, it was though death had caught me in its cross hairs. Fixing its intentions on me, this mysterious figure began to stir, moving closer.

Stepping out of the shadows, the mocking figure of a black shirted Viet Cong guerilla soldier stood across from me. I could see him clearly now. Looking into his eyes now, though, I saw only darkness. They were so deep set as to be non-existent. They were soulless, without any indication of life. Indeed, his face was just skin stretched over bone. This enemy soldier had gone over the line and had become the embodiment of death itself.

It was shocking, but I had seen this state in soldiers on both sides in Vietnam. Sometimes in war men descend so deeply into becoming killing machines they lose their souls in the process.

I knew I had come face to face, eyeball to eyeball with one of those responsible for so much evil around Hue. This enemy soldier held his razor sharp machete threateningly in the grip of one hand. I knew then this was the death dealer who had ended the lives of so many here in the citadel. He held up his other hand, pointing a long bony index finger directly at me. His words were fatalistic, "I've come for you, Jack." Waving his machete at the bodies on the floor, he added, "Yes, I killed your wounded comrades and the others you see here. Now it's time for you to join them."

I looked down at the slain and then back into this face of evil. Feelings for them that I could no longer suppress spilled over into my voice, "You have killed the wounded and the innocent. Why?"

"It was my orders to do so."

"Who gave you such orders?"

"The People's Army of North Vietnam ordered it to be done. I had to follow orders. I had to do my part in destroying Hue and in killing every living thing in it. Anyway, they were weak, and you are like them—a weak coward!" Pausing, his expression revealed complete contempt for me before continuing, "Where were you when I executed your comrades? Why did you not stop me? I believe you fled combat and hid in a bunker. It's true, isn't it?"

This was more than just the enemy, I thought. Thoroughly brainwashed by his superiors, this Viet Cong soldier had become the personification of evil, without conscience. Devoid of all compassion, he was capable of unspeakable atrocities. Many lost souls were reduced to such killers in what they thought was their line of duty. Some men became monsters in the Vietnam War, as they have in all wars.

"You're a coward!" He yelled at me again.

"I'm not a coward!" I reacted defiantly this time, feeling myself nearing the razor's edge.

"Well then, fight! Kill me!" he demanded. "Go ahead, now's your chance. Kill me!"

"I will not! I'm not a murderer, nor will I become part of the hate that surrounds you."

"As I have always thought, Jack Holden, you are a coward in war just as much as you are a failure in life." As he ranted on, there was something oddly familiar about the sound of his voice,

"How is it you know my name?"

"Oh Jack . . . Desperate situations require desperate solutions. That's what I said when I spoke to your mind on the bus. You were afraid then, just as you are now. You're afraid of life."

"That was you?" I thought about it, reviewing my past. There was something on the bus trying to get inside my head. Something was trying to stop my trip, which had become a journey of the soul. I had sensed it then. Though it was invisible, some sort of dark presence had been trying to make me kill myself. I felt the same presence in the form of this Viet Cong guerilla. It was then I realized, "I've seen you before, in my dreams and nightmares. If this is true, then you're not real. You're a figment of something that happened a long time ago, just a voice in my head now. I reject you!"

"You're such a fool, Jack! None of your words can harm me. You can't get rid of me. I'm more than just a voice in your head. I'm alive in your mind. Awake or asleep, I'll always be with you. The only way to kill me is to kill yourself. Go ahead, kill yourself!"

"I will not!" Remaining firm, I still thought about what he'd said. Thinking about this whole recurring nightmare, I asked myself, did it exist only in the distorted fabric of my mind, or was there more to it? All along, on the bus and before, it had been this thing urging me to take my own life. This was the voice I'd been hearing that was not my own. It came to me then. This was not just a bad dream about a confrontation between two men but something on a much larger scale. I thought I finally understood it: the whole world had become a battlefield on which a struggle between good and evil was taking place. I had become part of that struggle. What stood before me was not just a Viet Cong soldier bent on killing me but rather a demon trying to claim my soul for all eternity. I was not a coward and could face the evil that would make me believe this lie. More resistant than ever now, I declared, "Nothing you could say or do would make me kill myself or fight you."

"That's too bad, Jack. Didn't you know death conquers all?"

"What?"

"If you won't kill yourself, if you won't fight me, you leave me with no choice." The Viet Cong raised his machete menacingly, finishing in a cold and calculated voice, "You will die, and I will be the instrument of your death."

I looked deep into this cold, soulless face of evil to see if I could use my gift to get inside his mind. What I found was that he had long since ceased being human and was little more than a killing machine, fully intent upon killing me. Now I was sure of it.

In this most terrifying moment of my life, I heard Laurie's voice speak to my mind, *Listen to the Voice of God within you. Call on Him and you will receive all the strength you need to overcome anything. Jack, you must seek Him through prayer that is from your heart and He will help you.*

In my heart, I knew what she was saying was true. My spirit—my spiritual self—had been broken in Vietnam. The only truly permanent healing for such a wound is from God.

Sinking to my knees, I stared into the heavens, hoping to find God. I searched myself for inner strength. Finding it in prayer, I opened up my mind to the Infinite where all things are possible. From this core of my being, I found my innermost thoughts reaching into a holy place where the miraculous existed.

As the death dealer holding the machete loomed above me, my faith made connection with the limitless Spirit of God. I began to experience the same feelings I had felt under the tree in Meadow Wood when I truly felt one with God. From Him all things are possible. It was happening again. His Spirit was inside me, protecting and insulating me from this evil entity. Only He, who holds the power of life and death, could bring an end to this.

As I felt the blade of the machete edging closer, I knew then my initial feelings when I joined up with that Marine column were turning out to be true. I prayed my heart out, clinging to the words forming inside my head, "Oh God, please help me. Take this nightmare away. Take it away, forever." Trying to remember some of the 23rd Psalm again, I whispered, "Though I walk through the valley of the shadow of death, I will fear no evil: for thou art with me, thy rod and thy staff comfort me. Though I be in the presence of mine enemies, surely thy goodness and mercy shall follow me all the days of my life and I will dwell in the house of the Lord forever." Remembering some of the words my father taught me as a child, I concluded, "If I should die before I wake from this nightmare, I pray the Lord my soul to take."

Tears filled my eyes as the most powerful emotions I had ever felt surged through me. Reaching out, I was trying to connect with the ultimate source of hope. Faith took the place of my fears. I had spoken directly to God. He was out there beyond the boundaries of the earth, beyond human understanding. Praying with every thought in my heart and soul for His intervention, I had opened the closed door inside myself, letting the Lord's Spirit enter into my life. Keeping that connection, I found the secret of spiritual strength. It resulted in the purest form of Oneness with Him I had ever experienced.

Never before in my entire life had such feelings lingered so long within me as they were now. Expanding mental and spiritual forces allowed a new awareness and understanding to flow into my brain, enabling me to project my thoughts at light speed straight into the heavens where God might be. He was listening.

Then I heard His answer, *Fear not, for I will sustain and protect you.* In the flash of an instant He showed me what was about to happen.

Looking back up at the death dealer, I was no longer afraid. I had found the power and the glory of Almighty God. I knew what to say, "I rebuke you from my mind and soul, back into the dust of my past from where you have come."

In that very instant, the incomprehensible happened. Searching the night skies, there among the glittering stars I focused on a tiny pinpoint of red. Moving at incredible speed, this brilliant object shooting through the night sky began descending from a great distance. Stretching almost from the infinite, racing from deep space, the object left a trail of red streaking behind it. Glowing and looming ever larger, it was coming on a collision course straight toward us. This was no asteroid rock burning up in the atmosphere. Getting closer, a tremendous rumbling sound accompanied it. I could see it was a red fireball with a white center that was almost molten hot.

Plunging from the heavens, burning with the consistency of hot shimmering lava, it was becoming so blinding that I had to shield my face. In doing so, I still caught a glimpse of the face of evil above me. He seemed frozen and could not move. In those horrible seconds, I think even he knew this was his judgment day.

Upon impact, there was a sudden flash of light. The explosion was so great that as it burst outward intense flames completely and utterly consumed the death dealer. In a matter of seconds, this embodiment of all my nightmares was reduced to a burned out cinder, becoming a pile of dust on the ground. Then a powerful wind came up from out of nowhere, scattering the dust wildly about and away into nothingness. This personification of evil had been erased from all existence.

All was strangely quiet for a moment. By the grace of God, I had been thrown clear of the explosion. Only sprayed with dirt and debris, I rose shakily to my feet. Struggling, I staggered over to what was left of one of the battered walls. Bracing myself up against it, all my remaining energy sort of drained out of me as I fell apart. I lost it, crying uncontrollably. Feeling a release of many days of building tension, I became incredibly weak. I felt like I'd been hit with a sledgehammer. Losing all strength in my legs, I just slid down the wall to the floor.

Sitting there, I stared over at where the death dealer had been, and now where there was nothing. I had faced death and survived it. The evil that tried to consume me had in turn been consumed by a Higher Power. It was though it had been the finger of God. And indeed, it was. From that moment on, for the rest of my life, I would believe God IS God.

Humbled by this thought, I was quite overwhelmed. A curse had been lifted from me. I could actually feel the evil that had been an integral part of my PTSD letting go, its tentacles uncoiling from the vice grip they had held on my mind. God had saved my soul and saved me.

Fatigue had taken its toll. I lowered my head and wept again. After a bit, it came to me something was amiss. There was silence—silence inside my head. No more voices were battling for control of my mind. They were gone.

"Jack, they're gone for good," called out a familiar voice, agreeing with me.

I looked up and saw a hand reaching down in front of me. My watery eyes traveled up the extended hand of an American soldier in uniform, but blurred vision kept his face out of focus.

"Jack, let me help you up," said the familiar voice, speaking to me again. Emerging from the shadows was Johnny Sullivan!

My eyes clearing, I looked up at him in startled amazement. His face was so perfect now, unblemished by death. It was though the reflection of God was plainly visible in his features. I now found myself staring into the most transparent bluest eyes I'd ever seen . . . like Laurie's eyes. He glistened all over, revealing the more than human energy that was surging through him.

253

It was good to see him again, so very good. In disbelief, though, I had to ask, "Are you real?"

"I'm as real as you want me to be—or as God will allow."

Part of me accepted this. As I looked at him, studying his features, I started believing he was real. I told myself he was no illusion. My doubts were changing to joy, but I still wondered, "It's you, but yet how is it possible?"

"Don't be afraid. It is me," said Johnny reassuringly. "Don't you remember after we were blown up in the bunker, telling me to go with God and He would heal me? Well, He did."

"What!"

"Yes, Jack, it's true. Whatever you might think is impossible becomes possible with God. I'm no longer of the flesh but rather a spirit now—your spirit guide. He regenerated me so that I could come here. I'm here as sort of a guardian angel, to watch over and help you."

"I have to know, Johnny, was that a Viet Cong soldier? Or, what was he?"

"You prayed for help and called on the Lord. He struck down what was trying to consume you. No demonic presence in the entire universe can withstand the power of God. It tried to confuse you and take your soul. That's why I'm here now, to explain things and help you. The Creator has appointed me to be your protector and let me appear to you. Just as I was your friend in life, I am your friend in another way now. Jack, you may not have been aware of my presence, but I've been around you for a long time now, as a spirit taking many forms, watching over you."

"You were the white eagle in the valley?"

"Yes I was . . . and many other times as well, watching over you and my sister."

Sinking in, coming together in my mind, it was becoming clear to me. Staring deep into Johnny's spiritual eyes, it all made perfect sense to me now. Every little thing that had happened was part of a far greater whole: Mattie's vision of her brother behind me at Russell's store, what Laurie had said, why I came to the valley, everything—it was God's will being done in my life.

"Johnny, you've always been my friend, really more than I've ever known." Emotion and a surge of genuine feelings filled me as I whispered, "I love you."

"I love you too, Jack. We've been like brothers. That's true, more than you realize. I can tell you what has been revealed to me."

"What's that, Johnny?"

"Every soul that's ever lived is interconnected in ways human beings don't understand. The DNA thread that runs through each and every one of us—through all mankind—is a common thread. If one follows its path, it is a path that leads directly back to its Creator, Almighty God. I will explain: when He created man and breathed the breath of life into him, He left some of His DNA in him. Through Divine inspiration, Michelangelo knew this when he depicted it in his painting on the ceiling of the Sistine Chapel. The truth is we are all related, part of the family of man. We need to be more aware of this in actions in our own lives. Do this, Jack, embrace Him, and He will bless you for it."

"It's so profound yet so simple. I just had never thought of it. We are all related brothers and sisters, made so by the gift of life from the Lord."

"Yes, Jack. That's why God grieves at all this death and destruction, his children killing each other."

"What can I do? What must I do?"

"Do your own little part, by helping to bring peace and understanding to those around you. Remember, blessed are the peacemakers before God. For now, though, give me your hand."

I was reassured and reached up, taking his hand. Upon contact, what had appeared to my eyes as a flesh and blood hand, transformed into something else, powerful beyond description. This was the hand of a spirit, full of pure energy, warm and penetrating.

Johnny held on, helping me back up to my feet. As he did so, the strengthening warmth he possessed was released from his fingers into me. Surging up through my arm, it spread within me. It reached into every organ, every atom of my body, filling me with an immediate sense of complete wellness in every possible way.

Seeing this, Johnny explained, "You see, souls never die. I'm a ministering spirit now. I was permitted to touch you with His gift, which will help heal you. The Creator has ordained angels for such purposes since the beginning of time. In times of great danger, we are permitted to reveal ourselves to creatures of the flesh. So it is with the Lord's blessing I have touched you."

I felt it in ways far beyond any human touch. All that had been broken inside me was coming together, making me whole again. My PTSD was gone. It was a wonderful healing experience, far beyond anything humanly possible. Coursing through me, it gave me a true sense of peace. I wondered out loud, "What is it?"

Johnny answered, "It's in answer to your prayer. His Holy Spirit is with you now, inside you forever."

"It's like a strange form of energy flowing through me."

"It's the adrenaline of life—your new life."

"Johnny, I feel it inside my heart and mind. I feel closer to God than I have ever been."

"My friend, you were never really very far from Him. He was always there, waiting on you. The good Lord is always there for us. All we have to do is reach out to Him. Remember, He is an ever-present help in times of need for all mankind."

"I'm not really sure yet, but beyond His presence inside me I feel different, changing even as I speak to you. It's like my whole life is being redefined."

"You're free . . . free from the past. You wanted peace in your life, and you have found it with my sister in the valley. Now you must leave this place and go back. Mattie needs you far more than she realizes, and you my friend need her."

"Johnny, I'll be good to her."

"I know you will, my friend." He paused, becoming aware of something I wasn't. A sense of urgency filled his voice, "Quick Jack, the time portal to this place is closing. You must leave and return to your time."

Letting go of me, becoming transparent, he said softly, "Farewell." It was a word that lingered with me.

"Farewell, Johnny. I will remember you always." Both humbled and grateful, I added, "Farewell, my guardian angel."

A glowing light full of white brilliance surrounded this messenger from God. Rapidly becoming many spiraling smaller lights, they were dispersed into nothing. The vision of Johnny Sullivan was gone, beyond the realm of what is humanly possible to see.

For a brief moment, I realized where I had been was within a time portal in a place somewhere near the edge of eternity, perhaps even close to Heaven itself. If so, I thought for the briefest instant perhaps I should stay here. I even thought, would it be possible to approach the presence of my Lord? I knew the answer already. I had to go back and live out the rest of my mortal life as a human being. Yet I'd just been healed by the Creator. The urge to remain and be in His presence was overwhelming. What should I do?

In the midst of that soul searching moment, I heard a familiar voice reaching into my mind, *You must go back to the world of the living.*

I responded to it, "Yes, Johnny, of course I must go back. You're right."

Johnny's invisible spiritual hand touched me once more, and again I heard him, *You're a good man, Jack Holden. The Spirit of our Lord is going to be with you as a guiding presence for the rest of your life.*

A blowing wind came up again, and I was caught up in a shimmering brilliance that seemed to surround me. Swirling blackness engulfed me. Vietnam and my surroundings became a blur and disappeared. Momentarily, I found myself on a flat, level plateau that stretched into infinity. Still shaken, I felt all my inner strength flow right out of me. Weakened, I collapsed to the ground. Struggling, I raised up to a sitting position. Feeling dizzy, everything started swirling around me, becoming dark and turning into a raging storm again.

Beyond the boundaries of this darkness, there had to be light. I was determined to find it, finally understanding how to tap into the presence of the Creator: it was all around me and within my own soul now. I had faced death and discovered only God could overcome the evil that had crept inside my mind. Knowing this, I reached out for His help and guidance. I prayed again with all the strength I could summon, "Oh Lord, please help me back into the light. Save me."

Searching for some sort of salvation, I looked around and saw a brilliant spec approaching from a great distance, becoming a shadowy, somewhat blurred figure as it came closer.

CHAPTER 28
SALVATION

Increasingly weak, my hand trembling, I was barely able to stretch it out across the darkness toward the approaching figure. I was out of military uniform and once more the Jack Holden of 1989. About to pass out, I lowered my head, looking down as a hand emerged from the shadows into my field of vision in front of me. Gently touching me, the hand was kind and comforting, lowering me to the ground.

Wake up, Jack. Johnny's voice was clear and crisp in my mind, breaking the silence. Again, but louder and even clearer, hovering right above me, I heard Mattie's voice repeat the same words, "Wake up, Jack." As she cradled my head she added, "Let me help you."

With great effort I raised my head again, hearing Mattie's soft voice beyond the arm reaching for me, "Please come back to me." From out of the darkness she had come to reclaim my soul.

Returning to the world of the living, my eyelids flickered open, trying to refocus. I looked up to see her looming over me. She seemed to emerge from the darkness with a kind of glowing light surrounding her. Keeping in mind where I'd just been, it seemed to be a Heavenly glow around her. In any case, this image of her would remain in my memory for some time, and I still fondly recall it to this day.

An expression of growing concern expanded across her face as she attended to me. My exhaustion was so visibly apparent when I first returned to consciousness. I was so pale and washed out, almost drained of life itself. Breathing in and out very slowly, I was almost motionless, feeling weak and confused.

From a bottle of water and a small towel found in the root cellar, she was able to make a cool compress. Applying it, she patted away the fine beads of sweat from my forehead.

It was though the return from my time travel experience was like being spat out of the womb at birth. I was sticky and perspiring all over. I began to cry, becoming so caught up in this sensation of being reborn with a second chance for life. I immediately felt The Creator forgiving me for all my sins and shortcomings, strengthening me to the very core of my soul.

Slowly regaining my senses, I managed a faint smile and a response, "I'm back." My voice cracked and was very weak. I reached for her, snapping out of an alternate reality so real that it nearly killed me.

"I prayed for you, Jack, for your life. After all, prayer is at the center of my life. I believe all things are possible through it. It's the essence of who I am."

"Bless you, Mattie. Bless you for who you are."

Taking my hand, a rush of affection flowed from her, revitalizing me. Through Mattie's touch, her love became an active ingredient in healing me. Added to this, her prayers for me and mine for her joined together to become sort of a joint petition before God resulting in a healing that blessed both of us. In doing so, it became real and lasting. It was this extraordinary merging of our minds that would keep our kindred spirits intertwined.

I had to talk. "I saw the storm headed for the school. I knew I had to get here and save you. I thought I might lose you, and I couldn't bear it."

Her eyes responded with a look that mirrored her most internal feelings radiating from her face. "Oh, Jack, you'll never lose me." As she spoke, the glowing warmth still around her brightened and overcame everything. Nothing could diminish it.

As my vision adjusted, the dark background behind Mattie started to change. Surroundings became more clearly defined and answers came. Everything was bathed in increasing light from an unseen source. I looked around and saw that it was coming from the nearby lantern. Its warm rays permeated the entire root cellar. Realizing where I was, my attention returned to her. To me, she still had the face of an angel. What had taken place in that brief moment of time became an act of salvation I would remember for the rest of my life.

Coming out of the darkness, I had broken free from the shackles of the past. I knew everything had changed within me. I had faced the flashback that had paralyzed me for twenty years, overcoming the trauma and the nightmare within it. An inner strength, almost foreign to me, was building inside me. I could feel God's healing continuing. My ordeal had made me a stronger, much more spiritual person.

I knew I must tell her about it, but I had to find the right words. How could I explain it? I had been wrenched out of my physical body, occupying two planes of existence at the same time. While my physical body was back in the root cellar, my inner being was fully conscious on another plane of existence, reliving events back in Vietnam.

"Mattie, I want to tell you something . . . I'm back from a place I'll never have to go to again. I guess a part of me will always belong to what happened in Vietnam. But now I'm finally at peace with all that happened. I can leave it there, in my memories. I can go forward with the rest of my life. No longer broken, I can stand before you and feel whole. My soul was cleansed by the Lord. He healed me." Deeply humbled, tears full of gratitude formed in my eyes. The weight of all my nightmares was truly gone. I was free of all the negative symptoms associated with PTSD. I spoke with a new authority in my voice as I whispered, "I'm back, for good."

Mattie took my hand, slowly helping me up to a sitting position. Seeing I was groaning from the slightest move, she was very careful. Her total concentration on me, she sat down directly in front of my field of vision, keeping a watchful eye.

She was my whole world in that moment. I wanted to reassure her that my emotional and mental scars were gone. I spoke again of the miracle that had happened within me, "I'm no longer sick. I'm a better man than before."

Never letting go of my hand, the concern she felt for me lingered on her face. Then she put her worry into words, "For a moment you seemed to be dying."

"For a moment I thought I was, but you helped save me." Squeezing her hand affectionately, my wordless expression spoke volumes of my feelings for her.

She understood, her response again revealing the measure of her faith, "I thank the good Lord for bringing us through the storm and saving us both." Still shaking with lingering fear that wouldn't leave her, she added, "But on top of everything that's happened today, seeing you like that was almost more than I could take. It really scared me."

"Me too!" A wide-eyed Nellie Barnett spoke up, quite shaken. Sitting across from Mattie and me, silently listening and observing both of us, she was finally scared out of her silence.

I looked over at her, trying to reassure the little girl, "Don't be frightened Nellie, I feel all healed up now. Everything's gonna be alright." I reached over, gently squeezing her shaking hand in an affectionate manner.

"Thanks Mr. Holden," she said, smiling shyly.

"I think after all we've been through, we can be friends and you can call me Jack."

"I'd like to be your friend, Jack," she said, her shyness showing through, getting a little red in the face.

Feeling Mattie's gaze, I looked back around, facing her searching eyes. She wanted to know, "What really happened to you?"

Not holding anything back, I told her, "It was like I went through some sort of black hole, coming out inside a time capsule, reliving the worst nightmare I ever had. It was the most vivid flashback of the war I've ever experienced. Yet, it was more than that . . . It was real—or so it seemed. All I know is that a doorway opened inside my brain, and I relived events that had been closed off from me, what I could never remember from the war. I finally got to the end of that nightmare. In doing so, I realize all the PTSD episodes I've had since were born out of events I saw the rest of that day. Facing down an apparition of an enemy soldier who had gotten inside my head, I saw evil for what it really was and overcame it. Hopefully, it will be my final nightmare."

"Oh, Jack, by the grace of God it will no longer haunt you. I see it very clearly now: I believe the Lord wanted you to relive those events. It was through His will that you did, so He could heal you."

"Something else," I continued, "Your brother was there too. Not as we remember him, but rather more in spirit form. Johnny helped me get back here to you. Because of him, I understand the spiritual elements around me better than ever. Everything is much clearer now. You know, he said we needed each other."

Hearing this, she smiled. Taking my hand again, she said softly but firmly, "I do need you."

Looking into my eyes, she could see I was still struggling with something inside myself, and pressed me for an answer, "There was something else that really haunted you from that final nightmare. What was it?"

I hesitated, never taking my eyes off her. This was hard for me to discuss because it struck right to the core of my deepest fears. Wanting to tell her, I knew I must talk about it. I had to get it out, telling her about something that had been on my mind for years, "I was not even quite nineteen, perhaps too young for the awfulness I would see in Vietnam. There were so many killed in that war. My mind had suppressed some of the most horrible things I saw. Over time, it became even more horrific in my mind. But I've sorted out the truth of what really happened over there. In doing so, I know now one fear I was carrying around with me wasn't true."

"What fear was that?" she questioned.

"The fear that down deep, on some level I was inadequate to the task at hand, that I had been some sort of coward." At this point I could no longer maintain eye contact with Mattie. I hung my head, feeling weak and ashamed.

"A coward!" Nellie reacted, quite surprised at my statement.

Mattie and I turned sharply, staring at her, not quite realizing she had been sitting there listening intensely to every word being said.

Nellie continued with the truth in the way only a young child might know it, "Jack Holden! You're one of the bravest men I know, that is, except for my brother Leroy."

Even with that exception I felt my self-worth improving immediately. Nellie's words had unwittingly been a morale booster. A good feeling rose up inside me as the little girl's smile continued to radiate toward me.

Considering my actions, I realized that in braving the elements, going after them, I had acted with no thought of my own safety. It was just an instinctive reaction doing what had to be done. I had not been thinking about an act of courage but saving the lives of those who were in danger.

In coming to terms with my past, I realized the new focus for my future would not be possible unless Mattie was a part of it. We looked at each other, with growing feelings of affection filling both of us. Leaning closer to her, I explained, "I can live with my past, knowing what I know now."

"What do you know now?"

"You helped me out of the darkness and back into the light. You have been the anchor that pulled me back to the world of the living." Looking at Mattie, I saw her as a kind and compassionate, truly beautiful person. Knowing this in my heart, I loved this woman with every fiber of my being. I continued, "I found the one thing worth everything to me. It's what we have together. Without you, I'm nothing. With you, I'm everything I could ever hope to be. When you reached in and pulled me out of that nightmare world, you saved my life."

She sat there silent for a moment, my words reaching into her mind and heart. "I want you to look at me, Jack, really look at me. I'm just a country girl, but I'll tell you what I know. From the moment you first got off that bus here in Tyler Junction, you started changing—little by little—becoming a whole person again. If I had a part in that, I'm glad." Her innermost feelings rising to the surface, with tears welling up in her eyes, she added with emotion in her voice, "I truly believe that for some people in life, for the very lucky ones, there is that one special human being. You're that person for me."

I realized more than ever, how much she meant to me and spoke straight from my heart, telling her what I first felt coming out of the nightmare, "I think I have been given a second chance at life. I've gained a bit of wisdom here today and it tells me something very important."

"What's that?"

"I don't want to lose you, now or ever."

She moved even closer to me, whispering softly, "You're not going to lose me. You have me, always."

Going into each other's arms, we clung together in a tight embrace and found renewed strength in each other's support. She needed me as much as I needed her. Even more, we found our love was the glue that would bind us forever. Sobbing tears of joy, we kissed each other tenderly. Becoming overwhelmed with heartfelt emotions, we both felt freedom from the scars of the past. There would be no more sadness and nightmares for us. In its place was the most profound, pure sense of salvation, full of lasting feelings and love for each other.

Nellie's eyes immediately enlarged as she sat there, silently watching. "Miss Sullivan's got a fella!" she blurted out.

We were both startled by the little girl's outburst and turned sharply in her direction again, but only for a quick moment. Seconds later, we all had our attention drawn to the cellar door above us. Loud sounds of something heavy being moved were heard.

Though the voices sounded quite muffled, I thought I could hear Jerry Marsh talking to someone, "They may be down there! Let's check it out!"

I yelled in response, "We're in here!" Silence. I wasn't sure if they had heard me. I yelled again, louder this time, "WE'RE IN HERE!"

"Hang on, Jack!" Jerry yelled back, clearer this time. "Part of the old tree is blocking the door!"

There was tremendous noise as the shattered trunk of the old oak was pushed away from the cellar's entrance. We would later find out that the twister had picked up what was left of the massive trunk and quite literally slammed it over the cellar door.

As the trunk was being moved, we could hear Leroy's booming voice above the noise, "Please God, let my little sister be alive!"

Hearing him, Nellie reacted, screaming out in a loud voice that one would not suspect could come from such a young girl, "Leroy! I'm in here!"

Leroy could be heard enlisting the aid of others, "Quick men, help me!"

I didn't know for sure, but thought I could also hear the muffled voices of Dan Russell, Sheriff Bodeen, and Deputy Wilcox helping out.

The distant sound grew into an overwhelming continuous series of loud cracking, popping and snapping noises as the huge trunk was being rolled away. Then all was quiet.

Leroy's voice broke the silence, "Okay Holden, the tree's cleared away."

I advanced up the wooden steps toward the door. From behind, Mattie raised the lantern to light up the area. I yelled, letting them know, "Stand back out there! I'm unlocking the door!" Reaching up, I slid the locked bolts back. Backing down the steps, I rejoined Mattie and Nellie at the bottom of the cellar. I yelled upward once more, "Leroy! Jerry! It's unlocked!"

Looking up, we awaited their salvation from the storm, hearing a loud jerk and sharp tug on the door's exterior latch. As the door was pulled open and back, a tremendous amount of dust resting on it sifted down through the cracks. The three of us, captives of the root cellar, were all bathed in a shower of dust granules.

Where the door once was, two heads appeared in the opening, looking down. With a much clearer blue sky above and behind them, they were Jerry Marsh and Leroy Barnett.

Relief was audible in Jerry's voice, "Thank God you're all alive!" Then, as our eyes met, focusing directly on me, he recalled a promise, "I told you I wouldn't let you down."

At the same time, Leroy extended a hand downward toward me, raising his voice, "Holden, come on out of there!"

I looked up, not sure what was going to happen.

CHAPTER 29
HOPE

As their heads popped above ground, little Nellie and Mattie were covered in a whitish dust that made them appear almost ghost-like. Startled at first, Jerry Marsh helped them out of the cellar.

Following right behind, when I reached the opening the first thing I noticed was the fury of the storm was gone. Though it looked like a war zone, a strange calm had spread completely across the playground and beyond. Not even the sound of a breeze could be heard.

In front of me was Leroy Barnett, who helped me to the surface. Getting my footing back on solid ground, I moved cautiously away from the big fellow, not knowing how he was going to react. Almost immediately, Mattie stepped in between us with Nellie in hand.

"Leroy!" exclaimed a wide-eyed Nellie, looking up at her big brother, getting his attention.

The glare went out of Leroy's face, replaced by the persona of a kinder, gentler giant. He went to his knees, and with his big hand, wiped the dust away from her face. Seeing her features clearly now, he embraced her tightly. Looking up at Mattie, he was genuinely moved as he spoke, "Thank you for my little sister, and helping to make her the smart girl she is."

She patted him on the shoulder. "That's my job as a teacher."

Rising to his feet, he continued with the first nice things he had said to her in years, "I think you're more than a teacher, Miss Mattie. You're a truly good person."

In the meantime, young Nellie had been looking on. "Leroy! Leroy!" she persisted in a quite excited voice.

"What on earth is it?" he asked, turning to her.

"I know a secret about Miss Mattie."

"What is it?"

Her eyes widened as she told him, "Miss Mattie's got a fella, and I know who he is!" She then looked up in my direction.

Leroy followed her sight line up to me, where I was standing to one side of Mattie. Feeling both of them staring at me, I turned to walk off.

"Holden, wait up!"

Barnett's booming voice reached me. I stopped and started to turn back around, but again unsure of what was going to happen.

Following after me, Leroy was right behind me as I turned around. He explained, "With the storm and all, I never got a chance to talk to you. I, uh . . ."

"Leroy, no!" Before he could say another word, little Nellie was making herself heard again, stepping in between the two of us. Shaking an index finger at her big brother, she lectured him as only a child could, "Now you be nice to Mr. Jack, no more fighting between you two! He's my friend, and beside that, he saved my life."

"He saved your life?" Leroy's face took on a questioning expression as he looked at her, then up at me.

I reminded him, "I told you I'd find your sister and bring her back to you."

His attention went back to Nellie, trying to calm her. Leroy's attitude visibly changing, he spoke less like an angry Goliath and more like a gentle giant, "Everything's gonna be okay. I just want to have a word with your Mr. Jack. I promise."

Nellie leaned forward and got up in her brother's face, studying him closely. Knowing him all too well, she could tell if he was really sincere or not. Understanding his mercurial temper better than anybody, she told him how she felt, "Just remember, don't you lay a finger on him. HE'S MY FRIEND."

"Nellie, I promise," responded Leroy, appearing really sincere.

"Okay then." She seemed satisfied. Smiling, Nellie ran off to be with the other kids.

Leroy turned back to me, seeing the apprehension in my face. "No-no Holden, my fightin' days are over with. You were right about me. The day you licked me over at Russell's store, you set some events into motion that have changed my life. After Sheriff Bodeen took me off to jail for a week,

I hit bottom. I stayed awake day and night, the entire time, comin' to terms with the hate inside me. I had stored up a lot of anger. That's what got me into all the trouble I was in. It was all I could think about. The longer I lay in that small pathetic cell, the more I stared up at the ceiling. It was like I was looking at a vision only I could see. An image kept trying to form there. I saw things I will never forget."

"What sort of things Leroy?"

"The image came together in the form of little Laurie Marsh, staring back at me. She had my mother's family Bible in front of her. As she opened it, the vision went in close on a particular verse. It said, *Blessed are the peacemakers: for they shall be called the children of God.* After that the pages seemed to turn automatically. When they stopped, my eyes were drawn to another passage, *Do unto others as you would have them do unto you.* Then Laurie's voice whispered to my mind, *Read this book, it will do you good. Your mother told me to tell you this.* After that, the vision disappeared and I was alone with my thoughts again. Her words have haunted me ever since. I cried because my mother died last year. She was always trying to get me to read the Bible, God rest her soul. But I was too stubborn, too mean, too evil. Now though, since the day of Laurie's funeral, I've been reading it and thinking."

"Reading the Bible and thinking can be good for the soul," I observed.

Leroy continued, "I saw myself standing in front of a mirror. It let me look inside myself. I was forced to face the truth about my actions and have a chance to review all my sins. I saw how all the rage bottled up inside manifested itself in so much suffering. I had wronged so many. I didn't like what I saw, seeing the pain I caused others. It awakened something inside me. A new awareness of who I was and who I should be came over me. I prayed, and the hate just sort of drained out of me. I'm a changed man. I don't drink or curse anymore. Instead of the bottle controlling me, I'm controlling it. I've taken charge. I pictured myself standing before the throne of God on judgment day, feeling ashamed of myself. I still am. Jack, I had lost my way in life. I'd been walking through life dead to an awareness of God."

"I've never heard you talk this way before."

"I've never felt this way before. Where do I go from here? What do you think I should do?"

"You've been set free from your past to follow a new life the Lord is laying out for you even now. You were just someone who had become sick and confused. You were lost, but now you've been found. Knowing what you know now, you can live each day doing the best one can in all things."

"Jack, I think you're right. I understand now what it means to reap what you sow. In the future I just want what I've sown to be all good things. I believe you. I believe the Lord has a purpose for my life. You helped bring me around to this, showing me right from wrong. I'm thankin' you for that. I just wish my mother could somehow know I'm changin' my ways."

I could see that somewhere deep inside Leroy's mind, a light had come on, motivating him to change himself. He had met his day of reckoning the day we'd fought. His old life was behind him now, the anger and hate having gone out of him. His soul had started a journey that was transforming him into a decent human being. Looking into the former bully's face, I could see a gentler person who had been humbled before God, and I told him, "You're becoming a new man now, a better man than you ever were. As for your mother, I think she does know. She's looking down on you from Heaven right now, proud of you for coming back to the Lord."

"I think it takes a real man to admit when he's been wrong," Leroy admitted, opening up. "I'm sorry I ever raised my hand in anger toward you. I misjudged you, Jack. I was wrong about you, wrong about so many things. But I'm learning. You're not a stranger to me anymore." Tears came into his eyes as he continued, his voice choking with emotion, "You saved my little sister. I'm thankin' you for her life. I'll never be forgettin' what you did today. I hope somehow you'll find it in your heart to forgive all the bad things that have gone on between us. I'm proud to know you and want to be your friend, if you will let me."

I looked into his pleading face and saw a big man that was now more human than he ever thought he would be. The evil was gone, and a different person was standing in front of me. He had found the moral center of his soul. So I told him, "Leroy, you're becoming a pretty decent guy. Of course I'll let you be my friend."

For the first time ever, a genuine smile formed on the giant's face. "Jack, you're okay."

In what seemed a spontaneous moment, both of us were reaching out to each other. Leroy extended his hand directly toward me. Receiving it into mine, we buried the rancor that had existed between us forever. From that moment on a friendship was born. I observed, "You've let God into your life and you'll be better for it."

"Like you said, I was lost. I was just half a man before. Now I'm whole . . ." Leroy paused a long moment, staring deep into my eyes. "I've been telling you how I've changed, but I see it in your eyes too. You've been touched as well, haven't you?"

"What?"

"He touched you, the same as me."

"Yes, I was lost in my own way, but I'm healed now."

"You know, Jack," observed Leroy, "Me with my problems, and you with yours, we're kind of alike, in a spiritual sense that is, sort of like brothers as human beings."

"Well, sort of," I reluctantly conceded the remote possibility.

My concession seemed to delight Leroy as he came up with an even more pointed observation, "Isn't it wonderful how the Lord works Himself into our lives and helps shape our destinies?"

"It's wonderful what His power can achieve in all our lives, if we only let Him in. With every passing moment I feel myself changing for the better."

Understanding each other more than we ever had before, Leroy and I shook hands once more. At the same time we felt our mutual faith strengthening both of us. Initially of opposing beliefs, the act of forgiveness and forgiving had opened up our hearts to each other. We had been brought together in a common bond forged by the Powers of Heaven.

Hearing a commotion approaching, I turned to face a crowd of well wishers that were fast gathering around me, grateful that I was alive. I looked up as Jerry Marsh and Dan Russell got close. They patted me on the back, and shook my hand.

Jerry was first in line, leaning in close, "Something I didn't tell you this morning."

"What's that?"

271

"When Laurie's voice came to me this morning she said something I didn't understand then—that today she would be praying for both you and Leroy. I think I understand now."

I appreciated Jerry and his little angel more than ever, "Bless you my friend. Your Laurie is a peacemaker, even in Heaven."

Dan Russell came up along the other side of me, getting my attention, "You know, I still want to put your picture on the bulletin board with our town's other brave veterans."

"Dan, I'm still thinking it over, but I've got to talk with Mattie first. Then I'll get back with you."

"Very well . . ." Dan reluctantly agreed. Without saying it, his puzzlement was visible.

She was standing nearby, listening. Even then Mattie liked the idea of my picture being on Dan's bulletin board. I saw her face light up and reflect the feelings I believed she had for me.

Next, Sheriff Bodeen and Deputy Wilcox approached me from behind, getting my attention.

The Sheriff congratulated me, "Good work, Holden. You're a brave man, going out in the storm, saving Miss Mattie and the little Barnett girl, but . . ." His voice trailed off as his eyes scanned the playground. Shaking his head, he unintentionally revealed the strange way it affected him personally, "All this mess here sure has spoiled my domino game for today!"

"My sentiments exactly," Deputy Wilcox added, fully in agreement with the Sheriff. Dreading the upcoming cleanup, one word expressing the feelings from this trucker's heart escaped his lips, "Geeez!"

Debris and destruction, shafted and uprooted trees, stretched across every foot of the playground and on into the horizon. But the proud old school, even with the windows busted out, still stood defiantly against the forces of nature.

"Look!" Jerry Marsh shouted, pointing toward the high ground, closer to the school building itself. Something caught everyone's attention. The crowd that had gathered around me followed Jerry in that direction.

I was left momentarily alone. Standing there reflecting, I thought about the series of events that had brought me to this place. They had all been miracles of a sort.

Looking up at the incredibly blue sky, I spotted a rainbow and followed its trail across it. Taking on a special meaning for me, it represented an arc of hope reaching across the heavens ushering in a new world that had been cleansed by nature's powerful forces where new lives could begin. Everything below it was being blessed. A cool breeze passed over me. I realized something very important: I had not only been cleansed of my own self-guilt. I had been redeemed before my fellow men. Humbled, I bowed my head and whispered, "Thank you. Lord, for everyone who has helped me." After that I silently directed my thoughts to God, thanking Him for Laurie Marsh, Johnny Sullivan, my dad, and all of those souls who had been spirit guides and guardian angels for me.

In response, faint words formed, spoken only as a whisper to my mind. Frozen where I stood, I listened to the Voice inside me: *There is something else you must do to be completely whole. It's your destiny. You know what it is, don't you?* Thinking about it, I did know what it was. I kept hearing Leroy's words reverberating in my ears, "I was half a man, but now I'm whole." I wanted it to be true for me as well from this day forward. Destiny can only be complete when you fulfill the deepest needs of your soul. These thoughts cried out for me to do something. To complete my life, I had to talk to Mattie right now. Urgency and resolve to do so was filling me when . . .

"Look! There it is!" yelled Jerry Marsh again. All the excitement pulled me out of my thoughts and got my full attention. I was drawn to a small crowd gathering on the high ground near the school.

Jerry was bent over retrieving something half buried in the rubble. He held up a broken, shattered piece of wood. Still attached, though ripped and torn, was what was left of the American flag.

I realized what I'd been looking at. The storm's force had shafted the flagpole clear down to its base and broke it off. Though ragged, it had survived the elements.

Dan Russell, who was closest to Jerry, got excited, "I'm glad you found it! In one piece of cloth it's all we hold dear."

I felt the same surge of patriotism everyone seemed to be feeling. "It's still mighty beautiful to look at," I marveled.

Leroy glanced over at me, agreeing, "That's right!" Turning his attention back to the flag, he yelled words of encouragement, "Attaboy Jerry!

The sight of the grand old flag still standin' ought to give everyone what they need most—hope." It began here, Leroy using his forceful presence for good instead of evil. As if drawn by one gigantic magnet, he headed toward Jerry where a good portion of the crowd was gathering.

Raising it out of the rubble, Jerry admired the flag, "This represents Tyler Junction, the place in which we live, right here in the heart of America!"

He handed the flag to Sheriff Bodeen, who took it by the broken staff. Looking around, the Sheriff spotted a nearby place a little higher on the plateau. "Let's anchor it over there where it can be seen. It'll give everyone encouragement as we clean up this mess."

Sheriff Bodeen and Deputy Wilcox anchored the remains of the flagstaff in the ground on the plateau, bracing it up to a standing position. As the ragged flag waved defiantly in the afternoon breeze, everyone was caught up with enthusiasm.

It was though something from it in this special moment channeled right into Jerry Marsh, energizing him with a new sense of purpose. He immediately got the crowd's attention, "Listen to me people, everyone of us can make a difference. We can work together and make this town a better place. We can rebuild here!"

Dan Russell felt it too, making a promise, "We'll make Tyler Junction and the whole valley a better place to live!"

Leroy Barnett continued the thought, adding a touch of his new found faith in his booming voice, "We still have hope, and are alive by the grace of God. With the Lord on our side we can rebuild! I for one will help any man in the valley who wants to rebuild, starting right now. We'll make this town a place where we can live in peace and friendship with each other. We are all part of the family of man!"

There it was again, what Johnny had told me. It was a concept I embraced as it echoed in my mind the rest of my life.

I saw something else more clearly now. Looking at Jerry Marsh waving that ragged American flag, a sudden appreciation of it came over me. Seeing the strength of the human spirit in everyone brought back the love of God and country I had missed. It was a great feeling to see people rally around the flag instead of burning it. Right here in small town America I had again found the core values that made this country great.

In love there is forgiveness. After the storm, just such a circle of love surrounded and healed all the people of Tyler Junction. Out of that sprang the will and energy necessary to rebuild.

Right before my eyes, I saw the brotherhood of man coming together and restoring hope to the entire valley. The testimony of that fact was quite visible in their faces. The people around me had looked like they'd been kicked in the teeth by something awful. But like one gigantic Phoenix rising from the ashes, a glimmer of hope was forming on everyone's faces. I saw the visible change in all of them. Beaten people who had lost their jobs at the iron works plant, and had now lost their homes in nature's destructiveness, needed something. They found it in the voices that lifted their spirits here. They found hope. I must say there was no greater group of worthy souls than the folks of the town gathered on the playground that day.

Everyone was increasingly focused on the flag. The symbol of our country reached into the hearts of all who were there. It formed the basis of an emotional and patriotic bonding among them. Out of the greatest devastation, seeing all these people come together the way they did in the aftermath of the storm made me proud that I lived here. The town had been rocked to its very foundations, but by the grace of God had survived it.

I looked beyond the rubble, at the school building itself. Through everything that happened this day, the structure still stood. God's hand surely spared it, just as He had the children sheltered in its basement.

I looked around and saw tears in the eyes of the young and the old. They were all grateful just to be alive. From my own near death experience amidst the fury of the storm, this same feeling of gratitude surged through my mind as well. Full of a sudden wave of emotion, I whispered straight from my heart, "Thank you, Lord: for my life and for all Your blessings."

The impact of God's influence on everyone in the schoolyard that day was truly wondrous. There was something of a spirit of goodness in all of us. I knew we had all been swept up in a triumph of the human spirit, that Tyler Junction was exactly the right place for me to be at this time in my life.

Glancing around, I looked for someone to share these thoughts with. Aware of Mattie's absence again, I was immediately oblivious to those around me. While my eyes searched for her in the crowd I asked myself, *where is she?* Then the inaudible became audible, "Mattie, where are you?"

"I'm here." Her voice came from within a crowd of people nearby.

Wading my way through the sea of people surrounding her, I spotted her. She was talking to George Peabody, the school Principal.

"Thank God you're okay, Mattie," Mr. Peabody said, quite relieved as he tried to focus through his smudged glasses.

"I wouldn't be here," she explained, seeing me walking toward them, "If it weren't for this man coming right now."

Mr. Peabody glanced around as I stepped into view, now trying to look over the top of his interfering glasses, "Mr. Holden, thanks for your help today. We're so very grateful. I realize what you did today was at great risk to your own life."

"Mr. Peabody, I would have done whatever necessary to keep Miss Sullivan out of harm's way," I added. My eyes then traveled over, and saw even deeper feelings in her face.

Many more people were beginning to pour onto the playground, among them the parents and concerned friends of the school children, searching for their loved ones. Clinging to each other, Mattie and I worked our way through this growing crowd until we came face to face with a very worried looking Doc Peterson. He had just arrived on the scene and was making his way toward us.

Bare headed, teary eyed, the old Doc could barely suppress the knot in his throat. He gently examined her facial abrasions. His voice was full of emotion, "I never thought I'd see you alive again. It's a miracle."

"Oh Doc, it was a miracle." Choked up, tears filled Mattie's eyes too.

Reaching out, they hugged each other tightly, almost as if they were actually father and daughter. I always thought, the good Lord in His wisdom had brought them together.

Mattie explained, "I was caught out back with little Nellie Barnett when the twister hit. It was coming straight for us," she explained, revealing, "But Jack here, he rescued us and saved my life."

Doc turned to me, full of appreciation. Shaking hands warmly, the old man's feelings reflected his admiration, "Thank you, son, for Mattie. I'm so very proud of you. It took a lot of strength and courage to get out and brave the storm."

Glancing over at Mattie, she was the subject of my words, "When you love someone, no sacrifice is too much."

Doc looked at both of us knowingly. "I understand."

I told him, "I never want to lose the new life I've found here in the valley."

"Son, you're home, finally home."

"You've helped save my life. I think you know that." My feelings about the old country doctor rose to the surface as I continued, "With my parents gone, you've been more than a friend, kind of like a father to me. I love you for that, Doc."

"Jack, if I had a son I'd want him to be just like you."

Looking deep into each other's eyes, I think we both realized we had become a significant part of each other's lives. A surge of heartfelt feelings ran through both of us as we embraced each other like father and son.

"Doc, I've found peace. I'm a whole man again. You remember what you said about me, cleaning all those old cobwebs out of my head, finding the door to those blocked off memories in my mind?"

"Yes son, I do remember."

"Well, Doc, I found the pathway into my subconscious and went through that door today. I confronted all those lost memories. My past is finally behind me."

Doc's eyes travelled over to Mattie as she verified my claims, "It's true, Doc, I was with him in the root cellar as the twister passed over. Something happened. The noise of the storm was so loud, that it somehow triggered Jack's lost memories and they started coming back to him."

"I faced them, Doc, and now they're gone forever. I'm healed, fully and completely."

"Thank God. I told you, son, He's got a plan for you. Actually, He's got a plan for all of us." Glancing over at Mattie, Doc saw her edging closer to me. He added something perceptive to his original thought, "And I think— He especially has a plan for both of you."

I observed, "It's been you and Mattie that have helped me find myself."

Getting my attention, she added, "We did it because we love you."

Seeing her love for me visible in her face, I told her, "You know, I'm really one of the luckiest persons alive." Thinking about it for a second, my commitment translated into words as I told Doc, "With this woman here, the two of us will face the future together."

He had listened and understood our feelings for each other, telling me, "I'm glad for you, son." Then turning to Mattie, he reminded her, "Remember, you're my special girl always . . ." Pausing, he realized for sure now that her future was my future as well, he added, "I'm glad for both of you."

Just then, Mr. Peabody came up right behind us, putting his hand on Doc's shoulder, getting his attention. Still trying to look over his now definitely dust covered, horn-rimmed glasses, his frustration finally got to him. Taking them off, he muttered, "Need to get a new pair. Can't see anything through these things, they're bad!"

"What do you want, George?" Doc asked.

"Doc, will you take a look at a couple of these children? They've got some nasty looking cuts and bruises." Mr. Peabody gestured over by the back door of the school.

"Sure George, I'll be right there in just a moment."

Satisfied, Mr. Peabody headed back in that direction.

Turning back to Mattie and me, Doc concluded, "Well, it looks as though I've got some work to do. But before I go, I want you both to know that you're the two people I love most in this old world. I'll see you at sundown."

Starting to leave, he noticed we were holding hands. Reaching over, he patted our two joined hands, silently and approvingly, giving us his blessing. Looking at both of us, Doc's expression was full of love and warmth as he turned, heading back to the school building.

Now Mattie and I were alone unto ourselves, oblivious to the crowd of people passing around us. I was living intensely in this moment, my gaze totally on her. I knew this was my opportunity to talk with Mattie, and she in turn sensed my increased focus on her. Facing each other, we spoke what was in our hearts.

Taking my hand, she looked into my eyes, seeing the affection and depth of feeling for her that was there. "You said it, Jack, the long nightmare is over. Just think, we are standing on the edge of a bright new future together." Joy and happiness radiated from her face as she went on, "It's strange, though, how sometimes fate shapes our lives."

As she stood there in front of me, I knew it was much more than fate. All the spiritual and physical elements that make up the body and soul of an individual came together perfectly and completely inside me that day. My purification was complete. Equal measures of faith in God and love and support from those around me filled me. A wonderful feeling was going through me. I was truly a new person. I had emerged from the darkness of PTSD into a light where lasting healing was taking place. But for this part of the cycle of my life to be truly complete, there was one more dream to fulfill.

At the heart of my dream was Mattie, who at this same time was experiencing her own miracle in the schoolyard. It had been so long, but she never gave up hope. Though it hurt with each step she took at first, her leg was no longer weak and was becoming fully functional. There was a growing conviction in her heart that something good was happening. She was beginning to know this healing was going to be permanent. What rather felt like something out of socket too long, had snapped back into place, slowly but surely getting stronger.

We both realized we were not the same two people of just a few hours earlier. Many profound things had changed within both of us that day. The torn fabric of both our lives was being woven back together just as our hearts were being drawn into what would become a lasting relationship between us.

It was this hope, this dream that filled my mind. I knew I wanted it and told her, "I realized something I have to tell you Mattie. I was truly blessed the day you came into my life. Now I can't imagine my life without you in it. I want to be with you the rest of mine, right here in the junction of the three valleys."

"Jack, are you asking me to marry you?"

"I would be honored if you would walk through life with me."

We leaned closer together and saw our inner most feelings visible in each other's faces. We kissed each other as we came together in a moment that reflected the deep needs from within our own souls.

We both realized something very important about the love we shared. Relationships are to be treasured. They are the essence of the human experience. When people open up their souls to each other, they open up all they have. For us, this was a defining moment. We pledged to each other all the love in our hearts and laid the foundation for a relationship blessed by God.

Hand in hand, supporting each other, we walked out of the schoolyard and into the future of our lives together. The lessons learned and the knowledge gained from the events of 1989 would leave us both with inner peace and a happiness that would last forever.

CHAPTER 30
YEARS AFTERWARD

S ince the great twister of '89, seasons have passed into other seasons, and many years have gone by. Even though the flow of life has moved inevitably forward, memories have not faded. They have been passed on by the participants in those events.

One month later, Mattie and I were married. At the wedding, Doc Peterson gave Mattie away, and Jerry Marsh was my best man. She had done me the honor of becoming my wife, something I will treasure and hold so dear to my heart till the end of my life.

After the ceremony, Doc predicted, "Your marriage will be wonderfully successful because you both found the most perfect, kindred soul in each other."

After our marriage, Mattie and I bonded together in every way possible. Doc was right. Spiritually and physically, we fit together perfectly and helped heal the heartbreak in each other. God had brought us together and truly blessed our lives. The happiness wrought between us spilled over into the lives of our friends and loved ones.

Speaking of Doc, he continued serving the people and ministering to the spirits of those that lived in Tyler Junction. From an early age he'd decided to dedicate his life to the service of others. He could not escape the notion that a Higher Power had guided him in that purpose. He just recently retired, well over a hundred years old. At his retirement party he said, that like Joe Catlin, the good Lord had blessed him with a long life. He's never been alone, always having the love and respect of the people in the valley. In a way, they've all been his children.

Even at his advanced age, Doc's mind and vision have remained sharp. But he knew it was time to retire, sensing what was to come. Pulling me aside, he confided his premonition with me, "Son, this part of the cycle of life is very nearly complete for me. Yet my life experience is just beginning as I approach the time when our Lord will call me home."

The day of the great storm would be remembered as the day goodness and decency replaced evil in Leroy's heart. Before that day, he'd been feared and hated by some. After that day, he became a man loved and respected by all. Going through a spiritual rebirth, Leroy was baptized in the streams east of town that summer of '89. A growing religious fervor had taken him over. The word of God became the passion of his life for a season. He preached the Bible on the streets of Tyler Junction to all who would listen, including the unemployed and the homeless. His message of hope left the poor rich in spirit. He spoke to alcoholics, especially about the evil that existed inside a bottle of corn whiskey. He never gave up on his brother Kyle until, as he said, he stopped chewin' and drinkin'.

After summer's passing, another calling took hold of him. It too was an extension of this new found faith. He said his future came to him in a vision from Heaven: he was to help rebuild the town.

The people of Tyler Junction rose from the twister's devastation with renewed hope in their hearts. Leroy and Jerry became kindred spirits of enthusiasm, and together they rallied those souls and rebuilt the valley. They're still partners as building contractors and still friends all these years later. Dan Russell, fully aware of their old history, recently remarked to me, "Who would've believed it?"

Their first project became a building constructed on the vacant land directly across from Russell's store. It was the Joe Catlin Art Museum of Natural History. Those three paintings that were in Mattie's classroom had miraculously survived the storm, completely untouched by its destructiveness. Together, with almost forty other Catlin paintings and hundreds of his sketches, stored in the schoolhouse basement for years, they became the collection now appreciated throughout the art world. The storm had rendered the basement unsuitable for it to remain there much longer. Something had to be done. To properly display it, Leroy and Jerry constructed the museum as a labor of love. Mattie's grandfather finally achieved the recognition he always deserved. Attracting art enthusiasts and tourists from all over the country, his work has profoundly affected the lives of so many.

Leroy's little sister was also profoundly affected by the events of '89. It seemed that year was a turning point in her life. Becoming completely committed to a life-long goal until she achieved it, Nellie went on to become a schoolteacher at the Tyler Junction School in the last few years. Mattie had planted a seed back on the day of the twister that finally matured and blossomed into reality.

In 1990, Leroy and Jerry built our first home, and later built us a cabin over in Meadow Wood Valley, patterned after Mattie's old family home. Every year since, we've been returning to Meadow Wood for our summer vacations, renewing the special bond between us.

For me, this new cabin became more than a vacation retreat. It was where I could renew myself. I explained it once, "It gives me a feeling of peace whenever I come to this place. Just spending time here, enjoying the quiet within these walls, clears my head and restores a sense of balance to my life."

Mattie summed it up, expressing her feelings, "Everything that should be right in this old world becomes right when we're here in this cabin in Meadow Wood Valley." In this valley, our lives together have been filled with peace and happiness. We both feel the Lord's presence all around us here, healing us from day to day.

I'm no longer haunted by the horrors of war. Defeating the Viet Cong demon was a small victory. But within small victories there have been larger ones which have had far reaching consequences. From 1989 through these many years hence, I have never suffered another Post-Trauma flashback. Since the day of the twister and my experience in the root cellar, there have been no more nightmares. Banished by my faith, the complete eradication of my PTSD has changed me forever. The light of the Holy Spirit has transformed my soul. My new life has become a victory of the human spirit over the person I once was. One of the most important things that could ever happen to a person happened to me. I found lasting peace.

Marrying Mattie has been the best thing that could ever happen to me. With unwavering loyalty and support, she has never been far from my side, grounding me in the security of her love. What we have had together in the last twenty-plus years has not diminished but remained just as strong as that day in the schoolyard. In all these years since then, there has never been one day to pass that we haven't professed our love for each other. I believe we will always be soul mates for all eternity.

This same love that has enriched both our lives has been passed on down. Mattie has given birth twice, introducing two children into a family surrounded by it. In their early years, she told them, "Love is the lasting tie that binds. I told your father I loved him with all my heart, and he told me the same thing right back. Well, that circle of love keeps on growing, encompassing you kids. Later it expanded even more, to include all the people and things that are good about life here in the valley. Giving, receiving, and passing on that love can change lives, and maybe even the entire world, in the days and years to come."

Over the years, a brotherhood was forged between Jerry Marsh and myself and moreover a kinship with the entire Holden family. He was godfather to our daughter, whom we named Laurie. In more ways than one, she is the reincarnation of his little girl. It's as though some part of her essence has returned to earth as Laurie Holden.

Uncle Jerry—that's what our kids call him now—told them, "I love you two kids just as if you were my own. As for your father, well I love him just like a brother. He and your mom saved my life, and gave me hope to go on. In my mind, I'll love you all forever. You have become my life."

"Uncle Jerry," our children told him, "we love you too, forever."

"As I think on it," Jerry said, "perhaps my Laurie wanted it this way. As time passes, her spirit grows closer to my heart. Every now and then, in the quiet of the night, her voice still comes to me speaking words of comfort and wisdom. Something of her will always be in my heart and part of my soul. Most people don't understand this, but you do Jack. You lost your mom and dad. You know what it means to make connection with the spirit of a lost loved one. Just as my Laurie has visited me, so have you been visited by the spirit of your dad."

Listening, I told him, "Unless one has lost a close loved one, one can't possibly understand what you've gone through. But we know the miracles of God are infinite and far beyond human understanding."

Jerry agreed, "You're right. Just the other night I heard Laurie's voice in my head, comforting me. You know, you never get over the loss of a loved one. It just becomes more bearable with the passage of time."

"She is still there for you, Jerry, inside your mind. In a sense, losing her has proven not to be the end of her life. Rather a doorway into the eternal from which her spirit communicates with your mind has been opened. She'll always be there for you," I reassured him, "And we will always be here for you."

I really believe that Jerry's special relationship with my family has made a difference and helps keep him going. We have become a big part of his life, and he has blessed us with the most valuable thing he has to give—his love.

And now about our son, he was our first born child. We named him Johnny, after Mattie's brother. It's amazing to me how much he's grown up looking like his namesake. Mattie says that through him some of the spirit of her brother has returned to the valley.

Thinking of Johnny, a few days after the storm I talked to Dan Russell again about my picture from when I was in Vietnam. "I thought about it, and Dan you were right about my picture belonging on your bulletin board."

"Jack, it does my heart good to hear you say that."

"But Dan," I said, adding one important provision, "it can only go in one spot."

"Where's that?"

"Put it next to the picture of Johnny Sullivan."

Dan was curious, "Did you know him?"

I explained, "He was my very best friend in Vietnam. In so many ways he helped me to live again."

"I didn't know. I didn't realize you were friends."

"No one knew, Dan. No one knew . . ."

"So that's why you had to talk to Mattie about it. I understand now. Jack, I'll be glad to put it there. In fact, I'm honored to put it there."

"No Dan, I'm the one who's honoring Johnny and all the other veterans who made the supreme sacrifice."

So it was as time went by, Mattie and I would gather in front of that bulletin board every Memorial Day and say a prayer for Johnny and all our veterans who sacrificed their lives for their country. May God bless them all.

In a way, old friends were reunited, at least in picture form on Russell's bulletin board, where they remain to this day. Since that day in 1989, our friendship passed beyond the boundaries of life and death and continues even now, on a different level that exists in my mind. I don't think I'll ever be able to let the memory of Johnny Sullivan go. After all, he's my guardian angel.

As I look back and remember Vietnam, I think of it as the great tragedy of my generation. The human cost of it—and all the wars since—in terms of all the lives lost is the greatest heartbreak of modern times. In quiet moments I pray for all those souls that are in God's hands now. I pray for my son and all the young men of coming generations that they might be spared from future wars. I pray that our world might find God's peace.

Thinking about all the turmoil in the world brings my mind around to the one stabilizing influence that gives my own life peace. Looking over, I see Mattie as she is today. She is a towering figure of strength and wisdom. The old cane that she once was inseparable from now gathers dust and cobwebs in an obscure corner of our bedroom. Since that fateful day of the great twister, she has never used it again. Much the same as my own, she has often told me she too went through a spiritual rebirth on that day, being healed both completely and permanently.

In a life altering way, I was forever changed after that final nightmare. Almost overnight, I became more spiritual, with far greater insight into others, much more than most people have. Even Doc found himself coming to me for advice. As things happened in a small town, the word got around. Sooner or later, many of our neighbors came around seeking my insight on this or that subject. I believe the Lord redeemed and healed me so that I might help others. In doing so, I believe I'm fulfilling my destiny. Doc believes it as well and said it was a gift from God.

"This gift" has sort of led to something else happening in my life. Over the decade after the great twister, I became friends with most every family living in the valley. I earned a reputation for fairness that has endeared me to all. Just as I had been told that my life did have a purpose, I have found it through public service. Twelve years ago, Jerry and Leroy, along with Dan Russell, formed a committee, nominating me for mayor. Our town has prospered, and I'm currently in my third term as mayor of Tyler Junction.

Mattie says I'm more popular than ever, that everyone who has ever met me winds up respecting me, often for something they can't quite put their finger on.

I asked her, "What do you think it is?"

She gave me her opinion, "Several reasons. They sense your inner strength, wisdom, and honesty. They feel the power of your personality—and for want of better words—this wonderful aura that exists around you."

Our son chipped in, "It's your faith that has made you the man you are. People can feel the presence of God in you."

"Son, do you really think so?" I was intrigued by his insight.

"Yes, I feel it too. But there's something else I see in you," he explained. "You love people, don't you dad?"

"Yes, I really do. I give something of the best part of myself to others. In doing so, I believe I do my own little part in helping change the world for the better."

Reflecting on what I had said, my son thought about it and said, "And you succeed. You do so because you are a force for good. Others see it in you and admire you for that."

"Son, if that be true, God made it so. Embracing goodness and fairness to others has become part of the core of who I am. The old commandment, *do unto others as you would have them do unto you,* is just as important today as it was when the words were first spoken two thousand years ago."

"Dad, it's a good motto to have and live by."

I told him about my personal relationship with God, and something about life for all of us, "After the twister of '89, and in all these years hence, the good Lord has never left me or forsaken me. He is with me at this very moment, strengthening me, body and soul. It's been a miracle, not just for me but one we can all share in. If we just open up our hearts to Him, His Spirit will help us, giving us the strength and wisdom to change our lives. I feel like my life is now defined by the good I do for others. As each day passes I try—with all my heart—to walk in the footsteps of our Creator."

Now that I'm well into my 60s and Mattie is into her 50s, I look at our life together and marvel how it is still full of so much love. We have completed each other's lives. Our feelings for each other expanded and surrounded our children, making all our lives better for it.

At my birthday party, I caught our son staring at me. He said, "Even in your 60s, you have always looked remarkably the same."

Beside the graying hair, I knew better. Even if he hadn't noticed, I could see wrinkles that were not there a few years ago. But my discerning eye noticed something in him that demanded a father's attention. I picked up on something I saw in his face, perhaps a need for some one-on-one time with his Dad. In my son's case, it was as if I could pick up on this thought as well. I went over to him and whispered, "We need to spend some time together."

The next morning I took him out to the valley. As we walked along, I reminisced, "I've journeyed down this old road leading to Meadow Wood many times over the past two decades, but each time I travel it I see something new and wonderful. I'm reminded of something Jesus said, *Behold, I make all things new.* God does have a miraculous way of renewing nature for all time."

Shortly, we reached the junction of the three valleys where Mattie and I shared a picnic so many years ago. Standing there together on the plateau, my son and I gazed out across the valley as it stretched into the horizon in front of us. As guardians of this sea of natural beauty, we protect the secret of this place. In a sense it is sort of our legacy to future generations who will find inspiration here.

"It's incredibly beautiful," my son remarked, taking in all the dazzling colors.

"Yes," I agreed. "The whole valley seems to blossom like this every year at this time. Meadow Wood is putting on its best face to the world."

"Dad, I feel something as well."

"Son, it's the presence of God. Open the door of your heart and let Him in. Many people do not realize this is part of the secret to true success in life."

My son just looked at me for a long moment, studying me closely. I could tell the wheels were turning in his head until he finally spoke, quite moved, "Oh Dad, just listening to you lifts my spirits."

"No son, God lifts our spirits when we go to him. After all, we are standing on sacred ground, all around us here in Meadow Wood."

As we stood there, both of us were transfixed as a golden sheen came over the entire valley. It was though we had been blessed with a Heavenly light. Once more I felt renewed by the presence of our Lord. Now my son had been blessed as well.

The door I had spoken of was opening up inside my son. So he asked me, "Dad, I know you always come to the valley when you want to get close to God, but what about me? How can I get close to Him?"

"In the quiet moments here in Meadow Wood, I can hear His Voice speaking softly in my head. In such sacred moments, you too can experience this and find out what's God's purpose for you in life. Once you know for sure, stay on the path that will lead you to that goal. Listen to His Voice inside you, and He will guide you all along the way. He will keep you on the straight and narrow. This is the pathway of God."

"Dad, that's the pathway I want to walk through life."

Pointing across the valley floor to the ridge on the other side, I added, "It was when I was lying underneath those trees over there, I first consciously became aware that His seeds of wisdom and insight were growing inside me. From then on, I learned to live in a manner worthy of Him. His Spirit is everywhere here, but most of all inside us, guiding us in ways that will change our lives forever."

"But Dad, what if I'm not in Meadow Wood?"

"Son, you don't have to be in the valley to receive God's gift. All you or anyone has to do is open up your heart to the Lord. In the fullness of time, He will bless you with His wisdom and understanding. Concentrate, and in the quiet stillness that surrounds you, listen carefully and you just might hear the voice of your conscious, His Voice speaking words of wisdom to your soul."

Taking in my words, he wished for something that could not be, "It's a shame people have to die, that they can't live on, becoming permanent collectors of the wisdom of the ages."

Thinking about it, I told him what I thought, "In a way some of those we think of as dead are still with us. Their voices are still alive in our minds. Like Laurie Marsh and your Uncle Johnny. From time to time, especially when I'm here in the valley, I still hear them clearly, speaking to my mind. It took me a long time, but I finally realized even after death, that on another level—a spiritual level—their minds and souls are still alive. They do live on."

"Dad, God's wisdom is alive in you."

"My son," I acknowledged him with a great sense of pride in my voice. Looking deep into his eyes, I could see the Spirit of the Lord that was alive here in Meadow Wood was just beginning to touch him. As father and son together, we hugged each other in what was one of those special moments, one that I will remember for as long as I live. It was truly one of my life's golden memories.

Yet I am in the winter of my life. I will be approaching seventy as a hopefully wiser man than I was in my youth. Looking back, I do remember some other things fondly. At journey's end, I've found something more precious than gold. It consists of love that permanently exists in the deepest reaches of my soul. It is love for my wife and children and love for my friends around me. All of them in turn have paid it right back, making this circle of love complete. We have lifted each other up, transforming us into something better, changing our lives forever.

I look around me now and see the wonderful little town, the old general store, and the beautiful valley. Over the past twenty-plus years, outside of Joe Catlin's art museum and a new post office down by the old bus station, the rest of the town is remarkably unchanged. Just as it has been for decades, it has remained ageless and so well remembered in the minds and hearts of my family, friends, and loved ones.

We often look back at a time or a place in our lives and try to make sense of how it has affected us. Getting off the bus during that night of so many years ago certainly changed my life. The truth of the matter is: it was the people here—from a dying child to an old doctor and a school teacher—who brought me back to the Lord again.

God has been my compass. Little Laurie was indeed prophetic, when long ago she told me that the Lord would shape my life. I can clearly see now how much He has been actively involved in my life, in charge of my destiny. Since the beginning, He knew all along this is where I'd wind up being. My whole life has sort of been pre-ordained. Not a bad thing after all, that is to have the Lord on my side. More people should let God be their co-pilot in life.

In other ways, though, this whole town has affected me. There is so much to appreciate about it. The feeling of patriotism, caring, and decency alive in all who live here reached out to me. Most of all, it has made me part of it.

Tyler Junction is but a tiny spec in the heart of America, not even on most maps. If the adventurous traveler looks for it though, he will find it. Still here in all its glory, it's such a lyrical nostalgic place. Even the sands of time and modern progress have not been able to erase its charm. Images of the town and surrounding valley linger on in the memory of even the most casual visitor. It beckons the individual to come and spend some time among its peacefulness and serenity.

Writing this record of these events, it's glorious springtime as I sit at my desk in our family cabin in Meadow Wood. I know now what Joe Catlin meant about spending so much time here in the valley. I feel the same Spirit he spoke of inside my own heart and soul guiding me. As I look out the window of our cabin, a shaft of His light breaks into the room, warming my heart and making my life anew in His service. Few things are permanent in this world, but the power of the Lord is here, forever and always.

Putting pen to paper I have tried to recapture this tale of how I and the people I love most in the world attained a victory over pain and sadness, even the fury of nature. In telling this story, I have recalled a message of hope, how the healing qualities of faith and love came together with enduring friendships and formed a powerful force for good.

Now, after all this time, I stand here possessing the wisdom that only an accumulation of years gives one thinking about something for others. It's my hope, dear reader, that you too will find your dreams, your Meadow Wood.

—Jack Holden

Acknowledgments

In getting to the finished book you hold in your hands, there are many to thank who have helped me along the way. Their generous and unselfish input has helped make this work what it is.

Though fiction, much of this story has its origins in fact. Especially so, many aspects of the Vietnam narrative, in particular the siege of Hue, are true and real events that actually happened.

Completing this novel has been an undertaking over many years, through several drafts in which the story evolved and took the shape of what you now read. For this author, it became an inspiring experience full of healing.

It has been a very long journey that actually began many decades ago in the war torn 1960's with my service as a medical specialist in Southeast Asia. Over the years, my own encounters and countless interviews with veterans who graciously consented to discuss their PTSD experiences with me led to a compassion and understanding of this illness that would have not been possible otherwise. From those interviews and my own personal experiences, these seeds became the foundation of this book.

To a great extent, the fictional Jack Holden is a composite, an inspired amalgam of several real-life patriots whom I greatly admire. In this context, I believe we should honor all our veterans: common men—who through their courage, sacrifice, and faith—have found their way to uncommon greatness. Moreover, this book is for them, and the more than five million Americans still suffering from the invisible wounds of PTSD. May God comfort and give them hope.

In writing this novel, I want to acknowledge the support and encouragement of my extended family and friends down through the years, expressing my gratitude and heart felt affection for them. You all know who you are. I especially want to mention the love and support of my daughter and my son. Words are inadequate to express the love I feel for them and the sense of pride I have in them. Among others close to me, I want to extend my very special thanks to Canyon Russell for his generous and knowledgeable advice, always being there with quick answers to my questions.

Over the course of a lifetime, I have come to realize how much I am deeply indebted to my grandparents who raised me. The values they instilled in me as a child has helped make me the man I have become today. The advice they gave me and the wisdom they imparted, I will carry with me all the days of my life. In many ways this book honors them.

Finally—and above all—I wish to acknowledge my faith in God. His Spirit has guided me in the shaping of this work, and lifts me up to where I could otherwise only hope to be. He sustains and focuses me in all my creative efforts, for which I will be grateful all the days of my life.

—Sam Rawlins

About The Author

The author was raised in Oklahoma and Arkansas in the late 1940's and early 1950's in or near several rural communities. Later, he also spent time in Missouri, all an area known as 'tornado alley.' Soaking up first hand knowledge of small town life, he witnessed many destructive twisters in his childhood. These became some of his most vivid memories during those formative years. Decades later, he has been able to recount them in *A Return To Meadow Wood.*

In the war torn 1960's, after graduating from the medical training center at Fort Sam Houston in San Antonio, he served as a medical specialist in Southeast Asia. He was able to observe the destructive effects of PTSD in patients, friends, and in himself. Then, and through the years, the knowledge gained from these experiences has enabled him to tell this story with a degree of intimacy and understanding that would otherwise not been possible.

Later, after his military service, he was a full time bookseller for many years. During that time, his childhood interest in novel writing was rekindled, bringing with him a visual page turning quality to his style.

Subsequently, he experienced God's calling to write this faith-based, inspirational novel. Born out of his life's experiences, it has been a work of many years. During its development, he has felt the presence of the Lord inspiring him in his writing every step of the way.

He presently lives in the southwest, currently at work on a new book. Reflecting the very deep spiritual commitment in his life, his career goal is to continue writing novels that will impact readers in positive, uplifting, life changing ways.

CPSIA information can be obtained at www.ICGtesting.com
Printed in the USA
LVOW11s1327270916

506397LV00002B/106/P